W9-BVO-355

Sarah's Window

Sarah's Window

Janice Graham

Thorndike Press • Chivers Press
Waterville, Maine USA   Bath, England

This Large Print edition is published by Thorndike Press, USA and by Chivers Press, England.

Published in 2002 in the U.S. by arrangement with G. P. Putnam's Sons, a member of Penguin Putnam Inc.

Published in 2002 in the U.K. by arrangement with Time Warner Books.

U.S. Hardcover 0-7862-3891-7 (Basic Series)
U.K. Hardcover 0-7540-1764-8 (Windsor Large Print)
U.K. Softcover 0-7540-9159-7 (Paragon Large Print)

The text of this Large Print edition is unabridged.
Other aspects of the book may vary from the original edition.

Set in 16 pt. Plantin.

Printed in the United States on permanent paper.

British Library Cataloguing in Publication Data available

Library of Congress Cataloging-in-Publication Data

Graham, Janice.
    Sarah's window / Janice Graham.
        p. cm.
    ISBN 0-7862-3891-7 (lg. print : hc : alk. paper)
    1. Triangles (Interpersonal relations) — Fiction.   2. Flint Hills (Kan. and Okla.) — Fiction.   3. Large type books.
    I. Title.
PS3557.R1988 S25 2002
813'.54—dc21   2001057046

for Gabrielle

If our senses were fine enough, we would perceive the slumbering cliff as a dancing chaos.

FRIEDRICH NIETZSCHE

Acknowledgments

I would like to thank Mary Fisher, Sandy Helzer, Phyllis Malzahn, and their families for their friendship and support during our long, hot Kansas summers; Trish Hutchinson and Pierre Harbrant for their medical expertise and willingness to answer my questions; Jim Helzer for showing me the inside world of steer roping; Emily Lodge-Pingeon for her insightful suggestions; Wade Parsons for exploring the Flint Hills with me and sharing his extensive knowledge of prairie flora and folklore; Kurt Madison for allowing me to experience the actual workplace of a particle physicist; and my parents for always being there.

1

The Flint Hills have a gift for deceiving the eye. They are all illusion. They appear from a distance as an immense monotonous landscape, flat and barren, begging to be crossed swiftly and then forgotten, thus concealing their mystery and magic, secrets long kept to themselves.

The man who slogged along the shoulder of the county road that evening possessed an inner landscape not all that different from the one around him; but he was not inclined at the moment to make any such comparison. The stinging cold wind assaulted him, flayed the exposed skin of his hands and face with vengeful force. He could not walk upright lest he be knocked off his feet; he made progress only doubled over, where head and shoulders offered no resistance, and at times he found it necessary to advance by walking backward into the wind. With one hand he gripped the collar of his flannel shirt (he wore no over-

9

coat) but it offered little protection, nor did his run-down Nikes make easy progress on the crusted snow under his feet. With his other hand he gripped a red emergency gas can, and his bare knuckles burned from the cold.

His snow-blown hair whipped about his face. It was a wonderful face, a romantic face, quite unlike any to be seen around Chase County. It seemed somehow incongruous with his manner of dress; it begged a more formal, grander attire. It was the kind of face a Hungarian nobleman might own, features from some long since vanished line of counts and bishops. It was not the particular arrangement of features that was in itself so moving, but what animated those features — a kind of heightened spirituality that strangers easily mistook for arrogance. And then there were his eyes, remarkable eyes, an unripe blue that seemed to distance him from the world.

He was concentrated solely on reaching the cluster of houses several miles down the road. He could barely make them out in the dark from where he paused atop one of those gently rounded swells that characterized the land. There was a muted light in the window of a two-story frame house near the road, and this alone gave him a flicker of hope.

Billy Moon caught sight of the man as soon as his truck crested the hill. Billy pumped the brakes lightly, tried to control his skid as best he could, finally coming to a stop a good twenty feet past him. The stranger saw him and broke into a trot.

Billy leaned across the seat and flung open the passenger door. "Get in," he said. "Wherever you're goin', it's on my way."

The man looked up and thanked him as he clambered into the pickup, and Billy was a little blown away by that look, those ice blue eyes in that long, lean face.

Billy plunged the truck into gear and the tall stranger settled the can between his feet.

"That your BMW back down the road?" Billy asked.

"Yeah. Gas gauge is broken. I keep meaning to get it fixed."

Billy shook his head. "Runnin' low on gas is risky around these parts. You can go a long stretch without a soul in sight."

The man sat hunched forward, rubbing his hands together briskly under the heater vent. His windblown hair would have lent him a comic air were it not for those intense and anything but comic blue eyes. He gave a sudden, violent shiver and Billy glanced over at him. "Where's your coat?"

"I left it at my lab. I just flew in from California. In the seventies out there." He had a crisp, rapid speech that crackled like cold rain and seemed perfectly in tune with his eyes.

"If you're needing a gas station, you won't find anything open until we get all the way up to the state highway."

"Then do you mind dropping me in Cottonwood Falls?"

"No problem. It's on my way." Billy stole another glance at the man. "You live in the Falls?"

"Just moved there." The stranger smiled and held out a cold hand to shake. "My name's John Wilde."

Of course Billy knew all along who he was, had guessed as much when he saw the California license plates. Billy had heard it all from Sarah, how Susan Wilde was returning to the Falls with her husband and their newly adopted baby, hoping to find life a little simpler out here, and parenting a little easier.

"So you're Susan Blackshere's husband," Billy said.

"That's right."

"Never met your wife," Billy said. "She'd already gone away to school when I moved here. But I know your mother-in-law."

"Clarice?"

"Yeah. We've heard all about you." Billy gave him a good-natured smile. "Not too many secrets around here."

They were at that moment passing through the town. It consisted of a few simple frame houses, a church, and a farm or two.

"Not much here, is there?" John said.

"Nope. This is Bazaar. Population twelve and dropping. Nobody here under the age of sixty," Billy said with a short laugh. "Except for Sarah, of course."

John repeated her name. "Sarah?" But he wasn't really interested, was just trying to keep up his end of the conversation.

"Yeah," Billy said. "Sarah Bryden. Friend of mine." And he swung his head back in the direction of the house with the lighted window. "That's her place."

John glanced at the house as they sped by. Beyond it stretched monotonous, treeless hills and immense space now shrouded by night. He wondered what kind of person would live in a place like this. People born and raised here, he thought. People without much choice.

They rode in silence for moment, and then Billy said, "I hear you're a scientist. Is that right?"

"I'm a physicist," John replied. "I work with matter in its extreme state. Cold. Extreme cold."

Billy cut in with a dry laugh and said, "Now that would have been an ironic twist of fate, wouldn't it? Freezing to death out here."

But John only smiled and went on talking about how they could freeze gas down to a hundred nano-Kelvins. "That's one billionth of a Kelvin," he said. "Now that's cold." He smiled again. "Of course, we'll never get to absolute zero. We'll always be approaching it, but we'll never get there." He paused to run his long fingers through his hair, now wet from the melted snow, sweeping it back off his forehead.

And then John Wilde went on talking about his work with rubidium gas and magneto-optic traps, and Billy feigned an interest, but his mind was really on Sarah.

2

It was, of course, the light in Sarah's window that had caught John Wilde's attention, urging him down the road toward Bazaar. The yellow frame house stood near the road, and the dim light shining behind drawn curtains was the only sign of life in this shuttered and drawn little community. Had he been left to trudge onward, he surely would have stopped and knocked upon that door to ask for assistance. It was interesting that Billy Moon descended upon him at that moment, which served only to forestall by a few weeks something inevitable, as if destiny were playing games with itself, when it knew all along how things would end.

There was not much left to recommend the town of Bazaar. It had lost its post office years ago when the postmaster dragged his sweat-stained mattress out onto the railroad tracks behind his clapboard house and lay down on the icy rails in the middle of the night, waiting for the 3:12 to take him away to another life. A few faithful souls still attended the church, though they had no minister, so the ones who gathered brought their own Bible verses to read and recited their own prayers. Blanche Potter, who was ninety-two that year, still rang the bell every Sunday at nine o'clock sharp, although by that time everyone who was going to come was already seated on the worm-eaten pews.

It was not unusual for a light to shine from Sarah's window late into the night. She could often be found sitting where she sat now, on a chair in the corner of her room, a large sketch pad propped on her knees, her hand darting over the paper in brisk strokes, as if it were no more than an extension of her own mind. As Billy Moon's truck sped by on the highway there was emerging upon her paper a scene of marked contrast to the actual landscape that surrounded her: high, craggy pinnacles of rock rising into the air; steep, jagged cliffs falling off into darkness or mist, or was it water? It gave one the impression of a dreamscape rather than something earthly and solid, as if she had seen this land in a vision and was seeking to recreate it. Something in the power and urgency of her pencil strokes suggested the rocks were alive.

Perhaps she heard the truck, because just

after its passage she laid down her sketch pad and lifted her shoulders, then let fall a deep, weary sigh. She wore a heavy robe of forest-green, with a wide skirt that swept the floor and hid her bare feet. The sleeves of the robe were wide and loose and splattered with paint, as was the skirt. She settled her sketch pad on the floor and groped for the large tortoiseshell clip on top of her head, releasing it so that her long russet hair cascaded around her closed face like a veil. It was a striking face, perhaps not conventionally pretty, but the kind of face a discerning eye would follow in a crowd — its effect all the more mysterious because it worked on the senses as only beauty does, creating in the beholder an insatiable longing. (Indeed, the circuit preacher who came once a month to Bazaar to lead the tiny congregation in its devotionals was inevitably distracted by it, and he would forget parts of his sermon, so that the service was always shorter than he had anticipated, but no one seemed to care.)

Sarah stood and stretched and glanced casually about the room. Dozens of sketches and watercolors were tacked or taped to her walls in a desultory fashion, and on a pair of rusted metal TV trays set up next to an easel were scattered her painting materials: a daisy-shaped china palette, a peaches-in-syrup tin containing her brushes, two open paint boxes, a magnifying glass, pencils, and erasers. Nothing was calculated to be seen or admired, for no one ever came up here. The room itself was empty of all pretense.

Most startling, however, was the subject matter, for none of the watercolors bore the slightest resemblance to the towering craggy cliffs shown in the drawing she was now locking away in the bottom drawer of an old oak dresser. Many of the paintings were of grasses indigenous to the Hills — switchgrass and sand dropseed, and Japanese brome; others were wildflowers — coneflower and spiderwort, Indian blanket and plains bee balm. Captured here not as seen on the prairie but isolated and observed in great detail, with captivating delicacy and elegance.

In high summer, when the temperature pushed past a hundred and the wind swept like a furnace over the hills, she would rise early and take her truck as far as it would go down Little Bloody Creek road to the point where the road was no longer passable, continuing on into the open prairie, into the deep heart of the Hills where isolation from civilization was complete. Here she would sit, painting from her truck until the heat became unbearable, her long savage hair coiled at the back of her head, her watercolors spread out on the wide seat and a bare foot dangling out the open door, a stalk of butterfly milkweed propped on the dashboard or lashed to the steering wheel.

But during the cold, harsh winters she withdrew indoors and turned her thoughts inward, and saw things she did not want others to see, hiding away her visions in the old oak dresser under lock and key.

She made her way across the room and turned out the light, then passed through to the alcove, treading quietly so as not to awaken her grandparents who slept just below. The alcove was only slightly warmer than the adjacent room, for she would throw open windows even in winter, a habit her grandmother had attempted in vain to correct over the years.

Sarah did not change out of her robe but crawled between the rumpled sheets, sweeping the long skirt around her, settling into its warmth like a cocoon and falling instantly asleep.

3

It was her grandfather's accident up at Thut's quarry that had changed the shape of their lives. Just one of those freak things nobody would ever figure out, because Jack Bryden had shot rock all his life, and nobody shot rock better than him. When the guys would reminisce about the old days, they'd talk about plug 'n feather work and how Jack always knew how tight to drive the wedge by the sound of the ring, and how he'd squat under the hot sun pouring black powder into his hand, measuring it with his hawk eye so he got it just right. He always kept a Pall Mall dangling from his lips to light the fuse. Didn't inhale much. Didn't really like to smoke, although he kept the habit even after the accident.

Jack was drilling holes that cold October afternoon when Sarah was sitting in her art history class up at the University of Kansas. He had just stepped up to grease the spinning bit when he felt something swing low overhead, heard the soughing of wings and looked up to see a peregrine falcon pass so low he could see the titmouse in its claws. He'd been so excited he just stood there with a big grin on his face, shaking his head and wishing Sarah was there to see it.

What had probably happened was he'd stood for too long with his wrinkled neck craned upward in awe, and he'd tottered just a shade. Maybe that pesky wind had unsteadied him, and the drill snatched hold of his old work pants and grabbed him and jerked him off his feet, just set its claws into him like that raptor and spun him through the air. It was a terrible sound to hear, and the closest man, about two hundred feet away down at the bottom of the overhang, never forgot it, heard it in his dreams the rest of his life. He was a young trucker backed up to the rock crusher, waiting in line to fill his Dumpster. When he heard the old man's blood-chilling screams, he threw open the truck door so hard it bounced off its hinges, and then he fought his way up the cliff in a white panic. He said later he couldn't even feel his knees underneath him and he was afraid he wasn't moving because it all felt like a long dreamwalk. He had to claw his way up the last few feet of the face of that cliff and then he was racing toward the control box. When he got the drill stopped, there was an awful, paralyzing silence, and the young trucker looked up into the sky because he couldn't bear to look down. Then, suddenly, men appeared from everywhere, and the foreman was already on his cell phone and they were shouting at one another as they tried to disengage Jack's mangled leg from the drill. But the young trucker still stared up at the sky. His eyes were swimming with tears and he didn't dare look down because he knew then that what he thought were clumps of mud clinging to his shirt was the old man's flesh.

4

Sarah had nearly cut the class that afternoon, a tedious and uninspired survey course in art history taught by a mediocre professor, but on this day there was a guest lecturer, a Dr. Ernst Sebestyen, a Hungarian scholar of considerable renown. She had arrived late and found the auditorium full, and so she proceeded toward the front, finally squeezing into a seat near the center of the second row, directly below a wide motion-picture screen erected on the stage.

No sooner had she dug out a pencil and flipped open her notebook than the auditorium lights dimmed and an iron-tall figure in black strode slowly onto the stage. Without an introduction he advanced the first slide.

It was an image that stole her heart: a madonna and child with eyes like wounds, deep and dark and wide with suffering. It was the work of a little-known painter named Mikhail Vrubel, introduced by Dr.

Sebestyen as a Russian Cézanne. The voice on the stage was captivating, but it was Vrubel who spoke to her that day. There were his scenes of Portofino in Italy, and a nineteenth-century Spanish woman in gray satin that rustled in the silence of the auditorium. There was a bejeweled houri-eyed little girl swathed in red silks with a full-blown pink rose in her hand, a child with eyes so distant she reminded Sarah of herself.

And then there was the *Demon Seated*, a shirtless young man with long hair curled behind his ears, a painting so modern, breathing such life, that she found herself instantly infatuated with the image, found herself drawn in by the tension in his sculpted jaw and muscled shoulders and bare back, and the tormented look on his beautiful face.

Sarah had to hurry to catch up with the professor after class. The elevator was full and so she sprinted up three flights of stairs to the art history department. She found him down the hallway where a group of fawning graduate students surrounded him, and she waited, her wide eyes fixed on him, listening while they formalized plans to reserve a table at dinner where he would be their guest of honor. Finally, he detached himself and stepped into an office and closed the door.

Sarah knocked but did not wait for a reply. His head shot up, a startled look on his face when she closed the door behind her. She nodded a breathy "hello" and shed her heavy bag of books onto a chair. He fixed her with his dark eyes.

"Yes?" he asked. The voice tried, unsuccessfully, to hide his impatience.

But she did not know what to say to him, did not even know why she was there. Her shyness abruptly closed her down, the way it so often did.

"You were looking for Dr. Lungstrom, perhaps?"

She shook her head. For a second Dr. Sebestyen thought he had seen her somewhere before. But no, it was only that the face held such promise, such appeal.

"Was there something you wanted?" he probed, a little more gently.

"I'm sorry. I hope I'm not intruding."

"Well, that's a beginning at least." His mouth softened a little, and his shoulders, once rigid and square, relaxed.

"I just came from your lecture. . . ." She hesitated.

"Yes? And?"

"I was very moved by what I saw."

"Ah!" he answered in a booming voice, and his heavy eyebrows arched steeply. "You were moved!"

Sarah sensed he was mocking her. "I'm sorry." She reached for her book bag. "I shouldn't have come."

Her fair face seemed so earnest that he laughed.

"Wait," he said, waving her back. "Tell me. How were you moved? What did you see?"

She did not answer, but stood gripping the heavy bag with both hands, studying him warily.

"This isn't a test." He laughed a little gruffly. "There is no right answer. But I'd like to hear what you felt. Not what you heard me say. I want to know what *you* felt." He motioned to the chair next to his desk. "Please, sit down."

Sarah sat down on the edge of the chair, the bag between her feet. She looked down at her hands, and at that moment there flashed before her eyes the hands of the *Demon Seated*, and her nervousness faded.

"I felt . . ." She hesitated, then continued very softly, speaking barely above a whisper. "I felt as if I had seen into the depths of another human being. That I knew this man in the only way he really wished to be known."

She paused again, her eyes averted. "I felt like he'd done something I'd always wanted to achieve, but didn't know how to go about it." She looked up. "He found a way to voyage out of this world, didn't he?" She said this with complete assurance, and her eyes hung on his with intensity and directness.

"I think he must have been profoundly lonely," she went on. "And hungry. I mean spiritually." She reflected again, and then said quietly and deliberately, "It's as if he were able to take up paint and canvas and without any inhibition whatsoever, without any shame, cast his soul."

A long silence followed, and she looked down self-consciously.

When he finally spoke, Dr. Sebestyen's voice was low and gentle. "Are you an artist yourself?"

"I paint a little. But just watercolors. Landscapes. My home." She was surprised that she could say these things to him. Behind his gruffness, she sensed a warmth.

"Are you any good?"

"I have talent," she answered matter-of-factly. She paused, then fixed him with a steady, unflinching eye. "But I'll never be great."

"Ah, but perhaps your greatness lies in

your sentience. Your feeling. It is a gift, you know, to see and to be moved. What would Vrubel and his kind do without people such as yourself? Who would see them?"

She drew a great breath then, as one might after a confession, then rose and heaved her bag up on her shoulder.

"Please, sit back down," he urged.

"I can't. I have another class and I'm late already."

"Wait, just a moment."

He swept a large hand through his straight black hair, a gesture Sarah found strangely appealing. "If you're free this evening, there's a group of graduate students coming out to dinner. Nothing formal. The pizza place down on Massachusetts Street."

"I'm only a sophomore."

"That's not important. You'll be my guest. You know the place?"

"Yes."

"Can you come?"

Once again she hesitated, withdrew into shyness.

He added in a reassuring tone, "You'll sit next to me." Then he leaned forward in his chair, mocking her lightly. "And you won't have to talk. You can just listen. And watch us all."

She smiled. "All right."

"So you will be there."

"Yes."

"What is your name?"

"Sarah Bryden."

He rose with a jubilant, almost childish satisfaction on his face, and gave a stiff little bow, a gesture brought from the Europe of his childhood that resurfaced from time to time.

"Good," he said, and held out his hand and she shook it. "See you tonight, Miss Bryden," and then he turned abruptly away and began to remove his jacket.

Sarah wanted to skip, to dance, to fly all the way back to her dorm, but she contented herself with a brisk walk. Her future unfolded before her as she sped down the lane. She would learn Russian, travel to the great wide sweeps of the Russian steppes, journey into the heart of a great continent to see for herself this Vrubel's work. She would write monographs on him, bring his work to the attention of Western scholars and make him known. Not just Vrubel, but others, all kinds of great artists she would discover because she had this gift for seeing.

It never came to pass.

Even as she had sat in the auditorium reeling from the impact of the *Demon*

Seated, her destiny was being redrawn by the flight of a peregrine falcon over the autumn-brown sweep of the Flint Hills.

5

As Ruth Bryden watched her granddaughter enter the hospital room and hurry to her grandfather's bedside, she felt a strange sense of vindication surge through her. She had known so much hardship and disappointment in her life that she was comfortable with nothing else. Good fortune seemed to her a precarious and fearful thing; any second she could be plummeted down the cliff, swept away in a rushing avalanche of unforeseen disasters. "You see, Sarah, I knew something like this would happen," she might have said. "This is my lot." Her eyes, constant wells of unhappiness, said as much.

She tapped Sarah on the shoulder and motioned her into the corridor. Her old beige purse, discolored by the sweat of her palms, dangled from her elbow, and she poked around in it until she found a Kleenex and unfolded it with trembling hands.

"They had to cut off part of his leg," she

said, and her voice rose in a high-pitched whimper. She bent her head, and her shoulders heaved with sobs. She blew her nose, and her tired, pained eyes darted this way and that as she spoke. "His jacket tore . . . it was an old thing . . . you know the one." She blotted her eyes, but the tears kept flooding down her cheeks. "But his pants were those new ones," she spluttered, "and they just . . . wouldn't . . . it just chewed him up."

Sarah had been listening in heart-sickened silence. She reached for her grandmother and took the woman's thin shoulders and drew her close, but Ruth Bryden did not like to be touched, and Sarah met with tense resistance. Even in the heart of an embrace, Ruth kept her back stiff, her face turned away.

"I knew this would happen one day." She took a deep breath and broke free of Sarah's embrace. "He should've quit years ago. He was getting careless. He didn't used to be that way."

She stuffed the soiled tissue in her purse and pulled another out of the cellophane package.

"But he was doin' it for you. So you could go to college," she spit out bitterly. She looked back at the doorway to his room.

"I don't know how we'll manage now,"

she sighed wearily, shaking her head. Then she turned and darted back into the hospital room, leaving Sarah standing mutely in the hall.

Sarah returned to the university for one day, just the time it took to pack up her books and clothes and complete the necessary paperwork to withdraw from all her classes. She consigned her textbooks to her roommate, who had offered to cart them back to the bookstore and send Sarah whatever money they fetched in resale.

But Sarah kept her art history book. It sits on a shelf up in her room along with the few books her mother had left behind. It is a strange collection — Charles Doughty's *Travels in Arabia Deserta* and a much-used Greek guidebook squeezed in between volume one of Anais Nin's diaries and a trilogy of gothic fantasies by an obscure English author. At the end sits Sarah's book on modern art with a topographical map of Kansas marking the page on a Russian painter by the name of Mikhail Vrubel.

6

Not long after that, Sarah got herself a job waiting tables at the Cassoday Cafe, about seventeen miles down the highway from Bazaar, just across the turnpike. Unlike Bazaar, Cassoday enjoyed a bit of a cosmopolitan reputation, was indeed a crossroads of sorts in the Hills and drew an occasional cyclist from Seattle or San Francisco. Folks were quick to say it figured in somebody's guidebook of recommended bike paths through the Great American Wilderness, although who put them on the map remains a mystery.

Joy Bell was fond of saying Cassoday got into that guidebook because of her cafe, and it was true that the Cassoday Cafe had its charms. The faded signwall over the long, sagging porch read:

CASSODAY CAFE
GOOD FOOD AND GOSSIP
ESTABLISHED 1879

and it tried hard to live up to that reputation. Folks around here didn't much care that the once spiffy crimson letters had faded to rose and the paint was peeling off the clapboard walls, because talk was never in short supply, and the food, although unpredictable, was a cut above anything you could get for miles around.

Apart from Joy's little enterprise, the town wasn't too interested in drawing strangers to its dusty streets. There was a wind-washed two-room house across the street from the cafe that fronted as a makeshift dry-goods store, and a hand-lettered OPEN sign hung crooked in the window even though most mornings the place was dark as a grave. Kay Potts's antiques store down the boardwalk from the cafe had been around for as long as most folks could remember, although it saw only slightly more profit than the dry-goods store. There were a couple of hitching posts out front but they were there only to keep the men from ramming their trucks into the porch and bringing down the roof. Occasionally Wayne Tonkington rode over on horseback, but he always tied his horse around back on the clothesline.

Sarah knew the faces of her clients and the clothes they wore and who had to take what pills with his meals and who was diabetic and who was on a salt-free diet. She knew this as well as she knew the nicked-up tables and how Joy liked the chairs arranged, and the exact placement of the aging photographs on the walls: Billy Moon wrestling a steer, and Ethan Brown in his yellow slicker driving cattle down a ribbon of dirt road on a misty morning, and the sign over the entrance (removed from the old bridge at Cottonwood Falls) that read: "5$ Fine for Driving on More than 50 head of Cattle or 100 Sheep at one Time," and the one in the toilet (courtesy of Ray the Antique) that read: "Don't Squat With Yer Spurs On." Of a more recent vintage, placed conveniently next to the cash register, was the gallon pickle jar with a finger-smudged index card taped to the front that read: "Sarah's College Fund." Underneath someone had scrawled "Or Whatever." The fact that Sarah emptied it every Christmas and went on a shopping spree with Joy and Clarice up in Kansas City (they spent most of the little money there was on beer in a smoky Irish pub on the Plaza) didn't stop folks from contributing from time to time. Eventually that pickle jar entered into their myths and traditions, and no one really gave a darn if Sarah and Joy and Clarice (mostly Clarice) drank her college fund away every year.

7

The people of Chase County generally take their pleasures in things close to the land. They time their festivities according to the cycle of natural things, and their gatherings are mostly of the intimate and familial sort. So when Clarice Blackshere decided to give an open house in honor of her daughter, Susan, and son-in-law, and even went to the trouble of mailing out invitations to friends and family and old schoolmates of Susan's — some of whom resided as far away as Wichita and Topeka — the event began to take on a certain importance about town.

Of course, part of the draw was the old prairie mansion itself. Many of the guests who came that day had lived their entire lives in the county and never set foot in the historic Blackshere house. It was built of blocks quarried from Chase limestone, the same honey-colored stone that had been used to build bridges and churches and capitol buildings all across the country.

Great stone columns rose in simple symmetry supporting wide, airy porches on the first and second floors. You knew by looking at it that the old house was proud of itself, of its oiled cherry moldings and leaded glass door and red-tiled roof. There was a porte-cochère where horse-driven buggies had once drawn up to be handled by barefoot boys, and young women in long rustling skirts had descended into the dust and mud, grabbing their bonnets back from the wind, trying to make believe they did not really live in this place that most people just passed on by.

Clarice put her heart into the little party that afternoon, took particular care with the buffet (catered by Joy) and had an extravagant centerpiece of creamy orchids laced with red roses delivered all the way from Emporia in the snow. The old prairie mansion looked especially festive that cold January afternoon with huge logs blazing in the native-stone fireplaces, fresh pine garlands cascading over the doorways, and orange- and clove-scented candles flickering in every room.

Folks started pouring in at three P.M. sharp. Ladies with rouged cheeks gawked as they shed their coats and patted down their hair, and men with calloused, work-hewn hands greeted their friends and neighbors with self-conscious laughter at the sight of one another in sports jackets and ties that had long ago fallen out of style. They felt as though they were glimpsing a trace of their county's history — peeking like voyeurs into the proud past of the Hills's first cattle baron, and there was a touch of stiffness and perhaps a little make-believe in their steps and their manner as they plucked Joy's buffalo wings from a platter and gazed up curiously at the 1860s portrait of Jacob Blackshere, Sr., with his foot-long beard and seer's eyes.

Susan herself, a large woman, tall and heavy-boned with a delicately pretty face, welcomed the arrivals, taking their coats. Clarice stood at Susan's elbow, a little nervous, her eyes moist with pride. The baby, poor thing, had caught a cold and was running a fever, she explained, and had to be kept upstairs with a baby-sitter. John, they added apologetically, had driven up to KU's research library that morning and was expected any minute now.

The afternoon slipped by, and they finished off every last one of Joy's buffalo wings and her crab salad and jalapeño dip, and at five o'clock, when John had still not appeared, the crowd started to thin. Folks dug their coats out of the pile in the back bedroom and shrugged them on with furtive glances to one another, and thanked Susan — her mouth strung in a tight smile — for the invitation. (By that time Clarice had broken down in tears and Joy was sitting with her in the kitchen with a box of Kleenex on her knees, trying to console her but mostly making sure she stayed out of the gin.) The departing guests hunkered down against the cold blasts of wind and hurried to their cars and pickups to turn on their heaters and speculate as to what the hell had happened to John Wilde that had kept him away from a party planned in his honor, a party folks had driven long distances to attend.

Those who remained, however, changed the tone of that open house as if the old grandfather clock in the hallway had just struck the witching hour. Mostly it was a small crowd of friends close to Clarice and Joy who hung on, and when Billy Moon set down his glass and looked around the old parlor and said what a perfect dance floor it could be, Joy took the hint and dashed out to her pickup for her Garth Brooks tapes. Susan wished in secret they would all just go home, but she stood back while they shoved the chairs into the corners and the buffet table to one side and rolled up the carpet to bare the old hardwood floor; then everybody fell into a line dance. Wayne Tonkington emptied the last of the rum into the eggnog, and by five-thirty nobody gave so much as a passing thought to John Wilde.

After a while, somebody slipped in some Jimmy Dorsey tunes, and Wayne and his lady-friend coupled off and others followed suit, and without even bothering to ask, Billy caught Joy by the hand and spun her into his arms. He held her bundled tightly to his chest, grinning behind his dark mustache as he whirled her around the room with his hand pressed firmly to the small of her back. Sarah was surprised to feel a slight prick of jealousy as they swept by in front of her and Joy flashed a rapturous smile her way.

The room was filled with music and chatter and laughter, and Sarah looked around for her grandfather. Ruth had taken the car home earlier, but Jack had wanted to stay to watch the dancing. She spied him seated on the edge of a folding chair in a corner clutching a paper cup of eggnog. One of his favorite songs was playing, and he was smiling wistfully, his foot tapping out the rhythm on the wood floor. He swayed a little — whether from the eggnog or the music, Sarah wasn't quite sure.

There was a lull, and then strings and a French horn swelled, promising a slow dance. Billy appeared behind Sarah and swept her into his arms.

"At last," he whispered with his lips touching her ear.

"You could have had me earlier."

"I like to keep the best until last."

Sarah could still remember the first day she laid eyes on Billy Moon. She had been a senior and he all of thirty, and it was his first year teaching history at Chase County High. Sarah sat at the back of the classroom and doodled in her notebook, and you would have sworn she never once lifted her eyes, but she knew every move he made and could have told you how many times he walked up and down each row, and how many times he came within one foot of her and then turned and walked back to the front. She could have described with astonishing accuracy the colors of his plaid shirt or where he notched his belt, the scar on his hand from a bad rope burn and the Band-Aid on his thumb. She knew from the tiny white creases at the outer edges of his eyes that he had spent his summer in the sun —

undoubtedly roping steers — and she knew she was hopelessly in love with him. She also knew he was a happily married man with two young kids and that every other girl at Chase County High was equally besotted.

But after a long and painful battle with cancer, Maude had died tragically just before her fortieth birthday. To fill his empty hours, Billy had taken on the job of organizing volunteer tutors at Chase High — of which Sarah was one — they had been thrown back into each other's path, and what had once been a high school crush had, with time, grown into something undeniably adult.

Billy increased the pressure of his hand on her back, and they moved around the room without talking for a few minutes, content to be in each other's arms.

They did not hear John Wilde arrive. He had come through the porte-cochère at the side of the house and into the kitchen, and it wasn't until they heard voices raised in argument that they realized their guest of honor had returned. Billy grimaced, and Wayne let out a low whistle and said it was time to wrap it up. Clarice flew out of the kitchen with an embarrassed smile on her face and scuttled around the room in her stocking feet blowing out candles.

They were rolling back the rug when John Wilde rushed into the room. He carried a fat and tired-looking leather briefcase and a load of books under one arm, and he stopped in his tracks and looked at them all strangely with that blinding blue gaze of his. Everyone stopped talking then and the room grew dead silent, and Sarah was afraid even to breathe. She suddenly wished she was not there, wanted desperately to escape.

To her astonishment John's eyes found her, traveled quickly over the faces to hers, and she felt her pulse leap with the shock. Then he hurried on to his study but paused once more at the door to turn with a rather bewildered look and mumble something apologetic before closing the door behind him. Susan emerged from the kitchen and hurried after him.

Billy must have noticed the look on Sarah's face, because he slipped an arm around her waist and said loudly enough for everyone to hear that John Wilde didn't look a whole lot different than he had that night he rescued him from a blizzard. Still had that look of a doe caught in the headlights. Only difference was this time he had sense enough to wear a coat. Everyone laughed except Sarah.

John had only just switched on his desk lamp and dropped his books when Susan stormed in. She stood fuming silently in the doorway and then marched across the study toward him.

He was sifting through the clutter of papers on his desk, apparently looking for something. He glanced up, eyes bleary and bloodshot, and muttered, "I'm sorry. I really am."

She crossed her arms and gave an exasperated sigh. "You're hopeless," she said.

"So I've been told," he replied with a dry smile.

"Will you come out now? At least make some apologies?"

"Sure. Just give me a minute." He closed his eyes, and massaged them gently with long, lean fingers. "Will your mom ever forgive me?"

"Maybe. One of these years."

She approached him and smoothed back the lock of hair that had fallen into his face. "I need to sit you down and take the scissors to your hair again."

She leaned forward and gave him a quick peck on the mouth.

A sound from behind drew their attention, and John turned to see a young woman in the doorway holding a coat. She came forward into the light and John recognized her immediately; she had been standing next to Billy Moon, and it had crossed his mind that this was Billy's Sarah.

"I'm sorry," she said. "I was looking for my grandfather. I thought maybe —"

"There's no one here," Susan answered curtly, and Sarah apologized again and turned to go, but just then there came from the back of the study, where an old armchair was turned toward the fireplace, a kind of choked snort, followed by an incoherent mumble.

Sarah halted and turned.

"Grandpa?"

There was a slight commotion as the old man tried to stand and kicked over a bottle of whiskey beside the chair. He bent to retrieve it, staggered, and fell. There was a stream of muttered epithets as he tried to pick himself up off the floor.

John caught the expression on Sarah's face as she hurried toward the old man. There was no shame, only compassion and deeply felt sorrow.

She took the bottle from his hand. "Come on, let me help you," she whispered and crouched to get a grip on him. John dodged quickly around the end of his desk and hurried toward them. Jack had risen from his stupor, was staggering alongside Sarah with an arm slung over her shoulder. He narrowed his bloodshot eyes on John and told him he could manage by himself, thank you, and thanks for the Jack Daniel's.

"I'm sorry," Sarah said in a low voice with an embarrassed glance at John. "I just need to get him home."

John emerged from his study a few minutes later, but the remaining guests had scattered into the night. He stood on the doorstep and watched while Wayne chased Janie across the front lawn with a clumsily packed snowball raised over his head, and Billy Moon and Sarah helped Jack Bryden down the front walk.

Sarah drove home that night with her grandfather slumped against the window, snoring softly. She drove automatically, following the ribbon of road without seeing it, trying to summon up an image of John Wilde, but all she could recall was the penetrating set of those stone blue eyes.

8

Clarice had inherited the Blackshere mansion upon her husband's death — and a good deal of money besides — much to the outrage of the Blackshere clan. Clarice was certainly not without distinction, had a noticeable and lively charm about her, the very quality Jacob Blackshere, Jr. had so enthusiastically embraced. She had been Jacob's second wife, and by the time Susan was born, Jacob was sixty-eight and had already sired three sons and two daughters, and had five grandsons to carry on the name.

Now, the Blacksheres were a clannish people, and when Clarice had appeared on their horizon with her dark, glowing eyes fixed on their Jacob in no uncertain manner, they closed ranks and greeted her with cold smiles. Clarice was delicate and flirtatious and all those things the Blacksheres were not. She laughed too much and dressed in trim pastel suits and sling-back shoes; she wore gold charm bracelets that tinkled with her every move, and a cloud of soft, puckish scent always seemed to cling to her, inevitably leaving its trace on Jacob so that they could always tell when he had been with her, and it rankled them something awful. Eight months from the day of their marriage she gave birth to a nine-pound little girl, and that child, proof of Jacob's enduring manhood, became the crown jewel of his heart.

Susan looked and acted every bit a Blackshere, gave evidence even at the toddler stage of a single-minded determination and keen intelligence. But with Jacob's early death, Susan was tossed into her mother's camp, and after several years of empty gestures the Blacksheres snapped clean of them.

Clarice spent the rest of her days trying to whittle herself a chunk of life out of that tight-mouthed and judgmental little community. When a new man came through town, Clarice swallowed her pride and put a little color on her face, wriggled into a skirt, and went out and tried to catch his attention. But inevitably the town machine went to work on her. The nastiness always got back to her, came flapping around on the tongue of a dim-witted neighbor, and then Clarice would spend sleepless nights with those cutting words sluicing through her mind. More than once, Susan had watched her mother crumble to her knees and huddle childlike in the corner of her bedroom, sobbing her heart out in loneliness and despair.

It was like that until Susan and John had adopted little Will, and Clarice felt maybe her life still mattered to someone, maybe she was needed after all. Mothering had not come easily to Susan. The baby had needed surgery and his recovery had been slow, and Susan had the idea to come home for a visit with the baby. Then John got approval for a semester's leave of absence, and so Clarice volunteered to move into the renovated servants' quarters next to the old barn, offering them the old Blackshere house for as long as they wished to stay.

Despite Clarice's good-hearted intentions, Susan had few illusions about her mother's reliability, and so immediately upon their arrival in Cottonwood Falls, Susan had begun a search for a baby-sitter. The only suitable candidate was Joy's teenage daughter, Miss Amy Bell. During the school year, Amy lived with her father, Sheriff Clay Bell, up in the Falls. She spent her weekends and vacations in Cassoday, picking up a little extra money working at her mom's cafe. The Wildes had laid an early claim to her cheap although not always reliable labor. They had suffered her chewing gum on their carpet and her cigarette butts in their flowerpots, had shown extraordinary patience and considerable skill in decoding her garbled speech, because they recognized how lucky they were to find anyone who would stick it out for any length of time with little Will.

It was late in the evening on Valentine's Day when Sarah got a frantic call from Amy. Sarah recognized her thin whine when she answered the phone.

"Sarah, puhleeez . . . ," a plea followed by unintelligible babble.

"Whatever you've got in your mouth, spit it out and start over."

"I don't have anything in my mouth."

"Well then, just start over. Slowly."

"I'm baby-sitting for Susan and you've just got to come over," she repeated. "Please . . . I don't know what to do . . ."

Sarah could hear the baby crying in the background. She asked Amy what was wrong.

"He's been crying for so long, I'm afraid he's gonna have a heart attack and die. Can that happen to a baby? Can babies have heart attacks?"

"Where's Susan?"

"They drove up to Emporia to have dinner. I tried the cell phone but nobody answers. Then I called Clarice . . ." Amy paused. Everybody knew evenings were Clarice's worst times. "She couldn't help. She was useless," Amy finally pronounced with a sigh.

"You want me to come over?"

"Will you? Please? I'm so sorry. I just don't know who to call."

A light snow was falling when Sarah parked her truck in front of the house. The front door stood open, with Amy shivering on the porch and the baby's cries piercing the still night. Sarah had heard they were having a rough time of it. The baby had been born prematurely and with a weak heart, and he had spent most of his time in hospitals before the adoption. Now, at fourteen months, he wouldn't bond with Susan, didn't seem to take to anybody, wouldn't eat and just whimpered or fussed. The doctors called it "failure to thrive," but nobody seemed to know how to cure it or what to do.

"You know," Amy said as she led Sarah up the stairs, "I can see why Susan just comes unglued. He's impossible when he gets into one of these moods. He doesn't want to be held, doesn't want to eat." Her voice got all pinched, and Sarah could tell she was near tears. "I never knew a baby could cry the way he does, nonstop, and he just doesn't fall asleep."

Sarah opened the door to the nursery and looked toward the crib. His cries were muffled now; he had crawled to the corner of the crib and buried his face in the blanket.

"Hey, buddy . . . ," she said as she approached.

At first he didn't respond, but then she called him by name and he sat up. He was clearly undernourished, but there was something in his appearance, in the feral-like gaze of his pained eyes that spoke of a misery beyond hunger. His face was flushed from exertion, and his thin little shoulders shuddered in exhausted sobs.

Sarah stopped then, gripped by a powerful sentiment. She had known sadness and despair and read these things easily in others, but what passed between this abandoned infant and the troubled young woman now approaching him was something beyond logic and reason.

Will grew still and fixed his large dark eyes on Sarah, and the anger on his face gave way to a curious look.

Sarah paused momentarily with her hands on the crib rail, studying him as he studied her, as though they both were deliberating the next step.

Then she scooped him up, lifting him into the air, and felt a shudder run through his body. She was sharply aware of his slightness, as if he were more bird than child. He tilted back his little head and fixed her with a curious stare, then he grabbed a handful of the corkscrew hair and kneaded it in his tiny fist.

"He wouldn't even let me pick him up," Amy said. "I don't think he likes me."

Sarah answered, "Oh, it's just my hair," and felt a warmth flow through her body as he inclined his head on her shoulder. There were bald patches on his head, but the little bit of hair he had was dark and shiny and smelled sweeter than anything she had ever smelled before. She kissed the top of his head and said softly, with a faintly secretive smile, "I don't think it's anything personal."

"He's lost a lot of hair, I guess. Susan said they might have to put him back in the hospital."

"I hope not."

"They will if he doesn't gain any weight."

"Has he eaten anything?"

"No. He drank a little water. That's all."

"Let's go downstairs and give it a try."

Sarah rifled through the bags of home-made baby food Susan had so carefully pre-pared and stashed in the freezer. She pulled out one marked "Spinach" and waved it in front of his nose, emphasizing his need for such strong medicine, and while the cubes melted down in the microwave, Amy — now relieved of responsibility for Will — turned her thoughts to more personal worries and began to fret about her algebra exam the next morning. She carried on at length about her distaste for algebra, which, she believed, exceeded even Will's dislike of food, although, she astutely remarked, she would not expire for lack of it. It so hap-pened that Sarah was good at math, had great fondness for those things that came to-gether so neatly at the end, with just one simple, happy ending. So Amy fetched her book while Sarah settled Will on her lap with a dish towel tucked into the neck of his sleepers, and they sat at the kitchen table and went over several of the problems that had given Amy difficulty. Which is to say they did together the homework Amy had neglected to do in favor of evenings on the telephone with her boyfriend.

It was a while before they took notice of

Will. He had not fussed and had eaten a little of the spinach. He had not flicked it away, had not turned his head and squeamishly avoided the spoon as was his habit, but instead had nibbled at it, lolled it around in his mouth and even swallowed some. By the time several mysterious unknowns had been deduced, he had eaten more than half the rather inappreciable puddle of greens that had been placed on the table before him.

They were, of course, relieved, and a little amazed, but Amy was even more amazed by her ability to grasp one or two mathematical concepts that had up until that evening eluded her.

"He tried to help me," Amy said as she pushed her chair away from the table and stretched her legs.

"Who?"

"Mr. Wilde." She rose and pulled open the refrigerator door. "You want a Coke?"

"No thanks."

Amy popped open a can and sat back down. "He was very nice about it, but I couldn't understand diddly-squat, and then he started showing me what he was doing, you know, some of the stuff he's working on." She leaned across the table on her elbows to catch Sarah's eye. "He gets so intense when he talks about that stuff. I mean, the guy can actually make math sexy, I swear to God."

Sarah's reaction was immediate, a heat rising to her cheeks. She looked down at Will, away from Amy's quick eyes. "He struck me as rather . . . I don't know." She shrugged. "Detached."

"Oh, he's in the clouds, that's for sure." Amy giggled. "But damn, I sure wouldn't mind being up there with him."

"What's Susan like?"

"Oh, I don't know. Busy all the time. She's on the phone a lot. Does investment stuff from home. She works in the room upstairs." Amy paused to guzzle down the last of the Coke. "Not much of a cook, either. Fixes the same thing all the time. On Mondays it's this. Tuesdays it's that." She grimaced. "Yuck. How boring."

She removed a sheet of ruled paper from the back of her book and unfolded it.

"Here. I kept this. It's his handwriting."

Sarah lifted an eyebrow. "Did you get a lock of his hair, too?"

"Seriously, look at it. This is where he was trying to explain number twelve, and he just totally lost me."

Sarah took the paper from her. The script was surprisingly neat, even elegant. She found herself intrigued by it. As if she might read some expression of the man in his equations.

She folded it up and gave it back to Amy without further comment. Will had grown restless, and Sarah attempted a last swipe to clean his mouth, then lowered him to the floor.

"He forgets to eat, too."

"Who?"

"John!"

"Oh."

"I've taken lunch in to him sometimes and it sits there all afternoon."

Her mouth flew open in a great gaping yawn. She slid the Coke can aside and dropped her head on the table and mumbled, "I'm so tired. I wish they'd come home."

That's when Sarah suggested she go on home, leaving Sarah to finish out the evening. Amy took to the idea immediately, particularly when Sarah reassured her she wanted none of the baby-sitting money for herself, would gladly turn over to Amy all monies paid and received for an evening of suffering Will.

But Sarah was secretly glad when Amy left, and she carried Will around the kitchen and the parlor, talking to him the way one talks to things that listen mutely. She tempted her luck with a bottle of formula, and Will took a little of that, too. Finally, it seemed that sleep was winning out; his head rested heavily on her shoulder and his fingers slipped from her hair. But when she went upstairs to the nursery and approached the crib and attempted to separate him from her, even though his eyes were closed and his breath was giving way to slow, deep rhythms, he protested and grew agitated, and she could see he might easily throw himself back into a state.

In truth, Sarah was no more eager to part from him than he was to part from her, and so she turned out the lights and closed the door and went downstairs with Will curled up on her shoulder. She found her backpack on the floor in the parlor and pulled out a book, then looked around for a place to alight.

It was curiosity that drew her to John Wilde's study that night, and undoubtedly a wish to know him obliquely, to discover him refracted through the places he inhabited and the words he wrote and the books he read. There would be no harm in knowing him like this, with intent so innocent, while she might still remain unseen and unrevealed to him.

A trestle table had been set up to accommodate his computer, fax machine, and stacks of paper and files and books. She approached and stood for some time trying to make sense of the clutter. It did not surprise her to find that nearly everything was written in equations; all the notes and scribbles and printed pages were mathematical computations or graphs or measurements of some kind. Very little was expressed in words, and what was made no sense to her — "quantum memory," "atom-cavity state transfer," "vortex creation."

She was still standing in the shadows swaying gently with the baby when she noticed the rumpled throw-covered sofa shoved against the side wall below shelves of books. She was tired now, and the old sofa seemed particularly inviting. She flicked on the table lamp and sank down into the sagging seat. She worked off her shoes, then lay back and shifted Will onto her stomach.

She checked her watch. It was nearly eleven. She would read for a while, then put Will to bed and wait in the parlor until they returned. She opened her book.

9

Susan Wilde had always succeeded at anything she put her mind to. That's why little Will baffled her so, because he hadn't learned yet, hadn't been told, just how competent, how accomplished his mother was, how she always got it so right. For four months now John had watched her throw herself into the task of motherhood, but she confronted it like a battle, slogged into it with her mental armor and her clever strategies and her steeled will, only to meet with devastating failure. And on this evening, as they sat over their mesquite-grilled steaks in a corner booth of a steak house up in Emporia, they were unusually silent. They had both agreed earlier in the day not to talk of Will or his problems, but Will and his problems sat like a phantom at their table, and romance was nowhere to be found.

Susan looked up from her baked potato and eyed her husband's plate; the twelve-ounce porterhouse and mountain of home fries had vanished without a trace.

"You really should chew your food better."

He gathered up his napkin and wiped his mouth clean. Like many of his gestures, there was a suggestion of restrained energy.

"Still want to see a movie?" he asked.

"I don't think so."

"Too tired?"

"Tired?" A short puff of air escaped her nostrils. "That doesn't even come close."

"Shall we just go on home?"

"I'd rather. If you don't mind."

"No. I might work a little when I get back."

"Will you take Amy home?"

"Of course."

It was rare when John took much notice of the people around him, but on this evening as he waited in silence for his wife to finish (unlike her husband, Susan tended toward delicate, mincing bites), he found himself watching their waitress as she served the table next to them. She was a soft-spoken young woman with wide, slanted eyes, although he did not at first see the resemblance.

His mind was on his work, even as he pulled into the driveway and roused Susan from sleep, followed her into the hallway and took her coat from her shoulders, pecked her good night on the cheek.

She turned from the landing, leaning heavily on the handrail. "Please, honey, do be quiet when you come to bed," she whispered. "Don't wake the baby."

"I won't. You get to bed."

She nodded and trudged up the stairs.

Amy was usually to be found watching television in the old parlor, surrounded by a ring of litter, a Coke can or two, half-eaten bags of chips or bowls of popcorn. But the parlor was silent and there was no trace of the girl. It was not so much alarm as curiosity that swept through him, brought his thoughts back to the real world.

He called out in a loud whisper, "Amy?"

In the hallway he stood with his eyes on the stairs, wondering if she was in the nursery, hesitating to check for fear of waking Will, and that's when the door caught his attention. It was not at all as he had left it, but slightly ajar, with a sliver of pale light coming from the study.

He opened the door and looked across the room to where Sarah slept. The small table lamp cast a soft light that encircled her; the rest of the room was lost in darkness. She lay sleeping with both arms stretched behind her head, like a child waiting to be undressed. Quietly he approached and gazed down on her. The loose sleeves of her sweater had fallen around her shoulders, baring the insides of her arms, that vulnerable stretch of pale blue-veined skin, and he was overcome by a shocking urge to kiss her there. One hand hung poised in the air, the fingers gently curled; the other was hidden in the mass of her chestnut hair. The faintly exotic slant of her eyes and the high-winged brows were even more pronounced now that her eyes were closed, and it seemed her softly parted lips were offering up a kiss. He imagined with a kind of wistfulness the men who had seen her mouth just like this.

Will slept on her chest, his tiny body rising and falling with the rhythm of her breath, his flushed cheek on the pillow of her breast.

Never had the sight of a woman moved him so deeply; not even his wife, after all the years of intimacy, had ever appeared to him in quite this way. Will seemed to have tamed her just as she had tamed him, and there was a harmony in their togetherness, as if they were of the same mind, were dreaming the same dream.

She began to stir. The long, slender fingers came alive in a graceful, slow dance, and then she stretched and her body quivered as she took a deep breath, and her eyes opened.

He did not move but stood looking down at her with that penetrating gaze. Sarah awoke slowly, thinking this was still her dream, until he spoke.

He whispered low, "Shall I take him?"

She answered him with a quiet shake of her head, then she eased her way up, rising slowly, cradling Will to her breast. She swept back the dense tangle of auburn hair, then turned a groggy look on him.

"You're still asleep."

She nodded.

"Take your time," he whispered.

He waited while she worked on her shoes, and as she struggled to stand he reached under her arm and pulled her to her feet.

"Can you get him up to bed?"

She swayed slightly and he steadied her.

"Yes," she answered in a whisper.

He stood in the hallway listening to the old wooden stairs creak under her feet. It seemed like hours before she came down again, but it was only a few minutes. He had pulled a twenty-dollar bill out of his wallet and stood there with it folded in the palm of his hand, feeling a little silly and uncomfortable, the way he used to feel as an adolescent in the presence of girls. She descended the stairs with her eyes cast down, and when she reached the last step she looked up at him and said, "Amy called me. She was having trouble getting him to sleep. My name's Sarah."

"I remember you," he said as he held out the bill.

She reached for it and said with eyes averted, "Yes, from the open house. I'm sorry about that."

"I didn't mind."

She turned away and lifted her coat from the coatrack in the entrance.

"I'll give this to Amy," she said.

"I don't know if it's enough."

"I'm sure it is."

"Susan usually pays her."

Sarah lifted her backpack to her shoulder and turned toward the door.

"Do you need a ride home?"

"No, I drove."

"It's snowing heavily. Be careful."

"Thanks. I will."

"You want me to make you some coffee?"

"No, I'll be okay. Thanks."

She turned with a hand on the doorknob, and there was something in his look that gave her reason to pause.

"If you ever need me again, I mean . . . if Amy is busy, you can call me."

"Was he difficult?"

She seemed to be thinking over his question. "No, not really. He ate a little and then fell asleep on my shoulder. I think he just needs to be close to people."

He looked as though he was about to say something, but then his expression changed and he grew somber, but he did not leave her with his eyes.

Sarah could not last under that blue gaze, but looked down and mumbled a thanks, then opened the door and walked to her truck.

10

It was John's habit to work nights. After dinner he would return to his study to sleep for a few hours (on the same sofa where Sarah had slept), and then he would get up and work through the night when all was quiet and calm, slipping into bed just before dawn. After Sarah's departure he returned to the study, tossed a few pieces of kindling on the grate and settled a fat log on top, then watched as the kindling took flame. His thoughts were not on his work but on Sarah. He was only too aware of the lingering traces of her presence, perhaps even a slight heat left by her body on the very place where he was preparing to lie.

John Wilde had been an intellectually precocious youth, but girls did not interest him until late in high school. His popularity with women had always baffled him and left him a little uneasy. Even in the early stages of his marriage, the focus of his life had been his work, and sexual pleasure had always seemed strangely isolated from the rest of his life. It was not that he did not enjoy it, but that it seemed like something fragmented, not at all integral to his life.

His field did not draw a lot of women, but there had been a secretary in the physics department at Stanford who had flirted with him one winter, and she even tried to seduce him at the lab's Christmas party when she'd had a little too much to drink. At the end of the evening she stood in front of him in the crowded elevator and reached behind her back to work her hand between the flaps of his open coat. Unable, unwilling to resist, he felt her fingers drift between his legs, groping for him. John, in a daze, fixed his eyes dopily on the red digital numbers as they descended three floors, wishing they would continue into infinity. Several weeks later he walked into the office and found her flaunting a diamond and sapphire engagement ring, and the next month she moved to Seattle with her new husband-to-be — to John's great relief.

Then there had been Stephanie, a doctoral candidate from MIT he had met at a conference in Boston, and they had fallen into a long-distance affair that lasted the good part of a year, although they managed to see each other only twice after that initial encounter. It had frightened him terribly because she was on the verge of leaving her husband for him, and John felt nothing for her except a throbbing lust that spilled over into the rest of his life and sullied it. After those waters had ebbed, the guilt settled on the floor of his life like a sediment, and it lay there and hardened into a fine dark seam, a constant reminder of his betrayal.

He had never really questioned his marriage, had never really found it lacking by any measure. These occasional moments of temptation arose, but then they passed and were forgotten. That inarticulate no-name hunger that had driven him to rebellion as a young man had long since been channeled into his work, and — if not at peace with himself — he was at least reconciled to the life he was living.

The log burst into flame and John rose and went to his desk. He shuffled aside some papers, found the scientific journal he wanted, then settled himself on the sofa to read.

As soon as his head hit the pillow he noticed it — a faint sweet perfume from her hair. But he focused his attention on his reading and forced her out of his mind.

After a page he felt his eyelids fall under the weight of sleep. He struggled against the urge for a few more paragraphs, then rolled over and laid the journal on the floor.

It took him a moment before he realized his fingers had grazed something: it was the cold spine of a book, kicked under the sofa, only a hard-edged corner protruding.

He fished it out and looked at it.

It was an early leather-bound edition of Charles Doughty's *Travels in Arabia Deserta*. He had heard of Doughty, a nineteenth-century Arabist who had traveled the caravan routes. The book was a rare edition, one he judged to be of considerable value. There was no name, nothing to indicate proprietorship, but it could only be hers. He carefully opened it, and as he did so, a large envelope fell from the back cover. Within it were folded letters, their original envelopes discarded. The correspondence appeared to be typed letters to Sarah, and her replies, which were entirely handwritten. Her handwriting was erratic — at times an elegant, stylized script, at other times careless and nearly illegible. He knew at a glance it was an intimate correspondence, knew she would be exposed to him on these pages, and he was not sure if he wanted to know her like this, suspected he might be disappointed, that she might reveal herself to be dull, unimaginative, that the mystery would fade. It was more apprehension than conscience that caused him to hesitate; but finally, he sat up and began to read.

March 2

Dear Miss Bryden,

I am beginning to despair of ever having the opportunity to meet you. I know from your grandfather that you have tried to return my calls, and I confess this is one of the rare occasions when I regret my resistance to technology and my stubborn refusal to install an answering machine.

Therefore, I resort to this archaic — yet not unpleasant — form of communication and beg you to regard me as an acquaintance rather than a stranger.

I know that by now your grandfather has told you of my visit to your home and perhaps elucidated the reason for my presence in Cottonwood Falls. I'm sure countians secretly — or not so secretly — do not look with kindness on my attempts to unearth the lives of the living and the dead in my pursuit of literary glory. But I am used to my status as an unwelcome stranger; I lived it in

Baratzeland and shall live it in the Australian lowlands when I leave here.

It is a strange task I undertake, and although I am quite clear as to the shape and substance of my work, if you should demand my personal motives, I would reply that I will only know once it is finished, for the answer lies in the search itself and not in the final chapter.

Already I have strayed from my intent, which is to ask your cooperation in a matter of trade. I am sending you herewith a print of David Roberts's, which I obtained from a London gallery after visiting the site myself many years ago.

The drawing is entitled "Excavated Temple at Petra called El Ehasneh, or the Treasury" and is, I believe, one of the most beautiful among the 120 or so Roberts sketched. Apart from my own travels in Israel, Egypt, and the Sinai, my affinity with the subject is more than just a matter of taste: Roberts was accompanied on his journey through the Middle East by my great-great-grandfather John Kinnear in 1839, and I have among my papers in London some of the letters he wrote to my great-great-grandmother.

In exchange, I would very much like to have your pastel of the pale yellow-fringed orchid — the one above your bed.

Sincerely yours,
Anthony Kingsley

March 7
Dear Mr. Kingsley,

Your lithograph is worth more than all my efforts thrown together, but I am far too selfish to refuse it for the sake of form. Therefore, I am sending you, along with the yellow fringed orchid, one of my rare oils. It is quite different from my pastels, but I think it has merit. It is quite simply just another way of seeing things.

When I was at the university I wrote a paper on the Orientalists for an art history class. I mention this only as a way of connection. I am not a romantic — but I do believe in the power of myth.

My grandfather is always entertained by your visits. As for my grandmother, she makes everyone feel uncomfortable so please don't let her deter you. I regret I keep missing you.

Very sincerely yours,
Sarah Bryden

March 20
Dear Sarah,

I bought this for you last night at the Jitney Bazaar in Cottonwood Falls. It cost all of $1.00. In all my travels I think I have never seen such a tawdry teapot. But I fancied I saw just a hint of a grin on that camel's face, and I thought it was a secret bit of humour he might like to share with you.

Thank you for sending me your paper on the Orientalists. I knew you could find it if you searched long enough (although I suspect your reluctance was more a matter of timidity than time). It was, as I suspected it would be, quite impressive. You would have made a fine scholar.

I was very disappointed that you were called away last night just as I sat down at your table. I got a fair view of your face and your smile. But then you disappeared.

Fondly,
Anthony

April 9
Dear Anthony,

I applaud your determination, but I think your chances of finding a fringed orchid are slim. I haven't seen one in many years. Unfortunately, it can only be pollinated by the sphinx moth, which visits the orchid around twilight, drawn by its delicate perfume. The sphinx moth has nearly been exterminated by pesticides, and so these beauties may very well be doomed to extinction. Nevertheless, I urge you to keep looking.

I envy you your freedom on the prairie. And your fresh eye. I seem to have lost both.

I assure you, I am not averse to meeting you, but I do work long hours and my days off are generally spent drawing.

I am also completely absorbed by the book you lent me, so you mustn't blame me if I am reluctant to come out. I am particularly intrigued by the passages you chose to underline and your margin notes. More of a window onto your thoughts than the author's.

Yours truly,
Sarah

May 14

My dear Sarah,

I found Diamond Springs, but only after more than six hours of wandering. Not that I regret the wandering — it is, after all, my modus operandi. But I had hoped to have you for my guide.

I am now sitting in the shade of the big elm growing just north of the trough — I'm sure you know the one — and I am imagining this place throughout its centuries of interaction with man. Despite the buzzing heat and the hostile prickliness of these grasses I can't help but be convinced there is a genius loci here — just as there was one at Thut's quarry. Perhaps it is only that these places are somehow connected to you.

The old cowman I approached up at Diamond Ranch to get permission to wander out here without being shot told me a story about a little girl who used to run away from home and hide up here with a wild stallion. I made no attempt whatsoever to correct him and render his story more accurate. Instead I felt myself honored to be acquainted with a myth in the making, and I was determined to do nothing to diminish it. On the contrary, I drew him out as long as possible and, as I suspected he might, he took the bait and wove me a tale Mark Twain would have found tough to beat. But I refuse to be so easy as to write it to you; it will be had only in the telling, as oral literature should be had, and in exchange for your presence.

The wind has come up since I began writing, and I have to take great care lest these thoughts be lost to the wind.

Here, more than any other place, where there is nothing from the past to recommend it, no ruins, no monument, I sense the greatness of the ordinary that has tread here before me. Cattle paths approach this spring like the spokes of an old wagon wheel, and I see coming to me on the wind a Kaw buffalo hunter; a Czech immigrant; a Boston barber seeking gold; an army lieutenant sent to map topography seemingly endless, a land that haunted his nights with dreams of walking on the bottom of the sea; a mischief-loving ten-year-old girl (whom you would have liked); a Spaniard in chain mail with skin and mind the toughness of buffalo hide; and then those nomads of eras so long past they escape my imagination and I feel them only as spirits, with no faces, no history to define them.

There is, however, a vision that haunts me more than these, and it bears your face and your eyes and your smile.

Fondly,
Anthony

June 28

My dearest Anthony,

Your offer was providential; I hate to think what kind of misery my grandma might have brought down around my ears had I stayed under her roof one more night. We have times of peace and times of war, and we seem to be entering upon the latter.

Did I mention to you how, as a child, I used to imagine myself living here in this house of yours, daughter of a great landlord, with servants and ponies, and only once did I set foot in the place before yesterday, and that was in the dead of night the New Year's Eve of my senior year in high school, with a riotous gang of friends looking for ghosts.

Since you estimate your absence to be at least three weeks, I took the liberty of bringing over some of my painting materials and setting them up in the parlor. Rest assured that your privacy and your work will be completely respected.

Yes, the bed is spartan at best — on sleepless nights I think it not much better than the rack. But I have brought my David Roberts from home and hung it above the bed. It is quite serene here with your rugs, and the high naked walls seem to stand proud with a kind of forlorn beauty. I would dare not touch a thing in here.

I sense the sanctity of your solitude. I feel I am able to read you through what is absent — not what is visible. On these naked walls I feel there is written a part of your life.

I loved hearing your voice, all the way from London! But I see you so much better on the page. Please write me. Even though I am surrounded by you, I still miss you.

Love,
Sarah

P.S. I *am* going to repaint the kitchen, however. Would a pale buttercup yellow suit you?

July 10
My lovely Sarah,

You will receive this letter after my return, and should it come into your hands while you are by my side, I beg you to look away and shield me from your reaction should it be other than the one I desire.

My publisher here in London has agreed to do the next work in this series. My first was in Africa — in Baratzeland

— as you know. Then the Flint Hills. The next will be a region in the Australian lowlands. I haven't decided where. But it will be a small town. A prairie town like yours. And then, if all goes well, I will finish in the pampas in Argentina.

Come away with me, my dear Sarah. Come away with me and we shall travel these places together, you and I. I have made many attempts in my past to live this life peacefully with other women (as you well know) but I have not yet been successful. Could you see fit to forgive me my past and come with me — for as long or as briefly as you wish? I will be satisfied with whatever you can give me.

I do love you, my dearest Sarah.

Anthony

That was the last letter.

John sat for a long while in stunned silence, thinking about the lives revealed so intimately on those pages. Even though Sarah's replies were short, had her own letters been missing, he would have been able to measure the woman by the man. This was no common drifter who had passed through these parts, and the dignity and beauty with which he had announced his love for Sarah left John feeling vaguely envious, even inadequate. Who was this man who had tried to charm her? Lure her away with him? What had become of him? And why had her letters been returned?

He switched off the lamp and lay in the darkness with his eyes wide open, his mind in a muddle. It was a long time before he slept.

11

John generally slept late and heavily. Rarely was he disturbed by the racket of the family's morning ritual, the baby's wails and the sweeper running downstairs and the telephone ringing, but on this morning he was up in time to catch Susan in the kitchen tussling with Will over breakfast. He poured himself a cup of coffee and sank into a chair opposite her, and told her about Sarah Bryden.

"You mean she actually volunteered to come back?"

"She did."

"You're kidding."

"Nope."

"You must be."

"I'm not."

"Did she fly out of here on wings?"

He gave her a sleepy smile and ran his hand through his tousled hair.

"Took her truck."

"That's not very angelic."

Susan set down the bowl of cereal and tried to clean off the baby's mouth, but he resisted the wet cloth, stubbornly flinging his head back and forth until she finally gave up.

"So, somebody thinks they can handle you, Will." She gave a derisive little snort. "Imagine that."

"How do you know her?"

"I don't, really. Not very well. She's a waitress at the Cassoday Cafe. Amy's mother owns the place."

She sat quietly for a moment.

"That makes me think . . ."

"What?"

"Your dad's sixty-fifth."

"What about it?"

She rose to pour John another cup of coffee.

"What if we ask her to come along with us?"

"Up to Lawrence?"

"We really can't leave Will with my mom for that long. And I already asked Amy. She's got something on that day." She set the mug in front of him.

"What about her job?"

"It's on a Sunday. I think the cafe's closed Sundays."

"You'd pay her, wouldn't you?"

Susan laughed and reached over the table to brush the hair out of his face.

"Of course I would. Silly man. I'm sure she could use the money. I don't think they're very well off. You remember her grandfather?"

"Yes. The open house."

"She lives with him. And her grandmother. Rather pathetic, really." Susan paused, then, "I don't have the faintest idea why she's still living here. She doesn't fit in at all."

"Yes. I'd believe that."

There was a stiff silence while John sat hunched over his steaming coffee.

"What makes you say that?" Her voice held a twinge of something disagreeable.

He smiled up at her. "Oh, I think I know a thing or two about fitting in."

The doorbell rang just then. It was the boy from across the street come to shovel snow off the driveway, and the discussion of Sarah Bryden came to a close.

But talking about Sarah had started John thinking about his own life, and he lingered over his coffee that morning, and wondered about the turn of things in time.

Perhaps, had he been born at another place, another time, had his intellect been spared the straitjacket of an institutional education, it is quite possible he would have trod another path, would perhaps have become a great mathematician or even a sage. But his mind bore the birthmark of Middle America, and from infancy on, all that did not conform had been sweated out of him.

From the start John had been a source of anxiety and even disappointment to his rigidly conventional parents — both of them professors at the University of Kansas. First there had been the problem of muteness. At the age of three, when most children are becoming fluent (an age at which his older brother could already read), John had barely spoken at all. His parents took him to specialists, paid for test after test to assess and diagnose him, only to conclude his muteness amounted to no more than sheer stubbornness. They were reassured by child psychologists that their son would, when ready, speak. Which he did, of course. But this willfulness seemed to set the stage for the battle between his spirit and his rigid, autocratic family.

Soon, his extraordinary aptitude for mathematics became manifest, and later on, his fascination for the subtleties of physics, but even then his parents were not reassured. He was quite capable of failing a class if he found the subject matter dull or offensive (he told the school counselor he failed American literature because he had heard his father's voice in Cotton Mather's Puritan sermons). Yet he would finish exams in calculus or trigonometry in a third of the allotted time and spend the rest of the class period devising complex math puzzles on the back of his test papers and send them back to his teachers to solve. There seemed to flow through him a deeply intuitive and irrational current that his parents could never fully understand. All the standardized tools of measurement failed to define this quality of his, as if it lurked in some hidden recess of his brain, far away from the gaze of ordinary men.

The Ivy League universities his brothers had attended wanted nothing to do with this changeling (John seemed not in the least dismayed by the rejection), and he found himself dumped in the university in his own backyard, where his father, Dr. Armand Wilde, held the rank of full professor and past chair of the aeronautical engineering department. He tottered along through his undergraduate years, choosing to live a solitary and contemplative existence with another physics major in a small apartment near campus.

At one point he was on the verge of changing his major to theology, a prospect his parents found even more disquieting than the specter of failed classes, given his tendency toward independent thought. Only too clearly did they remember an incident when, in the course of his Saturday morning confirmation classes, Reverend Simpson had assigned the Apostles' and Nicene creeds to memorize, and thirteen-year-old John had come back the following week with a creed he had written himself. It was a wildly mystical monologue annotated with mathematical equations, and he spent nearly half an hour lecturing Reverend Simpson on the nature of the infinitesimally small and the infinitely large. For John, mathematical theorems were the scent (he was insistent on the metaphor) of God's presence throughout the universe. His parents feared no seminary would ever graduate him, let alone ordain him. Needless to say, they breathed a sigh of relief when John renounced theology and opted instead for theoretical physics.

His single-mindedness often left him insensitive to social nuance. He could ramble on about atomic vorticity and low-energy elliptical aberrations without ever suspecting it was all well beyond the understanding of his family and friends. But this is not to say he was without charm: on the contrary, everyone liked him, although few understood him. There was in his manner a directness, an unassuming innocence that melted the heart. This charm worked magic on women, particularly older women — at least those who were patient enough to attempt to communicate with him.

Eventually his studies in physics rose to meet the challenge of his precocity, and maturity tamed his eccentricities so that by the time he reached his senior year at university, his parents felt certain their son at long last fit the profile of the brilliant young scientist.

Appearances, however, were deceptive, and the spring before his graduation, a strange event occurred that put to the test what little remnants of rebellion still thrummed in his heart.

It was the last Sunday in April, just five weeks before commencement. He was slowly making his way down the grand stairs of the First Congregational Church behind the vast Gothic figure of his father as they flowed with the crowd to greet the Reverend Simpson on the sidewalk below, when he suddenly felt a cold, wrinkled hand slip into his own. He turned to see a shriveled creature gazing up at him from underneath a billowing mushroom of pale blue netting.

"You're the young Wilde boy, aren't you?" said a watery thin voice, her eyes pallid as the noon-washed sky.

"Yes," answered John. He was struggling to remember her.

"You're graduating this year, aren't you?" she asked pointedly.

"I am."

"What are you going to do with yourself?" She linked her arm in his and leaned on him as they advanced another step.

"I'm going out west. To Stanford. I'll be doing my doctorate in physics."

"Oh," she said, and her voice trailed. "Be careful."

John, misunderstanding, pressed his hand over hers to reassure her. "Let's go over here and use the handrail," he said.

She put on the brakes with a kind of stubborn heels-down jerk that let it be known in no uncertain terms that she was not what she appeared to be.

"I wasn't talking about myself. I was talking about you." She looked up at him with a severe gaze, full of indignation. "I was talking about you, young Wilde." She snorted back through powdered nostrils. "Boys need some time away from the father."

He indulged her with a condescending smile and gently emphasized, "But I'm not staying here. Stanford's in California."

"Oh, I know where Stanford is," she answered sharply, with an impatient flick of her blue netting. "But it's the same thing. It's the father. All your life you've marched to his drumbeat. It's time to do your own thing, young Wilde. Get out of yourself a bit. Go find the world. Fight in a war. Work in a soup kitchen. Join the Peace Corps. But don't go to Stanford. Not yet. You can do that later." She patted him roughly on the arm and gave him a smile that could scarcely erase the unsettling pallor of those blue eyes.

They were interrupted at that moment by a lady with pumpkin-colored hair who called her Hortense and bustled her away, chattering about the car waiting and how they'd looked all over for her.

"There was a Hortense Potter," his mother said when he asked about her in the buffet line at the faculty club where they lunched together once a month after church. "But she died quite some time ago. You probably wouldn't remember her. She used to work in the nursery when you were a baby. She always seemed to favor you. A very pretty woman. Even when she was old. Never married."

Armand was fishing a slice of ham from a silver domed dish and eyeing the eggs Benedict with restraint. Hortense? He sighed heavily and passed by the eggs Benedict. He could not recall a Hortense, did not much trouble his mind with the detail; it was, after all, of no importance.

But it was.

There had always been that other distinguishing feature about John, a sense of heightened spirituality that no memorized creed could ever invoke. Hortense played to that audience in him, and he took her quite seriously. Her look, filtered through blue netting, lingered with John, and with time the netting faded and there were just those eyes, and soon those eyes began to have a cunning resemblance to his own eyes when he leaned close to the mirror every morning to inspect his stubbled jaw.

He was a little at a loss as to how to proceed at this point in his life. His doctoral studies were very important, but Hortense had reawakened in him that intuitive streak, and he turned his mind inward and listened.

Only the idea of the Peace Corps truly appealed to him, but for the wrong reasons: its romance and slightly faded splendor, its association with the Camelot of the Kennedy presidency, its nobility of purpose, the lure of far-off, exotic places. But Peace Corps work generally involved teaching of some sort, and John's previous attempts at teaching had been, if not quite disastrous, then less than successful. During his undergraduate years he had taken an occasional tutoring job to earn pocket money, but most of his pupils left after only a few sessions, and always with the same complaint: instead of toiling on their level, clarifying the steps as they went along, he would wander off into complex theory, leaving his pupils thoroughly confused. Yet there was an intoxicating quality about him, and some students, particularly the girls, returned time after time just to be in his presence. When he spoke he would grow animated, the words tumbling out, his eyes deepening in hue, and whether or not they understood him became irrelevant.

He filled out the Peace Corps application almost as a lark, believing his responses to the questions would be far too vague. He floundered when it came to justifying his motive. He could not very well explain that Hortense Potter's ghost had told him to do this, but he was able to sound plausibly determined, and he sent off all the papers and the recommendations he had so stealthily solicited, and then tried to forget about it. Like some shameful misdeed committed in absolute secrecy.

A month later he was accepted.

To Kenya.

He had a choice now. He could act on his intuition, fly against the conventional winds that had directed his life until now, and it frightened him down to the marrow of his bones. At the same time, paradoxically, a kind of peace settled over him, and when he stared at his face in the morning he saw Hortense's eyes twinkle back at him, and he felt a release from all their expectations. As the weeks went by he began to see Africa as more than a mere experience or an interlude, but as a powerful determinant of his destiny.

A lightheartedness seized him during those last weeks before final exams, and it was undeniably this effervescence that had sent him off with a carload of friends to the Cicada Club up in Kansas City. John sat in the backseat with his roommate, Robert, a young Scottish physics major with a shank of greasy black hair and black-rimmed glasses, the two of them drinking straight gin from the bottle and feeling reckless and decadent.

It was Robert who brought Susan over to their table, because Robert didn't dance but he loved to show off his Anglican wit, and Susan was a good audience. With her long scarlet nails curled around a glass of scotch, she shot dry repartee right back at him. But Susan had her eye on John, even though he didn't pay her much heed that evening, was too busy moonwalking across the dance floor with a black-haired gamin to appreciate her many qualities. She called him a few days later, and the next time he saw her, in her own natural setting, sitting in a booth at the Ritz grill with a vase of lilies towering over her shoulder, glancing impatiently at the slender Rolex dangling from her wrist, he felt himself whisked silently and painlessly along that old Wilde current.

Susan Blackshere, National Merit Scholar and Phi Beta Kappa, had graduated summa cum laude from the University of Kansas, gone on for her MBA at Wharton, and immediately taken up a high-paying job with a prestigious Kansas City brokerage firm as an assistant portfolio manager. The fact that her father, although deceased when Susan was only five, had seen fit to make her trustee of her own estate upon her majority, and with title to a little land and more than a little wealth, showed either extreme folly or extraordinary insight on the part of the old man. The latter turned out to be true.

John was quick to recognize how Susan's many qualities complemented his own. She was cool, tempered reason to his energy and animation. When he tended to leap blindly ahead, she would calmly reel him back, settle him down, and start him off again. She was almost five years older than he, and she was the first woman he had ever met who held his attention past the third date. Her physical attributes were certainly not lacking, but their lovemaking was only a preliminary hurdle to be negotiated so they might proceed to the far more stimulating realms of the mind. For John, who had never had difficulty finding women who wanted to sleep with him, it was only natural that he confused this cerebral infatuation with love. It would take many years for that other side of him to be awakened.

John took Susan home to meet his parents one Saturday evening in June. Kansas summers are notoriously muggy, and that evening, like most summer evenings, the Wildes kept to the cool confines of their bay-windowed sitting room while Nancy's pot roast simmered away in the kitchen. John had taken the club chair while Susan stood at the bar next to Armand, who was ceremoniously mixing Bloody Marys, which they always drank in the summer, although John never really liked the drink much. Susan, it turned out, was truly fond of them, liked a sharp dash of Tabasco, which she boldly requested from Armand Wilde while she rattled off a complicated formula for managing the withdrawal of retirement funds. What John liked above all was the way Susan seemed to just step in and take over for him, like a human shield. She deflected all that terrifying focus of attention that had dogged him since his childhood. Now, for the first time in his young adult life, he sat in his parents' home, drank a gin and tonic instead of a Bloody Mary, and relaxed.

When Susan turned in mid-conversation and, seeing there was no seat beside John, lowered her long legs to the floor and settled comfortably at his feet, hiding her size-ten shoes artfully in the drapes of her black silk pants, John imagined he saw a glimmer of lust in his father's eyes. Then, a little later, while still in the throes of balanced portfolios, John dangled his empty glass next to Susan's ear and ever so discreetly rattled the ice cubes, a gesture he had watched his father repeat over the years to his mother who would, without batting an eye, step over and pick up his glass and refill it. John was waiting for a pause, waiting for her to turn a bemused eye on him and lance him with a dry smile, but she did not. Instead, she set down her own drink, rose to her full five-foot ten-inch height, removed the glass from his hand, and whisked across the room with a rustle of silk to the bar where she mixed John another gin and tonic as if she had been doing it all her life.

There could be no surer test of authenticity than this.

But the Wildes saw even more; they saw a potentially powerful ally, someone with a faultless guidance system, a characteristic Armand Wilde appreciated in humans as well as in defense systems. Her career, in one form or another, was viable in every region of the world, in every economic climate. She could follow John to Stanford, Columbia, even Copenhagen. She would be more than succor and balm; she would lay down the track upon which their son would travel.

Armand Wilde was not an intuitive man, but perhaps he sensed a certain hesitancy in his son that summer, because while John was busy at his old construction job and bedding Susan in her well-appointed brownstone near the Kansas City Plaza, Armand Wilde made an unannounced side trip to

Stanford. He was already in the general vicinity, had been called out West as a consultant for Lockheed and just thought it worth his time to check the classified ads and see what was coming up in the way of rentals that might be convenient for a young man in his first year of doctoral studies. He found just the thing, a little two-room duplex within walking distance of the physics department. He filled out the rental agreement, signed his own name, and put down a deposit that included the first month's rent.

Upon his return he presented John with this fait accompli as calmly as if he had just picked up a nice bottle of merlot for dinner.

That's when Hortense faded. Or perhaps she had faded earlier and John had been too busy to notice. That evening John shut himself in his room and dug out the papers from their hiding place in his closet: the acceptance letter, the instructions for training and interviewing that were to take place in August. He read them through again and again, trying to revive their plausibility. He sat on the side of his bed with the letter on his knees, rubbing his sweating palms against his jeans. He would look up at the door and see himself opening it, walking out, finding his father in his study, in his recliner, reading glasses riding low on his nose, smooth skull glistening in the light. John would thrust the letter into his gut and bellow like a drill sergeant, "Stanford be damned! I'm going to Africa to teach math to little Kenyans!" Then he would turn and walk back to his room and close the door and lie there in bed with his stomach squeezing out his breath while he waited for that battleship of a man to cruise into his dark waters and destroy him.

Instead, John destroyed the letter. He destroyed every trace of his folly. He had told no one about it; not Susan, nor his mother, nor Robert, not even the comfortingly anonymous workers on his construction crew. He took all the papers out on the job very early one morning, pulled them out from underneath the seat of the Ford Mustang his parents had given him as a graduation present, and burned them in an incinerator behind a new home they were building in Overland Park.

Afterward, he sat on the front steps drinking his Quick Trip coffee while he waited for the other workers to arrive, feeling all the ponderous weight of his decision. He knew all along Africa had been a myth; all he had really wanted was his freedom. Now, as he looked out across the sea of rooftops it occurred to him he might have just incinerated his soul.

He married Susan the week before Christmas in a candlelit ceremony in Lawrence, performed by the most Reverend Simpson in that very church where Hortense had visited him. The First Congregational Church welcomed 512 guests to its sanctuary decked in holly and flocked pine, with tall, flickering tapers playing against the solemn shadows. John had returned from school just two days prior to the wedding, and the whole affair struck him as something out of a dream.

John would be the first to admit that his life set its course at that moment. As his parents had predicted, Susan — the wind in his sails — directed him. Not so much overtly but subtly, because of who she was. Sometimes it seemed to him that she was a Wilde before she was a Blackshere, and so John followed in his father's footsteps. But even if he had wished it, John could never be that battleship he so feared; he was much more like the deep and darkly perplexing waters through which it sailed.

Hortense rarely visited him anymore. Only in rare and troubling dreams, and then she was always disguised somehow, and she no longer had a name.

12

John had not intended to drive up to the university until later in the week, but he changed his mind that morning while he had his coffee and listened to the shovel scraping against the concrete walk and thought about things past, and wondered some about the future. The encounter with Sarah seemed to have set things in motion, to have flooded his consciousness with a peculiar awareness. Even Will appeared to him in a new light, and when he looked at the strange child crawling around on the floor at his feet, there would flash across his mind the image of Sarah sleeping, and the child didn't seem quite so strange anymore.

He rose and set his empty mug in the sink. He looked out the window at the snow-blanketed lawn and the morning sky full of dazzling light, and he thought it would indeed be a good day for a drive.

He had intended to break in mid-afternoon, but he lost track of time as he usually did. He slapped shut his laptop and quickly gathered up his work and dashed down the walk behind the research library with his coat open and flapping in the cold wind. It was getting close to nightfall when he exited the turnpike at Cassoday and cruised slowly into the town. The lights were out at the Cassoday Cafe and the place was dark inside. There was an OPEN sign hanging askew in the front window, but when he tried the knob the door was locked. Just then the red-checkered curtains stirred, and Amy's face appeared in the window. The door opened, and she greeted him with a shy smile.

"Hi."

"Is Sarah here?"

"Nope. We're closed."

John motioned to the book and the large envelope under his arm. "I just wanted to return this. She left it over at our place last night."

"Oh, I can give it to her."

She held out her hand, but he only stared blankly at her. She couldn't help but notice the way disappointment washed over his face and troubled his blue eyes, and there was a sudden boyishness in his demeanor that twisted at her heart.

"She'll be in early tomorrow. I can give it to her then."

"Yeah. Thanks," he answered. But just as he shifted the book to his hand, there was the sound of tires crunching on the snow, and he glanced over his shoulder to see a white Bronco with the Chase County Sheriff logo emblazoned on the door pull to a stop behind him.

"Sorry, I gotta go," Amy said as she struggled into her coat. "My dad's here." She turned to lock the door behind her. "You know, she lives just up the road in Bazaar. It's on your way. If you want to take it by yourself."

"I guess I could do that."

Amy stole a sly glance at him as she sprinted down the steps to the waiting Bronco. "It's the yellow house. You can't miss it."

There is an enchantment that settles over the Hills at twilight. It is rapid and fleeting and can only be seized at just the right time in just the right confluence of light and shadow. As John drove slowly up the road to Bazaar, he sensed such a moment was on him. He took his time, glancing often at the snow-patched winter-brown hills shrouded in ever-deepening hues of violet as the sun pulled its last light from the sky. As he rounded a bend or climbed to a plateau it seemed the face of the land was always changing. The north wind blasted his car from time to time, and he had to grip the wheel tightly to keep it on the road. The stars were already out and shining with cold brilliance in the clean sky. He thought again of the letters he had read and the man who had written them, and the seductive power in the words that passed between this man and Sarah. He wondered what kind of woman Sarah was and how it could be that he had never in his thirty-some years felt quite this urgency about anyone before.

Even in the penumbra of dusk he could make out the yellow house with peeling white trim. He slowed and turned into the driveway.

An old man on crutches answered the door and John didn't recognize him right off, only when he gave a little hop forward out of the shadows and his face came under the porch light. A screen door separated them, but John could still catch a glimmer of mistrust, a seasoned wariness in the old man's eyes.

"I apologize for dropping in like this . . . ," John began. "Is Sarah here?"

"Nope."

John had sealed the batch of letters in a large manila envelope, and Jack Bryden cast a suspicious look at the package John now gripped in his hand.

"You sellin' somethin'?"

"No, I'm returning some things she left at our place last night when she baby-sat my son. I'm John Wilde."

Recognition lit up the old man's face and smoothed out the deeply furrowed brow.

"John Wilde! Well, come on in. Too cold to be standin' out there."

The room reeked of stale cigarette smoke only partly masked by the odor of roasting meat wafting in from the kitchen. A hand-sewn quilt covered the worn seat of a chesterfield sofa, and limp lace doilies hid the threadbare armrests. Next to the recliner sat a metal TV tray littered with the old man's essentials — a sand-filled Folgers coffee can in which to extinguish his cigarettes, this week's *TV Guide*, nail clippers, a tin of Altoids. The room was dark except for the flickering light from the television tuned to the evening news. Beside the recliner, lodged between it and the chair, rested a prosthetic leg.

"Sorry I didn't recognize you. I was a little under the weather that night of the open house," apologized Jack. With the rubber tip of his crutch he jabbed at the switch on the base of a floor lamp behind his recliner and light flooded the room. Only then did John notice where his denim overalls were turned up and pinned just above the knee.

There was an awkwardness in the encounter, and if Jack Bryden, who was generally a convivial man even with strangers, found himself looking with vague suspicion on this man with the unsettling blue eyes, it was because somehow Sarah figured into the equation. He looked down at the leather-bound volume John held out to him, shifted his weight a little on his crutches.

"This is what she left?" His voice was edged with surprise.

John handed him the envelope. "And this, too."

He gave a cursory glance at the envelope but made no move to take it, just hung there on his crutches cradling the book in his hands.

There was a movement across the room, and John looked up to see a gray-haired woman standing in the kitchen doorway, a woman as drab and ordinary as a sparrow. A housedress hung loosely on her thin shoulders, and she stared warily at him as she dried her hands on her apron.

"This here's my wife, Ruth," Jack said.

Ruth gave him a curt nod.

"That's a rare book, isn't it?" John said, shifting his gaze back to the old man.

"Well, it's a pretty special book if that's what you mean. It belonged to Sarah's mother." He shifted his weight and then went on softly, "She drowned. Off some damn island in Greece . . . hell if I can ever remember the name of the place. Even though I been there. Had to go over to pick up Sarah and bring her home. She was just a baby. Not even a year old." His voice had turned gruff and he was thumbing the soft leather of the book.

"Don't need to talk 'bout those things in front of strangers," spat Ruth, and just as she turned back into the kitchen they heard snow crunching underfoot and footfalls on the porch steps, and Jack shouted, "Hold onto that handrail, Blanche!"

There was a flurry of stomping feet and mumbled curses as the door burst open, and John stepped back to make way for a bundle of fur swathed in yards and yards of muffler. A gloved hand unwound the knitted wool from her head and neck, and Blanche shook out her softly curled white hair, and John looked down into the face of a vision.

"John Wilde, meet Blanche. Bazaar's one and only registered historical monument."

108

But it was not Blanche, it was Hortense, with the ice-blue eyes.

John muttered a greeting, but Blanche didn't take note of the awe in his voice. She was too busy trying to untangle the cat from her feet.

"Damn her hide, she's gonna be the death of me."

"Well, if you'd feed her once in a while . . ."

"Jack, I feed that damn cat three, sometimes four times a day and she's still between my feet."

"She loves you, be thankful you've got somethin' loves you, Blanche. Somethin' you don't have to stick dollar bills in their birthday cards every year so as to get their attention."

Blanche had finally unwound her muffler and stuffed her gloves in her pocket and was unbuttoning her coat.

"Well, I've never liked cats, so how is it I got myself three of 'em."

Ruth appeared from the kitchen with a scrap of cold ham. "Here, give this to her." Blanche held open the screen door and tossed the ham onto the porch, but the cat was not interested. Finally Blanche gave the animal a swift kick with her black rubber overshoe and sent it hissing off the steps and into the front yard.

"Blanche!" cried Ruth.

"Oh, hell, she ain't hurt. She'll be right there when I come out. Never seen a cat like that. Acts like a damn dog. Only worse."

Only when she was relieved of her coat and the cat did she turn her twinkling eyes to John and hold out a bony hand.

"What's your name?" she said, squinting at him through fogged glasses. John was surprised she didn't already know, didn't set about cursing him right then and there for his betrayal all those years ago.

"John Wilde," he answered.

"This here's Clarice's son-in-law," clarified Jack. "Married to Susan Blackshere."

Blanche flopped down onto a chair and bent over to remove her overshoes. She looked up at him and the look unsettled him just as her first appearance had done, for the resemblance — although not perfect — was stunning.

"Where you from, John?"

"California for the last ten years, but I was raised in Lawrence."

"Ah!" She lit up. "I've got family up in Lawrence. Good town," she said.

"You look a lot like a lady who used to attend our church."

Blanche was massaging her toes through

thick wool socks.

"The Congregational Church, by any chance?"

"Yes. It was."

"That was my twin sister. Hortense."

She looked up at him and John felt the back of his neck tingle.

"Did you know her?" she asked.

It took him a moment to answer. "She seemed to take an interest in me."

"That doesn't surprise me. She didn't have kids of her own and she was always meddlin' with those youngsters at that church, tellin' 'em what they should and shouldn't do. But they loved her for it. She had the best darn Halloween parties. She'd get all dressed up and do these haunted house things, 'n kids'd come from all over the neighborhood to parade through her house." Her voice had softened from the brusqueness of earlier, and she engaged John with a direct look and said, "You must've been a little boy when she died."

He answered gently, "Yes. I was."

John just stood there staring blankly at Blanche while she rubbed her foot.

There was a brief, uncomfortable silence, and then John excused himself politely, said he should be going. As he left he deposited the envelope on a table next to the door.

It was a confluence of events, to be sure, happenings that slowly seemed to construct an awareness of a place, a person. And so it was that he felt himself drawing closer to a world that was not his, and at the center of this world was a woman.

13

At the end of February, invitations went out announcing a reception to celebrate Armand Wilde's sixty-fifth birthday. It was to be held at the Wildes' home up in Lawrence, a stately colonial-style house set well back from the street in a grove of birch trees just behind the university chancellor's residence. The guest list included the chancellor himself, along with deans and high-ranking professors from a multitude of disciplines. Several of Dr. Wilde's former aeronautics students who were now in prestigious positions in academia or the corporate world had flown in for the occasion, which included a colloquium planned in his honor.

Sarah rode up with Susan and the baby early in the day; John, who was to leave early Monday morning for a conference in Minneapolis, was still working feverishly on the paper he was to present. He was to drive up in the afternoon in time to attend the reception.

Sarah spent the latter part of the morning and the early afternoon sequestered with Will and the other three grandchildren in the spacious third-floor attic of the Wildes' home — one long, undivided room under the eaves stretching from one side of the house to the other. The wife of the previous owner had been a dancer, and the space had been converted to a studio. Now the hardwood floor was littered with toys, and the two boys were huddled in front of a television monitor battling over turns with the PlayStation. Ashley, the youngest, had been the only one to show an interest in the baby, and she had tagged along while Sarah walked around the room with Will that afternoon, trying to lull him to sleep.

Sarah had not had time to eat since morning, had only nibbled a few of the carrots the children left on their plates. When, around four in the afternoon, Will finally fell into a sound sleep, she laid him down in the playpen, left instructions with the children to keep the video volume low, and slipped downstairs to get something to eat.

She could hear the din of voices and low-pitched laughter as she descended the stairs, and she paused, hand on the rail, and looked around. The wide French doors at the back of the house had been thrown open and a shifting sea of bodies stretched from the chandeliered foyer through the living room to the sunroom beyond. In a corner of the living room stood John's father, hemmed in by a phalanx of professors and a few eager graduate students. Armand Wilde was, in all respects, a giant of a man — over six feet four inches — and he had a way of carrying himself with his shoulders thrown back and paunch dead ahead, as if he were accustomed to ramming out of his way any and all obstacles. Watching him move through a crowd of students, one had the impression of a heavily outfitted battleship slicing through frozen seas. At the top of this bulk sat a rather delicate, rosily handsome face and a dazzling pate. And a smile. Armand Wilde always smiled. Even when he tore apart brilliant theses and reduced doctoral candidates to tears, he smiled. He was the stuff of which dictators were made — a man convinced of his own superiority and righteousness, determined to fashion the world in his own image. But Armand Wilde had no political ambitions, and so he wielded his considerable influence only within the sphere of work and family. Those who survived knew themselves to be of exceptional mettle and grew in time to admire the man; those who did not were simply destroyed.

John Wilde was one of those who stood in that elite circle at his father's side, but he seemed vaguely distracted, smiling wanly and belatedly at the pleasantries, glancing about the room. He did not hear half of what was said.

He noticed Sarah as soon as she entered the room, although he pretended not to see her at all. He had been restless and bored, and suddenly the room came alive for him. He saw her weave through the crowd quietly and noticed how she made eye contact with no one, murmuring polite apologies as she squeezed around the piano, behind a cluster of women, unsmiling, detached from them all. She made her way to the buffet table and picked up a plate from the stack. Suddenly, Susan appeared from the kitchen, nervous, her face drawn up tight with worry. There was an exchange of words; Sarah hesitated, then with some reluctance she put down the plate and followed Susan into the kitchen.

John turned away from his father's side, set his glass on the mantelpiece and headed across the room, but a stooped, florid-faced gentleman — a classics scholar and an old family friend — caught him in mid-stride and begged to hear about his recent work. But even then, engaged in conversation about that which he loved most in life, he noticed her immediately, as soon as she re-appeared with a tray of champagne-filled glasses balanced effortlessly on one hand. There was a certain pride about her, an air of dignity; he had noticed it earlier, a kind of gravity tempered by grace. He excused himself and made his way through the crowd. She looked up, and he thought he saw a flicker of pleasure in her eyes. Then she smiled.

"Why are you doing this?" he said in a low voice.

"I don't mind."

"Where's the server?"

"She went home sick. And they were shorthanded to begin with."

"People can serve themselves."

Her smile broadened just a little. Then she turned away, toward a cocky graduate student who was reaching for a glass, and he caught the faint perfume of her hair.

She turned back to him and just at that moment the smile faded and her face clouded.

"What's wrong?"

"I'd better go check on Will." There was unmistakable urgency in her voice. "I've been gone too long," and she looked around for somewhere to set the tray.

"Here, give it to me."

She murmured her thanks and pressed through the crowd and dashed up the stairs.

She nearly collided with Ashley clattering down the stairs from the attic.

"What is it? What's happened?" Sarah asked.

"Aaron did it!"

"Did what?"

"Put the pillows over his head."

She took the child's hand and flew up the stairs. They reached the top and Sarah gripped the knob, but the door to the attic would not open.

"Did they lock this?"

"I don't know." Ashley was crying now. Sarah rattled the door.

"Open up, boys," she called out firmly.

She could hear muffled laughter behind the door, and Will's wails.

"He was crying and Aaron got mad and said he was tired of listening to him cry all day. And he said he didn't want an ugly little dark baby for a cousin."

Sarah felt anger surge through her, and she tried to keep her voice calm and low.

"Aaron? I know you can hear me. Open this door. If you don't, I'll have to go back down and get your father. If you open it now, I promise I won't say anything to anyone."

The laughter subsided and she could hear footsteps approaching, and finally the sound of the latch, and the door opened.

They had piled blankets and pillows on him, and she was amazed that he had not suffocated, that he was only hot and sweating. The wailing ceased and the panic in his eyes gave way to relief as she picked him up and cradled him to her shoulder.

"Oh, baby," she whispered, kissing the sweat from his scrawny little neck, thinking once again how delicate and birdlike he seemed. "You just don't want to be left alone, do you?"

She stayed with him the rest of the afternoon, watched from the curtained attic window as the guests departed, and let him sleep nestled against her neck.

It was well after dark when John found her sitting near the window at the far end of the attic. The other children had long since been allowed outside, and Will was now asleep in his playpen. She looked up as John approached, his footsteps echoing on the bare wood floor.

"You still haven't eaten," he whispered.

"I have now." She pointed to the empty jar of Gerber chicken and peas on the window ledge.

He grimaced. "Baby food."

"It's not bad." She grinned. "It's just the texture that's a little off-putting." She rose, straightening her sweater. "Is Susan ready to go?"

"Susan's staying on for a few days. With Will. I'm taking you home."

Sarah dropped her eyes. "All right. Just give me a minute to get my things."

"I'll meet you downstairs."

14

Wigner [contends] that only when somebody becomes conscious of a phenomenon is it really "actual." . . . My own feeling is that there is an area where it is true, especially in human relationships; people becoming conscious of each other can have a tremendous effect on each other.

DAVID BOHM,
THEORETICAL PHYSICIST

Armand Wilde had long since retreated to his study, but John's mother stood shivering beside one of the tall white columns that graced the entrance, watching as her son backed down the driveway. John turned and waved goodbye one last time, then she stepped back inside and closed the door.

Even then he avoided looking at Sarah, and yet he saw nothing but her. Her head was bent forward slightly as she rearranged her hair, sweeping up a long strand that had escaped the casually coiled knot at the back of her head. It was this gesture he kept seeing as he shifted his old BMW into second gear and cruised down the steep hill.

A fine, dry snow was just beginning to fall.

Nancy Wilde loved Susan as if she were her own daughter, and she had a tendency to worry just a little more about Susan and John than she did her other sons and their wives. This was perhaps why, as the two women sat at the kitchen table a short while later trying to tempt Will with some mashed potatoes, she blurted out a warning to Susan that, in its candidness, took them both a bit by surprise.

"Maybe it wasn't such a good idea to send John off alone with that young woman."

"Oh, Mom, you must be joking!"

"Well, she is rather attractive."

"Do you think so?"

"She's unusual-looking."

"I think I know the kind of woman John would go for, and she's definitely not one of them." Susan threw her head back and brushed a strand of hair out of her face with the side of her hand; there was a touch of arrogance in the gesture, of absolute self-assurance. "Not at all his type." She glared down her nose at Will, who was very slowly mouthing a spoonful of mashed potatoes.

"You want to try?" she asked, proffering the spoon to her mother-in-law.

"No, honey, you're doing fine."

"No, really, I can't imagine they'd have more than two words to say to each other."

"I'm sure you're right."

"Actually, to tell you the truth, sometimes I almost wish he would have an affair."

"Susan!" Nancy's horror was real. "What an awful thing to say!"

"Mom, he's just so . . ."

Nancy rose quickly and plucked the kettle from the stove.

"Tea?"

Susan saw the look on her mother-in-law's face and knew she had best drop the subject.

"Yeah. Sure. Thanks."

As she filled the kettle with water, Nancy Wilde scolded herself for having unleashed an unwanted confession of this sort and resolved henceforth to keep any suspicions to herself. For all her reserve, she had an eye for the subtle and was especially keen to even the slightest aberrations in the normal behavior pattern of sons and daughters, and husbands and wives. And she felt there was something not quite right about that young woman and her son, a tension in the way they seemed to avoid each other's gaze.

★ ★ ★

"Look in the backseat."

Sarah gave him a curious glance, then turned to look over her shoulder.

"The plastic bag. It's for you."

He turned to catch the look on her face and was rewarded with a smile that made him forget the road and the stoplights strung out along Iowa Street.

"Be careful. It might drip."

"What's in here?" She was peeling off the aluminum foil.

"Is it still warm?"

But she didn't answer, only shook her head as she bit into a crisp spring roll. "Delicious," she mumbled after a moment, then, with thumb and forefinger she lifted a shrimp from the plate and popped it into her mouth. "Delicious," she said again.

"Chinese food is all my parents do, I'm afraid. Apart from Mom's pot roasts."

She tilted her head sideways. "Am I complaining?"

"And I thought maybe you'd like some wine." He reached behind her seat and handed her a small Thermos. "Mom thought it was coffee."

"You are sweet," she said as she took it from him, but she avoided his eyes.

After a while he asked her if she would like

to listen to some music, but she declined, said she preferred the silence on a night like this, preferred watching the snow in the headlights.

It is a common enough occurrence in places where roads slice through open prairie that creatures cross those paths unexpectedly, most often at night; but it was unusual in this particular part of the country because the highway was fenced off for the protection of cattle and wildlife, and there was little woodland cover here, only that afforded by the cottonwoods and burr oaks down near the creek beds.

They both spotted the white-tailed buck at the same time. A thing of such grace always startles the eye, but here on open road on the plains of Kansas, on a snow-blown winter's night, the buck seemed to both of them a thing of rare beauty. The swift, graceful arc his body made as it cut through their headlights left its imprint on their mind's eye even after he had crossed the road and bounded down the ditch and over the fence. John shot forward in his seat and let up on the accelerator, suddenly alert with his hand tensed on the wheel, but the buck was already gone.

They caught the doe by the hind legs; she

had nearly made it past them. One more stride and she would have been across the highway and out of danger. The impact was so light — a muted thud — John was not quite sure what had happened until Sarah gasped.

"What was that?" he cried, easing the car off the road.

"It was the doe! We hit the doe! Drive back! Please!"

He came to a full stop and turned to look at her. "We can't do anything . . ."

"Do you have a flashlight?"

"In the glove compartment."

But she already had it in her hand. She tore off her seat belt and threw open the door and jumped down.

"Sarah!"

She stumbled down the embankment and disappeared into the darkness. John shifted into reverse and backed along the highway until he had her in his headlights. She was on the other side of the ditch near the fence. She had taken her gloves out of her pockets and was spreading apart the bottom strings of barbed wire to clear an opening.

John rammed the BMW into park and jumped out.

"Sarah! There's nothing you can do!" he shouted as he jogged down the shoulder.

"Come on back!"

He stopped and watched as she carefully maneuvered through the barbed wire. Once through, she turned back toward him and cried, "But she must still be alive!"

"Just let her go!"

Her hair blew over her face, and he thought how wild she looked standing there in the headlights, slightly out of breath, her arms raised at her sides in a pleading gesture.

She turned and waded off into the snow, disappearing again into the darkness. All he could see was the circle of light from her torch as it panned the bleak curves of the land.

John hurried back to the car, cut the engine, and pocketed his keys.

He had a rough time getting through the barbed wire; he snagged his sweater and mumbled a few curses, but when he made it out he found her easily enough. She had not gone far. The doe had finally fallen up the hill near a clump of switchgrass. Sarah was squatting a few feet to the side, the flashlight trained just above the doe's head.

"Incredible. That she made it this far," she said softly. "Look at her leg."

John looked to where the disk of light fell on the animal's hindquarters. There was a deep gash down her haunch where the hide was laid open, and the bone below the knee was hanging loose; it had been snapped clean of the joint.

Sarah looked out into the black night.

"He's waiting out there for her. He knows something's wrong."

Then she turned her face up to him.

John's heart was felled with that one look, doomed like the dumb panting creature at his feet. He dropped down on one knee and they knelt side by side in silence in the snow while the wind whistled through the barren hills.

She said, "Down near El Dorado, there's a place where they rehabilitate wildlife."

"This late? On a Sunday night?"

"It's a prison. I'm sure we can get somebody to answer the door."

"They do this kind of thing?"

"The inmates do it. I've taken animals to them before. A snow owl I found once. And a fledgling bald eagle. But this . . ."

A strong gust of wind blew at them, and she lost her balance. She put out her hand to steady herself, and it fell on his knee.

"You tell me how to get there, we'll give it a try."

"You don't mind?"

"No."

As if she had heard them deliberating her fate, the whitetail lifted her head off the ground and focused her bewildered brown eyes on them. She made a last effort to right herself, pawed at the hard earth with a hoof and struggled to get her footing, then collapsed back into the snow.

They saw the very moment death came over her. It swept across her body just as a gust of wind blew a cloud of fine dry snow past them, and when the wind had died the doe lay still.

Sarah snapped off the flashlight, but they lingered beside the animal, stunned by the abruptness of death and the puzzling vacuum that follows. John reached out and placed his hand over Sarah's where it still rested on his knee. They could hear the wind in the distance, moving toward them over the prairie like waves on the sea, moaning low and growing louder as it approached. A strong gust swept over them and Sarah shivered. John took her hand and they rose and slowly made their way down the hillside back to the car.

With the heater running they sat for a while, but Sarah was still shivering so John shrugged off his coat and laid it over her lap.

"I'm fine, really," she said. But she did not refuse the gesture.

They pulled back onto the road, and for the longest time neither of them made an effort to speak. The warm car, its steady motion and thrumming engine, lulled them into silence, yet all the while they were thinking about what they had witnessed. It was not so much the event itself that had affected them, poignant as it had been, but their shared reverence for the moment, the way both of them had seized upon something wordless and simple and eternal.

He wanted to see her to the door. Sarah told him it wasn't really necessary, but she thanked him all the same. Inside the house she waited, listening to the sound of tires on the gravel as he backed out. Then she bent down and removed her boots, and, carrying each in one hand, she climbed the stairs in the dark to her room. She lay in bed that night and thought about it all, and her thoughts kept returning to the dark outline of a doe against white snow, and the feel of his warm hand around her own.

15

Although he was firmly grounded in the ways of rural living, Billy Moon was a man of thoughts and ideas. He had been born and schooled in Oklahoma, but that didn't stop his imagination from strutting down the Hall of Mirrors in Versailles and stumbling over bodies at the Battle of Agincourt, and doing his absolute best to drag his students along with him. He paced the aisles of his classroom in a caged walk with his fingers splayed on his hips, engaging the sons and daughters of wheat farmers and feedlot owners in critical thinking about things far removed from their daily lives, things their parents ignored or ridiculed.

Sarah admired this about him, admired many things about him, but even after Maude died she never dreamed he would see anything in her but the girl she had once been, a solitary kid at the back of the class who never raised her hand and never looked him in the eye.

It was the tutoring job that moved them into new territory. Sarah had begun volunteering the previous September, and soon both of them began to anticipate those Tuesdays when she came to school. Sarah got into the habit of dropping by Billy's room between classes to say hello. If one of her students was out sick or taking a test and she had some time on her hands, she would settle herself at the worktable next to his desk and enter scores into the gradebook or grade some of his quizzes. Then one Tuesday she came early and brought him a pastrami sandwich, and then lunch just became a part of the order of things.

And then there was that day when Sarah wore pink.

It was lunchtime, and Sarah had arrived at his door with a plastic bag slung over her wrist and her coat buttoned up the front.

"Lunch is here!" she called out as she stepped into the classroom.

"Be right out!" cried Billy from the storage room at the back. "Lock the door, will you?"

She turned the lock and wended her way through the chairs toward his desk. Billy's classroom was like a world unto itself, and walking in there always gave Sarah a rush. There was not one square inch of wall that wasn't covered with a poster or a piece of trivia scavenged during the trips abroad he organized for his European history students every two years. Strung across one wall was a blue, white, and red Tour de France banner snatched from the finish line on the Champs Elysées after the last cyclist had cruised by. Stick-pinned to the back wall — straddling a Salvador Dalí poster and a Coca-Cola advertisement in Spanish — was a blue and yellow jersey he swore he had bought off the captain of the Leeds rugby team. The kids' favorites, however, were the few scattered photographs of a much younger Billy riding the bulls, caught in the boneless attitude of a rag doll, one hand gripping the cinch, the other flapping overhead.

She turned around to see Billy in the storage room doorway with a couple of paper plates in his hands.

"What do you want to drink?" he asked.

"What do you have?"

He turned his back to her and swung open the door of a small refrigerator.

"Got some 7UP and orange juice. Couple of Perriers been sitting in here for months."

"Then let's knock off the Perrier."

When he came out she was removing her coat and the look on his face made her blush and clasp the coat back around her as if she were naked.

"Oh, don't, Billy." She laughed nervously.

"Don't what? Don't look at you?"

"Yes."

"Sarah, you were made to be looked at."

He said it so darn seriously, gripping a Perrier in each hand, his legs squared like a boxer.

"Oh, don't start."

"Start what?"

He was so intent, forcing her to heed that stance of his, and she saw there was no laughter in his eyes; but then he broke free and set the bottles on his desk.

"I know you don't like to be looked at," he said.

"How do you know that?"

"I watch you. And I think I've gotten to know you pretty well these past few months."

"Have you now?"

"And I think you haven't changed a whole lot since you sat at the back of my classroom — what? — twelve years ago? . . . and drew caricatures of me."

"Not of you. I never did that to you."

"You did a great one of . . . What was her name?"

"Kathy. That little witch who sat right in

front of your desk."

"But not me?"

"I would never have made fun of you."

Abruptly, he popped the lids off the Perriers, and his mouth was hidden behind the dark mustache, but she could see he was pleased.

"Let's eat these things while they're still warm," she said. She removed the foil from the ribs and dropped a slab onto each plate.

Now, Billy Moon had a knack for storytelling, and as they sat at the worktable and savored Joy's baby back ribs, Sarah was treated to a few of Billy's observations and theories on the interaction of the sexes at Chase County High. Sarah listened to him that noon and watched the way he hunkered down over his ribs and blotted at his mustache with a napkin, watched the way his eyes twinkled and thought maybe she was falling in love.

Billy expounded the theory that Chase County High's teachers' lounge was a microcosm of interpersonal interaction, that in many ways it was an accurate reflection of the social fabric of Chase County at large. The two sexes were not all that fond of one another, he claimed. The women wanted to be like the men but couldn't, and the men were a lot more like women than they wanted to admit, and this confusion led to a rather ugly animosity that slunk around most days with its tail down and its hackles up just waiting to be provoked. Inevitably someone would say something — the menfolk would express their humor in terms of women's morphology, and then the womenfolk would take offense — and then everyone would see how that critter could show itself downright nasty, with a front lip that pleated up as neatly as venetian blinds to show a finely aligned row of butcher-sharp teeth and vocal cords that rumbled in Dolby stereo. On these occasions of ruptured civility, which occurred as they did from time to time in the teachers' lounge, the two sides settled like foot soldiers into their respective trenches, with occasional defectors slipping out under cover of dark and forming compassionate and human bonds — Miss Morgan of home ec and Mr. Fleming in the math department, for example — and then slipping back to their own side at dawn to prepare themselves for the daily battle.

Billy had long observed this segregation of the sexes during the lunch hour. The men always sat in a lineup along the wall in, as the ladies had often noted, the most comfortable facilities in the lounge, a long orange Naugahyde sofa flanked and faced by several chairs of the same fabric in faded avocado and citron — a formation that bore a remarkable resemblance, Billy noted, to the old Conestoga wagon-train circle of defense, with a newspaper-cluttered coffee table where the campfire would have been. The women camped on the other side of the lounge in a huddle of small circular tables surrounded by upright chairs, a formation that revealed their natural inclination toward communication and signaled right off their skills in synthesis and cooperation, all of which — Billy knew for a fact — the menfolk lumped into the general category of gossipmongering. A few women on occasion would brave the male defenses and sit for a few moments around the campfire with the fellas, but it was usually when a bit of official business was taking place, and the incident was viewed as a pleasant anomaly. But under no circumstances, never, ever, did a man who saw himself as a man wander into that female labyrinth, settle himself down among the plentiful designing Ariadnes with their skeins of threads they were constantly rolling up and unrolling, knotting and unraveling.

Sarah's amused laughter had rallied him on, and Billy lost track of the time. Before they knew it the bell had rung and the halls were full of students rushing to class.

Billy sat back and wiped his hands on a paper towel.

"How'd you like to come over and ride Warlord this weekend?"

Sarah paused with her thumb in her mouth. Warlord had been Maude's horse.

"He hasn't been ridden all summer," Billy added. "Gettin' wild."

"He was always wild."

"Yeah. Maude was always a little scared of him."

"I can see why. He's young and he's a stallion."

"You used to own a stallion."

"That was when I was a crazy kid."

"Want to ride him?"

Sarah dabbed a bit of sauce from her mouth and lifted her eyes to meet his. Her smile held a faint air of challenge.

"I'll give it a try."

Billy began to clean up the clutter, folding up their paper plates and tossing them into the trash. He was standing there, looking down at her as she cleaned her fingers, when he said, "Take off the damn coat, Sarah."

It was a startled look she gave him. But she did as he asked, slipped the coat off her shoulders and let it fall onto her chair. He thought she looked a little like a virgin disrobing before her first lover, but he knew better.

He had never seen her wear anything like that before. It was a stretch top that molded her breasts, cut low enough to reveal cleavage. And the color put roses in her cheeks.

"Why are you so embarrassed?" he said gently.

"I'm too pink." She grimaced. "Joy talked me into buying it. I should know better than to listen to her."

"Joy was right."

Sarah shook her head vehemently, flinging her corkscrew curls from side to side.

"I'm too pink."

"No. You're not too pink," he said, and he turned away quickly before it had an effect on him.

That weekend she went out to ride Warlord and stayed for dinner. The following weekend she was invited to dinner and ended up staying the night. At Christmas Billy tied a big red bow on Warlord's saddle and set it under his tree with a note to Sarah saying the stallion was hers.

16

It was a bright March morning and Sarah was in the stall thinning out Warlord's mane when she heard the stable door creak open and felt a rush of cold air. She heard Billy approach, the sound of his boots muffled by scattered straw, and she peered over Warlord's withers.

"Morning," she said, then disappeared behind the horse's long neck.

"Hi, stranger." His voice was still a little gravelly, not quite awake.

He ducked under the rope and stepped up beside her to give Warlord a firm pat on his neck. He wore a sleeveless down vest over a wool shirt and he smelled like soap.

"Sun wasn't even up when I heard you drive in."

"Sorry. Hope I didn't wake you."

Sarah wound a section of mane around her comb and tugged hard, loosening a strand of horsehair.

"You gonna ride him?"

"Planning on it."

"That's good."

"It's just been so cold."

"He still needs to be ridden."

"I know."

"And so do I."

She avoided his eyes, then, abruptly, dipped under Warlord's neck and disappeared on the other side of the animal.

"I'm sorry," he said then, and there was honest contrition in his voice. "That was crude."

"Yes. It was. And not at all like you."

He laid his hand on the chestnut Arab's muzzle and stroked him fondly. "You've been avoiding me."

She had moved around to the horse's rear and had begun combing out the tail.

"Sorry."

There was a pause, and Warlord turned his big head around and eyed the two of them.

Billy answered, "Would you like to elaborate on that a little?"

She paused, then came around to face him.

She looked down at the comb in her hands. "Maybe it's just, well, things got off to such a quick start . . ."

"You didn't seem to feel that way a few months ago."

She was still avoiding his gaze.

"What is it? Be honest with me. You been seein' somebody else?"

She shook her head emphatically.

"No."

"Where you been evenings? I call and your grandpa says you're gone."

She shook her head again.

"I'm there. I'm just up in my room."

"I thought so."

She shrugged. "It's not that he's lying, it's just he knows I won't answer if he calls. And so he says I'm not there."

"You're too withdrawn, Sarah."

"It's just winter. Winter does it to me."

"What better time than winter to come to my bed?"

He did not try to touch her, but when she looked up she met his dark eyes and felt the passion surge again, and she was so relieved that tears came to her eyes.

"Oh, Billy . . ."

She reached out and stroked his jaw, and he kissed the palm of her hand.

"Come on," he said gruffly, and she dropped the comb onto the stall floor and followed him out of the barn.

But after they made love, she was in a hurry to leave him. He mistook her impatience for enthusiasm. The sun had come out strong, and the March wind held just the faintest hint of spring, and she was eager to ride.

She warmed up Warlord in the arena, and then, against Billy's advice, took him out on the open range. He was strong and full of pent-up energy, and she had to work to keep him contained; but the struggle did her good, and she wore him down and wore herself down, and came back in the afternoon, both of them exhausted. Billy was furious at her, told her that even though the horse was hers now, and he wouldn't go back on his word, if she did that again he'd never let her up on his back. But she only laughed and said she'd come in the dead of night to ride him if she had to.

17

*When two particles interact with each other,
they exchange energy and/or momentum.*

K. C. COLE
*FIRST YOU BUILD A CLOUD
AND OTHER REFLECTIONS ON PHYSICS
AS A WAY OF LIFE*

It had been three weeks since she had closed the door on John Wilde, but he had struck a presence in her heart that she could not erase. There had been only little Will to bring them together, and Will had been put back in the hospital for an indefinite period. She knew there would be no continuation of what had begun, that the stirrings in their hearts would be left to slowly wither and die with time. And yet the days passed by with a kind of renewed hope for some vague, undefinable happiness, and what had manifested itself on that wintry night traveled on through the core of her being like a deep tremor.

During this time, during the nights, she

stayed awake to paint in oils, and she watched new things appear on her easel — landscapes of lonely houses perched among fierce hills and peopled with elongated shadow-like forms. Minimal, barely more than silhouette, but they were there, easily distinguished as man and woman and child. It had been many years since she had painted even the faintest abstraction of the human form.

Her restlessness was not easily appeased. The familiar faces that made up the tapestry of her days, the routine amusements and distractions, appeared now to her like a pale, wintry world. Everywhere she turned there was a blinding sameness. She could no longer distinguish one moment of her life from another, and the events of each day were forgotten as soon as they had passed. She began to take short trips up to Lawrence, where she had once gone to university. She had always loved Lawrence from the first time her grandfather had taken her for a visit as a little girl and they had wandered hand in hand through the campus, along footpaths winding between stately old halls of cream-colored stone. The town itself was a lively place, animated by a peculiar mix of academics, artists, cowboys, and old hippies, and Sarah never grew tired of it. And so, that spring, she began spending her days off up there. Removed from prying eyes, she would take her sketch pad with her and sit on a bench with the March wind scattering dead leaves at her feet. Here she could make believe life held hope and promise.

When John was in Lawrence he generally ate a late lunch, if he ate at all. He avoided the funky old cafes on Massachusetts he had frequented as an undergraduate; even more fastidiously, he avoided the affluent West Lawrence neighborhood, steered clear of the shops and restaurants enjoyed by his parents and their friends. There was a new bakery and deli on Louisiana Street that he liked, a clean, sunny place called Wheatfields that reminded him of his favorite bakery in Berkeley. He usually tried to time it so that he missed the lunch crowd; it was generally quiet then and he could find a booth to himself and spread out his work and read while he downed a sandwich and a salad. He liked the ambience, the lack of pretense and the way the sunlight angled through the slats of the venetian blinds.

He heard the door open and casually glanced up from his journal. When he saw Sarah walk up to the counter and pause to read the chalkboard menu on the wall, there was such a sudden change in his countenance that any casual observer would have noticed the effect she had on him.

He waited, following her with his eyes until she had paid and then paused to pick up a napkin from the service corner. When it seemed she was moving toward a table near the door and might not see him, he laid aside his journal and rose.

She saw the movement, turned her head. Her eyes held a look of disbelief, utter amazement; only slowly did she smile and walk toward him.

She was dressed as he had seen her before, in worn denim jeans and a loose, heavy-knit sweater, a backpack slung over her shoulder, the uniform of those who wish to blend in.

"Here," he said, "please, come join me," and he cleared room on the table.

"I won't disturb you? Were you working?"

"No," he answered and quickly rolled up his journal and stuffed it down behind the worn leather briefcase near his elbow. "Please, sit down."

"Thanks," she said, and set down her tray.

He hid his hands under the table, tried to hide his nervousness.

"I never expected . . . ," he began, then her backpack knocked over his iced tea and he grabbed for it.

"I'm so sorry," she said, quickly mopping it up with her napkin.

"It's all right."

Finally she was settled, the sandwich and Coke removed from her tray, and both of them took a deep breath and looked at each other and smiled.

"I like this place," Sarah said.

"So do I. One of my favorites."

"I used to work over at the Paradise Cafe. When I was in school here."

"You went to school here?"

She nodded. "Didn't graduate, though."

Carefully, she picked up her sandwich. There was a conscious reserve about her, and he wondered if she was as nervous as he.

He had forgotten about his own sandwich, had lost his appetite.

She cleared her throat. "How did your conference go?"

He smiled, relieved to have the conversation turn to something he could handle. "Very well. The paper'll be published next month."

She put down her sandwich and turned an inquisitive gaze on him. "So, tell me, what does a physicist do in a typical working day?" Then, with narrowed, smiling eyes, "In five words or less."

He leaned forward on his elbows. "I'll give it to you in one."

"Only one?"

"Math."

"I should have known."

"Why?"

"From what Amy said about you."

"Oh, yes. Amy. She tells me you helped her a lot more than I did."

"Only because I'm on her level."

"I should think you were a good deal above it."

"Perhaps because I enjoy it."

"Math?"

"Because it's logical. There are answers." She lowered her head and bit into her sandwich, but her eyes were still on him, watching him.

"My math isn't logical."

"It isn't?"

"No, not at all. Not in pure math. Like when you're dealing with integers and primes. Then it's really more intuition than logic. I come up with these theorems that work and I know they work, but I can't prove how. It's all really very mysterious. Which, I suppose, is why I love it."

Sarah had fallen into his eyes, was lost in their gentle blue gaze, and suddenly her appetite was gone and the roast beef sandwich she had eyed so hungrily seemed dry and tasteless in her mouth.

She put down the sandwich and reached for her Coke. "I thought you needed laboratories. Don't you? Things like . . . I don't know, electron accelerators?"

"I fly back to Berkeley every so often."

"And the rest . . ." She fingered her straw. "The rest is in the math."

"Yes. In the equations."

"What can you see?"

"A lot. Its own kind of imagery. Certain things, certain physical realities. Things that are easier to describe with an equation than with words."

She nodded. "Yes. I think I see what you mean."

She glanced toward the window. The afternoon light streamed through the blinds, falling in narrow, bright shafts across the room. She pressed the backs of her hands to her flushed cheeks.

"Goodness, it's warm in here."

"Yes, it is bright, isn't it."

She unzipped the pocket of her backpack and removed a wide green clip and, with the same gesture he had observed in his car that night, wrestled her sorrel hair into a loose knot and secured it on top of her head.

Suddenly, he could think of nothing else

to say, nothing that made sense. He rose and offered to get them some ice water, and she thanked him.

She watched him while his back was turned — the lean, muscular body, the brittle energy that seemed locked in every movement. In his absence she scanned his belongings, the scuffed briefcase with his initials engraved on the bronze latch, the old leather jacket thrown over the heap, the scientific journal, as if she might find the answer to why he so intrigued her, why she could not get him out of her thoughts.

He set down her water and she thanked him.

"Now," he said as he settled back opposite her, "tell me about Doughty."

It took her a moment to follow him.

"Doughty?"

"Your book."

"Oh, yes . . . ," and he noticed a faint blush rise to her cheeks. "I never thanked you."

"No need to."

"I kept meaning to. And the envelope."

"I sealed it."

"Thank you."

"I assumed they were personal."

"Yes." Then, with a slow shake of her head, "I can't believe I did that."

"You were still half-asleep when you left."

"I guess I was." She took a sip of her

water, eyed him over the rim of the glass. "Did you read them?"

"Yes," he replied without hesitation, freezing her with a look of such directness that her heart fluttered in her chest. "You seemed like a different person. In the letters."

"I was."

The blue eyes warmed inquisitively.

"I was different with him. I became someone else."

"And did you like who you became?"

She narrowed her gaze on him and smiled. "Yes. Very much."

"He was English?"

"Oh, yes," she replied, lifting one of her fine, arched brows. "Very."

"You didn't leave with him."

"Oh, but I did. For two years."

"Married?"

"No." She took a deep breath. "We had serious disagreements."

He watched her closely, could read the shadows of some not-yet-forgotten pain, saw it between her eyes, the way she furrowed her brow. He was aware of a sensitivity toward her that he had never felt toward any other woman, a kind of tender curiosity.

"Are you still . . ."

She shook her head. "No," she replied. "The last time I heard from him, he was in

Argentina. That was almost," she paused to calculate, "three years ago."

There was a clatter when a busboy rolled his trolley up to the booth behind them. When he had cleaned off the table and squeaked on by, Sarah continued.

"I think in many ways we were well suited to each other. But we wanted different things. In the end."

All this while he watched her fingers caress the glass, and now the fingers grew still.

"He lives only for himself. But that wasn't apparent at the beginning."

She raised the cold glass and pressed it to her cheek and then to her neck.

John said, "God, what a fool he was."

Again, the color rose to her cheeks, and she kept her eyes lowered.

"I think maybe now he regrets it. Maybe."

She shrugged and leaned back, finally lifting her eyes to meet his, and said, "He will become what he is to become, and fatherhood will not be part of that experience."

"I see," John said, a shade embarrassed, and looked away, at the young man with the trolley.

After a moment he added, "And you're still here."

"Yes."

"No desire to leave."

"Sometimes."

"But you don't."

"I will."

"But not now."

"I have ties here. Ties that bind."

"Are you waiting for that to change?"

She looked up at him, a little off guard.

"Good question."

He searched her eyes for the longest time, and once again it seemed as if a wordless communication flowed between them.

"Why we do what we do," she said.

"Mystery."

"Yes. Mystery."

She smiled, and he returned the smile. He would have liked to reach out and take her hand, but then he thought it wasn't really necessary.

John had always been drawn to the invisible: more specifically, the invisible connections between things. As a child he had puzzled over the phenomena ordinary men take for granted in modern life: the connection between a flick of a switch and the sudden appearance of light, or sound, or image. He tore things apart — old lawn mower engines, radios, watches — looking for the connections. But his interest went beyond the engineer's obsession with mechanical cause and effect, with deconstructing and reconstructing physical reality: he searched for things that would leave him awestruck, things residing in mystery and obscurity. Invisible connections.

It was this fascination and a high tolerance for ambiguity that led him to the doorstep of the world of particle physics: here there were no absolutes, no unequivocable rights and wrongs. Truth took a meandering path, and what appeared absolute one day could be refuted or proven to have limitations the next. In the world of physics, rules broke down beyond certain parameters; in extreme states — at extreme velocities or extreme heat or cold, in extremely massive or minute dimensions — matter behaved strangely, bizarrely.

He had devoted his life to observing the invisible and constructing mathematical devices and inventing terms to describe the indescribable. The subjects of his research could be neither touched nor measured, scarcely even imagined. And these things did not frighten him.

But what he was beginning to feel for Sarah frightened him. He had always been the observer, and now he was the phenomenon itself.

18

The last thing Sarah wanted that Saturday morning was a scene at the Cassoday Cafe. John Wilde had come in around eleven and taken a corner table. She brought him the menu and tried to keep her hand steady as she poured his coffee, tried to keep her voice just kind of quiet and neutral while they talked briefly about little Will who had just come home from the hospital. She caught him watching her a few times, discreetly, nothing that drew attention, but she could feel the heat in his eyes and it made her go weak at the knees. Then Billy Moon came in with a couple of guys from his baseball team, and they took the table next to John. When she brought their order, Billy cracked a joke, hinting that Sarah had been over at his place the night before. The guys gave Billy a good ribbing, which embarrassed Sarah something awful since she knew John could hear every word of their conversation. Right after that the strangers walked in, and that's when the trouble started.

She tried to let off a little steam to Joy, but it wasn't enough, thought it best not to tell Joy how the beefy guy had pressed his elbow into her crotch while she was taking their order, and how he had stacked the menus on the far side of the table so she had to lean in front of him to retrieve them. Then he had made a move as though to pass them to her, timing his gesture just right so he brushed her breast with the back of his hand. It was so casual, one could easily believe it inadvertent. But Sarah knew better; she suspected he had perfected it over the years on many a waitress.

"They're sick!" She picked up an order of baked ham from the counter and stabbed the scalloped potatoes with a sprig of parsley. "And so crude! First all these vulgar jokes about women, now they're on to the Mexicans."

"Buncha slugs," Joy muttered as she ladled gravy over an order of meat loaf and handed it to Sarah. "Good dose of pesticide. That's what they need."

"They're so loud. Like they want everybody to hear. Millie got up and moved to another table. It really upset her."

"Calm down, honey. They're not from around here. Probably won't ever see 'em again."

"We'd better not."

"Just ignore 'em. Don't get all worked up. Spit in their coffee if it'll make you feel any better — that's what I do — but don't say anything."

She approached the table with plates balanced on both arms. They saw her coming and quit talking and sat back in their chairs. The big man tucked the edge of his napkin into his belt and laid his hands on the table and stared at his paper place mat like a dog waiting to be fed. At the sight of them something in Sarah snapped and she knew she was going to do something she'd probably regret.

When she hesitated they thought she couldn't remember their order and so the big guy looked up at her with a lewd grin and said, "I got the ham, honey."

"The ham," repeated Sarah, and he nodded. So she served the cheeseburger with extra fries and the meat loaf to the other two, then she smiled at him and set the ham plate down in front of him and said, "Gentlemen, this is on the house."

They looked up at her like they'd heard wrong. The big man leaned back in his chair and grinned at the other two, and the little man with plaster-splattered arms sneered and said, "Why? You got cockroaches back there?"

"No," intoned Sarah, with her hands on her hips, "we've got roaches out here." She paused just a second before adding, "Three of them." Then she looked them all in the eye, rapidly, one after the other, and said very sweetly, "You gentlemen don't need to come back here. If you do, you won't be served. Now eat up, 'cause it's gettin' cold."

She turned away then and the room was dead still.

"You callin' us names, little bitch?"

It was the big man talking, and as he spoke he lunged forward and grabbed Sarah's arm, squeezing it tight like a vise so that she gave a startled cry of pain. He yanked her back around like a whip, and she lost her balance. There was a sudden crack that might have been her arm, or might have been the sound of her head as it hit the table.

Even before she fell, John was on his feet and knocking over chairs to clear a path toward the guy. Billy had his back to them and hadn't seen a thing. When he looked up from his scrambled eggs, John already had the beefy guy by the scruff of the neck and had slammed him facedown on the table. The plaster-splattered man had scrambled to his feet with a knife in his hand.

Randy, the county's undersheriff, was just

coming out of the men's room, double-checking his fly, when he heard a commotion — dishes breaking and bodies rustling — and saw John Wilde wrestling the big guy and Sarah crumpled on the floor. On reflex he popped the snap on his holster and in three strides was there with his gun drawn in their faces, and then things got real still again. The plaster-splattered man dropped the knife and it fell, breaking one of Joy's dishes. That was the only sound they heard — that and the sound of John Wilde's breathing as he held his face right down on the beefy guy's ear. Randy ordered everybody to stay right where they were. He asked Sarah if she was all right. She was struggling to her knees, one hand pressed to her forehead, as Billy Moon bent over her and helped her to her feet. Randy was more worried about what John Wilde might do because he had the beefy guy in an armlock and his shirt twisted so tight around his neck that his eyes were bulging something awful. Randy thought the big guy had "heart attack" written all over his face, and then wouldn't that put them in a fine fix.

"It's okay . . . ," Randy said in a low monotone, but he couldn't remember John Wilde's name. "It's okay. Just back off now."

John moved slowly, but finally he calmed

down a little and let up on his bulldog grip, and the beefy guy stumbled to his feet.

Nobody got nasty, what with Randy's Smith & Wesson aimed steady at the big guy's back, and he was able to persuade them in but a few short words to kindly take their business elsewhere. The strangers responded swiftly, although not without some crude parting words, and in a minute they were out the door and gone.

Upon hearing Sarah's cry, Joy had burst out of the kitchen gripping a bottle of ketchup by the neck. Randy was holstering his weapon when he looked up and saw her standing there in her chef's apron smeared with raw meat loaf and the bottle poised in midair. He chuckled and said, "What the hell were you gonna do with that thing, Joy?"

That just sort of knocked the tension right out of them and the dining room exploded in laughter; then everybody started talking at once.

Billy lifted Sarah onto a chair, but she had a little blood on her forehead and scalloped potatoes all down the front of her apron. She looked up at Billy and Randy with tears in her eyes and mumbled how sorry she was, but she was still trembling.

Then Sarah turned to look at John, and

even through her blurred vision she could see the way he was looking at her. His eyes no longer seemed blue and pale and distant, but angry and dark and pounding like the sea.

Billy dropped down into a squat beside her chair.

"You okay, kid?"

Tenderly, he cupped her chin in his hand and tilted it up so he could see her face.

John saw that gesture. It was a strange feeling, on top of the blood pumping through his temples, the adrenaline still on the rise, to feel this sudden plummeting sensation in his chest, a kind of free fall of the heart.

Joy was bending over Sarah. She swept the hair off Sarah's face and examined her forehead. There was a swelling already, a red knot just above her eyebrow.

"Let's get some ice on that."

"I'm okay," whispered Sarah.

"You'd better stay down for a minute," said Billy.

"I'm fine," she answered, pushing them away with a shade of annoyance.

Millie had the good sense to wrap up some crushed ice in a dish towel for Sarah's forehead. She, for one, was glad the jerks were gone, she said, and thought Sarah had done the right thing. Everybody voiced their agreement and pretty soon everything was back to normal.

Apart from her red eyes and the lump growing on her forehead, Sarah behaved as if nothing had happened. She took their orders and served their hotcakes and sausage and refilled their coffee and even took a minute to look at the photo of Millie's new grandbaby. But John left not long after that. When she cleared his table she noticed he had barely eaten a thing, had left most of his pancakes and a full cup of coffee. Next to his plate was a twenty-dollar bill to cover the four-dollar breakfast. When he walked out the door that morning without looking back, he took the sun out of the day, took the light right out of her heart. No amount of good-natured joking or laughter could bring it back, and Sarah had no smiles left for anyone.

Joy didn't say much to her about the incident, was oddly silent about the whole affair. That evening when everyone had gone and Sarah was upending the chairs on the tables so Joy could sweep the floor, Joy paused and turned to her and said, "Did you notice the way he was looking at you?"

Sarah gripped another chair and swung it up on the table and said calmly, "Who?"

"Oh, come on."

"You mean Billy?"

"No. John Wilde."

"I didn't see anything. I was down on the floor."

"I can't believe you didn't notice. Jeez, the way he dove in there."

"He probably just saw it happen before anybody else."

"I never imagined him that kind of guy."

Sarah shrugged and turned away and changed the subject, although she didn't miss the look on Joy's face, the look of one who suddenly sees things in a new light.

19

John was in Berkeley for the better part of that week. He returned home late Friday in an animated state, stood in the kitchen unzipping his leather jacket, his briefcase wedged between his feet and his eyes afire, telling Susan how well the research was going, that it required only a few more trips before he polished it up and sent it off for publication.

"Where's the little guy?" he asked as he hung his jacket over the back of a chair.

"He's in his room."

"Asleep?"

"I suppose so."

He looked around the kitchen. "Where's the monitor?"

"It's up in the bedroom. I didn't turn it on." She saw the look on his face and turned away and went back to the pile of laundry she had been folding on the kitchen table. "I can hear him. I don't need it."

"It's a big house."

"And he's got a damn loud voice, John." She flung down the sleepers she had in her hand and turned back to face him squarely.

"You can't imagine what he was like these past few days while you were gone." Suddenly she was on the verge of tears, and waving her hands in the air. "And Mother! God, she's more trouble than help! She's always inviting people around, and I can never get any rest!"

"It wasn't such a good idea, was it?"

"Don't start coming down on me."

"I didn't mean it that way, I just meant your mother —"

"I know! I know she's useless."

"She means well."

"Everybody means well, but it still all falls on me! You lock yourself away in your office or run off to KU for the day and . . ." She stopped and her shoulders sagged. "I'm sorry. It's just that . . . for a while I thought he was getting better. . . ."

"He's not eating, is he?"

"It's not only that, it's just, whatever I do it isn't enough. I can't make him happy. He's just totally listless or he cries, and when he does sleep it seems like I always have something I have to get done and so I don't sleep. . . ."

She sank into a chair and took one of his

hands in both of hers and looked up at him.

"John, tell me, how attached are you really to this child?"

"What are you suggesting?"

"Your mom says we should give him back. For readoption." She hurried on to say, "People do that. It can be done."

She caught the disturbed look on his face, and tried to hold onto his hand but he withdrew it.

"Is it worth our marriage?" Susan said.

"What do you mean?"

"I'm unhappy. He's making me unhappy." She went on, her voice cracking. "He's making our lives miserable and he's tearing apart our marriage."

A tear inched down her face and John felt his heart ache for her. But he could not bring himself to kiss her and so he touched her cheek and gently wiped away the tear.

"But I thought you wanted a baby."

"Not like this," she whispered. "Not at this expense."

"I knew it wouldn't be easy."

"We were so happy. Just the two of us." Her eyes were swimming in misery. "Am I so awful? Am I such an awful person?"

"Of course you're not," he said gently, touching her hair.

"Your mom said it could just get worse

when he's older. If he doesn't bond with us now, imagine what he'll be like when he gets older."

"He will bond with us."

"But *when? How?*" she cried, and in a sudden outburst of frustration she grabbed an armload of laundry and flung it angrily onto the kitchen floor. "I don't want him in our lives anymore! I just don't!"

John stared at her mutely while she sobbed into her hands. Lightly, he stroked her hair, then, after a moment, he picked up his briefcase and took his jacket from the back of the chair and walked out through the kitchen to the entry hall. He hung up his coat, then climbed the stairs to the top floor.

The door to the nursery was closed, and when he opened it he found Will sitting in his crib, clinging to the rail, his dark thatched head peering out between the white bars and his eyes full of unfriendly fire. His smooth, tawny cheeks were covered with red splotches and his frail little body shuddered with each breath. John knew he had been crying for a long time, had finally just worn himself down to these muffled sobs.

"Will, my boy," John said as he closed the door behind him, but he didn't in the slightest feel like Will was his boy. He stood at the side of the crib and reached down to take him, but the baby turned away, crawled into a corner and drew his scrawny little legs up under him and lay there with his white-diapered rump in the air like a hedgehog in the headlights.

John remembered how he had looked the first time he saw him, lying all wasted and frail in the clear Plexiglas crib with his chest still bandaged and plastic tubing up his nose and his tiny arms strapped to the aluminum rails. No one else had wanted him. He was so ugly, barely the size of a newborn although he was eight months old at the time.

He had been adopted by a South African diplomat, a woman working for the UN Assistance Mission in East Timor. She'd found him when she was on a visit to Sri Lanka with her American husband. He had needed heart surgery and she offered to send him back to the United States and pay for the procedure with the understanding that she would adopt him. They arranged to have him brought back to the KU Medical Center in Kansas City, where her husband had done his medical internship, but the woman was delayed in East Timor because of political unrest in the region. A few weeks later the mission office was attacked and she was stoned to death, leaving Will recovering from his surgery in Kansas City with no family to return to.

The surgeon was a friend of John's brother, and John and Susan had flown out from Berkeley just to see the baby. John had never had much occasion to be around children, had no special affinity for kids in general, and certainly not for babies. But even before he saw him, he had felt there was some connection there, something beyond mere circumstance that had brought him into that hospital room.

Susan had been more cautious, but John won out in the end, and they brought him home, convinced they could pull him through.

But nothing was as they had hoped it would be, nothing was as they had planned. And now John stood in defeat looking down at his son.

"Oh, Will," John whispered again, and this time a wave of pity swept over him. He wanted to reach out and take him but he was afraid if he did he'd set him off. Gently, he placed his hand on the baby's back, and the size of his hand over the little being amazed him. He wondered, beyond the muteness and the helplessness, what kind of consciousness lay under his palm, if it was great or small, if it was full of powerful instinct or spirit. If it had issued forth from elsewhere, drawn forth "from out the vast," as Tennyson liked to believe, or if it was a temporal consciousness only, and would, with time, cease to exist.

Will was still whimpering, but he was tolerating the touch of John's hand, and John wished he knew what more he could give him, what would soothe him and lull him back to sleep. Once again Sarah stepped back into his thoughts, and he saw her face up close looking at him unsmilingly, with a knowledge that was somehow to Will's liking. But no, it was just the hair, the soporific effect of her hair clutched in his tiny fist.

20

When John left the following week, Susan was on the verge of despair. The first day went smoothly enough, but come nightfall the child became agitated and irritable. Susan tried repeatedly to get him to sleep, but he would doze off only to awaken a short while later and start to cry, and then she would race back up the stairs to rescue him from his misery. He sat up in his crib and wailed and pleaded with large dark eyes, but there was little she could do to soothe him.

Susan was lost. She could not know, nor could anyone, what consciousness directed his body and mind. She knew he was uncomfortable, that he was mute and dwelled in a world of instinct; this she could forgive him. But that he had rejected her so absolutely, this she could not abide.

Throughout the evening she appealed to the child. She brought him things to drink and eat, piled gadgets and cuddly toys before him. Then, finally, feeling herself growing frantic, she turned off the monitor, closed the door, and went back downstairs and turned up the stereo. But still she could hear his cries.

She was in the kitchen chopping onions for a spaghetti sauce when suddenly all her frustration and resentment erupted. She slammed the knife down on the chopping board and threw her head back and shrieked at the ceiling, "Stop it, Will! Damn you, just stop it!"

She brusquely dried her hands on her apron and marched down the hallway to the stairs.

"I've had enough of you!" she shouted at him from the bottom of the stairs, and for a moment he seemed to stall, but then he started up again, and she went on.

"I've had enough of your tantrums! Now shut up!"

She started up the stairs once again, fueled by rage, threatening him with each thundering step. When she rammed open the door and came charging in, he looked up at her, stunned and fearful.

"What do you want?" she cried and swept up a toy from the floor and flung it across the room, knocking the little teddy bear music box off the dresser and sending the lamp crashing to the floor.

She advanced, and Will shrank from her and crawled to the back of the crib.

"What did I ever do to you to make you hate me so?" she screeched. She sprang at his crib. "I'm not evil! But you make me feel that way!" She gripped the crib railing and leaned menacingly toward him, and Will cowered in the corner and wailed.

"Stop it!" she screamed, and she shook the crib railing. "Stop it!"

Then, suddenly, she paused. She felt as if she were teetering on the edge of a dark and terrifying moment. Something had stepped into her mind just then and brought her up short, and she felt as if she were dragging herself back with all the mental courage she could summon. In those agonizing seconds she did not see Will; her mind was focused on what lay beyond, on her next gesture, her next action. And she was horrified at what that might be.

She deliberately lifted her hands from the railing and took a step back. Then she turned and fled down the stairs.

Her hand shook as she dialed the number. "Mama?"

Clarice answered, and Susan knew she had been drinking, and her heart sank. Oh, Mama, she thought, for God's sake, why can't you be sober tonight?

"I'm coming over to get you. Right now. I need to get out of here. I can't stay cooped up with this child."

"Susan, honey. Are you okay?"

"No, I'm not okay. And I need you to put down whatever it is you've been drinking and get your hair combed and put on your shoes and come out with me."

"It's late. And it's raining."

"I don't care if it's a blizzard. Get yourself dressed."

She found her mother lying on her bed flat on her back, sound asleep. It appeared she had tried to get herself ready and passed out before she could finish. She was wearing her raincoat over her nightgown and a shoe on her left foot; the other shoe lay on the floor beside her bed.

21

Jack Bryden didn't sleep most nights. When it finally got to the point where the sheer tiredness of being just hung around his neck like a horse collar throughout the day and weighed him down, then he'd sleep like a baby. But most nights he'd just lie in bed, trying not to fidget too much and wake up Ruth. He'd listen to whatever song was running through his head, hoping it would be Cole Porter or Emmylou Harris, but sometimes it was something dumb he'd heard on the radio and didn't even know the words to and then he'd get irritated.

Occasionally, when he couldn't stand it any longer, he'd roll slowly out of bed onto the floor and snake his way on his belly into the other room. These actions required a good deal of strategic planning and mental resolve, and he would sometimes fall back asleep just thinking about it. Inching to the edge of the bed, slowly drawing back the blanket and suffering the shock of cold air, then twisting his front half down and off the bed, the hind part following, slithering onto the cold hardwood floor, grinding over onto his back and lowering his hips ever so slowly. Once while doing this he caught sight of himself and got the giggles and had to hurry and get his rump off the bed because he was jiggling the mattress and was sure Ruth would wake up and think he was playing with himself again, after which nights she wouldn't talk to him for weeks.

Once his body was safely on the cold wood floor, he would begin his serpentine crawl, using his elbows the way he had done in the army except now he didn't have to carry a rifle. He'd maneuver past the sleeping enemy, around the foot of the bed and out the door, which, if all went as planned, he would manage to catch with the toes of his lone leg and pull neatly shut behind him. One night he had fallen asleep, exhausted, right at the foot of the stairs, and Sarah found him when she came down in the early hours of the morning. But Sarah was good about those kinds of things, never harped at him or acted wounded. She had helped him to the sofa and covered him with a blanket before she left for the cafe, and he'd gone right back to sleep.

Most invertebrate nights, however, he'd

lift himself on a crutch and slip on a coat and make his way to his old pickup, where he'd sit with the heater on and listen to Ella or Louis on the Discman Sarah had given him for Christmas one year. And in the spring and summer he'd just sit in the porch swing, and then he was glad to be alive.

There was a thick mist creeping silently through the Hills that night, moving through the darkness like something predatory, and the sweet smell of spring hung in the chilly air. Jack ventured out onto the porch and lowered himself onto the cold slatted swing and laid down his crutch.

He hadn't been out there but a few minutes when he heard the stairs creak, and the screen door hinged open and Sarah came out, wearing her long green robe and dragging a coverlet behind her.

She laid the coverlet over his lap and sat down next to him.

"It's sweet out tonight," she said.

"Sure is." He paused. "Can't see a damn thing, though."

She took the Discman from him and flipped it open to see what was inside, then gave it back to him.

"I need to get you some new CDs."

"No point in doin' that. I always listen to the same old ones."

There was a long silence between them, and then Sarah kicked the swing into motion and they swung together without talking.

Finally she said, "Did the phone ring?"

"Nope."

"I thought I heard it ring."

"Must've been dreaming."

"I wasn't asleep."

They could hear the sound of the engine long before they saw the red-and-blue light swimming through the fog. The vehicle slowed and turned off the highway and cruised down their street, coming to a stop in front of the house.

A cranelike figure wearing a badge and uniform strolled toward them out of the mist.

"Evenin', Jack. Sarah," Randy said politely, pausing with one boot on the bottom step of the porch.

"You got trouble written all over you," Jack said.

Sarah said nothing but planted her bare feet on the ground and leaned forward just a little in a manner of expectation.

"Somebody already notified you?" Randy asked.

"About what?"

"Well, since you're up, I thought maybe

Clay'd already given you a call."

"Nobody's called," Jack answered.

"Had us a little accident down the road a piece."

"That's a nasty road," Jack said, squirming to get comfortable.

"What happened?" Sarah asked.

"Well, now, I'm gettin' to that, Sarah. Just hold your horses."

But Randy was a talker, and he had a certain way of thinking. He had to start at the beginning and tell them the whole story, about how Susan Wilde had run her Land Cruiser into the ditch and flipped right into the low drystone wall that ran next to the road for the length of Donnie Henryson's farm. It woke up Donnie and his wife and terrified the kids, set the hounds to barking for the longest time. Donnie's wife didn't want to go outside, so Donnie had to go out alone and wade across the ditch in the dark with his flashlight.

"Who was in the car?" Sarah cut in anxiously.

"Now, I'm gettin' to that, Sarah."

"Then get to it," grumbled Jack.

Susan had been wearing her seat belt, he said, and didn't appear to have sustained any truly serious injuries, thought she might have a broken bone or two. But it seems she'd lain there in the ditch, pinned back with the air bag, and then it deflated and she was part floating in water. Donnie Henryson had stood out there with her until the fire department came, trying to help her keep her head above water, because she couldn't hold it up herself after the air bag went down. He kept talking to her, and praying for her. Couldn't do anything himself, trapped the way she was. And the worst part was that the baby was in the back crying his little heart out, and Donnie said Susan was saying some pretty awful things to that baby, but that was the shock, of course.

Sarah drew in a sharp breath. "He wasn't hurt, I hope."

"Not a scratch." He turned and pointed to his patrol car parked in front of the house. "He's asleep in my backseat."

Sarah shot up and tightened her robe around her waist, then loped barefoot down the porch steps and over the wet lawn toward the car.

"Now, wait a minute, Sarah . . . ," Randy shouted, but she was halfway to the car.

Will was asleep with a blanket tucked around him. Very gently she peeled back the blanket and lifted him to her breast. He awakened just a little and whimpered, and his tiny limbs shuddered; then he fell back asleep.

Jack and Randy were in a low conversation when Sarah came up to them with the baby in her arms.

"Where's the father?" Sarah asked.

"Well, now, Sarah, if you'd hung on a bit, I was gettin' to that part. I was tellin' your grandpa here that John Wilde's out of town, out in California, and we got ahold of him and he asked us to bring the little tyke to you, if you don't mind."

"I don't mind," she answered.

"Won't be for long," added Randy.

"I'll keep him as long as it takes," she said, with a glance over her shoulder.

Jack twisted around in the swing. "You better check with your grandma before you go takin' on anybody else's baby."

"I'll take care of him," she said again, quietly, but with a firmness neither man missed. "He won't be in anybody's way."

Then she went inside and left the two men staring at the ground. Jack asked Randy if he had a cigarette on him and Randy did, and they smoked in the dark. By the time they finished their cigarettes the fog had rolled back and the clouds had spun away. The stars sparkled brightly in the blackest of skies, and the night was a marvel of beauty to behold.

22

It was just after noon and a spring storm was moving in from the south as John drove down 177 toward Bazaar. Heavy clouds flew overhead like timid souls fleeing the wrath of the storm. When he drove up their driveway the sky had turned an ominous black, and he dashed up the front steps just as the rain began to fall. He rapped lightly on the screen door frame and peered through the mesh into the shadows.

He heard Sarah's voice call, "Come in."

John went inside, set down the playpen, and slid the bag off his shoulder. He found Sarah in the kitchen. Will was strapped firmly to her chest with a dish towel. He had seen photographs of Kenyan mothers wearing their babies like that.

"I'm so very sorry," she said.

If his eyes betrayed any weakness, it was only for a moment. When he spoke he made sure there was nothing in his voice that hinted at the brightness in his heart.

"Thanks for taking Will. I don't know what we would have done."

"It's okay." She was pouring coffee into a mug and she held it out to him. "I'm glad I can help."

John took the mug from her and her fingers brushed his.

"How's Susan?"

"She's fine. Physically. A fractured wrist. That's all." He took a sip of the hot coffee. "Considering how bad it was. She's very lucky."

"What happened?"

"She went out for a drive. Thought it might help put Will to sleep. She said she turned around to check on him, and when she looked back at the road . . ." He paused. "She'd driven right into a patch of fog. Couldn't see a thing. I guess there's a bend in the road right there."

"Yes, there is. I know it well."

John's eyes were on his son. The child's cheek was resting on her breast, and he was deep in sleep.

"Thank God he wasn't hurt," muttered John.

"Oh, yes," she said.

There was another pause.

"Have you had any sleep?"

"No. Spent the night at the airport

waiting for the flight."

"Sit down."

There was such sweet firmness in her voice; it calmed him immediately. He pulled out a chair and sat down at the kitchen table.

"Have you had lunch?"

"I'm not hungry."

She had her eyes on him for a moment, then she stepped over to the refrigerator and pulled out a covered dish.

"We've got homemade chicken salad."

"I'm really not hungry."

"I'll make it for you all the same."

There was silence while he watched her lay out two slices of bread and spoon the chicken salad over them.

"I can keep him as long as you need me to," she said.

"What about your job?"

She dropped a handful of chips onto the plate and turned to place the sandwich before him.

"Water? Iced tea?"

"Water's fine."

"Joy and I already discussed it," she replied as she filled a glass with water and set it down in front of him. "I can take him into work with me."

"I'll pay you. We'll work something out."

"Don't worry about it."

"I'll pay you," he insisted, through a mouthful of chicken salad.

"Eat your sandwich."

Sarah looked down at Will; he hung there in the dish towel, his bare arm dangling, and she lifted it and kissed it and said gently, "He has the most beautiful skin I've ever seen. The color is absolutely exquisite."

John looked up at her and wiped his mouth with the napkin she handed him. Then he smiled and said, "I think so, too."

When he had finished she cleared away his plate and John picked up the bag with Will's things and the folding playpen and offered to take them where she wanted.

Sarah hesitated a long moment before motioning him to follow her upstairs. She paused at the bottom of the narrow staircase and turned to him and said, "It's not very tidy right now. Not really suitable for a baby. But I'll rearrange things."

The stairway opened into an alcove underneath the eaves. A small bed, still unmade from the night before, stood against the wall. At the foot of the bed was an old oak dresser, its top buried under clutter, and a straight-back chair shoved under a dormer window served as a catchall for her clothing. There was a monastic simplicity about the room.

"This is where you sleep?"

"Yes."

The alcove had a sloped ceiling, and John had to stoop slightly as he stood beside her. Through the dormer window he could see the dark rain clouds scudding by.

He stepped past her into the bedroom.

"We do have a crib," she said. "Down in the basement. I'll bring it up this afternoon."

John set down the bag and leaned the playpen against the wall, then looked around. Sarah had paused in the alcove to lay Will on her bed, and when she appeared he said, "So this is what he was writing about."

"You mean Anthony?"

"In his letters."

"Yes."

"May I?"

"Of course."

The hardwood floor creaked as he carefully made his way across the room, lifting his feet to avoid the paint-caked glass jars and bowls that were scattered around. As he passed from one painting to another she named the grasses and the flowers for him. He was stunned that she had found all this color in the drizzled browns and greens of the prairie. She explained how difficult it was to find some of them, that several of the wildflowers were especially rare and grew only on real prairie, in the conservation projects or along the edges of pasture outside the fences where the cattle couldn't get to them.

The rain fell in a downpour, pummeling the roof, as he quietly studied a gouache of a pink filamented prairie smoke. He said, "Why do you hide all this?" He turned to look at her. "You do, don't you?"

A faint nod.

"Does anyone know you paint?"

"Yes. But nobody comes up here. Not anymore."

"You mean no one ever sees this?"

She shook her head.

"You must know how good these are."

She paused, gave a tired shrug.

"You don't believe me?"

"It's not that." She hesitated.

"What?"

"I don't like people to see what I do."

"Because of what they might say? Their criticism?"

She shook her head. "No. Because of what they might see."

His eyes held on hers, and it seemed to her the blue grew very intense; then he turned and walked to the center of the room, where the easel stood, and bent over to look closely at the painting of a clematis.

Sarah said, "Da Vinci thought if you look closely enough at a stone, at the variations of color as light touches it, then you'll see there all of God's creation — mountains, woods, plains, hills . . . even the expressions of the human face. He said the same applied to the sound of bells. Listen to church bells, he said, and in a single stroke you'll hear every sound in every language ever uttered on earth."

John straightened and said, "You know what I see when I look at this flower?"

"What?"

"I see an entire landscape." He paused, and then added, "I see you."

The smile hovering on her mouth faded.

"I think I've never seen anyone as clearly as I see you," he murmured.

They both stared at each other for the longest time. Thunder rolled in the distance, and a car rolled in the driveway and then the screen door slammed. Ruth called out Sarah's name, but Sarah did not answer.

Finally John approached her and looked down into her eyes and hesitated a long while before he raised his hand and brushed her hair back from her face.

"How's your head?" he whispered. He found the bruise and touched it with his fingers. Her eyes closed at his touch, and John lowered his mouth to kiss the raised place

189

above her eyebrow. When she felt his warm, dry lips against her skin, she thought the world had slipped away.

"Are you in love with Billy Moon?" he whispered.

She opened her eyes at the question, hesitated a long while, and then she answered softly, "I thought I was."

He swallowed heavily.

Her lips were poised and parted, waiting for him. He wet his own lips nervously with a flick of his tongue and then, ever so slowly, he lowered his mouth to meet hers.

There was in that kiss such tenderness and desire longing to be expressed that neither of them could breathe. The world withdrew from around them and sounds receded into the distance — the water running in the kitchen downstairs, the driving rain, the old beams creaking in the wind.

When at last John withdrew, there was a glimmer of sadness in his eyes, and he brushed her hair from her face and took a step back. She looked down then because she did not want to see the guilt on his face. She said nothing, nor did he. She kept her eyes lowered, her hands clasped in front, at her waist, and she did not look up when he left the room, nor when she heard his footfalls on the steps.

23

Clarice felt responsible in no small part for the accident, felt it never would have happened had she been in the car. But what really devastated her was that Susan chose to convalesce up in Lawrence at the home of John's parents.

Clarice had long been aware of the special bond between her daughter and Nancy Wilde. Even before her marriage to John, Susan had seemed to fit into their family as naturally as if she were their own flesh and blood. On more than one occasion, Clarice had found herself outvoted and outmaneuvered by Susan and Nancy Wilde, and there were times when she felt her daughter was not her own. By their complicitous smiles and their disregard for her meekly tendered suggestions, by their increasing familiarity and enthusiastic solidarity, Clarice knew they saw her as an unnecessary outsider with poor taste and insufficient education. Often she would force a bright smile and nod (perhaps a little too eagerly) in agreement with them, watching as her daughter moved into yet one more degree of separation. Clarice would never forget how she had sat in Nancy Wilde's kitchen while they planned the wedding, blinking back her hurt while they talked of florists and engravers, trying desperately to steady her trembling hand and silence the rattling saucer when she raised her coffee cup to her lips.

Susan's retreat to Lawrence after the accident was more than Clarice could bear. With John frequently up in Lawrence with them or in California, and Will in Sarah's care, Clarice again found herself alone. Much to everyone's surprise, she did not sink into a depression. Instead, she called her brother down in Dallas and asked him to find her a good rehab center. Said she'd pay whatever it cost, stay as long as necessary. She wrote her daughter a long and maudlin letter apologizing for how she had botched up her life, then, disgusted with her own self-pity, she tore it up again. Joy drove her to the airport early one morning, and on the way out of town they stopped by Sarah's house so Clarice could say goodbye to her one and only grandchild.

Joy thought the whole incident had been a

wake-up call, and she had great hopes for her friend's rehabilitation. But bets were made at the Cassoday Cafe that week, and most folks thought the odds were not in her favor.

May arrived, the growing season, and the land was restless with change. The wind swept across the grassy ocean and the prairie moved like the sea, rising and falling in swells of ever-shifting tones of green. The warm wind stirred the grasses into perpetual motion, coaxing birth and renewal from the land. Patches of tiny blue bird's-foot violets that seemed to have sailed in overnight blanketed the greening slopes. There were sudden bursts of color all around in wild, unexpected places.

Joy wheedled her sister Jeannine into working a few days at the cafe, and she added hours to Amy's schedule so Sarah was able to cut back to part-time. When Sarah did come in to work they set up Will's playpen in the kitchen, but more often than not he was bouncing around the dining room on Sarah's back, yanking at her hair and staring wide-eyed at the customers. John neither called nor passed by, but he sent her money and a brief note expressing his thanks and saying he was leaving for

Berkeley and would see her when he returned. But he did not say when this would be, and so the days passed slowly by and Sarah lived each one in anticipation of seeing him again.

He gave her no warning, just showed up one Saturday morning out of the blue. It was a perfect day for it, warm with a cool breeze that played with the white curtains at her windows so that they seemed to beckon him inside. The sprinkler stuttered on the front lawn, dashing cool water over his face as he hurried up the sidewalk. No one answered his knock, but the front door stood wide open, so he went inside and called her name. He heard music coming from her room and he went to the bottom of the stairs and called again, and then she heard him and answered, told him to come on up.

There was nothing she could do, dressed in shorts and one of her grandfather's old shirts and covered in paint as she was, and so she just sat there with a rapturous smile on her face listening to his approaching footsteps.

She sat poised on the very top of a ladder in the center of her room, smiling down at him. Her auburn hair shone with the soft radiance of the morning light, and her beauty struck him speechless. She put down her palette and asked him if he'd hold the ladder steady while she climbed down. He set down the tulips he was carrying, a large bouquet wrapped in clear cellophane with a pink ribbon tied around the stems, and walked slowly toward her with his head thrown back, studying the ceiling.

It was not just the ceiling — the entire room had been thoroughly purged. The walls had been swept clean of her work and washed in a whispery blue, and over this was sketched in pencil the outline of fields of grasses and flowers. It was the beginning of a mural.

"Look," she said as she touched the ceiling, directing his gaze to a face peering out from behind the shoulder of a large figure only hazily sketched.

He stood below her, his hands on the ladder.

"It's Will."

"You recognized him."

"Right away," he said, his smile broadening into a grin. "Couldn't miss him."

"He hasn't quite got those fat little cherubic cheeks," she said as she cautiously made her way down. When she reached the floor, she dipped under his arm and tried to turn a bright smile toward him, but she was trembling inside.

"Thank you for the tulips," she said.

"I see they're wasted. You have a room full of flowers."

"They're not wasted," she replied. "Thoughtfulness is never wasted." She crossed the room to where Will sat in his playpen in a pool of toys, mouthing a plastic horse.

"Did you see him?"

When the child saw Sarah approach he dropped the horse and crawled to the rail to meet her. She knelt down and peeked at him playfully through the mesh panel, pressing her nose through the netting, and he smiled and reached out and pressed his palm against her nose.

John stood transfixed by what he was seeing. Sarah reached down and picked him up, and Will came eagerly into her arms.

"He looks good."

"Yes, and he's eating," she said brightly. She shifted him to her hip, and he perched there, easy and comfortable and content. Will's eyes did not leave her face. There was something primal in the way he read her, following her movements and gestures and words. Suddenly, for the first time, John sensed an intelligence in the child, a wordless, natural intelligence that had escaped them during those first months.

Sarah rummaged through a cluster of glass jars full of pencils and paintbrushes, and finally came up with one tall enough for the tulips. She emptied it and handed it to him and asked him to fill it with water, pointing to the small bathroom off the alcove.

He returned with the tulips in the jar and set them on the card table in the midst of all her paints and brushes and rags.

"That's a good place for them." She smiled. "Right in the middle of all my mess."

After that they stood quietly for a moment, Sarah rocking the baby on her hip and John studying the walls and the ceiling.

"It's from the Sistine Chapel, isn't it?"

"Yes. *The Creation of Adam.*" She pointed up at Will's portrait. "In the original that's Eve. Cowering behind God."

"Cowering?" he laughed.

"I think so. If you look at her eyes. Of course, all I have are reproductions in books."

She had clipped to the ladder a page torn from her art history book, and she plucked it from the clip and passed it to him.

"What do you see? In her eyes."

John studied it quietly for a moment.

"She does look a little anxious," he smiled.

"Yes. Like she's very unsure about the whole thing."

"What whole thing?"

"Oh, all that man business. And earth. I think she's much more comfortable with God. It's like she's saying, 'Can't we just leave things the way they are? This is fine with me. Why mess with things?' "

She laughed lightly, but then grew quiet when his eyes swept over her face. The curtains whispered and a cool mist blew in from the sprinkler. Even Will perched quietly on her hip.

"I can't have children, Sarah. It's me. Not Susan. One of those classic cases of mumps when I was young. It didn't really bother me. I thought fatherhood was reserved for more ordinary men. Not someone like myself. I always had this belief that I was a chosen one, that I was destined to make some great discovery, work out some theorem that would make history. But when Will came along, he turned my head. Despite what's happened, I still can't help but feel he was meant to be in my life. That he's brought me here."

Sarah took a step toward him but he held up his hand and stopped her.

"No, Sarah," he whispered. "I'm not trying to seduce you."

"I didn't mean . . ." She paused, mildly flustered.

"Don't be embarrassed," he said quickly. "God knows, I dream of you all the time. I dream of making love to you. But it's more than that, and I don't know how to define it, or what I'm supposed to do with it. I don't know why you're so important to me. But I know you are. And I'm confused."

Will was distracted by a sudden movement in the tree outside the window, the rustle of leaves as a bird took wing. He turned his head, pointed to the open window.

John smiled at the child. "Bird. That's a bird."

He leaned forward and kissed him on the head, then strode swiftly out of the room and down the stairs. Sarah took Will to the window to wave, but John did not look back.

24

The circumstances of her accident had left Susan with a bitterness that worried her mother-in-law, and so Nancy Wilde urged her to consult a therapist, believing this might help Susan deal more effectively with her anger. Early in the week the therapist had called and asked to meet with John privately. John drove to Lawrence that day, expecting the session to be an update on her progress.

Dr. Redpath took a seat in an armchair next to a table scattered with a few *Field & Stream* magazines, and John sat on the other side. The doctor lifted his glasses off his nose, rubbed his bloodshot eyes with the back of a hairy fist, and apologized for keeping John waiting ten minutes. Then he began to ask questions. He asked about their marriage, about their plans for the future, for their family. They were not threatening questions, but John found them disturbing. They were questions he had never really pondered until these past few months, and now he had no convincing answers. Had Dr. Redpath asked him to explain Bohm's theory of invisible morphogenetic fields or Ramanujan's partitions theory, John would have acquitted himself with much greater ease.

Dr. Redpath listened carefully to what John said, and he could sense that behind his cautious and sometimes vague answers was a man of deep moral integrity. After he had asked many questions and listened to John's replies, he poured a glass of water for himself and took a drink, then he began to speak.

"Your wife is a very intelligent woman."

"Yes. Of course she is."

"She's quite capable of assessing what is happening to her right now. And she knows, and I know, and I thought you should know, that it is not just an issue of trauma we're dealing with here. It's about parenting. It's about the little boy."

John felt his stomach roll over and a sudden nausea sweep through him.

"His name is Will."

"She doesn't refer to him by name."

"Why not?"

"She needed to create a distance from him. I helped her do that."

"Why would you do that? Why would you

try to create a distance where there needs to be warmth and closeness?"

Dr. Redpath reached again for the glass of water and sat up a little in his chair.

"Susan confided in me some of her behavior with regard to Will. She came very close to some actions that would have had severe consequences."

"What was that? What are you referring to?"

"Well, she came rather close to a violent response. On several occasions, I gather. She's been honest with me."

"Has she hurt him?"

"No. She was able to pull herself back. She recognized what was happening."

John leaned forward in his chair with his elbows on his knees and clasped his hands tightly. "I didn't know. I knew how frustrated she got. I think she neglected him sometimes. She'd ignore him when he got too much for her." John looked up, quizzical. "Don't other parents ever get like that?"

"They do. Especially with children as difficult as Will."

"He's not that difficult anymore." John leveled his eyes on Dr. Redpath. "He's made a lot of progress since she last saw him."

"I'm sure he has."

"He's calmer. He sleeps better. He's eating. He's gained four pounds."

Dr. Redpath watched the body language, the way the man became animated when talking about his son. He realized it was going to be much more difficult than he had imagined.

"That may be in part because of the young woman you've placed him with. I understand she's developed a bond with him."

John dropped his eyes. "Yes. She has. But I'm hoping it'll carry over."

"Affection . . . bonding . . . does not necessarily carry over. Sometimes unique bonds are created . . . or not created . . . as the case may be."

There was a long silence, and Dr. Redpath noticed the blank stare.

"Mr. Wilde?"

There was not an immediate reaction, only a slow, tentative response.

"I can't give him up."

"John, not everyone wants to be a parent. Not everyone needs to be a parent. Not everyone should be a parent. I think your wife falls into all of those categories. This is not a judgment on her. It's just a fact of life."

"No," muttered John under his breath, his eyes still fixed in space. "No."

Dr. Redpath hesitated before he said quietly, "You have to make a decision. You chose to marry Susan, and you've lived, from what I can gather, some very good years together. You strike me as an exceptionally compatible couple. And your family is extremely supportive of you and your wife. Would you say this is true?"

John nodded slowly.

"These are assets that only become more important as the years go by, as you grow older together. You have to decide how important that is to you."

"You're saying I have to decide between Will . . . between my son and my wife?"

"That's what I'm saying."

"Is this your professional opinion? Or is this what Susan wants?"

"She wanted me to talk to you before you saw her. She didn't feel she was strong enough emotionally to put it to you as clearly as I could."

"You mean give me an ultimatum."

"The mental health of your wife is at stake. And, of course, Will's safety, too."

There was another long silence, and then, abruptly, John rose and nodded his thanks to Dr. Redpath. Dr. Redpath followed him to the door, and then John paused and turned and met the doctor's gaze.

"I know you mean well," John said.

Then he turned and left.

He sat in his car for the longest time. Flint-colored thunderheads advanced swiftly across the sky, and he could hear deep thunder in the distance. It started to rain, and he watched as another patient arrived and scurried down the walk with her purse clutched over her head. Finally he started up the engine. He drove slowly, trying to make out the road through the steady down-pour.

He pulled into the driveway of his parents' home and cut the engine. The windows of the old BMW had fogged over and he sat locked in his thoughts, hidden from the world, when suddenly the car door flew open and Susan hopped in and quickly slammed the door behind her.

"God, this rain!" She lowered the raincoat from her head and turned to him with a wary smile. "How about if we go for a drive?"

He looked up at her and only gradually the blank look lifted and he seemed to see her and he smiled.

"Hi," he said and reached out and touched her hand.

She gave a sigh of relief and swallowed nervously.

"Shall we go for a drive?"

He wiped a patch of fog from the windshield with his hand.

"In this?"

"Your mother's home."

Her wrist was still in a cast, supported by a sling, but she looked rested and much happier than he had seen her in a long time. She had lost weight and had taken to sunbathing at the club and her skin had a robust, healthy color.

"Oh, John," she whispered, holding his gaze. "I tried so hard . . ."

"I know you did."

"I thought it was because I was doing something wrong. I thought it was all my fault. But it's not . . ."

She paused, waiting to hear some word of absolution, but there was none.

"Dr. Redpath helped me see that," she went on. "He said —"

"He explained it all to me."

Timidly, she reached out and laid a hand on his arm.

"But you still blame me."

"Things can still work out. It's not hopeless." His voice was colored with such optimism that Susan withdrew her hand and stared at him in stunned disbelief.

"You didn't understand anything at all,

206

did you? You didn't hear what he was saying."

"But he doesn't see things —"

"No, John," she whispered through a strangled voice. "You're the one who's blind."

There was a long silence, and when she spoke her voice was low and unsteady. "We have something worth fighting for in our marriage. I think it'd be a tragedy to throw it all away. This has been a horrific time for me. For both of us." She tugged the raincoat up around her shoulders and reached for the door handle. "Let's give us time to heal."

She left him sitting there. The sun came out and turned the car into a steam bath. He sat with his hands on the wheel and sweat trickling down his face and fog steaming up the windshield until he could no longer bear it. Then he went inside to shower and get ready for dinner.

25

The Flint Hills Rodeo drew contestants from all across the country — steer ropers from Texas and bull riders from Colorado and Wyoming, bronc busters from California. In his younger, wilder years Billy Moon had done a little of it all, had ridden the bulls and wrestled the steers, but now he kept to roping, stayed pretty much on the back of his horse, counted on his skill with a lasso and his good timing to bring home the silver buckles and the big money prizes. It was the young drifters who went for the bull riding and the bronc busting, traveling the circuit from one rodeo to another, arriving all tough and grim-faced with their saddles hoisted over their shoulders and their overnight bags in their hands, with just enough money in their pockets to cover the entry fee, a few beers, and a cheap room for the night. But the steer ropers like Billy Moon were a different breed, many of them professional men, educated attorneys or dentists or businessmen, men with homes and wives and families, a little older perhaps, with reason to be a little more cautious.

The Grand Entry with its horseback pageantry of rodeo queens and waving flags had taken place earlier in the afternoon, and it was now getting on in the evening. Billy was sitting with a few buddies on the tailgate of a truck, sipping beer while they waited for their events. Billy had always enjoyed the company of cowboys, but this spring he found their camaraderie to be just the antidote he needed, helped him keep his mind tuned to something other than Sarah and the way she'd been avoiding him. He liked the heat and the dust and the grit on his skin, liked listening to their lumbering conversation, liked the way they prodded one another along with sharp wit and dry laughter, and silences punctuated by the sound of spit hitting the dirt. They never talked much about themselves or about people, unless it was how one-armed Ward Butler liked to test an electrical outlet by spitting on his thumb and sticking it in a live socket, and how one day he got shocked so bad he went into a coma and lay on the closet floor in his boxer shorts for two hours before his wife came home and found him. Or how the woman at the car wash up in

Strong City was almost strangled to death when she dropped the water gun and it went crazy on her, flipped and flopped until it wrapped itself around her neck, and it took three guys to get it off her. For the most part they talked about the mechanics of things, things that broke down and could be fixed, pumps and air conditioners and alternators and the like. They talked about their cattle, their horses, their dogs, and their trucks. They never talked about their cats or their women.

Somebody checked his watch and noted the time, and Billy slid off the tailgate and tossed his empty beer bottle into the front seat and headed back to where his horse stood tied to the side of the trailer. A truck hauled a trailer by, kicking up a cloud of dust, and when the dust settled he looked up and saw Sarah coming toward him across the field. She was carrying the baby on her hip, John Wilde's kid, and Billy turned away and heaved the saddle up onto his horse. The sight of that kid called up all kinds of resentment. He knew all about how she had taken him on this spring, knew the whole sorry situation, about Susan and the baby's poor health, but Billy felt there was something more to it, felt Sarah was hiding behind her new status as mother to avoid settling some things that needed to be settled between them. Billy liked things to be simple and clear. Sarah had never been simple and clear.

He didn't turn around right away, even after she greeted him, just sort of grunted out a reply and reached under the horse's belly to grab the cinch and buckle it up. She was talking to the horse, trying to get the kid to pet him. She took the baby's hand in hers and stroked the horse's nose, then tickled the soft, velvety muzzle.

"Careful. He bites," Billy said.

"I know that," answered Sarah, but she said it sweetly and he could tell she was in a good mood. "I know this horse."

Billy watched her for a moment, then shook his head.

"You're tempting fate, girl," he said, and she backed away while he unfastened the halter and worked the bit into the horse's mouth.

She had bought the baby a straw cowboy hat that was too big for him, and she'd tied a red bandanna around his neck. Billy thought he looked ludicrous. But he seemed content, didn't seem to mind that the hat kept falling down over his eyes.

"I'm a little surpised to see you here." He slung the bridle over the horse's head.

"Why?"

"Didn't think you were very fond of rodeos."

"I came to see you ride."

He fastened the chin strap and then held the reins out to Sarah.

"Can you hold him for a minute?"

"Sure."

"Don't turn your back on him."

He stepped into the trailer, and through the doorway she could see him strip off his T-shirt and slip into a white Western shirt. He was a small man but muscular, and Sarah caught a glimpse of him as he buttoned up the shirt, white against his sunbrowned chest, and she looked away.

He came out, tucking in his shirt.

"I'd better get over there if I want a good seat," Sarah said, handing him the reins. Quite suddenly, she leaned forward, laid a hand on his shoulder, and kissed him gently on the lips. Then she turned and hurried across the field toward the stands.

She bought a corn dog from a vendor and found a place on the bleachers near the starting gate, just a few rows up. She sat there with Will, the two of them nibbling halfheartedly at the corn dog while they watched the first of the contestants. It was always the horses Sarah loved to watch, more than the riders, the way they burst out of the box with their necks stretched long and their ears up, all long-legged muscle and pounding hooves as they zeroed in on the steer up ahead and closed in on him. They boxed him in, a horse on each side, the hazer and the bulldogger, careening along beside him as he shot back and forth, adjusting their gait to the speed of the steer so they were dead even and holding him in place. Then the work fell to the horse on the left flank, the bulldogger's horse. He'd feel the shift in weight as the rider slid to the right and hung from the horn by his left hand, right foot still leveraged in the stirrup until his left foot was over the saddle and he was down in the hole. A good horse stayed the course, despite the man dangling from the saddle, kept the steer right there off his right eye while the rider got his right arm underneath that horn. There was always that moment's hesitation, and then, arm locked around the horn, the bulldogger cut loose. His feet popped up in the air and he was on the ground with the steer. The rest was up to the man, and the horse was riderless and running free.

Sarah kept her eyes peeled for Billy, and finally saw him arrive on horseback alongside his partner. She watched him line up with the other teams beside the box. She thought what a fine-looking man he was, and she knew then she didn't love him, wondered why she couldn't, wished to God she could.

26

During John's visits to Berkeley he made it a point to check up on their home in San Francisco. He and Susan had purchased the house following his promotion to tenure track, but the timing was ceremonial rather than financial. He never could have afforded such a place on his income alone. After all, it was her six figure salary they spent to renovate and decorate, her taste that prevailed, and in the long run it was her pleasure it procured. It was a long commute for him but convenient for Susan, who worked in the city, and in the back of his mind John had always felt it to be more her place than theirs.

Now, his office up at the university, that was a different matter. He had moved in an old sofa so he could nap during his nocturnal stints at the lab, and he had installed a small refrigerator and a microwave to enable him to catch a bite to eat without leaving the premises. His work had always been a veritable emotional and mental fortress against invasion from the outside world, against tumultuous passions and disturbing events, those things he spent his life trying to avoid.

Whenever he came into town he would generally pick up a rental car at the airport, drive straight to his office, and work long into the night. He preferred to catch a few hours' sleep on the sofa and then walk down to the faculty club gym for a shower and shave in the morning rather than commute back and forth to the city. Nevertheless, he made it a rule to stop by the house at least once and visit with the neighbor who was keeping an eye on the place in their absence. The lights had been set to an automatic timer and a security company was being paid to keep watch. A gardener came by once a week to maintain the lawn. Most of their furniture was still there; they had moved only their personal belongings and the desk and chairs from John's office.

Most of the time John whisked in and out, but on this particular evening he found himself lingering at the bay window, pausing to take in the ocean view that had sold them on the house. They had achieved an enviable lifestyle, both of them with prestigious careers, and Susan's skilled investment decisions had already netted them enough personal wealth to assure their financial security.

As John watched twilight settle over the ocean he tried to imagine their return to this house in the summer, what it would be like to carry on as they had. With or without Will, it seemed to him equally strange. Uncomfortable. Instead of setting foot back in an old, familiar place, a place filled with bright hopes for their future, it seemed to him a dead place, a place to be rid of. When he thought about it he realized that — outside of his work — the only passion he had experienced in his life, and what little joy he had known as a father, seemed to be bound up with Sarah, in a little town of no consequence in a remote part of the country. Things had happened to him back there that had never happened to him before, and he felt connected. Whereas this place that he called home left him with an emptiness as vast and barren as the hills he had gazed upon from Sarah's window.

Quickly he locked up the house and hurried out to his rental car. After fighting the Friday-night traffic all the way back to Berkeley, he arrived tired and out of sorts, ate a sandwich he had picked up on the way, and then lay down on the sofa in his office. He awoke a few hours later and worked through the night and all the next morning in the lab, taking apart and rebuilding the magneto-optic trap, a procedure that normally took him days of intensive work. He left a long, detailed memo for his colleague and then, without shaving, drove directly to the airport and waited in the lounge until he could get a flight back to Kansas City.

He tried to call Sarah from the airport in Kansas City but there was no answer. He knew her well enough now, knew this did not necessarily mean she was not home, and so, heedless of speed limits and lurking highway patrol, he sped down the turnpike to Bazaar with the accelerator of his old BMW flat to the floor.

It was after nine o'clock when he pulled up to her house. There were still lights on, although not in her window. He tapped lightly on the front door and the porch light came on and Jack answered the door. He spoke gruffly, said Sarah wasn't home, and John apologized, thinking he'd probably woken the old man. John asked if she'd be home this evening, but Jack said something about her being her own free agent and his not keeping tabs on her. Yeah, Jack said, she had Will with her. Never went anywhere without him, and then, seeing the troubled look on John Wilde's face, Jack asked if there was anything wrong. John answered that there wasn't, just that he was missing his boy, he'd been out of town and hadn't seen him in a while, although Jack suspected there was more to it than that.

An hour passed and Jack was on his way to bed when he looked out the front window and saw John Wilde's BMW still parked in front of the house. He told Ruth he was going outside for a smoke and then he hobbled out and leaned against the porch railing while he lit a cigarette. He pocketed the lighter and glanced around the front lawn. The BMW appeared to be empty, but as he moved to the side of the porch, he caught sight of John Wilde sitting on the curb on the other side of the street.

John stood and crossed the street.

"I thought I might wait for them. If you don't mind," he said as he came up the front walk.

"She might not be home till late," Jack answered as he picked a flake of tobacco off his lip.

"I don't mind."

Jack motioned to the front porch swing.

"Wanna sit for a while?"

"I'm imposing."

"Naw. Once I get to bed I'm not sleepy

anymore. Can't seem to sleep except in front of that damn TV."

Jack laid down his crutch and settled himself onto the swing, and John sank down next to him.

Jack started rambling on about his accident, about how he lost his leg and how the gangrene had been eating away at him all these years.

"Doctors tell me if I quit smokin' it might help. But a man's gotta have some pleasure left, don't he?"

Then he talked about Thut's quarry, the place where he lost his leg, and said how it had been one of Sarah's favorite places when she was a kid. Back when she was little it wasn't being worked, he said, had been abandoned since the 1800s.

"She loved to wander out there," he went on, "and when I got her her pony, she'd take him up there. A little Connemara stallion. Black as pitch. You shoulda seen her ride that fella. Those little Connemaras are jumpers, and she'd take off over the open fields with him lookin' for fences and ditches and scrub brush to jump. She used to come home all bruised up from fallin' but she never said a peep about it 'cause she was afraid we wouldn't let her ride. She'd just hobble up to her room and close the door and we'd never hear a complaint out of her. Never broke anything. She was lucky for that.

"When she got older, she'd just light out on her own. It got so the neighbors used to call up to let us know what part of the county she was roamin' in. The Prathers at Tetersville, they'd call and say they'd seen her down their way; or old Dirty Shirt Sam, who worked several of the ranches, he'd call me and say she was over on the Verdigris. Come summertime she'd disappear all day long. Sometimes even all night. That's when her grandma put an end to all of it."

Jack paused, took one long pull from his cigarette, then snuffed it out in a coffee can on the floor beside him.

"Her grandma sold the pony. Without a word of warnin' to Sarah." Jack shifted in the swing. "Sarah was fifteen then and Ruth was worryin' a lot about her. She looked grown, like a young woman, and she was wild. But that was the end of it for Sarah and her grandma."

Jack shook his head. "She hasn't really changed much. Still wild. She may seem tame 'cause you don't know her. But I figure she's just biding her time until the waters return, and then she'll be gone. Not really the kinda girl a guy can depend on. Got her own way of seein' things."

Jack fell silent. After a moment he picked up his crutch and rose from the swing.

"Time for me to be turnin' in."

John stood abruptly. "I guess I might as well go," he said.

Jack thought maybe he was waiting to be contradicted, the way he lingered there, his hands on his hips and his eyes still on the road. But then he mumbled a good night and marched quickly down the steps.

Jack hobbled back inside and switched off the porch light.

27

John slept on the sofa in his study that night and woke around four in the morning and worked for twelve hours straight. He needed to get out of the house after that, so he walked up the street and over a few blocks to Broadway and got himself something to eat at Hannah's Cafe. He wandered up and down Broadway a little, then went back home where it was cool and turned on the television and watched the evening news.

Around nine-thirty he called her. There was no answer, and so he got in his car and drove over there again. This time there was a dim light shining from her window.

He knocked on the door but there was no reply. Jack's truck was gone and he guessed she was alone. He went back down the stairs and stood out on the wet grass and called out her name. After a moment there was a shadow at the window, and she drew back a curtain and peered out.

"Sarah?"

"John!"

"May I come up?"

"Of course. Door's open. Come on in."

The living room was dark and he tripped over Ruth's shoe boxes stacked on the floor in the hallway. She heard the clatter and his confused muttering as he came up the stairs, and she laughed.

She wore a white summer dress and stood barefoot in the middle of the floor with a book in her hand. A soft, muted light came from a lamp on a nightstand beside her bed. John noticed the crib against the wall.

"Is he asleep?" he asked, keeping his voice low.

"Yes."

"Am I disturbing you?"

She did not answer right away, but dropped the book onto the nightstand and looked back up at him. "No, of course not. I was just trying to tidy up a bit."

"I came by last night."

"You did?"

"Your grandfather didn't tell you?"

"No, he didn't."

Sarah avoided his eyes and pulled up an old wicker chair for him to sit on.

"Sit down."

But he remained standing, a little more relaxed now, finally tearing his eyes away from her and turning his attention to the mural.

"You've finished."

"Not really. But I needed to move everything in. Couldn't take forever."

"It looks so different."

"Yes, it does," she said brightly.

"My God," he whispered.

"What?"

He shook his head, mouth agape. The figures were only lightly sketched and filled in with pale gouache, nothing like the vivid hues of the original, but even without all this detail she had managed to capture the spirit of the work.

"I was just playing. Really. Having fun with it."

His eyes fell back to her, and then her smile faded.

"Can I offer you something to drink?"

He hesitated. "No," he said at last. Then, "Sure. Why not?"

She laughed. "It was only a gesture."

"I understand."

At that moment he gave in, stood in the middle of the room with his head lowered and his hands on his hips.

"Sarah," he whispered. "I took marriage vows. And I take them seriously. I've broken them in the past. But I did it thoughtlessly."

He lifted his eyes and met her gaze. "If I had known I would ever feel about a woman the way I feel now, I never would have married."

She crossed the room to him, and he drew her into his arms. They stood in the dim light and held each other in a tender embrace.

Nothing more was said. Slowly, his lips found her forehead and her hair, and his fingers brushed back a curl and he kissed the top of her ear. Her hands moved slowly over his body, over the rounded curve of his shoulders and down his back and around his waist. When he tried to speak she closed his lips with a kiss. Deftly, she worked her hand under his belt. He groaned softly, and she quickly unfastened his belt and opened his trousers. He groaned again and whispered her name.

She drew him over to the bed and lifted her white skirt, raising a bare leg, and eased herself down on top of him.

Never had he experienced the kind of loss of self he felt just then; he thought he knew love, assumed he had known passion, deep in his heart had no great regard for either, until this moment. He gave himself over to her and she swept him away, obliterating all he thought he knew about himself.

In the dim lamplight, with the cool night breeze fluttering the curtains from time to time and the cicadas harping senselessly outdoors, they lay naked on her narrow bed and completed what had begun in heart and mind.

The pleasure they gave each other that evening was the greatest either of them had ever known, and it was given with such full hearts, and yet achieved so simply and naturally. All of John's anxieties vanished; he sensed it was not so much that he was in the hands of a greatly experienced lover, but that he was in the hands of a woman who was capable of great love. He knew it from the way her eyes sank into his when he rolled her onto her back and she grew so terribly still, as if she were listening with her entire body when he entered her, and reading his heart through his eyes.

For a long while afterward they lay wrapped in each other's arms. He kissed the sweat from between her breasts, and she raised her head and swept back her hair across the pillow. He lifted himself on one elbow so he could see her better in the dim light, and then her eyes and the way she moved told him she wanted him again. He found himself aroused, not gradually but quickly, and he laughed a little, surprised at himself, but she did not laugh. There was an urgency that overtook them then, and their bodies were wet from sweat and she gasped and closed her eyes and raised herself to him, begging him to look at her body as they made love a second time.

This time her pleasure exploded in cries she had to stifle against his shoulder. When he had finished he looked down at her face and saw tears in her eyes. He took her in his arms and cradled her against his body and kissed her and held her, and still not a word passed between them.

At last, they slept.

She awoke first, and she gently roused him. He had been sleeping deeply, more soundly than he had slept in months, and for the first few seconds he did not know where he was. Then he realized he was with Sarah, and he opened his eyes.

"You must go," she whispered. She was caressing his face with her fingers and he found her lips and kissed her deeply.

"Really," she repeated, pulling back from the kiss. "It's almost five. It'll be getting light soon. You have to go."

"When can I be with you again?"

He saw by the look in her eyes what the answer would be even before she whispered it.

"Never."

She sat up, swung her feet over the side of the bed, and sat quietly for a moment, feeling his hand caress her waist and her hips. Then she stood and he watched while she pulled her dress over her head and walked toward the bathroom.

When she came back he was dressed and leaning over the crib, watching Will sleep. She led him quietly down the stairs and kissed him softly goodbye, and waited while he walked barefoot down the front walk with his shoes in his hand. When the taillights disappeared from sight, she shut the front door and went back upstairs to bed.

28

Nancy Wilde was surprised to find her daughter-in-law already up, sitting in the hearth room with the morning paper spread across the coffee table and a mug of coffee in her hand.

"You're up early."

"John called," Susan said, looking up from the paper.

"I didn't hear the phone."

"He called on my cell phone."

"So early? Where is he?"

"He's home."

"In San Francisco?"

"Cottonwood Falls."

Nancy was pouring herself a glass of orange juice, and she glanced over the counter and said with a twinge of surprise, "I thought he wasn't due back until tomorrow."

"He wasn't."

"And he didn't come by here?"

"Got in too late, he said." Susan set down

her coffee. "He wants me to come home."

Nancy came around the counter into the hearth room. "Have you finished with the front page?"

"Right there."

Nancy set down her juice and retrieved the paper from the floor. "If he wants you home, then you should go home." She settled into an armchair opposite Susan. "When's your mother coming back?"

"Not for a while, I think." They never spoke about Clarice's problem, and Susan had not told them her mother had gone into rehab. Susan shook her head in dismay. "I just don't think I can handle it yet."

Nancy watched without comment while her daughter-in-law rose to get herself another cup of coffee. Susan paused with the carafe in her hand, set it down, and looked at her mother-in-law. "He just doesn't understand," she said in a strained whisper.

"About the baby?"

"Yes."

"How did you leave it?"

"Unresolved."

"Then go home and resolve it."

"If I go back there I'll have to take Will back. And I'm not ready. Not physically, not emotionally."

"If your husband wants you home, then

you go home. The rest, you'll work out." When Susan did not respond, she said, "He's trying to tell you something."

Susan looked up in alarm. "What do you mean?"

Nancy Wilde was not comfortable with intimacy, even among women, and when her daughter-in-law had settled back down opposite her and sat peering at her over the rim of her coffee cup with a worried frown, when Nancy finally spoke, it was with great difficulty.

"Once, before John was born," she began, and she grew very still. "Actually it was right after Nick was born — Armand started behaving strangely. I can't tell you precisely in what way, not now, although at the time I could have chronicled every little thing. The most minute details, the things he did differently for no reason whatsoever. For a while I thought it was just me. You know, postpartum stress. That kind of thing. But my instincts told me otherwise.

"Then, one weekend we had one of his doctoral students and her husband over for dinner. Armand did that very rarely. He didn't socialize with many of his students. Right then and there, that should have tipped me off. But there was some justification for it — I don't recall now what he said.

Anyway, that evening, during dinner, we had a terrible blizzard. Snow just wouldn't stop. Their car got snowed in. Armand invited them to stay the night."

She removed her reading glasses and rubbed her eyes, then put them back on. When she spoke at last it was with averted eyes, and her voice was forced.

"That night your father-in-law slept with his underpants on. He has never slept with his underpants on. Even when we had family visiting, or other guests. He had never done it before that night, and never did it again. And there were other things that night that were different between us."

She screwed up her mouth, as if the memory were still on her tongue, sour and biting. She straightened in her chair, an attempt to regain a dignity she had momentarily sacrificed to a greater good. "But I knew who it was then. I knew who the woman was."

Susan left that morning. She packed up her bags and drove back to Cottonwood Falls in the new Range Rover she had bought to replace the Land Cruiser.

She found John working in his office. He smiled up at her, and she thought she read an eagerness in his eyes that looked a little like apprehension, and she felt a faint stab of fear.

She leaned down and kissed him on the lips.

"You're back," he said.

"Yes. You moaned loud enough."

"I'm glad," he said. "I've missed you."

"Have you had lunch?"

"No."

"Tuna sandwich sound good?"

"Sounds very good."

Around one in the afternoon she took a tuna sandwich in to his office. As usual, she quietly set down the tray and started to leave, but he turned away from his work and asked her to wait a minute, said he had something he wanted to discuss.

She sat down on the arm of the sofa.

"Yes?"

"I've given a lot of thought to all this," he said.

"You mean Will."

"Yes."

He told her he thought he could finish his paper this weekend, and then they could bring Will back home.

"This isn't a discussion, then."

"Let's just get him back. See how things go. I'll have more time now. I can help out. I'll look after him."

"And if it doesn't work out?"

"I think it will."

Then he turned away, back to his calculations. Susan felt an odd relief, as if she had been expecting something else, something much worse than this. She sensed this was not the time to contradict him, thought it perhaps best to placate him a little for now. She would find time over the next few days, draw him out, make him see how impossible it was.

She rose and placed a hand on his shoulder.

"You really want him badly, don't you?"

"Yes. I do."

She gave his shoulder a slight squeeze, a conciliatory sign, and turned to leave.

"Wait," he said. Then, rifling under a sprawl of papers, he held out a postcard to her. "This came in the mail yesterday."

She took it from him. "What is it?"

"An invitation."

She glanced at the postcard, a rather spectacular image, lightning splitting the skies over open prairie, then turned it over and read the handwritten message.

"A barbecue?"

"Memorial Day. That's this weekend."

"Who's Billy Moon?"

"Sarah Bryden's boyfriend."

"I didn't know she had a boyfriend."

"We don't have to go. I just thought . . ." He shrugged. He had still not looked up to meet her gaze. "She's done a lot for Will. It would be a nice gesture. To accept."

"Will she have the baby with her?"

"I'm sure she will."

Susan gave an exasperated sigh and rolled her eyes. "God, this is so uncomfortable."

"We don't have to go. Your call."

"Let me give it some thought."

Over the next few days Susan observed him closely and concluded her mother-in-law was wrong. She noticed nothing unusual about her husband's behavior. He was as he had always been: preoccupied with his work, distracted around the house, little inclined to make love.

29

Billy Moon's Memorial Day Barbecue Bash was a kind of institution among his friends and family. It was rivaled in popularity only by Wayne Tonkington's Fourth of July Bullfrog Fry. Maude's protracted illness and death had brought about only a hiatus, not an end to the tradition, and Billy was determined to make it as grand as ever this year. His elderly aunts and uncles came shuffling in, and his grown daughters trailing their current beaux, and his cousins with their teenagers and toddlers. The entire faculty at Chase County High was always invited, as were many of the steer ropers and wrestlers he met year after year on the rodeo circuit.

Billy's place sprawled down the backside of a hill, backed up onto one of those many crooks and crannies that rivers carve out of the land. In the drier months of summer the Cottonwood kept to a deep and narrow course along the south bank, leaving a playground of exposed sandbars on the north.

When Billy was of a mind to mount his tractor mower and trim the tallgrass, you could walk right down that slope and across the sandy riverbed to within a stone's throw of the south bank.

As Susan and John marched down the gravel drive and rounded the house — John with a six-pack of chilled Coronas under his arm — they could hear children's muffled shouts and laughter from the pool. Near the back door two little boys looked on while one of Billy's daughters sprinkled rock salt into the barrel of an ice-cream maker. Under the trees, two women were spreading a plastic tablecloth over a sun-warped picnic table. On the patio, an older set brooded over a game of rummy in the shadow of a white-fringed parasol.

There was a deep metal tub of iced beer and sodas under an umbrella on the back patio, and when John stepped up to bury the Coronas in the ice, one of the rummy players looked up from his cards and welcomed them, introduced himself as Billy's uncle, said to make themselves at home.

John took Susan by the hand and led her across the closely clipped lawn toward the river. It was a peculiar gesture — the first of several she noticed that evening — because John was not the romantic type, did not generally hold her hand in public. It felt awkward to both of them, and he wished he hadn't done it, but it was too late.

Billy had seen fit to engineer all kinds of paraphernalia to tempt one to play. There was a rope-and-tire swing suspended from the limb of a mammoth cedar where kids could swing out over the river and drop into the water. A few old tractor inner tubes, heavily patched, still survived, and as John and Susan made their way across the lawn they were met by a gang of children racing up the hill while a young man in a bathing suit dragged a canoe onto the shore.

He did not see Sarah at first, did not pick her out from the mothers kneeling around the plastic wading pool, not until she rose to her feet and with a flick of the hand brushed her hair back from her face. She caught sight of them and waved.

Susan was all smiles and charm then, walked up to Sarah and thanked her effusively for all she had done, said she was looking forward to getting her baby home, gestured to her arm covered wrist to elbow in a brace (she wore her sling that day although she hadn't worn it in a week), and said she would be getting this off soon and then would be able to cope. Then she squatted at the edge of the wading pool and pretended an interest in the little boy, pretended to be so very pleased with how well he looked, so healthy and active.

John glanced at Sarah, hoping to catch her eye. But her attention was focused on Will, and the expression on her face pinned him to the ground. It was a kind of rapture that shines from the inside out, the kind of bliss that comes only from loving a child.

That was exactly what Susan saw when she looked up, and that's when she knew. It was peculiar the way she realized it, because Sarah was not looking at John just then, she was looking at the child, but the effect was the same. That her husband was in love with this woman did not occur to her immediately, but grew out of the realization that this woman truly loved her son, loved him in a way one could never imitate, or force, or conjure. She saw then all she had strived to feel, saw it come so naturally out of Sarah's heart.

Will took a spill just then, found himself all tangled up with the others. Sarah bent down, laughing, and retrieved him. Will clung to her, the way John had seen him do so many times, as if his little life depended on her.

Susan stepped back and — slipping her good arm around John's waist — beamed at him and said how fantastic their child looked.

"I think we should be able to bring him home next week," she said with a tight smile pasted on her face. "I should be able to manage by then."

Sarah's face darkened, and Susan felt an instant rush of satisfaction.

"We've really been looking forward to getting him back," she went on, eyes fixed on Sarah. Then, to John, "Haven't we?"

She glanced back to catch the look on Sarah's face, but Sarah had her mouth on the baby's neck, teasing him with kisses. Susan could not read her eyes. John stood stiffly at his wife's side, immobile. Susan tore her eyes from Sarah and gazed up fondly at him, but he was watching Sarah, and that was when it all came together. The realization was instant and total, and she stared at him in horror. She felt herself swallow involuntarily, her body in some spasmodic withdrawal from this awful truth. She flung her gaze back at Sarah, but Sarah had wrapped Will in a towel and, without a word to them, had turned up the hill, the baby still clinging to her hip, his eyes gazing darkly at them over her shoulder.

"She's a strange one, isn't she?" Susan said as she watched her move away, but John surprised her by agreeing. Yes, he said with a smile, Sarah was a little odd, but there was admiration in his voice. Susan did not like at all that he had used her name. The very naming of her hinted at a certain intimacy.

John detached himself from her grasp and strolled down the slope toward the river's edge, and Susan hated him for that gesture, all of a sudden hated this entire event, this place and these people, their rural pleasures and simple ways.

"John," she said, striding quickly to catch up with him, "this heat's getting to me. Let's go. Let's just leave."

He turned to face her and shrugged. "Sure, that's fine. We put in an appearance. We don't have to stay."

But then he glanced up the hill at the trestle table now laden with dishes.

"Looks like they're getting ready to eat." He reached for her hand again. "I'm starved," he said. "Let's eat first, and then we can go if you want."

But the call to table was slow in coming. It was early in the evening when they finally sat down to eat, and everyone filled their plates with coleslaw and baked beans and hunkered down over slabs of mesquite-smoked ribs. Susan and John found two empty chairs at one of several folding tables set up on the lawn, not too far from where Billy had pulled up a chair for Sarah and Will.

Several times during dinner John glanced aimlessly Sarah's way, hoping to meet her gaze, but she studiously avoided looking in his direction. However, when folks finished eating and the table emptied, Sarah remained, sitting alone with her chin resting in her cupped hand, staring out toward the river.

Susan had revived a little, surprised him by appearing to enjoy the company of the man next to her, an English teacher from Chase High. When John rose to get another beer, Susan caught his hand and whispered that it was time to go, but he ignored her and broke free and strolled up the lawn. He was screwing the cap off a bottle of Corona when Susan appeared beside him.

"Let's go," she said, and without waiting for him she turned away and headed toward the road.

Susan was behind the wheel of the Range Rover with the engine idling when he finally appeared. He hesitated, hand on the door, then leaned down to look at her through the window.

Never in all their years together had Susan seen such a look on his face. His jaw was set, and in his eyes burned a mutinous fire. It had flamed up once before, back when he was becoming his father's son, when they were all out in full force beating down that irrational self of his, the one that Hortense had recognized and greeted on the steps of a church all those years ago.

She pressed a switch and lowered his window.

"What's wrong?" She said it casually, but her stomach felt like she had just plummeted down a steep amusement park ride.

Susan watched through the window as he straightened and turned away and slowly walked back down the road toward the house. She called after him, and when he did not respond she stamped on the accelerator and the Rover sped away, spitting gravel in its wake.

He did not return to the party. He wandered a little in the dark, finally slumped down on the fender of a truck and remained there with his head in his hands until night fell.

30

The sun dropped behind the hills and drenched the land in apricot light. The air cooled down and mothers urged their children out of the water, and they sat sulkily on the lawn, draped in towels, teeth chattering and lips the color of blueberries. Fireflies danced in the woods behind the house, and a group of children clutching jelly jars and a dip net ventured off to trap them.

Cicadas set up a high whir, filling out the orchestra of night music, and thunder rumbled to the south. Folks settled down on the lawn, some on aluminum folding chairs, others on blankets. They talked little, answering one another in short grunts or lazy laughter, and when Wayne got a hankering for argument, tried to stir up a debate about federal funding of the prairie reserve, Joy kindly told him to pipe down and eat his ice cream.

When John finally returned to the gathering, he noticed how the mood had changed. The talk had slowed and the night was spinning its magic. For a long time he hovered in the doorway to the kitchen, a bowl of melted ice cream in his hand. Sarah was sitting with Will on a quilt out on the lawn. Moments earlier, Billy had knelt down next to them and laid a hand on her shoulder, but then he disappeared down toward the river. Will was fussing, needing sleep, and Sarah was trying to bed him down there on the quilt with his bottle and a stuffed giraffe he had taken a liking to. From a distance John watched as Billy's old hunting dog, a sag-bellied bitch who had borne him four litters, singled them out of the crowd and dropped down next to Sarah. Will shot up from his reclining position and began pounding her skull with his bottle, an abuse she bore in wincing silence until Sarah snatched away the bottle. Then Will set to whining, which the dog, despite her seasoned patience, could not tolerate. When she stood up and slunk away in the direction of her lair underneath the house, Will darted off after her, quick as a beetle. Sarah flung herself onto the ground and caught him by a leg just before he crawled out of reach.

She was sprawled facedown on the grass when John stepped forward from the shadows of the house and bent down to scoop up Will, sweeping him into the air, and Will gasped with surprise and delight.

"How about a walk before I take off?" he asked quietly.

"I thought you'd gone," she said, her eyes wide with surprise.

"I came back."

"I see."

"Lost my ride, though."

She stood, brushed the dirt off her shorts. "I can drive you home." She slipped on her sandals. "I can take you anytime."

"After our walk."

"How about if we take Will into the woods? To see the fireflies."

"Then, to the woods," he said, lifting Will onto his shoulders.

For an instant Will strained toward Sarah, stretched out his arms to her with a little bleat, but then he felt his daddy's strong hands on his back, reassuring him. He gripped John's head, curled his hands around his chin, and together they moved down the sloping lawn, Will bouncing along on his father's shoulders.

At the edge of the woods John lowered Will into his arm and took Sarah by the hand. Moonlight filtered through the swiftly scudding clouds, lighting the path dimly.

The children had long since tired of chasing fireflies and had fled indoors to lounge wet-haired before the TV. Now the only sounds were the gentle humming of cicadas.

"Better stop here," warned John after they had gone a certain distance. "Too dangerous in the dark. Unless you want to go back for a flashlight."

"Oh no," she whispered. "That would ruin it all."

They were in a clearing, a savannah in the midst of the burr oaks. All around them danced fireflies, tiny pulses of golden light darting through the dense, warm night air. John reached out and caught one, snatched it out of the air like a wizard, and then held up his clenched fist before Will's eyes.

"What's in here?" he whispered. Will reached for his hand, attempting to pry it open.

John relaxed his fist and Will won the game. The boy peered into the cradle of his father's hand and there, resting on his palm, lay a dot of golden light. The little boy's eyes widened, and his long, dark lashes blinked back wonder. The firefly crawled across John's palm; then, sensing freedom, it flew off into the night. Will watched in silence, and then he dropped his weary head on John's shoulder, sighed deeply, and shut his eyes. He popped his thumb in his mouth and his other hand fanned the air, searching furtively for a handful of hair.

Sarah saw what he was doing, and she drew close and silently began to unbutton John's shirt. John started to speak, but she hushed him with a kiss, and then she took Will's hand and laid it on his father's chest. The little boy dug his fingers into the thicket of hair and then grew still.

"You stay with him a little longer," she whispered. "I'll wait for you in my truck."

Then she crept quietly back down the path.

At the edge of the clearing was a log, an old cottonwood weakened by wind and age. John sat down on it and listened to the breath of his child and watched the fireflies dance in the moonlight.

After a while he rose and slowly made his way back to the house.

Most of the guests had gone home, and he heard voices on the patio and saw the glow of cigarettes in the dark. He avoided them, kept to the side of the house and cut around to the front where a truck waited with its headlights on.

"You aren't going to be missed?" John asked as he slid into the front and settled the sleeping baby into the car seat next to Sarah.

She reached up to adjust the rearview mirror. "I said my goodbyes."

For several miles they drove in silence. They rolled through Elmdale, and a short ways out of town at the top of a swell, Sarah slowed the truck and turned off the road, passing through a gated entrance. It was a moment before John realized they had entered a cemetery.

"I'd like to show you something," she said.

They left Will sleeping in the truck, and John followed her across the grassy knoll, between marked graves. Stars shone brightly in the windswept sky, and the moon had risen higher and shrunk to a cold white orb. The place seemed not at all morbid but beautiful in the pale moonlight.

Sarah took his hand and led him to a grave on a gentle rise. She stood at the foot, staring down at the small marble marker. Cut tulips had been placed in an urn beside the marker, but they had long ago wilted and the wind had scattered their petals over the grave.

"My daughter's buried here."

By the moonlight John could only just make out the inscription on the marker:

REBECCA ANTONIA KINGSLEY

Sarah knelt down and began to clear away the dried petals.

"Anthony didn't want children," she said quietly. "He was adamant about it. He was furious at me. When I was three months pregnant he went away. Into the outback. He didn't really have to, but he said he did. I couldn't go . . . I was too sick. And then I didn't hear from him for so long. Finally, I came back here. There really wasn't anything else I could do."

She paused, brushed the dirt from her hands. When she continued, her voice was calm, restrained. "It was a very difficult pregnancy at the beginning. Then there was a time when everything seemed fine." She paused for a long time, kneeling with her hands pressed against her thighs, collecting her thoughts. "But then . . ." She shook her head sadly, a shade of recrimination in her voice. "I keep thinking I should have known, if I'd known they could have done something, but they didn't discover anything was wrong until that last visit." She paused then, and John knelt beside her.

"She had died. She was full term, but she was dead. There, inside me. I remember the doctor going out and coming back in with these young med students. They all just marched in and looked at the screen — the ultrasound. I was looking at it, too, and I was watching their faces. I couldn't read the screen, I didn't know what to look for, but I could read their faces."

She sat back on the grass and pulled her knees up to her chest and continued in a clear voice. "He went on, telling me what they'd have to do, but I didn't hear anything after that. The nurse had to tell me again, later, after the men had gone. She sat with me and held my hand, and she was crying, too. Anthony wasn't there, and there was nobody to grieve with me, except this nurse, and finally I just reached out and she put her arms around me and held me, like mothers do. They'd have to induce labor, she said, to expel the fetus. I'd have to go through all of that."

She sat back and wiped a silent tear from her cheek. "It was a nightmare." At that moment John pulled her close to him, and she laid her head on his shoulder.

"They didn't want me to see her. They just sort of whisked her away. I was trying so hard to get a glimpse of her. I remember turning my head, stretching my neck so I could see her go out the door. I just wish I'd had something to remember her by. Anything. If I'd heard her cry, or seen her fingers or hands or feet, or her little face. She had a pretty little face, the nurse said. And a pretty little rosebud mouth. I guess that's why it's been so hard to let go, because I never really had anything to let go of."

Sarah took a deep breath, and then went on.

"I began to hemorrhage. I remember the doctor sitting on his stool with his hand inside me, trying to keep my insides clamped down while they waited for an anesthesiologist. Then they put me to sleep. When I woke up the doctor explained what had happened. If I were to get pregnant again, he said I'd be high-risk. He said he was being honest with me, that I probably wouldn't ever be able to have children."

She tilted her head and gazed up at the night sky.

"I wrote Anthony. I asked him to come back. Just once. To see her grave. He wrote back that he was very busy. He said he'd try to find some time. But he never did. He never came back.

"I had resigned myself to so much. Until you came along, and Will. You gave me hope." She turned her face toward him and smiled sadly. "Not hope that I would ever be able to have you. Or Will. That's not what I mean. But I knew then my heart hadn't died."

31

She fussed with his clothes that morning, put him into something stiff and new, and put shoes on him and took them off again. She could read his eyes, saw that intelligence that no one believed he had, and she knew he was confused and a little scared. He didn't want to be put down that morning, and he fussed over his breakfast. Finally she just gave him a bottle and sat in the porch swing rocking him, singing him silly songs and lullabies, waiting for them to come and take him away.

She did not know if Susan would come or if John would come alone. She tried to be generous, tried with all her heart to wish the other woman well, but when she saw them pull in the driveway, saw Susan's drawn face turn toward her then glance away sharply, she felt all the goodness drain away.

But Susan remained in the car, and John strode up the front steps and did not look her in the eye.

"Can you come in?" Sarah asked as she

rose from the swing. "Grandma's made a peach cobbler."

John stood awkwardly with his hands on his hips, his eyes on Will. "I think it would be easier for everyone if we just took him and went."

"I know. That's what I told Grandma. But she insisted." She gestured behind her. "His things are all there. Just inside the door."

She had packed up all his clothes and toys in brown grocery bags, and she waited on the steps while John carried them out to the Range Rover. When he came back for his son, he paused at the foot of the stairs, wanting to say something, but then she realized Will's eyes were on him and Will was smiling, and his little brown arms were straining for him. Sarah smiled and leaned toward John and let Will climb into his father's arms.

"There," she whispered. "I knew it would be okay."

Sarah turned and went inside and closed the door. She did not wait to see them drive away.

She worked a long day that day. She flew around the cafe, whisking out plates of the Mexican special and refilling glasses of iced tea, and if there was a smile on her face, there was no joy in her heart. As she bent down to serve Lew his chicken-fried steak and gently remind him he had ordered the green beans, not the corn, and he asked where her baby was, she felt her face fall, and she turned away and set down the pitcher. Then she strode through the kitchen and out the back door into the backyard and hid behind the old throw-away fridge Joy had dumped there. She leaned back against it and put her face in her hands and cried. She slumped to the ground and huddled there with her head on her knees and the hot sun beating down on her hair. She opened her eyes and her gaze swept across the backyard, the wooden produce crates stacked next to the trash can, Joy's stunted peach tree, and the sagging clothes-line. For a long time she sat with her face turned up to the blistering sun, with the deafening roar of cicadas in her ears, until Joy came out and called her name. Sarah rose and came into the open, shielding her eyes from the sun, and said, "I'm sorry, Joy. I wasn't feeling well. Heat just got to me. But I'm fine now."

She swept around Joy and into the kitchen, leaned down to the sink and dashed some cool water on her face, picked up the dishes that had backed up on the service counter, and strode tall into the dining room.

That night Billy found her out in Warlord's stall saddling him up to ride. It had rained earlier in the evening and the ground cover was wet and slick. He sat out on the front porch for hours in the dark waiting for her to come back, praying she wouldn't take a fall and be lying out there in the hills with her head split open. At one in the morning he finally went up to bed. When he shuffled downstairs the next morning he found her asleep on the sofa wrapped in an old horse blanket, her red hair tangled and matted and flecked with bits of dried grass.

She clung to him after that night, seemed to need his presence if not his love, cooked his dinners for him, spent her evenings with him in front of the television or playing rummy, or working Warlord in the cooler hours of twilight. But she never came to his bed, hadn't shared his bed since that morning back in early March. She slept in his daughter Angie's room some nights; some nights she slept on the sofa, some nights he didn't know where she was. She seemed to go a little wild those weeks, wouldn't go back home, told him something about a mural she'd painted on her ceiling that she couldn't bear to live with. Even called in sick a few days and worried Joy so much that Joy came out to Billy's place, dropped by one evening after she'd closed up the cafe to check on Sarah. But Sarah just got annoyed by all the fuss, said she only wanted a break from everyone.

Her grandpa kept tabs on her, called Billy from time to time just to see how she was doing, but if Sarah was around she'd get upset, said she didn't like to hear them gossiping about her like two old crones. A few times Jack spied her truck parked right down the street in Bazaar and thought maybe she was visiting Blanche, but Blanche hadn't seen her. It was Jimmy Baird who recognized her coming out of the old Methodist Church around the corner, and the next time her truck appeared Jack hobbled down to the church, slipped up around the back and peered in one of the windows. There she was, alone, kneeling at the end of the second row. He waited awhile, thought perhaps he might catch her coming out, but he waited for nearly twenty minutes and all that time she didn't move so much as a hair. He went back home then.

32

Hardly a year goes by when the Cottonwood River doesn't overflow its banks at one point or another along its serpentine route through the Flint Hills. In the dry season it's a sluggish old river, and Jack Bryden would fish the South Fork on a late summer day and drift no more than a quarter mile downstream before twilight. But when the rains come, the Cottonwood swells with the runoff from hundreds of square miles of uplands. Once the high plateaus drink their fill and the earth is saturated with early summer rain, the waters trickle down those gentle green shoulders in rivulets and streams and wind their way into the gullies and creeks, and then the Cottonwood goes on the rise.

In a bad year, with heavy rains, the tributaries slough their water downstream only to meet with an already swollen waterway; then, mile after mile of river begins to back up. With nowhere to go, the Cottonwood gathers itself up in great roiling currents; it climbs higher and higher, clawing away at the banks, ripping the earth from beneath the trees and tearing off ledges until it has broken free of its man-mapped boundaries and reclaimed the land.

Then it begins to move over the land like the living thing it is; it creeps up the fields, between the rows of corn and maize, and farm wives barely sleeping at night listen for the water rising. They look out their windows and hear it coming up the fields toward them in the dark, and they open the door to the basement stairs and see the black water glistening on the bottom step. The next time they get out of bed to check, it's risen three more steps and so they stay awake then, sit in the kitchen by the light of an oil lamp and listen to the radio and wonder how high it'll rise this time. Come morning it has swept away the chicken coop and the doghouse, and the farmer's wife watches with her waders on, the water now eight inches up the ground-floor wall, while an eddy roils past the barn and carries off her old stove, and she wonders whose land she'll find it on once the waters recede.

That summer they recorded the longest rainy spell in white man's history of Chase County. Nearly all of Kansas was affected, and the panhandle of Oklahoma, but Chase

County had the worst of it. The intensity varied from hour to hour, but the rain never stopped for long. At times it lightened to a drizzle, but then turbulent clouds would harden into a mask of gray and the sky would empty itself with such torrential force that Donnie Henryson, who on the second day started moving equipment to higher ground, commented later to his wife he feared he might drown if he so much as dared to look up. The skies are vast in Kansas, and there were times when they could see sunlight flooding Marion County to the west, or stars in the eastern night sky over Lyon County. Overnight the river rose from eight feet to seventeen feet, and since seven o'clock that morning the sirens in Cottonwood Falls had been wailing. Folks had been up since before dawn erecting a wall of sandbags down at the end of Broadway where the Cottonwood winds by the town.

John was taking books from his shelves and packing them into boxes when Billy Moon called. John could hardly hear him over the deafening roar of the rain on the roof.

"John?"

"Yeah?"

"This is Billy Moon."

A drawn-out pause, the sound of rain cutting in and out.

"Hello?"

"Can you hear me?"

"Barely."

"I'm on my cell phone in the barn. Phone line's out. I need to ask a favor. When you leaving?"

"Tomorrow."

"Oh. Well, I imagine you're pretty busy."

John shot a swift glance around the room, at the jumbled piles of books and boxes strewn over the floor, at Will toddling toward him gripping a wad of papers in his fist.

"Yeah," he said with a twist of humor as he leaned down and swept the child into his arm. "I've pretty much got my hands full right now."

"I won't keep you then. I was just calling around to see if we could round up some extra help over here at my place."

Another strung-out pause before John replied tersely, "I wish I could help."

"Hey, no problem. I wasn't even sure you were still in town. Sarah said she thought you'd already left."

Another silence, this one taut with tension, punctuated by the sound of pelting rain.

Billy asked, "You think you'll get some flood damage?"

"Not here. We're up too high."

"Sorry, didn't catch all that."

"No, I think we'll be okay. How are you doing?"

"Well, tell you the truth, I'm afraid that river's gonna make it to my back door before we get finished. Trouble is, everybody else's got the same problem."

"Sorry I can't help."

Billy said something else, but the line was cutting in and out and John couldn't make any sense out of it and so he hung up.

John had seen them only once over the past two weeks; he had been coming out of the convenience store up in Strong City and found Billy gassing up his truck at the pump. Billy was wearing a cowboy hat, sunglasses, and faded jeans, resting a boot on the bumper while he pumped the gas, and looking very much like a cliché, John thought. They exchanged a tense but cordial greeting, and as John passed by he caught a glimpse of Sarah in the truck. The look that came over her face, the way her expression suddenly froze at the sight of him, all of it made his stomach turn over and he nodded a greeting at her and hurried on to his Rover and sped off, trailing a wake of gravel.

Since seven o'clock that morning, Susan had been scrambling around behind the movers, dashing from kitchen to parlor to bedroom to make sure nothing was forgotten. At long last, Clarice had decided to put the house up for sale. She had come back from Dallas the week before, having gained a little weight and looking years younger. She had quietly confided in Joy that she had not had a drink since she'd left Cottonwood Falls, and she planned to return to Dallas and settle down there. Susan was to take what she wanted out of the old prairie mansion; Clarice wanted only to purge herself of the place and start anew.

The two of them had spent the previous week going through the house, and with the exception of a few antiques Susan was shipping back to their home in San Francisco, and some old clothing and linens they had donated to the Salvation Army, the rest was to be left behind to go into an estate sale.

Obsessed as she was with detail and organization, Susan compulsively sorted and categorized and labeled every item in the mansion. Nothing was too small or insignificant to escape her attention. These tasks energized her the way nothing had done since her accident. She rose early, fairly popped out of bed chatting before her feet hit the floor about all that needed to be accomplished that day. She tackled room after room, closet and drawer, surrounded by packing boxes and lists and labels, by yellow and pink Hi-Liters and all the paraphernalia she deemed necessary to establish order. Even though Clarice was home, John had kept his word and taken on nearly all responsibility for child care, and tranquillity was momentarily restored to their lives.

The movers had arrived early that morning. The truck was backed up to the porte-cochère to provide shelter from the rain, but this necessitated moving everything through the narrow kitchen pantry. When John came into the kitchen with Will riding on his hip he found Susan watching with an eagle eye as they maneuvered an antique buffet out the back door.

He asked her, "Do we have any rain boots?"

"Rain boots?"

"Yeah."

"I don't think so. Why?"

"How about fishing boots? Does your mom have any old waders or anything like that down in the basement?"

"We gave all that stuff away. Why?"

He shook his head. "Just wondered."

"You're not thinking about going out . . ."

He seemed to be hesitating, his eyes cast down.

"No. No, I'm not going anywhere," he said and turned to leave the room.

"Who called?"

"Billy Moon," he answered over his shoulder.

She called after him, "What did he want?" but he was out of earshot and all she heard were his footfalls as he jogged up the stairs with Will.

Susan stared after him, the movers momentarily forgotten. He had been distant and taciturn since the night she had driven off and left him at Billy Moon's place. He had made no excuses, and she had asked for none. They had always forged through difficult times like that. Brushed off those troubling incidents, neither of them wishing to confront the other. They had just simply moved on with their lives, and this had always worked for them, until now. Ever since that evening things had been different, and Susan could feel it. In her own mind she felt an urgent need for familiarity, to have things the way they had been before, insulated by their own small coterie of friends in San Francisco and John's colleagues at Berkeley. She sensed that Will was somehow the key to holding them together until they came through this tempest. She had done her best to act the part of the loving mother, although most of the time she resented the child with all her heart.

John no longer had the slightest doubt about Will, knew his instincts had been true from the start, knew he had done the right thing to make him his son. If he had failed Hortense once, all those years ago, he redeemed himself now.

And then, of course, he could never smile at Will without seeing Sarah, and every time he held the child in his arms there was a connection to her that went beyond the tangible, and he felt he was loving her, and she him.

Susan had followed the movers back upstairs to supervise the dismantling of Jacob Blackshere's old four-poster bed, and when she came back downstairs she found John rifling through some boxes stacked near the front door. He straightened, pulled an old baseball cap out of the pile, and fitted it on his head.

"John!" she scolded. "What are you doing?"

"I was looking for a raincoat." He bent over to dump the pile of clothing back into the box and she noticed then that Will was dressed in the little slicker they had bought for him back in San Francisco. It was still too large for him, but he tottered there next to his father, gripping John's pant leg to steady himself, his dark little face peering out with bright anticipation from underneath the yellow hood.

"Where are you going?"

"I thought I'd take a ride into town. Check up on the flood situation."

"You're taking Will?"

"You don't want me to leave him, do you?"

"No . . . I mean, I can't keep an eye on him and keep up with the movers."

"No problem. I'll take him." He bent down to pick up the child, then opened the door and stepped out onto the front porch. A gust of cool wind blew a fine spray of rain over them, and Will recoiled and buried his face in his father's shoulder.

Susan followed them outside.

"You'll get drenched like that."

He seemed not to hear her, was following the clouds with his eyes.

"You won't be gone long, will you?"

"I don't know. I may drive over to Billy Moon's place. Give him a hand sandbagging."

The look on his face stalled her rising frustration. She said nothing to him about the movers or his books or his office.

"You'll call me if you do."

"Of course."

He turned and, drawing the yellow hood over the little boy's face, darted down the front steps to his car.

There was a sense of urgency gripping the town as John drove down Broadway. Storefronts had already been sandbagged, and merchants were scrambling to move their goods out of the reach of the oncoming waters. There was a pickup truck backed up to the doorway of Cleo's Antiques, and two men in rain ponchos were hoisting a heavy oak dresser into the back.

Parked at the curb in front of the Senior Center were a half dozen cars and pickups with hastily loaded belongings — dry goods and cookware stuffed into bags and crammed into backseats, clothing and tennis shoes plastered up against rear windows — all signs of families fleeing disaster. The center had been transformed into a community flood watch, gathering information from throughout the county — what towns were being evacuated and where the evacuees would be sheltered, what roads were impassable — giving advice and counsel and serving coffee and doughnuts around the clock.

A hand-drawn graph was tacked to the door charting the flood level, and a tall, gangly farmer clutching a cup of coffee in one hand and a tattered straw hat in the other had his nose up against the chart. Ray turned, settled his hat on his head, and shuffled down the sidewalk. John recognized him then, had seen him at the Cassoday Cafe, and he stopped and rolled down his window, shouted a greeting through the rain and offered him a lift. Ray said he would be grateful if John would take him down to the bottom of Broadway, down to the old bridge to check the flood level.

"Hell, I ain't never seen it like this," Ray said as he settled into the front seat. He laid his hat on his knees and smoothed back his sparse white hair with a huge liver-spotted hand. "This is gonna be worse than the flood of 'fifty-one, I can tell you that for sure."

He had taken on the job of monitoring the flood level every few hours, he explained, and when John asked where he wanted to go, Ray pointed straight down Broadway. "To the old bridge. 'Course you can't see it no more. Went under two days ago."

"You think it's going to rise much more?"

"No way of knowin'. That's why everybody's takin' precautions." He raised the cup to his lips and took a gulp of coffee. "I remember back in 'fifty-one my daddy had a pool table in the basement and he wasn't 'bout to let that flood ruin it. He had us all down there takin' that thing apart. Spent darn near all night unscrewin' those bolts and draggin' the big heavy oak legs upstairs to the attic. Then him and my mom and my brothers, we carried that slate top upstairs and laid it across my brother's and my bed, and my brother and me, we slept on the floor for a week until the waters went down and Daddy moved it back down to the basement."

Ray took a breath and then eyed his coffee. He was old and getting a little slack of memory, and he'd told his stories so many times that nobody paid much heed to him anymore. So he was pleased to have a fresh captive ear, not at all in a rush to go the three blocks to the end of the road.

Only then did he seem to notice Will in the backseat, and he craned his leathery brown neck around to glance at the child and commented on how Sarah'd seemed a little down since she didn't have that baby to fuss over anymore.

John answered that they'd been lucky to find her, said she'd done miracles with the boy. There was a silence while John rolled cautiously through an intersection, then he said, "You've known her for a long time, haven't you?"

Ray was squinting through the rain, eyes focused on the road ahead. He chuckled to himself, a caustic, dry sound.

"Hell yes. I can tell you stories 'bout Sarah'd make your hair stand on end. Like when her dog bit her. Tore open the side of her leg. Know what that kid did? She went and heated a poker in the fireplace and cauterized the wound herself. Didn't want to have to go to the hospital." Ray shook his head in wonder and turned his face to John. "Well, when Jack found out what she'd done, you know what he did? Think he'd scold the kid? Not a chance. He took care of the burn best he could and sent her up to her room, and then he made some cockeyed excuse to Ruth so Sarah wouldn't have to come downstairs to dinner. Then he called me, and the two of us took that husky up into the hills behind the railroad tracks and we put a bullet between his eyes. That dog'd been a birthday present to Sarah, and Jack'd spent a chunk on him and he was a beauty. Beautiful dog. But Jack couldn't have that dog around after what it did to Sarah. Never could tolerate anybody hurtin' Sarah." He swilled down the last bit of coffee. Then he crushed the paper cup in his big hand. "Jack's like an old mother hen with that girl. Sometimes I think that's why Sarah don't move on with her life."

"What about Billy Moon?" John asked.

Ray shrugged. "I don't know. Billy's a good man. Be better for her than that English fella. That jerk broke her heart and darn near killed her. But she was crazy about him. It showed all over. She just sort of came alive. Had a different face on her. I ain't never seen her look like that since." He shot a glance back at Will again. "Except maybe since you folks came to town."

They had come to a stop where the road dead-ended at the old bridge. Before them, stretching along the bank of the Cotton-wood River from the bridge on past the Mill Stream Resort, lay a three-foot-high wall of sandbags. John leaned forward on the steering wheel and wiped the fog from the glass.

"Jeez," whistled Ray.

The once benign river had turned ugly. The waters were swiftest along the old main channel, racing downstream in great roiling currents, carrying with them branches and debris. The dam and old bridge had disappeared and the river had leveled out and started moving across the valley. Bates Grove Park north of the river was completely submerged. Now, only parallel rows of sycamores marked the entrance to the park from the highway, and picnic tables bobbed like rafts in the eddies.

"There's no way that river's gonna go down, even if it quits rainin'. Those creeks still got a lot of runoff to dump on us. I seen water move in on Saffordville when it hasn't even rained out there."

Ray pulled out a pair of binoculars from underneath his raincoat and leveled them on a tree at the edge of the river.

"Lord Almighty," he murmured, and then he took the strap off his neck and passed the binoculars to John. "Take a look at that. See that gauge there stickin' outta the water?"

He pointed to a wooden post notched and marked with hand-painted numbers.

"Yeah."

"That's the official river gauge. What d'ya read?"

"Looks like just a shade under twenty-one."

"Yeah." Ray took back the binoculars and buried them under his raincoat. "In 'fifty-one the river topped out at twenty-one feet one inch. And we're almost there. Hell, that scale don't go above twenty-two feet."

On the way back, John told him Billy Moon had called, said he was thinking about heading over to his place to give him a hand sandbagging, and Ray said that would be a real neighborly thing to do.

When John drove away he saw Ray with his nose screwed up inches from the flood chart tacked to the door of the Senior Center, clutching a pen and carefully noting down his findings.

33

It had been Sarah's idea to give John a call. She had been in the kitchen making a fresh pot of coffee while Billy was on the telephone with him, and she listened through the doorway. She could tell from Billy's end of the conversation that he wouldn't be coming. She looked up and forced a smile when Billy came in, held out a mug of coffee to him and urged him to sit for a few minutes. Jer Meeker had been over earlier in the day, and they'd moved the tack and feed up to the loft. Jer had loaded the horses into his trailer and taken them up to high pasture, but the river was rising fast and they were shorthanded. Anybody who had land sitting high and dry was over helping a neighbor, but most of the population resided down in the valley cut out by the South Fork of the Cottonwood, and they were all busy shoring up their own property.

"He can't come," Billy said as he took the mug of coffee from her and lowered himself into a chair.

"Well, it was worth a try." She glanced out the window, trying to keep her voice casual, disinterested. "When did he say they were leaving?"

"Tomorrow."

Billy peered at her over the rim of his mug. He had never questioned Sarah about it, but he knew she had feelings for the man, had known for sure ever since the night of the barbecue, knew something had gone on between them, didn't really want to know how much and when and where.

She turned back around to him then, smiled and said not to worry, they'd get the job done. Deep down Billy was relieved John Wilde wouldn't be coming, thought perhaps he'd rather lose a few things to the flood than witness the two of them together again, watch the way they tried to avoid each other's eyes, then stole glances when they thought he wasn't looking.

They were still in the kitchen when they heard the car drive in, and Sarah's heart leaped at the sound of tires on the wet gravel, but it was Billy's youngest daughter, Angie, who had driven down from Manhattan, although Billy had cautioned her to stay where she was because the roads were too dangerous. Billy's neighbor dropped by right after that, said he could spare an hour or two, and so the men carted the sandbags down the drive and the women set about unloading concrete blocks and lugging them into the kitchen to raise the appliances. Sarah tried to give Angie a hand emptying the china cabinet, but Angie was quarrelsome and seemed to resent Sarah's presence, took offense at Sarah's every move, so Sarah went back outside to help the men.

She had the hood of her vinyl poncho over her head and the rain was beating in her ears so she didn't hear the car, didn't even know he was there until she looked up and saw Billy talking to John on the front porch, and John holding Will in his arms. Little Will was like a church steeple in a thunderstorm, a safe channel for that electrifying love of theirs. When Sarah saw them she came sloshing up the hill, her jeans splattered with mud and the green vinyl poncho flapping at her sides so it looked like she might take wing and fly. She came up the steps toward them, her face exploding with joy, and without lifting her eyes to John she threw off her hood and held out her arms to take the child from him. Will recognized her instantly, stretched out his hands to her, and John moved closer and shifted the child into her arms. They spoke in low voices, a complicity of which neither of them seemed to be aware hanging over every word.

"I'm sorry I had to bring him."

"I'm so glad you did." She nuzzled the baby's neck, avoiding John's eyes.

"I didn't know if there would be anyone to watch him."

"I'll take him inside. There's a lot to do in the house."

"It won't be a problem?"

"We'll manage," she said, and she glanced up at him and smiled.

John slogged up and down the muddy drive that afternoon bent double under the weight of sandbags. He paused from time to time and looked out over the low sloping land, and marveled at what the river had done to this seemingly immutable landscape. Plowed fields had slipped out of sight, fence posts and barbed wire vanished. The river had broken the south bank first, filling in the lower valley. Now it was rising quickly up the steep north shore, and men like Billy who had never had the river in their homes were waging a futile battle, had not yet learned to give the river what it wanted, to wait and see what it left behind when it was gone.

By mid-afternoon the rain had finally ceased and the sun was pressing hard through thinning clouds, but no one seemed to notice. They were all working at a frenzy. The women had cleaned out the basement, hauled up Christmas decorations and boxes full of rusted gardening tools and sleeping bags. More than once Angie, deluged by memories of her mother, had broken down in tears and Sarah had left her alone with Billy, had gone up to the kitchen to clean out the lower cabinets, bag and box everything and cart it upstairs to the bedrooms. She had penned Will into the corner with a few boxes and put Billy's dog in there with him to entertain him and keep him quiet. The old dog seemed to sense she was a necessary sacrifice in time of crisis, and when Will yanked her ears and tugged on her fur and force-fed his cookies to her, she would only wince and turn her sad brown eyes up to Sarah in a silent plea.

It was a hectic afternoon, and emotions and tempers ran high. The men came inside and raised the kitchen appliances and the furniture up onto the concrete blocks, and when they ran out of blocks they used tall juice cans; when they ran out of those they stacked the peaches and tomatoes Maude had preserved in glass jars and stored down in the basement, which upset Angie again. Billy was afraid they hadn't raised things high enough, and Angie was worried about her mother's piano, so the three men hauled Maude's piano upstairs.

By dusk Billy felt they'd done as much as they could do. The afternoon had been dry, but at sunset the wind came up and the air turned cold, threatening more rain.

John was preparing to leave, had already settled sleepy Will in the back of his car when he saw Sarah come out onto the front porch and pause at the railing, studying the sky. She was exhausted, her face drawn from lack of sleep and hunger, but she smiled at him as he approached. They exchanged a few banalities about the weather, and she said something that made him laugh, about how the countians really thrived on these disasters, needed their annual floods and fires and tornadoes to give them a sense of self-importance.

He held her look for a long moment after their laughter had faded.

"And your grandparents are all right?"

She nodded. "They're on high ground."

"That's good."

She smiled. "You'd better go before it gets dark."

"I will miss you, Sarah," he said.

He could not bear to tell her goodbye, just stood there in the dim light getting cold, the rain trickling through his matted hair and down his face.

"Go," she whispered finally.

34

The windshield wipers batted away at the light rain as he barreled down the county road, fishtailing in the loose gravel, eyes keen on seeing into the darkness along the tunnel of his headlights. The only living creature picked up in the beams was a wet and bedraggled dog loping alongside the road, but even he ignored the passing vehicle, just kept up his measured trot as John drove by.

John got a little confused once or twice, in the rain with such poor visibility, wasn't sure if he was still on the right road, and he breathed a deep sigh of relief when he finally met up with the state highway. It wasn't but a few miles down the blacktop when he spotted red flares in the distance, and a little farther down he came upon two highway patrol cars stationed broadside across the lanes. He had to wait while a pickup truck pulled a U-turn and headed back in the opposite direction, then a state trooper in a rain slicker advanced toward the car. Road up ahead was out, he said tersely as he leaned down and squinted through the window at the man and the baby in the back. Two miles of state highway submerged.

"Where you headin'?" he asked.

"Just down the road. Cottonwood Falls."

"Sorry. This area's pretty much cut off. Unless you want to head back through Florence. Fifty's still open that way. You can cut south to El Dorado and then take 177 back up to the Falls."

"How long would that take me?"

"Oh, I'd say a good two hours."

John frowned up at him. "Two hours?"

"Sir, I suggest you head back where you came from. Weather's pretty freaky right now. Got some serious fog coming in."

The trooper stepped back with an impatient wave of the hand to move John on his way.

John sat at the side of the road for a few minutes with the engine idling while he thought about what to do. He had called Susan from Billy's not long before he left. The movers had finished and the truck had gotten safely on its way. But she was uncomfortable, she said, all alone in the big empty place. He had expected her to be angry, but she had only sounded apprehensive, wanted him to hurry back.

He knew there were back roads through the hills, thought maybe Sarah could draw him a map. If there was a way to get home, keeping to high pasture and avoiding the floodplains, she would know it for sure.

He headed back down the highway and turned off onto the county road, and just past the cemetery he saw the approaching fog. It floated eerily across a field of maize, passed effortlessly through barbed wire and fence posts, crept up to him and wrapped itself around him, carrying him along in its silent grasp. He had to slow down to a crawl and feel his way back along the gravel road. From time to time, emerging abruptly into a pocket of black night, he would catch a glimpse of the land and sky. A thin sliver of cold moon hung distant and high in the heavens while fine wisps of cloud sprinted below, whipped along by the wind. The treeless hills were caught in a shifting bed of pale dappled light. Just as suddenly he would plunge back into thick fog, and land and sky would disappear.

At times it seemed as if he were not advancing at all, as if this forward motion were but illusion and it was the land that was in motion, and the land had returned to its watery origins, the flint-colored sea. Once he yawed too near the edge, careened off into a rain-swollen ditch. He sat with his heart thumping and his tires spinning in the mud and fear sounding alarm in his head, until finally he was able to coax the car forward, up the shoulder and back onto the road. He had lost all notion of time and distance, and he wondered if it was possible to get lost in such a place.

He knew he had taken a wrong turn somewhere, because the gravel road to Billy's place stair-stepped down range and township lines at right angles in a gridded, orderly fashion. But the road he was now wending along resembled the old Indian trails, had a natural serpentine flow to it that fit the contours of the land: at times it was no more than uneven ruts of flinty limestone.

He thought he must have come down off the plateau, was somewhere near the river. When he cranked down his window he could hear a swollen creek rushing by in the distance. He was hoping to find a section of road wide enough to allow him to turn around, but the mist hung over him like a shroud, and he could see no more than a foot beyond the hood of the car.

There was a sudden break in the fog, and he was briefly able to see ahead. The road had faded to a rutted cattle trail, gradually losing itself in a sea of swaying prairie grass. But there, just to the right of where he had stopped, stood an opening in a dense thicket of thorned honey locust. It was an entrance onto the land, with nothing more to discourage passersby than a rusted barbed-wire fence coiled around a pole near the road and a buckshot-riddled sign warning TRESPASSERS WILL BE PROSECUTED. John backed up, then swung around into the opening. A patch of fog drifted by, and when it cleared he saw in his headlights a truck parked far ahead in a clearing. He recognized the truck instantly. It was an unusual color, a faded apple-green — Sarah had bought it used years ago from a rancher who had been particularly fond of it, wanted to sell it to someone who had a liking for things that stay the same.

He turned off his engine and sat a moment with the truck in his headlights. In the back, Will began to stir. John reached back, tucked the blanket around him, then opened the car door and got out.

Sarah's truck was unlocked and he opened it, checked inside. There was nothing to suggest vandalism, only clutter, a bit of trash, an odd Coke can and coffee cup on the passenger seat, and maps refolded and stuffed into the pocket on the door.

There was even a sketchbook.

He stepped around to the front of the truck and tried to get his bearings, but he could see no farther than a few feet ahead. The fog crept around him in slow, sinuous swirls, and there was the dull roar of the creek somewhere off to the left, and a faint rushing sound, as of leaves high overhead, but he could see no trees.

Will had begun to cry; the sudden absence of motion had woken him. As John turned back toward the car, he stumbled and sent a rock clattering into the thicket. There was a sudden rustle of branches and a soughing of wings, and then the distant yipping of coyote. Suddenly, with dramatic abruptness, the fog rolled back and he found himself standing on a great yawning stage of bare limestone. All around, massive blocks quarried in years past rose in colossal mounds like ancient ruins. In the darkness with wisps of earth-bound clouds floating through it, the old quarry resembled an ancient Greek theater.

Sarah used to come here, not only to sketch but to connect herself in a visceral way to the land, to dream her way into it.

"Sarah?"

He did not recognize his own voice.

"Sarah?" he tried again, with more force.

It was absurd, she was not out here, she was safe with Billy.

Yet, ignoring Will's wail, drawn by curiosity, he moved a little deeper into the enclosure. The wind passed through again, a strong wind that rattled the leaves on the cottonwoods and set them chattering. Far in the distance where an arm of the ledge curved around, beyond a labyrinth of blocks stacked in giant columns, a white-haired figure stood erect, Christlike, at the top.

He advanced along the ledge toward the figure, and the mist seemed to follow him, twisting and turning through the narrow lanes. The figure seemed to move, and then it disappeared in the mist, and the fog crept up and closed around him. John halted, alarmed, his breath caught in his lungs. He reached out but his hand met with nothing but air, yet only seconds before there had been rock at his fingertips. He blindly groped around in the mist, stepped forward, hands still outstretched, took another step. Finally, his fingers found solid rock. He breathed relief and advanced another step. For a split second he felt the shock of empty air below his foot, and then he flew forward, propelled into the darkness.

35

John lay unconscious for a long time, and all the while the creek was rising. The waters found the shallow quarry easily, spilled freely over the ledge, cascading down the rock face to fill up the basin where he lay facedown on the stone floor. He looked quite unlike himself without that brittle energy that had always animated his face, and in this state he bore a chilling resemblance to the lifeless form that had lured him here — a sun-bleached coyote skull nailed to the exposed root of an upended cottonwood, an old tree weakened and toppled by the wind. From time to time the airborne root swayed and creaked and groaned, and the skull bobbed in the darkness.

But the wind was silent now, and the fog had lifted. A baby cried in the distance.

He grew conscious gradually, as he felt the water move up his face, felt it rising around his head, over his fingertips, climbing up his legs. He panicked and choked. Finally, he was able to lift himself on one shoulder, draw his leg up and brace himself with a hand, but his head began to spin and he collapsed into the water. He took a deep breath and rose again, crawling through the water on hands and knees. When he tried to stand, nausea broke over him and his head filled with awful pain. He sank to his knees in dry heaves, his stomach gripped with convulsions. For a moment all he could feel was his sickness; he waited until it passed, then cleaned his face with the muddy water.

He made it to his feet and staggered through the water, but whenever he tried to look up and get his bearings, he grew dizzy. He wasn't even sure which way he was heading, didn't know how far he had come. The floodwaters were spilling quickly into the quarry, dislodging branches and loose stone from the rock above and sweeping them over the ledge in a steady cascade. Stumbling through the swift current, he found a place where the limestone ridge had faulted and began to pull himself up the side of a rubble-strewn bluff, fighting against the force of the rushing waters. Time and again he would slip, and he would curse the river and then curse himself. At last he dragged himself to the top, only to find the current so powerful he could barely stand.

The road and the fields had disappeared underwater and the quarry had been transformed into a wide and treacherous crossflow of rapids and eddies. He slogged forward, through twisting, narrow lanes between columns of stone blocks, wishing with all his heart Will would cry that loud, racking cry of his so he could find his way back. He scanned the darkness for his car and tried in vain to orient himself. At last he caught a glimpse of a bulky shadow low in the water, and he stumbled forward, pressing against the force of the flow. He could see it was the car, gliding slowly with the current. The headlights still glowed, but only faintly, like two dim, watery moons. It struck him he must have been unconscious long enough for the headlights to drain the battery.

Plowing through the current, he reached the car, caught hold of the bumper, and pulled himself alongside the back. Will was only barely visible through the window. The child had managed to squirm out of his car seat and had slipped to the floor, snagging his yellow raincoat on the latch, and now it was wound around his body. The water was rising around him, and he huddled there, exhausted and terrified. John tried to open the door as the BMW bobbed along, but it would not budge. He shoved away from the car and plunged underwater, fishing blindly on the bottom of the quarry floor until his fingers found a loose stone. Stone in hand, he shot back to the surface and dragged his way around to the side of the car again. He slung his head back, shaking the water from his face, and when he peered inside again Will was no longer visible. In that brief moment the waters had risen over the edge of the seat and he had sunk beneath them.

John fell upon the car with a fury, pounding until the glass shattered. Bashing away the shards from the frame he plunged inside and grabbed his son's hand. At that moment the car was caught by an eddy, and with John hanging through the window it began a slow spin. It hit a block of stone and tilted, and water spilled through the window. John could feel the jagged glass cutting into his stomach as he worked frantically with both hands underwater to free his child. Finally, Will's raincoat gave way, and John lifted him out the window.

There was no time to do anything because the water was up to his thighs and he could barely hold himself upright. Unless he found a high place quickly, out of the reach of the flood, they would both surely be swept away. Holding Will over his head, he staggered through the water toward the columns of quarried blocks silhouetted against the sky.

The water was hip level now, and the current swept him along with an alarming force. He plowed forward, holding steady against the flux, struggling to keep his balance with the child still held aloft. The dizziness returned intermittently, and he knew he was losing blood and was afraid he might lose consciousness, but he made it finally to the base of a cluster of quarried blocks.

Stretching to the full length of his height, he lifted Will onto one of the tall columns, dragged himself up after him, and collapsed facedown on the stone block. Then he raised himself on his elbows, put his mouth to the child's face, and breathed what little breath he had left into him. He kept it up as long as he could, even when he grew faint. The child felt so different now, all the energy released, the muscles relaxed, not tense and fighting, and John wished with all his heart for even a whimper, just one small sign of life. He struggled to remain conscious, trying to revive the child, but then everything around him seemed to recede. The water sounded distant and he couldn't feel himself any longer, couldn't feel the pain in his stomach or the pounding of his skull. It seemed there was just this tiny child, so small, and still.

The wind chattered in the cottonwoods nearby, and the stars blinked overhead. The quarry filled and the river moved on, and John was not alert to a great energy moving toward him.

36

There were other deaths that night, and others gone missing, and the county was in turmoil, hadn't lost any lives in a flood since 'fifty-one. The pilot who found them just after dawn wasn't sure what he was seeing at first, the body curled around a bundle of some sort atop a strange formation of cut stone in the old abandoned quarry. He had to swing back around to take another look, and as he hovered just overhead with the chopper's blades whipping the floodwater into spray and laying the cottonwoods low, there was no movement, no sign of life, and he prayed he wasn't too late. They'd had reports out, and he was pretty sure he could identify the man, knew that bundle under his arm must be a baby.

Sarah had spent the night on the sofa downstairs, stretched out on her back in her jeans with Billy's oversized waders on her feet and his cell phone clutched to her stomach.

Susan had called the house around ten and spoken to Billy. She was worried sick about John, said he wasn't home yet and she hadn't heard from him. Then Sarah got on the phone to Joy, and Clay promised they'd begin a search at dawn.

Around midnight the muddy water crept into the house, covered the floor and brought with it a damp chill like the outdoors. Billy kept checking on her, urging her to come upstairs to bed, but Angie had reclaimed her room and the other bedroom was crammed so full there wasn't space for a rodent to bed down there. Sarah wasn't about to share Billy's bed and he knew it. He only annoyed Sarah and she grew impatient with him, told him to stop fussing over her. Angie heard them arguing and came and stood in her bathrobe at the top of the stairs glaring down at Sarah, then scuttled back to her room and slammed the door.

"Sarah?" Joy said.

"Yeah."

"God, it didn't even ring."

Sarah hitched herself up into a sitting position. "Yeah, so? Where is he?"

"He's safe, honey. They found him."

There was a long silence on the line while Sarah fought back a sudden rush of tears.

"Thank God," she muttered.

"He wasn't very far from you. Just down at Thut's."

"What was he doing there?"

"Don't know. Maybe got lost in the fog."

"Is he okay?"

There was a slight hesitation. "He's in a coma."

Sarah dropped her feet over the side of the sofa, and they splashed softly in the water. "In a coma?"

"I don't know all the details."

"Where's Will?"

In the silence that followed Sarah seemed to freeze. She was aware only of the sound of her heart pounding in her chest.

Joy softened her voice. "He didn't make it, honey."

"What do you mean? What happened?"

"He drowned."

"Will drowned?" Sarah asked in a small voice that made Joy's stomach twist in knots.

Joy took a deep breath. "All I know is they found the both of 'em stranded up on top of one of those columns in the quarry, and John was unconscious and almost dead." Joy couldn't finish. "Oh, baby, I'm so sorry. . . ."

Time slipped away from her, and Sarah

sat there with her feet in the water and pale morning light filtering through the drawn drapes, Billy's cell phone to her ear and her hand over her eyes. She sat there listening to the silence, conscious of her own breathing and Joy's patient presence on the other end of the line. She heard Joy light a cigarette, heard her cough a time or two. Joy didn't hang up on her, though, was ready to wait as long as it took, didn't try to rush her. Finally, Sarah's voice cracked across the line.

"I need to get out of here," she said.

"Where's your truck?"

There was no reply.

"Honey, where's your truck?"

The hand slid down the face, over the mouth, and her eyes stared blankly into the shadows of the house.

"I can't stay here," and her voice grated against the silence.

"Sarah, where'd you leave your truck?"

"Up at Thut's."

"The quarry?"

"It died on me a couple of days ago. I just left it. Didn't have time to mess with it."

"Well, it's a goner now. Clay said the quarry's flooded."

"Come get me."

"I can't get in there."

"I'll walk out. I can cut up across high pasture over to the highway. You can pick me up out on 50."

"Honey, practically the whole damn highway is washed out! All the way to Florence! This county's one big lake right now!"

Sarah stood and waded over to the large picture window and drew aside the drapes and looked out at the overcast sky.

"If I can get to Florence, will you come get me?"

"Sarah, you be careful."

"Just come get me," she answered, and she sloshed toward the kitchen with the telephone crimped to her shoulder while she zipped up her jeans. "Okay?"

"What are you gonna do?"

"Don't worry about me."

"Well, I do!"

"Do something for me, please. Call Clay and see if he can find out where they've taken him."

There was a heavy silence. "Which one?"

"Both of them."

Despite her tenacity and stubbornness, and her intimate knowledge of that place, Sarah could not best the river. She stood on a bluff that morning and surveyed a land strange and foreign to her. She had seen the hills transformed and molded by the seasons, painted in the muted browns of fall and the vivid greens of spring, blanketed in white snow and baking in the scorching light of an August day. But she had never seen them like this. The lowlands were now a continuous ribbon of water wending through the valley, and of human settlements there remained only the top story of a house or two or the roof of a barn. Out of this sea the low hills rose like islands, like something cut loose and set adrift.

It took her until nightfall to get back to Billy's house, and all she could do was pace, sloshing from room to room while she tried to reach Joy on the cell phone. Billy was concerned about the battery running low since they were without electricity now and he couldn't recharge it, and they got into another argument. Sarah left the house with a sleeping bag under her arm, waded to the barn, and climbed up to the loft and spent the night there.

It took nearly a week for the floodwater to leave the house, and all the while they were kept busy sweeping, had to keep the muddy water in constant motion so it wouldn't settle and dry to a hard sediment on the floor. During that time Sarah learned they had buried little Will up in Emporia, some cemetery nobody'd heard of. Joy thought it wasn't proper, thought they should have given Clarice a say-so in the matter, or at least buried him in Lawrence, where the Wildes lived. But Sarah said there wasn't any point in that, said none of them would ever visit the grave.

37

He felt Susan's hand gently squeezing his own and heard her reassuring him, telling him he was going to be all right. For a long time he lay there with voices swimming around him. He heard his mother and thought he might have heard his father, and there were sounds of doors opening and closing and brisk footsteps and sharp voices echoing down hallways.

"Don't try to talk, honey." It was Susan's voice, and he heard the rustling sheets and the scraping of a chair.

"Where's Will?" he whispered groggily.

He tried to turn his head toward her and felt a sudden dull pain.

"Stay still, John. You had a skull fracture," she said.

He opened his eyes, but the light was bright and painful and he closed them again. Sounds were jumbled and loud. They were whispering and he could only pick out certain words.

He tried again to open his eyes. They were all there, looking down at him with worried faces. Susan was sitting at his bedside, holding his hand.

"Honey, the baby didn't survive. But you did. It was a miracle. Your skull was fractured and you'd lost so much blood. . . ." Her voice cracked and his mother put a hand on her shoulder. Before he closed his eyes he saw his father step up to the bed. His father's face was white like a ghost's.

This is his dream: a treeless landscape of high prairie, but it is also a river. He feels himself enclosed as if in a vast room, and yet there is an incredible sense of space. He is floating downriver on his back, as though on a bed. Everywhere there are people coming and going, around him all the time, people he knows; he senses this about them, that they are familiar. Still, this sensation of moving along with the water, of floating. There is a boat on the river, a fishing boat. Hortense sits in it, upright, and she is sleeping. She has tried to fool him but he recognizes her by her white hair. She wants to make him think she is Blanche, but he knows better. He struggles to draw himself closer to her, but he cannot raise himself because of the weight on his stomach. All the while he is distracted by the presence of others around him. Then the water is gone and Hortense is gone, and there is just this vast room and he is standing among all these people. He looks down at his body and finds he is naked. The heaviness has disappeared, and he is stunned to find he is healed. He is overcome by a profound sadness, intensely felt.

They whisked him away, took him straight from the hospital to the airport and put him on a plane back to California. Armand Wilde had arranged for one of his graduate students to drive the Range Rover back to California for them, sparing them the long two-day-plus haul. The moving van had already arrived in San Francisco, but John knew there was more to their urgency. They closed ranks around him and secrecy informed their every move. He suspected they were rushing to remain one step ahead of him, making the decisions for him before he had time to reflect, giving him no opportunity to take up a position of opposition, to resist them. When John regained consciousness, Will had already been put in his grave, and from that moment on the child's name never crossed their lips. It seemed as if Susan and his parents were making every effort to erase an unfortunate episode in their lives, to weaken whatever power it still held over him.

They were busy that first week settling back into their home, moving in the few pieces of furniture Susan had kept from her mother's estate, unpacking John's books and all their clothing and linens and dishes. Still, Susan found time to meet with a head-hunter, and by the end of the week she had set up four interviews. There was a brightness to his wife during these days that she tried in vain to soften with a mask of sobriety, but John knew better, knew she had no burden of grief to bear.

She came home one Saturday with three business suits from Saks, poured John a glass of cold Chablis, sat down with him in their living room with a view of the ocean, and told him about two job offers, both high-level positions with investment firms.

He sat and listened, drank only a little of his wine, and when she tried to solicit his opinion he turned lusterless blue eyes on her and said, "I need to talk about him. We never talked about it. Not once."

The smile left her face, and she sat back and crossed her legs. John thought her shoes seemed new, too, but he could have been wrong.

Susan fingered the sweating wineglass. "It was just so painful . . ."

"Was it?"

She glanced up sharply. "Of course it was. I felt it deeply." She ran her hand along the smooth leather back of the sofa. "But not as deeply as you did. I'm aware of that."

"I need to talk about him."

With pinched lips he looked away, and she knew he must be fighting back tears.

"John . . . ," she whispered, and she reached for his hand.

He fell quiet, as though he were sifting through troubling thoughts, but he seemed to be getting control of himself and she felt relieved.

She patted his hand, then rose and picked up her glass. "I need to start dinner."

His eyes followed her as she crossed the room.

"What did you do with all his things?"

She turned and answered soothingly, "I gave them away."

"When? Where? I never saw a thing. Not one box."

"I took care of it all."

"You didn't save anything? Not a single toy? Nothing? Not the damnedest little thing to remember him by?"

She hesitated, eyes averted, then sat down

in the club chair opposite him. She set down her glass on the coffee table and leaned forward with a level gaze.

"I didn't do it callously, John. I asked. I asked your mother, and the chaplain . . . and my therapist . . ."

"Why didn't you ask me?"

"I wanted to spare you the pain." Her eyes fixed on his, and he tried to read sincerity in them, but he could not. "John, through all of this, we put you first. We had your very best interests at heart."

"And you're so damn sure you know what's best for me."

Susan sat back, crossed her arms at her waist, and turned a tight mouth toward the wide bay window where the hues of sunset spilled into the sky.

There was a tinge of bitterness when she spoke, and restrained anger. "You would have self-destructed long ago if it hadn't been for people who had your best interests in mind. And by that I mean your mother and father and me. People who love you most in the world."

He turned a stunned look on her.

She laughed sharply. "What? You think I don't know that about you?"

She leaned forward again, and a veiled anger shone dully in her eyes. "I did not wish for this to happen, even though you might think I did. And I don't take one god-damn minute of pleasure in that little boy's death. But I won't deny that I'm relieved, and I don't feel in the slightest bit guilty because of it. I intend to get on with my life and be happy, and I wish you'd do the same." She rose abruptly to her feet, snatched her glass, and strode out of the room.

That evening he took himself off to his study with his books and a bottle of scotch. When he'd had enough to drink he picked up the telephone and called. Jack Bryden answered.

"Jack?"

"Who wants to know?"

"John Wilde. Is Sarah there?"

"Nope."

John waited for an elaboration of some sort, thought it would be forthcoming if he gave the old man a minute, but there was only a heavy silence coming down the line.

"When would be the best time to call back?"

"She's not here."

"When will she be back?"

"I don't keep tabs on Sarah."

He could see the old man's face behind

the gruffness, see the downturned mouth and the eyes like shields.

"Yeah, okay, well, tell her I called, will you?"

There was no response, and John wanted to take the telephone and slam it into that awful wall of silence. Finally there was only a click on the other end, and then the dial tone.

After that, John never tried to call her again.

He threw himself back into his work that summer. He even took up handball with a professor new to the theoretical physics group, a high-strung, fast-talking young man with neither wife nor children and little interest in either subject. The two men would reserve a court for the entire evening and play one brutal match after another, pushing each other to the limits of endurance until they were worn down. Afterward John would drag himself to the campus cafeteria and eat a hot meal before he crawled back to the lab and collapsed onto the sofa. He would go home every few days to pick up some fresh clothing which he kept in his locker at the faculty club, and if Susan was home they would speak pleasantly, congenially, to each other, about their work, their day, but it was all anecdotal. There was never anything of substance, nothing heart-felt. It occurred to John one night as she slipped into bed beside him and turned off the light that things were very much as they used to be, and it seemed to John she was not discontent.

38

"Mrs. Sullivan," she'd say, *"leave no one near it. It is my nest and my cell and my little prayer-house, and maybe I would be like the birds and catch the smell of the stranger and then fly away from ye all."*

FRANK O'CONNOR
THE BRIDAL NIGHT

The line advanced and Joy kicked the suitcase forward a few feet.

"Damn, I wish you'd put this off."

"I can't. Can't change my ticket," Sarah said.

"You go sit. I'll hold your place in line."

"I'm fine."

"I bet you've got a fever."

"I'm just fine."

"You should've seen a doctor before you left."

"It's just the flu."

"It's probably some strange virus you got from the floodwater."

"It's just the plain old flu."

"There is no such thing as the plain old flu. Back in the Middle Ages entire populations of Europe were wiped out by the plain old flu. And you're probably *importing* some rare strain with you."

Sarah wrinkled up her face, gave Joy a suspicious look. She was sounding conspicuously unlike herself.

"Where'd you read that?"

Joy adopted a smug expression. "In that guidebook you bought. You left it in the kitchen the other day. I was reading it."

The line advanced another foot, and again Joy nudged the suitcase forward.

"Hell, you could've at least gotten a new suitcase."

"That one's fine."

"Won't hold up."

"It's fine."

"I want you to go to a doctor as soon as you get there."

"I'll be over it by then."

"Promise me."

"Yes, Mother."

They checked her bag, and then they sat at a coffee shop in the airport terminal and Sarah had a cappuccino while Joy picked apart a banana-nut muffin with her red-lacquered nails.

"Honey, really," she said, "I'm worried about you."

Sarah kept her eyes lowered, ripped open her sugar packet and sprinkled the sugar over the foamed milk.

Joy leaned forward across the table, peering up into Sarah's face. "You just get so closed up. The times you should be reachin' out to others and instead you just pinch that old shell of yours shut like a clam and God help any of us who've got their fingers in there."

Sarah dismissed this with a shake of the head. "You're trying to read all kinds of things into this. It's just . . . well, it's time for me to do it. It's something I've always wanted to do. I'm going to see things I've always dreamed of seeing." Her eyes swept past the faces at the counter, fixed on some distant point in space. "Always it's been books. Reproductions. Now I get to stand in front of the real works of art. The very names of these places are like magic to me. Lord, I've put it off long enough."

Joy held out a chunk of muffin.

"Sure you don't want anything to eat?"

Sarah shook her head. "I'm sure."

"Look, hon, it's not that you're doing this, that's not what worries me." Joy popped the bite of muffin into her mouth and washed it down with a swig of coffee. "You're still grieving. And for more than just that little boy, I think."

Sarah's eyes darted away, fixed on the back of a man counting out change for the cashier.

Joy dropped her voice, spoke gently, and her eyes were gentle, too. "You've never talked to me about him."

"There's nothing to talk about. Nothing happened."

Joy prodded. "I'm not gonna judge you. You know me better than that."

But Sarah's face was closed, and Joy knew that look well, so she shifted to the present, to the future.

"You will send me postcards?"

Sarah relaxed, broke into a weak smile. "I just wish you could come."

"I know. I'm sorry. Timing's just rotten. But you'll meet people. It's always easy to meet people when you travel alone."

"Yeah, right, like you've done so much traveling alone."

"That's what they say."

But then she noticed the tears in Sarah's eyes, and how she was struggling to blink them back, and she felt her own throat swell.

"Come on," Joy said, patting Sarah's hand. "Let's go take a look in that gift shop.

Find you a good magazine to read on the plane. Something fun."

There was a baggage handler strike when the plane arrived in Paris the next morning, and she waited at the baggage claim for well over an hour, sat on a metal bench next to a white-scarfed Muslim woman with two small children and waited. It was almost noon by the time she boarded an Air France bus to take her into the city, and she found a window seat and pressed her nose to the glass, full of expectation. But as they approached the outskirts, all she could see in every direction was urban sprawl, ugly pollution-streaked concrete blocks, and her heart sank.

The bus dropped her in a busy street at the foot of a cluster of high-rises on the outer rim of the city. From there she took a taxi to her hotel in the Latin Quarter. Under an overcast sky, Paris struck her as a place without a beyond, enclosed in monochromatic stone and dense gray light. But then the people seemed to compensate for this, and Sarah, who was used to vast, unpopulated space, found a certain beauty in the way their lives were organized, with the shops and markets and cinemas and churches just below their windows, along the wide boulevards and down the narrow streets.

There was nothing exceptional about the hotel, and her room was small, but it had its own bathroom and had been recently papered in a cheerful floral print. She sat on the edge of her bed with her open suitcase behind her and thought perhaps she might take a shower and then go for a walk through the streets, maybe over to the fountain where she had glimpsed a crowd of young people loitering beneath a statue of St. Michael slaying his dragon, perhaps try one of the sticky sweet cakes from the Tunisian bakery on the corner. But after her shower she crawled into bed and lay there shivering, curled tightly in a ball, smothered in a down comforter she had found in the armoire. She felt ill, and lonely and afraid. Still, homesick as she was, she could not bear the thought of returning to Bazaar, to a room with a view of treeless hills and vast skies, to the portrait of a child hovering over the shoulder of a poorly executed God.

Tucked back in a residential neighborhood of nineteenth-century town houses, the hospital had not been easy to find. But it was well known, she had been told, and many notable and wealthy Americans went

317

there to be treated by American doctors. Nevertheless, she had been wary, had conjured up an image of a shabby waiting room with peeling walls and broken chairs, but she found instead a thoroughly modern and comfortable clinic, and a doctor who greeted her with a southern accent.

He said little but examined her thoroughly, then sent her back to the waiting room while lab tests were run.

It was a long while before he reappeared in his white coat and flashed her a tired smile and gestured to the door of his office.

He sat down behind his desk and waited, hands crossed over his stomach, while she took a chair opposite him.

"Miss . . ." He hesitated, bent forward to check the file in front of him.

"Bryden," Sarah prompted.

"It is 'miss,' is it not?"

"Yes."

"Well, as I suspected, it's not the flu."

"It's not?"

"You're pregnant."

She sat motionless before him, as if he had spoken not to her but to some other woman sitting in that chair facing him at this moment. It took her a few seconds to find her voice.

"You must be mistaken."

"You didn't suspect . . ."

"That can't be."

"I'd say from the size of your uterus you're a good nine weeks."

"It must be something else . . ." Her voice trailed off.

"It's not a tumor, Miss Bryden. Your urine test is positive."

"That's impossible."

"I'm afraid not."

"But it's not possible."

She struggled to keep her voice from shaking as she told him about John's medical history, about his infertility and the subsequent adoption, although she omitted anything about Will's death.

After she finished, she listened in stunned silence while he clarified a few points, explained to her that the gentleman in question apparently was not completely infertile, that oligospermia was easy to misdiagnose, that chances of conception were so slim that lab tests fail to indicate any possibility whatsoever.

"But in this case" — he smiled expansively — "you beat the odds. I've seen it happen. Couples try for ten years, then all of a sudden the woman becomes pregnant. The chances are there, you know. Somewhere in the universe at some point in time, someone beats the odds. It does happen."

He could see she was in shock, the waves of confusion, of disbelief, passing across her face.

"So, all these aches and pains I feel . . ."

"Just another symptom of pregnancy. The first trimester is the most difficult."

"It doesn't mean I'm going to lose the baby?"

"Not at all."

A smile flickered on her face, and she grew calm.

She rose to her feet.

"Thank you," she said, fumbling with the zipper on her backpack, and he noticed her hands were shaking.

"You might want to rest a bit outside, Miss Bryden," he said kindly, rising from behind his desk. "Or maybe get something to eat or drink. There's a cafe across the street."

"Thank you," she said, and this sudden kindness overwhelmed her and she broke down in tears.

She wasn't quite sure where she was going. But it was a sunny, glorious day and the idea of a bus ride appealed to her. She found a seat at the back and perched there with a Cheshire-cat smile on her face while she watched the neighborhood roll by. They passed a small park, and from her window she caught a glimpse of a playground hidden among the trees, circumscribed by bright flower beds and cleanly clipped shrubs. It was purely spontaneous, a gesture that fit her mood; she shot out of her seat and dashed off the bus just before the door swung shut.

Following the sounds of laughter, she came upon the playground. Children romped noisily from swing to slide, hung from rope ladders, squatted in sand piles. Their mothers, seated on freshly painted green benches, watched or read or chatted among themselves, from time to time raising their voices in warning or to break up a squabble.

Despite what doctors had told her years before, Sarah could not believe anything would happen to this unborn child. It was not that she was trying to delude herself, but rather, for some obscure reason, the startling news brought with it a profound serenity. Had she been visited by angels, she could not have been more reassured. As she sat there she recalled how she had lain awake one night in the loft in Billy's barn, had lain in the straw curled up with Billy's gentle old hunting dog she had dragged up there to keep her company, recalled how she had cried herself to sleep with the dog in her arms. Her heart had been drained of hope that night, and yet, without her knowledge, she had been carrying within her this miracle.

She sat on the bench until noon and the park began to empty; mothers settled toddlers into strollers and trundled back home for lunch and naps. It was very much an insider's world, Sarah thought. So banal and prosaic to the outsider, so often belittled and scorned. But there was for Sarah in that sun-dappled deserted playground the fulfillment of a dream and a reason to be alive.

39

Of all escapes from reality, mathematics is the most successful ever.

GIAN-CARLO ROTA,
MIT MATHEMATICIAN

It was around the middle of July when John first made the acquaintance of Dr. Shelley, a British physicist who was joining the faculty at Berkeley for the fall term as visiting professor. Rupert Shelley was an unassuming man with pallid skin and drab brown hair, and so soft-spoken one had to strain to hear him. Shelley was one of the first to develop a system of thought that synthesized quantum theory and traditions of mysticism, and his books were now classics in the field.

The two men were introduced in the hallway outside the physics office, and the encounter stretched through the afternoon, continued through dinner and late into the night. As they shuffled through the empty parking lot toward their cars sometime after midnight, Shelley extended a personal invitation to John to join a small group of colleagues and friends on a retreat scheduled for the first of August. Shelley's retreat was a well-kept secret, open to a select few involved in research across a wide spectrum of interests — cosmology, chemistry, biology, particle physics — and devoted specifically to the interfacing of those fields and, above all, to the search for unity. It was held every summer in an ancient monastery in an isolated region of northern Greece. He and a group of like-minded benefactors had restored it to a certain degree, hardly luxurious by Western standards, but it was adequate for their needs.

"What we really like about the place is the vacuum," he told John while they sat in Shelley's office the following day eating ham sandwiches. "There's bloody well nothing up there. And that affords us a certain freedom from artificial needs — you know, all those countless things we're told we need to keep us happy and functioning. We have no fax, no television, no automobiles. Now, you can bring your PC and your mobile telephone," he grinned sheepishly, "but they must be turned off during the day."

Susan liked the idea, said she thought it was just what John needed.

"You should do it," she called to him as she came out of the bathroom that evening, briskly towel-drying her hair. "Vacation's out of the question for me this summer. I told you that when I took this job." She plopped onto the bed beside him, her wet, tousled hair sticking out in short shocks around her face. She looked more youthful these days, seemed to have regained her old buoyancy and vigor.

"Your passport's still valid, isn't it?"

"Should be."

"We've got a good travel agency at the office. I can see what kind of fares they can get you."

"If you don't mind."

"Where is it?"

"Place called Meteora. I'll have to fly into Athens. Take a train from there."

"I think it's a fantastic idea," she said brightly, and John looked over at her, admiring the confidence that lent her such credibility, thinking how impressed they must be with her at work. He smiled warmly.

"My God," she said in a breathy voice, and her hands fell limp to her lap and lay there in the folds of her wet towel. "That's the first time I've seen you look at me like that in ages."

She held his gaze for only a minute, then leaned forward and kissed him lightly on the lips, a kind of impatient, hurried kiss, before rolling off the bed. She threw him a rueful grin over her shoulder and scuffled back to the bathroom, reminding him a shade apologetically that she had to be at the office by six when the markets opened on the East Coast. But John knew all this, for she was always gone when he awoke, and it struck him she might have been just a little anxious there for a moment, might have imagined he wanted to make love.

Caught up in his work during the days prior to his departure, John gave little thought to the trip. He rummaged through his drawers, found his passport and set it aside with the plane ticket, and stopped by the cleaners to drop off a load of shirts to be laundered. Just before Shelley left he dashed into John's office to say goodbye and leave the necessary travel information, but apart from a reminder to bring warm clothing and sturdy walking shoes, John had no idea what awaited him. So when the train to Kalambaka rounded a bend in the track and he first saw the place, he was so mesmerized that the book he had been reading slipped from his hand to the floor, remaining there until the woman next to him picked it up and laid it on the seat beside him.

"Isn't it spectacular?" she said, and John turned to look at her. She was young, with glasses and a quirky smile, and she seemed to bristle with that enthusiasm he always found so engaging in his students.

"I had no idea," he murmured, his eyes shifting back to the window.

After a few minutes of rummaging through the backpack wedged between her legs, she withdrew a water-dimpled brochure and handed it to him.

"Here," she offered. "Keep it. I don't need it. This is my third trip up here."

The Kalambaka train station was a shoddy, decrepit piece of bureaucratic work and decidedly unpicturesque. There was no footbridge spanning the tracks, and he noticed the Greeks were lugging their suitcases across the rails, so John did likewise. At the gated exit he looked around, but Shelley was nowhere in sight. After a moment he noticed a dark-haired boy moving toward him, fighting the current of bodies and all types of conveyances pouring from the station. The boy scrambled up on a boulder, swaying from foot to foot while he surveyed the crowd. He caught John watching him and there seemed to be an immediate recognition; he broke into a disarming grin, ripped off his baseball cap, and fanned it through the air. John picked up his suitcase and wended his way down the road.

"You must be waiting for me," John said as he approached and set down his bag. "John Wilde."

"Hello, Dr. Wilde," grinned the boy. "I'm Yannis. Dr. Shelley's very sorry he couldn't meet you himself. He's having some problems getting the rooms opened up. It happens every year. The old monk in charge locks things up when we go, with these huge medieval locks and keys, and Dr. Shelley has to run all over the place tracking down the keys."

The boy's British syntax was weighted with a thick Greek accent. John suspected he was older than he had appeared from a distance; judging by his speech and ease with strangers he might be all of twelve or thirteen. He pointed to John's bag. "Is this all you have?"

"Yes. Just this bag."

"Here, let me take it for you."

John protested, but the boy was strong, of tough mountain stock, and he lifted the bag with ease.

"It's good you don't have much luggage.

It's a bit of a climb."

They had little chance for conversation after that. They walked several blocks to a taverna, and Yannis disappeared inside while John drank a tepid beer at a wobbly table out front and enjoyed fleeting moments of sun between clouds. All around the edges of the town, the strange outcroppings of rock rose like dusky sentinels. From time to time there would be a break in the mist and he would catch sight of a redroofed monastery clinging to a distant pinnacle high in the clouds.

After a while, an old car pulled to the curb in front of the taverna and Yannis hopped out, snatched up John's bag, and motioned him into the car. It was nothing as official as a taxi, but the man took directions from Yannis and drove them the short distance through the bleak, ramshackle town to a farm at the foot of a cliff. As John removed his bag from the trunk, Yannis darted off to where a muleteer was busy lashing a load onto the back of a mule.

"Hurry." Yannis waved. "He's getting ready to leave. We can go with him."

Day was quickly fading, and the towering cliffs seemed rooted in darkness while their peaks bathed in the glow of late-afternoon light. They were unlike any form John had

ever seen. He had read about their formation in the brochure pressed upon him by
the young woman, the result of millions of
years of erosion, cut out of the mountains by
the Piniós River. They appeared, however,
not so much a result of a wearing down, but
rather a rising up — as if the rock had
sprouted these formations, the rebellious
manifestation of something unaccountable
in the very earth itself. A place so spectacular that theories of erosion do not suffice,
and the mind wants to believe a mysterious
force at work.

John had thought to make the trip to the
top on foot, but he soon mounted the mule
they had brought along for him; Yannis
walked at the head of the mule train, chatting in Greek to the muleteer. It was a long
climb, and at times perilous, but the sure-
footed beasts plodded at a steady pace. The
sun was setting when they finally reached
the monastery walls.

Once inside, they passed through a series
of gates and inner courtyards. The village
had once been organized for work, survival,
and defense, and Yannis briefly pointed out
the old bathhouse and fountain, and the
domed church, explaining that it had been
started in the late 1300s with additions built
over a period of three centuries. At one of

the gates Yannis stopped and spoke briefly to a bearded monk seated on a chair in front of the porter's lodge before they continued into the cloisters and down a covered arcade, finally entering a long refectory with a smoke-blackened ceiling.

"I'll take your things on up to your room," Yannis said as he turned to go. "And I'll find Dr. Shelley and tell him you're here."

Rupert arrived in minutes, out of breath and more agitated than John had ever seen him, but there was a freshness, a glow to his normally pale skin that had not been there in California. He still wore his proverbial sweater, but the bow tie was gone, and he had not shaved for several days.

"Terribly sorry I couldn't meet you at the station, John," he said as he rushed forward to shake his hand. "Hope my young assistant took good care of you."

"Yes, he did. Excellent care."

"Brilliant boy. Met him when I gave a series of lectures at the British School in Athens." Rupert paused to brush some rock dust from his trousers. "A prodigy in math. It's amazing what he's been able to do with so little formal education. I told him about you. Said you'd have much in common. He's been looking forward to meeting you."

"He's Greek?"

"Yes. But his English is impressive, isn't it?"

"Very."

"So much potential. I've been trying to get him out of here, place him in a good boarding school in England. I think I've found some sponsors, but what he really needs is a mentor. Someone to champion his cause. Parents are peasants. Don't really see much use in his toying around with numbers." He paused and rubbed his hands together excitedly. "Tell you what, I still have some business to finish. I'll show you to your room. Then you'll be on your own for a while. Take a look around. Get yourself acquainted with where things are. Sorry, old boy, no running water. No electricity, either. Rather primitive. But we manage. Ever used a gas lantern?"

"Not since Boy Scouts."

"Yannis will show you. Nothing too complicated. Even for us scientists. Although last year Nigel Boote damn near burned the place down. You'll do fine though. Just ask Yannis if you need anything. If you want to send any mail out, he'll take care of that, too. We'll meet back here at seven-thirty. The monks are feeding us tonight. They take care of us for a few days until we get in all our supplies. It's a bit of a hike, so wear your boots. You'll work up an appetite."

Yannis had taken great care to prepare John's room, had lit the gas lantern and laid out a box of candles and matches, had even turned down the raw cotton sheets and plumped the down comforter at the foot of the bed. A pitcher of water had been left next to a metal basin with a bar of soap.

John washed and changed his clothes, then went to look for Yannis, but the boy was nowhere to be found. He looked for him along the arcade, down steep paths and up steps cut into the stone, coming at last to the church. The church was empty, but rows of votive candles flickering in an alcove testified to the presence of spirit in the absence of man. John was about to turn to go when he was startled by the sudden rustling of wings — sounds of bird or bat frightened from its perch. He paused and raised the lantern, followed with his eyes where the lantern cast its light. There, gazing down upon him from the high gilded dome were sober-faced prophets and saints and angels, resplendent in still-vivid colors of the past, in ocher and sienna and jewel blue. He thought of the ceiling in Sarah's room, and the way she had climbed down from the ladder, down out of the clouds and into his arms. He had not thought about her all day, not since boarding the train in Athens that morning, and this sudden recollection of her startled him. She seemed distant to him up here, the once sharp and poignant pain now blunted.

His thoughts were interrupted by the sound of the portal creaking open, and he turned to see Yannis in the doorway.

"Dr. Wilde?"

"Yes?"

"It's time for dinner. Dr. Shelley's already gone ahead. I'll take you there." He reached for the lantern. "Are you a religious man, Dr. Wilde?"

"Yes," John replied without hesitation. "I am."

"I thought you would be."

Night had fallen sharply and the high cloistered walls surrounded them with an impenetrable blackness, so that the eyes were drawn immediately heavenward to the starry sky.

The boy scampered up the steep rocky path ahead of John, the lamp swinging from his hand. After a while he paused, turning back toward John. "I've kept a notebook," he said. "It's all my formulas. Everything I do on my own during the school year. But there's no one in my school who understands what I'm doing. Would you take a look at it?"

"I would," John answered as he paused to catch his breath. There was in the boy's exuberance a strong echo of his own childhood passion. "I used to keep notebooks."

"You did?"

"Yes, and nobody ever understood mine either." John laughed then, and his own laughter felt surprisingly honest and good. They started up the path again.

"What was your favorite thing?" the boy called over his shoulder. "I mean, to work with. What did you like best?"

"Infinite series."

The boy stopped in his tracks, spun around to face John. "Mine, too," he whispered, his wide eyes eclipsed with wonder.

John had been eagerly anticipating an informal and relaxed exchange of ideas between men of science, but it was his evenings that brought him the greatest satisfaction. He would devote an hour or so to the boy, discussing the notebooks; then, after Yannis left, John would put aside his computer and sit with paper and pencil, working in that elementary way he had worked as a student, playing with equations, turning them inside out and upside down to see the possibilities inherent in the medium, looking for connections and relationships he knew intuitively were there, waiting to be found. As the days went by he felt it returning to him, that old self-assurance, that belief in his God-given gift. Thoughts of the world beyond scarcely penetrated the chamber of his mind, and he did not think about the time when he would have to return. Were one to crack open the door and steal a glimpse of this tired-looking man in a wrinkled shirt bent over a narrow table scratching down long trails of numbers, it would have been impossible to detect behind the blank, focused stare what joy, what ecstasy burned within.

40

It is a peculiarity of man that he can only live by looking to the future.
VIKTOR E. FRANKL
MAN'S SEARCH FOR MEANING

As the place became visible through a break in the trees, Sarah decelerated and shifted her eyes away from the road and stole a long look. This was how she had first seen it, and although she now lived there and knew its true derelict condition, its dank, gloomy rooms and mildewed tapestries, and the tall, slender chimney on the south wing that had been raked off during last winter's windstorm — despite the ruinous effects of years of neglect for want of funds, it never ceased to inspire her with awe. She had since learned a bit about architecture so she knew this late-sixteenth-century château was a rather motley version of the early Renaissance style, perhaps lacking a little of the purity of its Italian ancestors, but striking all the same, the aesthetics of symmetry and harmony captured in rose-colored brick and slate and stone. Classicism, she had learned, was the architecture of power, privilege, and wealth, and even had the château been abandoned and in ruin, it would have retained an aura of glory.

She glanced over at Joy, whose mouth was hanging wide open. Sarah knew exactly what she was feeling. Joy had ceased talking minutes earlier, was leaning forward, gawking through the windshield.

"No . . . ," she drawled, her voice thick with incredulity. "Don't tell me that's it."

"That's it," said Sarah, and she pulled to the shoulder of the road to allow a motorist to overtake her.

"I thought you were kidding."

"No. I said 'château.' That's what it is."

"Yeah, but I thought you were exaggerating."

"Well, parts of it are really run-down. A lot of the rooms are empty. All the really valuable antiques are in the rooms open to the public, and the family lives up there," she pointed through the windshield, "on the south wing."

Sarah checked her rearview mirror for traffic and pulled back onto the road. "You'll see it better in a minute."

Joy kept muttering, "My God, oh my God," as they turned into a long, poplar-lined drive. The château had been built in alignment with the solar movements, Sarah explained, so that come summer solstice the sun's arc would trace a path dividing the residence into two perfectly symmetrical sections. She stopped at the bottom of the drive and pointed to the upper windows.

"Look. They're aligned front to back. You can see all the way through to the trees behind the house."

"Oh my goodness . . ."

"Midsummer, if you stand out on the back lawn, you can see the sun rise right through that upper window there."

"Wait," Joy cried when Sarah began to accelerate. "Just wait one more second so I can take it all in."

Joy fell silent, her hand over her heart in what Sarah knew to be a totally unconscious reaction, and honest to its core.

A moment later, after she'd recovered, she laid a hand on Sarah's arm and grinned. "I can't tell you how much mileage your grandpa's got out of this."

At the mention of her grandfather a tenderness washed over Sarah's face. "How does he look?" she asked.

"Very good," Joy reassured her. "Fire in

his eyes. Every time he gets one of your letters or postcards he brings it into the cafe and passes it around."

"Does he?" Sarah asked with a bright smile.

"Oh yes. He's so proud of you. You're all he talks about. His granddaughter the governess to a count and countess . . ."

"Fréderic's not a count," laughed Sarah. "The title went to his cousin."

"Well, your grandpa's made him into a count, and if I were you I'd let him have his way."

Sarah sat there a moment longer, hands fixed on the wheel, her smile fading as she stared blankly ahead.

"Don't worry about him, honey," Joy said softly. "He'll be fine."

"I feel like I abandoned him."

"No you didn't, and he doesn't think that at all. I'm sure he doesn't," Joy said.

"I know. And he tries so hard in his letters to let on like it doesn't bother him. But it comes across. Maybe because I can tell he's trying so hard."

"Well, of course he misses you. But that's okay. This is what you should've done a long time ago. Get on with your life."

"It's just that whenever I try to get on with my life, it's so far away from them."

"Do you ever hear from Ruth?" Joy asked.

Sarah shook her head. "Not really. Sometimes she adds a few lines at the bottom of Grandpa's letters. That's about it."

They sat in silence for another moment, then Sarah shifted into first gear and the car crept up the incline.

As she parked the little Renault on the gravel drive around the side of the house, three brindled hunting dogs came loping up the slope from a cluster of old stone barns. Sarah climbed out of the car and bent down to pet them, and they grew excited and jumped up on her. A man dressed in a blue work smock and boots called from the doorway of the nearest barn, and they turned tail and trotted back to their master. The man watched from the doorway, a piece of machinery in his hand, and when he saw the women trying to ease the bulky suitcase out of the backseat, he set it down and hurried up the slope toward them, the dogs at his heels.

"*Bon, laissez-moi faire ça,*" he said, shooing the women back and wiping his grease-stained hands on a filthy handkerchief. "*Vous ne devez pas faire d'effort comme ça,*" he scolded, wagging a finger at Sarah. He stuffed the handkerchief into his pocket and then retrieved the suitcase.

"What'd he say?" whispered Joy as they followed him inside.

"I'm not sure," smiled Sarah. "I don't understand a lot of what they say. But it's okay. I'm getting used to it."

With a manly display of strength he swung the heavy suitcase onto his back and followed the women up three flights of a creaky wooden staircase to a long hallway running the length of the top floor. Dormer windows under the steeply pitched roof looked down on the sweeping grounds, the front lawn with its circular drive, and the long tree-lined entrance and the forest beyond.

"My room's down here," said Sarah.

She flung open the door to make way for the blue-smocked man, whom Sarah thanked by name, and he set the bag on the floor and shuffled out.

Sarah had already warned Joy not to expect much in the way of amenities, and she apologized that the toilet was at the end of the hall, adding that it was always, even in summer, bitter cold. A sink and a modular shower had been installed in the corner of the room, and a tiny refrigerator was crammed between the two, but these things had been discreetly concealed by a folding wicker screen. A four-poster bed engulfed the center so that one was constantly maneuvering around it. Facing the bed was a small television set perched on a cracked marble-top dresser. The room, traditionally that of the governess, boasted a fireplace with a decorative marble mantel on which Sarah had placed a few small prints she had purchased from vendors along the Seine. An old leather armchair had been pulled up to the hearth, and another chair served as a catchall for mail and newspapers and magazines. A glass trolley (by far the most unsightly piece in the room) positioned next to the armoire held an electric coffeepot, an assortment of crackers and cereal and some fruit, a few pieces of cutlery, cups, and plates. Sarah's underwear was strung to dry over an electric radiator rolled into the corner.

It was impossible to move without running into something.

"It's small," Sarah said with a bright smile, "but there's a gorgeous view." She nodded to the dormer window. "Actually, I have another room, behind that door, but I use it as a studio and there's no fireplace and I was afraid you'd be cold. So," she shrugged, "this is it for a week."

Joy was standing next to her suitcase with her hands on her hips, in her denim jacket and gold hoop earrings and high heels, looking very much like a gypsy.

"Honey," she shook her head, "I don't care how small it is. It's fantastic." She spread her arms and wheeled around. "I can just see you here. It's just you, all over."

She stepped up to the window and peered out. "Look at this view!" Then she spun around and swooned, "And what a bed!"

"It's not as comfortable as it looks."

Joy stepped around Sarah and flopped backward onto the bed with her arms flung over her head. But Sarah would not let her rest, took her by the hand and pulled her back to her feet. They had only a few minutes before they had to pick up Justine from school, Sarah said, and she wanted to show Joy the gardens.

They passed through the sprawling kitchen and Sarah stopped to talk to a stout little woman in an apron hunched over a cutting board. It seemed that Sarah was going to great lengths to make herself understood, something about a piano lesson, but the woman never looked up from the apples, just nodded and went on chopping.

Outdoors the sun had disappeared behind a low bank of clouds. They followed a path through a tall hedge into a rose garden, and Sarah talked about how she had come to live with this family and take care of their children.

"Sometimes it just gets to be too much, because I live on the property and I'm always around, and they've found that I'm flexible and don't have a problem with taking the dogs to the vet or helping prune the rosebushes." Sarah paused and pointed to a pale pink rose. "Look, the roses are still in bloom." She leaned in to smell it and Joy watched the way she moved. She knew there was something about her that was different, strikingly different, but she couldn't put her finger on it. She seemed older, with a kind of maturity, although she was more exuberant than Joy had ever seen her.

As they left the rose garden and cut across the lawn to a cluster of stone buildings, Sarah explained how Victoria, Fréderic's American wife and a former publicist for a haute couture house in Paris, had a difficult time keeping employees. "She's the center of her own little universe out here. She has only her family's interests in mind and everything else just completely escapes her attention. It's a terrific amount of work. Three small children and overseeing the estate, and her husband."

They had passed behind a greenhouse and Sarah led Joy down a short gravel driveway to a narrow street while she talked about Fréderic. "He had polio when he was a boy. He's paralyzed from the waist down. I drive him into Paris occasionally, and we have good chats. He's really a very funny man."

They had been forced to walk single file along the narrow sidewalk, and suddenly Joy stopped and grabbed Sarah by the shoulder and spun her around.

"Sarah, just listen to yourself."

"What?"

"You're going on like a magpie."

Sarah laughed brightly. "I suppose I am."

"I can't believe how you've changed."

"Have I?"

"You're . . . I don't know . . . you're, like, radiant. You look . . . *happy*."

"Well, I am."

"It shows, all over you." She looked down at Sarah's loose-fitting sweater and her soft, flowing jersey pants. "Put on a little weight, too, I can see . . ."

Sarah blushed, stammered something about the bulky sweater.

"But it looks great on you. Honestly. Look at those cheeks!"

"Joy, I'm pregnant," blurted Sarah. She smiled, a little hesitant and unsure. "The baby is John's."

Joy stood motionless, her expression frozen on her face.

"What?"

Sarah threw back her head and laughed.

"You're what?"

"I'm going to have a baby."

"John who?"

"What other John do we know?"

"John *Wilde?*"

"The one." Sarah turned back up the street. "Come on, we need to hurry."

"Sarah," Joy cried, rushing along behind her. "Sarah, how on God's green earth can that be?"

"Joy, believe me, it took a long time for the shock to wear off, but I'll explain it all this evening, when we have more time to talk." They turned a corner then, onto a wider street, and Sarah linked her arm through Joy's and briefly ran through the schedule for the evening. When Fréderic was away, Sarah explained, she would eat late with Vickie. It gave them time to talk about the children. "But he'll be home tonight, so we'll eat early with the housekeeper and the children. Once I get them bathed and to bed, then we can go up to my room and I'll tell you all about it."

"My God . . . Oh my God," Joy mumbled as she tripped along at her side.

41

There was little chance for them to talk that afternoon. Sarah's day was a busy one, feeding lunch to the youngest and taking her in the stroller into the village while she ran errands, then picking up the boys from school and walking them home, and overseeing their homework, and the eldest son's piano lesson on the Pleyel in the salon with the young music instructor from Prague (he played Brahms's Hungarian Dance for them), and then there was dinner and getting the children bathed and into bed. Joy did not meet Fréderic de Beauharnais but she met the lady of the house, briefly, at the end of the day in the vast book-lined salon that functioned as informal dining room and family room and office. Victoria was on the telephone when Sarah came in, but she took a minute out from her conversation and welcomed Joy, then exchanged a few words with Sarah. Joy was a little disappointed, had expected a great beauty, not this rather ordinary matron, a little on the heavy side, with broad shoulders and a square, Slavic face and pale hair.

All afternoon Joy's thoughts were dancing around this news of a baby, but it wasn't until late that evening when she heard what the doctors had said (Sarah had seen several of them since her first visit), heard all about the improbabilities of such things happening, and heard, at last, Sarah's confession.

Joy was in bed, knees tucked under her chin, watching Sarah stack kindling in the fireplace to start a fire.

"I loved him," Sarah said quietly, without the slightest trace of regret. "I think it began that night Amy called and I went over there, and I fell asleep with Will in his study. From the moment I opened my eyes and saw him staring down at me . . ."

The bed creaked and Sarah looked over her shoulder.

"Are you falling asleep?"

"Hardly," answered Joy.

Sarah dusted off her hands and set a match to the newspaper she had stuffed beneath the kindling, then waited for the wood to ignite. "We never talked about it," she said quietly. "We just knew it was there, between us. It didn't need words."

The kindling began to blaze and Sarah laid a log on the fire. "We were only together once. Just one night. After that . . ." She paused, remembering. "He's a good man, Joy, and a moral one, and I think it was very hard for him. It was hard for me, too. I didn't want my happiness at the price of someone else's."

"Does he know?"

Sarah hesitated, staring silently into the fire. Joy thought perhaps she had not heard, and so she repeated it. "Sarah, does he know? About the baby?"

Joy saw her shoulders rise in a deep sigh, and her head swung from side to side.

"No."

"Well, are you going to tell him?"

"I've thought about it. So many times. But I wouldn't know what to say. It's a very delicate situation, isn't it?"

"Honey, he's got to know."

Sarah picked up the poker and nudged the log into place. "Does he?"

"What do you mean?"

"It would be awful, if he left her because he felt obligated."

"But he loves you."

"Yes, but I'm not sure he knows what to do about it." Sarah smiled a little sadly, then glanced up at Joy, a candid look on her face. "What do you do with love, Joy? Where do you go with it? Where does it take you?"

They were silent for a long while. Out-doors the plaintive call of an owl marked the silence.

"But what about the baby?" Joy asked. "He wanted a child so badly, didn't he?"

"I think so . . . especially later, when Will improved. He loved Will very much." She hung up the poker and turned to look at Joy. "But then, we never talked again, after Will died."

There was a long pause, and the flames crackled in the silence.

"Sometimes I hate him for that," she whispered.

Joy sat up in bed. "Oh, honey, you can't blame him; he tried so hard to save him."

"Not for that," she said in a voice paper thin.

"I don't understand."

Sarah looked down again, seemed to be contemplating her hands, the long slender fingers, the cuticles stained with paint. "I didn't have anyone to grieve with. I was alone. I felt Will's death just like I'd felt my own child's. It was all there again for me and I had to bear up alone. The father was gone, and there I was with all this sadness. This unbearable sadness. If he'd just called, or written, or done anything to let me know he felt it as deeply as I did."

"You know he did."

"And then sometimes I think, what if I lose this baby? What then?"

"Don't talk like that."

"But I think about it all the time. It's like I'm waiting for things to flip around and for it all to come crumbling down. Then what would be the point of him knowing?"

Sarah rose abruptly, replaced the fire screen, and announced with determined cheerfulness that she was going to have a shower. She peeled off her sweater and bared her stomach to Joy, and Joy placed her hand on the baby and smiled. Sarah's mood brightened then, and she disappeared behind the wicker screen and stepped into the shower, all the while babbling on over the noise of the spray, telling Joy about the work she was doing.

"I'm doing some documentation for the botanical garden in Paris. On my day off I go in and do sketches of their exotic plants. They're really pleased with my work. And they're so nice to work with. I'm very excited about it."

She turned off the water and stepped out and grabbed her towel, peeked around the wicker folding screen.

"Are you still awake or am I talking to the walls?"

"Half 'n' half," Joy mumbled from the bed.

"I also had an offer from a publishing house that specializes in natural history. They wanted to send me down to the Pyrenees in the spring to do a series of brochures on the wildlife and the flowers, but of course I won't be able to go."

She stepped out from behind the screen and walked naked across the room to the armoire and opened it. Joy watched her, thinking of all the times she had seen her scurry back and forth in the Cassoday Cafe with plates of the daily special, and that was always the way Joy had seen her, that was her Sarah. Now, here she was with swollen stomach and breasts, the firelight glistening on her skin, reaching for her nightgown, slipping it over her head and closing the door of the armoire. She stood in front of the mirror brushing her hair, and Joy couldn't imagine a man on the face of the earth who wouldn't fall in love with her.

Sarah turned all of a sudden, hairbrush in hand, and said, "Don't think I'm deluding myself. I know what the risks are, trying to have another baby. I've been told by enough doctors, but I try not to let it get me down. I just pray a lot and hope for the best. I have confidence in Dr. Faure. He's the one who introduced me to Victoria. They're close friends."

Joy shot up in bed. "You're not planning on having the baby over here, are you?"

"Yes."

"But why?"

Sarah paused and lowered the hairbrush. "You don't see why?"

"No! I don't!" Joy sat up in bed. "What reason could you possibly have for staying here? You've got no family or friends here."

Sarah's face clouded. "I just couldn't go back," she whispered, and Joy saw that this newfound happiness, although real, was fragile. "Think about it, Joy. Just think about it for a moment. All the implications. Especially for my grandparents. Not to mention John and Susan, and Billy. Everybody knows everybody. It'd be a slap in the face to all of them."

"Bunch of hypocrites."

"I don't begrudge them their feelings, Joy. I was raised like they were, with the same kind of scorn for adultery. And it's more than just John. It's Will's death, and everything that happened to me before John . . . with Anthony. I came home in this state once before." She grew silent and started picking nervously at her hairbrush.

"I'm sorry, honey," Joy said gently. "I

didn't mean to open old wounds."

"I just can't do it. The very thought of going back sends waves of darkness over me."

"Oh, honey . . ."

"It's not like I have any great affection for this place as opposed to any other place." She picked up her damp towel, draped it over the radiator, then turned again to look at Joy. "It's so different from what I know. I used to see trees as an eyesore," she said with a smile, and Joy could see the sadness lifting. "But I am growing to like it. I'm beginning to like it very much." She turned off the lamp next to her chair and came to bed.

"My feet are cold," she warned as she crawled in next to Joy.

"You keep them off me."

Sarah giggled and then they settled down.

The fire had burned low, and the room had fallen into darkness. A moment passed, and she turned to Joy and whispered, "It's just that I'm happy now, and I guess that's how we judge a place, isn't it? Not for what it is, but for what we are when we live there."

But Joy's breathing had slowed and deepened; she had fallen asleep.

Sarah smiled. " 'Night, my friend," she whispered.

42

Joy left at the end of the week, having tasted a good slice of both town and country. They saw the Eiffel Tower and Notre Dame, strolled the Champs Elysées and shopped at the Galeries Lafayette, even took a Bateau-Mouche down the Seine and popped into the Louvre for a few hours so Joy could say she had seen the *Mona Lisa* and the *Winged Victory*. The rest of the time Joy puttered around the château, visiting the exotic gardens and the gift shop and the petting zoo, tagging along on tours of the public rooms, and generally delighting in her role as guest of Fréderic and Victoria de Beauharnais. Mealtimes were strictly observed, and even though they ate with the children and the housekeeper, a certain formality reigned, and a rigorous etiquette was required of each of them, down to the smallest child. They ate well and drank the fruity Beaujolais from the family's small vineyard, and Joy took back to the Cassoday Cafe enough gossip to serve up for years to come. As for Sarah's pregnancy, she was sworn to secrecy, but she extracted from Sarah a promise that Sarah would keep her informed of all progress, for better or worse, and — regardless of cost or inconvenience — Joy would be at her side for the baby's birth.

Autumn brought the smell of burning leaves and wood smoke, and the crack of hunters' rifles in the nearby forest. The forest within the estate was a designated wildlife reserve, but poaching was common and Monsieur Cassat, the groundskeeper, spent many a sleepless night stalking trespassers and confiscating the kills they abandoned as they fled his searchlight. More than once Sarah had seen him coming out of the woods in the morning, scowling grimly, a wild boar slung over his shoulder and blood dripping onto his boots.

Very gradually the seasons passed, marked by the changing colors of the countryside and a forest mottled with crimson and gold. The winters here were green and mild compared to those in the Flint Hills, and even when the leaves had fallen and the forest stood brown and unclothed, there were still blue firs and pines and moss-covered rocks to gentle the eye, and the grasses sustained their greenness and did not die out. On the first of December, as she crossed a meadow on a walk with Justine, Sarah spied a lone yellow butterfly darting among a few spindly dandelions and tiny white daisies still in bloom, and she was amazed to see the azalea on her window ledge in full flower until mid-December when it was finally struck down by the first frost.

December announced itself not with brittle sunlight and numbing cold but with ever diminishing days and increasing rain, always rain. It seemed to Sarah she barely got the children home, their boots, book bags, and coats removed, before night fell, and they took their snacks and spread out their schoolwork on the long hardwood table in the vast hearth room, sequestered by the darkness and rain. Sarah would go around the room switching on all the lamps and piling logs onto the fire. More than once the housekeeper complained to Madame de Beauharnais about this useless waste of electricity, and Victoria, ever frugal, would reprimand Sarah. But light was Sarah's weapon against depression, and she stubbornly persisted in her habits, leaving a trail of lighted lamps wherever she most frequently passed in the evenings, so that from the outside the south wing of the château shone brightly in the darkness.

In December Sarah began to work into her daily schedule an hour's rest on the worn sofa in the huge hearth room, the one where the dogs and children camped on Friday evenings to watch videos — this being the only room where a fire burned all through the day. Even if Fatima was running the vacuum or Madame was on the telephone at her desk in the far corner, Sarah would stretch out, cover herself with a wool throw, and go to sleep. The room was so vast and sounds so muffled by the encumbrance of massive book-covered tables and chairs and sideboards and hanging tapestries, that conversations were rarely overheard; neither were Sarah's light snores.

If Sarah had a champion that winter, it was Dr. Faure. It was he who urged Victoria to relieve Sarah of some of her duties, who insisted, in the later months of her pregnancy, she use Fréderic's private elevator instead of the stairs, and who suggested Victoria provide her with a cell phone for use in case of emergency. Victoria, always a little slow to respond to the needs of her employees, was nevertheless accommodating, for she truly liked Sarah, found her particularly good with the children (even ten-year-old Henri, who had given such grief to their previous *au pairs*) and hoped she would stay on after her baby was born.

But the true test of this arrangement came in late December, only five days before Christmas. Sarah had driven the children in to Saint-Germain-en-Laye to ride the carousel and do some last-minute shopping. The excitement of Christmas hung in the air like the smell of snow. A giant pine tree decorated with huge floppy bows and shiny red ornaments the size of basketballs had been raised in the small *place* at the end of the Rue de Pologne, and garlands of flocked greenery woven with gold-and-silver ribbons decorated the doorways of *boucheries* and *boulangeries,* wine merchants and the Monoprix, and the fishmonger with his squid and raw oysters and salmon on white beds of cracked ice.

Always at this time of day the streets were full of shoppers, but never so many as in this season, and now they overflowed the sidewalks and spilled into the streets with their strollers and dogs and shopping caddies. The local beggars had their corner, and the harpist his, and the chestnut vendor had staked out a space for his coal brazier. There was always a bottleneck at that corner, and the smell of roasting chestnuts wafted all the way down the street.

It was five in the afternoon, and darkness had already fallen. Henri was gawking at a wild boar suspended from a hook next to the entrance of a butcher shop. Sarah suspected he was fondling the long needlelike fur and inspecting the snout and huge ears just to annoy Justine, and so she took the younger children by the hand and herded them on down the street toward a chocolate shop. All of a sudden she felt a painless rush of warmth between her legs, and she looked down to see bright, fresh blood trickling down her knee, staining her pale stockings. She called back to Henri, but he stubbornly ignored her, and she had to rush back to get him. He was only ten but he could tell by the look in her eyes as she hurried toward him that something was wrong, and then he saw her legs and he went white. Someone jostled him, and he got pushed aside, though he caught a glimpse of her face before she slipped to the ground. He heard someone cry out and he shoved his way through the shoppers and found her sprawled on the wet pavement, her bulky body blocking the way and the children beside her, Antoine pale and Justine wailing. Henri grabbed Justine by the hand and shook it hard and told her to be quiet, and then a lady from the *parfumerie* came out and helped Sarah inside. She was conscious when they sat her on a chair and Henri reminded her she had a cell phone in her purse. He dug it out but she was too weak to hold it, so he took it away from her and called home.

They were able to avert a miscarriage, but just barely. Two days later Sarah returned home. The children were out of school for the holidays and there was much excitement and much to do, but Sarah was confined to her bed. Only Justine was allowed up to her room, and Sarah read her Christmas stories and let her play with her watercolors. The housekeeper complained bitterly about the extra work, suggested Mademoiselle Bryden should be kept in the hospital where she could be tended to properly, or better yet, that she should return to her own country, that it did no good to hire someone to care for the children if she could not get out of bed, and that Madame de Beauharnais was being terribly inconvenienced by this turn of events. But Victoria had a soft spot for Sarah, so she turned a deaf ear to Madame Fleury and instructed the household to tend to Sarah's needs.

Their inconvenience was short-lived, however, for Joy arrived the day before Christmas with a suitcase full of macaroni and cheese, Oreos, two tins of Libby's canned pumpkin and evaporated milk to make pumpkin pies, candy canes and American videos for the children, two bottles of Sarah's favorite shampoo, and hastily wrapped presents from her grandfather and grandmother, all of which did Sarah a world of good.

Christmas dinner was a formal affair served in the grand dining room, but it was reserved for the immediate family. The employees had their own dinner service at the long table in the sprawling kitchen, and Sarah and Joy were invited to this, but Sarah could not leave her bed. So Joy carried up trays of food to her room, filled their plates full of foie gras and smoked salmon, took a little of the fish course and a lot of the turkey and chestnut dressing. She came back down later for the cheese and the traditional *bûche de Noël*, and of course two good-sized pieces of her own pumpkin pie.

Joy laid out their feast on a small drop-leaf table covered with a white tablecloth and lit with a single red taper. They sat before the fire in Sarah's room and were happy like this, just the two of them.

"I can't believe they didn't invite you to eat with them," Joy said.

Sarah shrugged, cut off a bite of turkey. "I told you, that's the way she is."

"What if I hadn't been here? What would

you have done?"

"They would have brought me something."

"Not that old Madame Fleury. She's got it in for you. She'd see you starve before she'd lift a finger."

Sarah shrugged again. "Really, I understand. They have so many people they entertain all year-round."

"Still, it's not very charitable. And that's what Christmas is all about."

Sarah set down her wineglass and smiled. "You're the best Christmas ever, Joy."

"Are you sure you should be drinking?"

"Absolutely. Just wine. The doctor prefers it to medication. 'A stitch in the cervix, bed rest, and wine,'" she mimicked lightheartedly. "That's what he said." But Joy could see from her eyes she was taking none of it lightly.

Later that evening she and Joy exchanged presents. Sarah watched from her bed while Joy unwrapped her gift — framed watercolors, one of the château and another of a spray of pink dog rose.

"Oh, Sarah," Joy sighed, her eyes wide with delight. She set the paintings on the mantelpiece where she could admire them. "These are beautiful. And to think that all those years, you never let anybody see anything you painted."

"John saw them."

Joy crossed the room and sat down at the foot of Sarah's bed.

"Did you ever write him?" she asked.

Sarah gave a light laugh and threw her hands up in the air. "What would I say to him?"

"That you need him."

"Do I?"

"Very much so."

"Your presence does me a lot more good than his would."

"That's different."

The mock cheer on Sarah's face gave way to a worried look. She reached for Joy's hand. "Oh, Joy, how could I possibly draw him back into my life again just to share this?"

Suddenly Joy could find no more words of reassurance; tears stung her eyes and she blinked wide and looked down at Sarah's hand in her own, hoping Sarah had not noticed.

Sarah hoisted herself up on an elbow and turned to Joy. "I don't know if I'm doing the right thing, I really don't, but I know this much: If I lose this baby, I'll be losing more than John's child. I'll be losing the person I most want to be."

There was a solemnness in Sarah's eyes that Joy had never seen, a kind of heartfelt confession of her own frailness.

"Oh, Sarah honey . . ."

"Without this child," her voice lowered to a pained whisper, "I'll be nothing. My life will be worthless."

"That's not true. Look at what you're doing now. Look at your beautiful paintings."

But Sarah only shook her head. "They don't mean anything."

"Sarah honey," Joy murmured, smoothing down her hair.

Sarah laid her head back on the pillow and slid her hand down her belly. "You know what I do? I keep track of every movement he makes and I write it down in that notebook." She gestured to the bedside table. "I write down the exact hour and minute. Every time he squirms or kicks. I do it even at night. That's why I don't sleep."

They were silent for a moment, and then Joy said, "Sarah, you need that man. You need him here, with you, now."

"Joy, have you forgotten he's married?"

"Well, maybe he won't be able to come. But you need to give him the chance."

Joy straightened, and a look of firm resolve spread over her face. She patted Sarah's hand. "You just let me take over from here."

The next day Joy called Clay and woke him up at three in the morning to tell him she'd be staying on in France for a while. Joy's sister had agreed to come in and run the cafe for her, but she'd need Amy to put in extra hours, and she wanted Clay to drop around whenever possible to keep an eye on things. Clay was bad-tempered about being awakened in the middle of the night by his ex-wife, was particularly annoyed by her inability to explain herself, but he was downright baffled by her refusal to say exactly when she would be home. He couldn't get back to sleep after that, just lay in bed until dawn, listened to the wind rise and watched the morning light creep in between the slats of the blinds. Then he got up and put on some coffee and sat in the kitchen wondering what could have prompted such foolhardy behavior in that woman. When he told Amy over breakfast, his daughter's head shot up from her bowl of cereal. She stared at him wide-eyed, milk dripping from her spoon, and breathed, "Oh my God, Mom's fallen in love."

And so it was that word got around that Joy was staying in Paris, and within a week the tale was embroidered with all kinds of colorful twists and turns, and folks were saying the Cassoday Cafe would soon be up for sale, and Joy was to marry a count.

43

Joy exercised more courtesy and self-restraint than usual when it came to calling Jack Bryden. She didn't want to jar the old man out of sleep in the middle of the night, particularly given the kind of news she had for him. It was tough to break it over the phone, but she didn't want to wait for a letter to reach him. She knew Jack would be terribly wounded that Sarah had hidden all this from him. But he surprised her by saying he had suspected there was something wrong, had suspected it for months now, was dead sure of it when she didn't come home for Christmas. Jack had hoped that whatever it was, Sarah'd share it with him in good time, and now he was just relieved that she was not ill, or in danger. He asked why Sarah herself hadn't called, and Joy explained that Sarah didn't know she was calling him, said she was using her own judgment in this matter and needed his help. She wanted him to find John Wilde.

Ruth had gone to the store that morning, and Jack was on his second pot of coffee, checking the newspaper ads for after-Christmas sales with a mind to picking up some new tires for his truck, when Joy called. After he had hung up he sat at the table picking at a callus on his palm and thinking it was silly for an old man to cry like this. The tears just slid down his cheeks and dripped onto the table, and he sat and stared at them as if they weren't his own.

He didn't really spend a lot of time pondering the thing, knew what he had to do, what he should have done all along. Tediously, he hobbled up the stairs to Sarah's room and opened her top dresser drawer. At the back was a small manila envelope. He took it downstairs and sat back down at the kitchen table. He tore open the flap, then dumped the letters onto the table.

There were only three, and they were still sealed. He had shown that much respect for the man that he had not opened the letters. He turned them over and read the return address. The first two had been written from Greece. He instantly recognized the postmarks, remembered Sarah's mother writing from places in Greece, remembered the strange alphabet. He remembered how he had felt sitting here at this same table talking to a man at the embassy who was trying to tell him his daughter had drowned but Jack hadn't been able to understand him. He knew where Greece was. He'd been there. Only place he'd ever been in his life outside of Kansas. He'd stood on a pristine white beach among a bunch of sunbathing tourists and looked out to sea where his daughter had last been seen. He'd stood there in the new shoes Ruth had bought for him with sweat trickling down his back underneath his shirt, with children running into the water and laughing, and he'd cried then, too.

He wondered if Sarah would ever forgive him. It wasn't right, what he'd done. Maybe if the letters hadn't been written from Greece, maybe if John Wilde had written them from California, maybe then he would have forwarded them. He didn't know. He wasn't really sure why he'd done what he'd done. All he knew was that his granddaughter had suffered enough, and this tall man with stone blue eyes who had lived among them only briefly and yet seemed to know her so well, this man would only break her heart.

He turned over the last letter. It had been postmarked only a month before, from Cambridge. In England.

He got up and took a knife from the drawer, sat back down, and slit open the envelope. He would do what he had to do. Go wherever he had to go. She would have done as much for him. Had already done it.

44

In design and discipline, Cambridge was not all that different from Aghion Oros. For centuries a monastic sort of life had prevailed. Like the holy mountain, its colleges — surrounded by walls of stone and brick — presented a closed face to the world. One entered through a great arched gate, down a dark passage past a lodge where a porter admitted visitors and kept keys. Here men wore robes and lived in cloistered halls with chapel bells chiming the hours, and young boys with angelic voices sang old Anglican liturgy. There was a cloying nostalgia in the green quadrangles and the sound of bicycles rattling across cobblestone paths, in the very sound of the names — King's College and Trinity Hall. Here were nurtured young men of finer intellects and higher spirituality. John Wilde was suited to such a place.

He did not miss the holy mountain. The monks had been indifferent to him. Even with Yannis as interpreter he had not been able to draw them out. He had expected his choice to stay on the mountain to be questioned, but it seemed to rouse not the slightest bit of curiosity. They passed him daily in the courtyard, sweeping by him in their long robes with their dark eyes full of intrigue. Each evening they ate their meals in silence, content with their salt fish and black bread and pewter jugs of wine. He had felt deeply the isolation and utter foreignness of the place, but in the end, this was what had set everything in motion.

At first he had been tormented by guilt and a sense of having betrayed family and colleagues and friends. He had endured long torturous telephone conversations with Susan and his mother and — most painfully — his father. His father had threatened to fly to Athens, to come out there and talk some sense into him, and John knew it was only the remoteness of the place that had stayed him. And then there were the tedious conversations with the chair of the physics department at Berkeley as they sorted out all the implications and what could be done to replace him at this eleventh hour, and most important, the repercussions of such an action with regard to his career. Their letters had been full of astonishment and anger and disappointment, accusing him of all kinds of weaknesses, of self-indulgence, even cowardice, but none of them had come close to the truth. Only Sarah would have understood. He remembered how he had set about writing her, knowing she would see the need for his decision, would understand and encourage him. How eagerly he had waited for a reply that never came.

When, by the end of September, his family realized they had lost the battle, there was a last-minute frenzy of telephone calls and then, abruptly, all communication with him ceased. In October he wrote Susan asking for a divorce, which set off another round of agitated calls from his parents. But John no longer feared their disapproval. No longer did their voices live inside him dictating his conscience. When Susan wrote back, a curt and bitter letter of consent, he felt as if his psyche had at long last thrown off an invisible burden, something weighty and cloying, and he had been set down in a new world a naked and free man.

Early in October he had begun collaborating electronically with two Cambridge mathematicians from Trinity College introduced to him by Rupert Shelley. With their backing John had been awarded a grant from the Royal Society — Britain's most distinguished scientific body — and Rupert Shelley had made available his small house near the university, an arrangement that would enable John to move to Cambridge and devote himself entirely to mathematical research.

All of this would have been gratifying in itself, but when John was able to obtain a scholarship for Yannis at a private boarding school near Cambridge and to persuade the boy's parents to give their consent, John felt he had in some small way made penance for his failings. John's affection for Yannis was honest and real. The boy was more than just a clever pupil full of promise, a mirror image of John as a young man. He represented John's frustrated altruism and all his awkward attempts to love. He was the Peace Corps and Kenya, and Sarah and Will.

Cambridge was full of distinguished and unusual faces, faces such as John's, and he drew no attention as he stood in the cobbled courtyard of the pub with a pint of ale in his hand waiting for Jack Bryden. The old man had refused to discuss the purpose of his visit, despite John's probing questions. He only said he was coming to see him on a matter concerning Sarah, and he asked John to be good enough to suggest a hotel where he might stay for a night.

John had reserved a room in a quiet guest house with views of the river Cam and Jesus Green and suggested they meet at the Eagle, an amusing pub, he claimed, of historical significance, where the scientists Watson and Crick had first announced their discovery of DNA. But John suspected Jack Bryden was not in Cambridge for his amusement. John had detected a strange note in Jack's voice when they had spoken on the phone, not quite remorse, but a kind of concern behind the gruffness.

For nearly half an hour John waited in the courtyard, then he went in to the bar and ordered an ale. At that moment the door flew open and a crowd of punters barged noisily into the pub. He looked up and saw the old man standing in the doorway. There was a striking vulnerability about him, the way he stepped inside with a self-conscious glance around the room, and for the first time, seeing the old man with fresh eyes from a distance, he saw a strong resemblance to Sarah.

John raised his hand and waved to him. He had never seen Jack Bryden in anything but jeans and a work shirt or old overalls, and he was a little surprised to see how well street clothes suited him, saw the man had once been handsome in a rough kind of way.

John waved him over to a table near the wall and Jack worked his way through the crowd. The limp was more pronounced than John remembered it. Jack held out his hand for John to shake and then he dropped down onto the booth with a deep sigh of relief.

"Leg still bothering you?"

"Don't have no leg left. Took off the last of it couple of months ago," he said as he unbuttoned his jacket. He kept his eyes averted, but John could see he was in pain.

"Damn," muttered John. "Why didn't you tell me? I could have come to your hotel."

"No need for that. I been through this before. Muscles just need time to get used to walkin' different." He glanced up then and forced a smile, and John could see the beads of sweat on his forehead.

"What can I get you to drink?"

"What they got up there?"

"Anything you want."

"Whiskey?"

"How do you want it?"

"Get me a double. Straight up."

When John came back he saw that Jack had removed a thick envelope from the inside pocket of his jacket and laid it before him on the table. John set the glass of scotch in front of the old man and sat down opposite him. Jack lifted the glass and muttered, "Cheers," then took a long drink. He set the glass down gently and looked up.

"I owe you an apology, John Wilde."

John watched while Jack lifted the flap on the envelope and poured out three letters.

"You wrote these to my little girl. She never got 'em."

John scooped up the letters and turned a dark look on the old man but said nothing. They were all there. All three of them. Only the last one was opened. Jack motioned to it, then drew back with a weak shrug of contrition.

"I only opened that one to see if you'd given a phone number."

"You never sent them on."

"You're a married man."

"Not anymore."

Jack kept his eyes averted, but John could see there was a softening around the mouth.

"That makes things easier, I guess," Jack mumbled.

"Makes what easier?"

"What I have to tell you."

Jack's glance fell on his glass; he lifted it and quietly studied the amber liquid, then bolted the last of it down.

"Is Sarah all right?" John asked in an anxious voice.

"I don't know how to say these kind of things to make 'em sound pretty."

"Where is she?"

"Paris."

"Sarah's in Paris?"

"Been there since this summer. Went over on vacation and ended up staying."

A light crept into John's eyes.

"She's gonna have a baby."

John didn't even flinch. His look remained fixed on some point in the distance. "Is this what you came to tell me?"

"Yes."

"Why should this concern me?"

"Because the baby's yours."

"That can't be."

Jack gave a little chuckle. "That's what I said. And I imagine that's what Sarah said, too."

"It's Billy Moon's."

"Ain't Billy Moon's baby. Sarah wouldn't have a thing to do with Billy Moon after she met you. I know that much to be true."

"When's the baby due?" John asked.

"Middle of February."

John made a quick mental calculation, and then he began to feel a kind of warmth seep through him, a kind of rosy glow, and he knew it was not the beer.

Jack added gruffly, "Sarah don't have no reason to lie about that kind of thing. And besides, I'm only here 'cause Joy called to see if I knew where you were. Nobody even knew Sarah was pregnant. Sarah was gonna have the baby on her own. Wasn't gonna tell you or me or nobody."

John took this in, then glanced up, worry etched around his eyes. "Is she okay?"

"Joy says she's doin' fine, but the doctor won't let her get out of bed." Jack fingered his glass, glanced down.

"Somehow you don't reassure me."

"Well, I don't know much more than what I've told you."

"You haven't seen her?"

Jack shook his head. "Not yet. I'm takin' the train to Paris tomorrow."

It was a tacit invitation, and it hung in the air between them. Jack was thinking he'd hate the man forever if one more second of silence slipped by.

Jack leaned back against the booth and stole a glance at John, but there was none of the uncertainty, the indecision he had anticipated. A radiant smile had crept into the man's eyes, and their color had softened.

"You know, many years ago," John said, "way back when I got married, there was one doctor who told me this kind of thing could happen. I had mumps when I was thirteen. Bad age for mumps. And this doctor said that sometimes the tests don't really show if the damage is only partial or complete. He said couples go for years . . . even adopt a few kids, and then, suddenly it happens." Then he turned that look on Jack and added softly, "And it happened with Sarah. Sarah's going to have my baby."

And right then Jack knew from the look in his eyes that John Wilde loved Sarah, loved her as much as any man had ever loved a woman.

Suddenly Jack was keenly aware of change, thought perhaps he had never felt it as sharply as he did at this moment. He wondered maybe had this conversation taken place somewhere else, someplace familiar like the Cassoday Cafe, then maybe he could have taken it better, absorbed the shock without feeling as if he were made of something brittle and fragile that could crack and fall apart. He saw then that things would never be the same again, and as the realization flooded over him it seemed to sweep his heart right out of his body so that he felt empty and terribly alone.

45

Joy said it was a shame they were arriving after dark and couldn't see anything. She chattered away with great excitement, attempting to paint a picture of the place for them as the taxi crawled up the snow-packed drive toward the château. John sat in the front next to the driver and so had a more spectacular view, but if he was struck silent at that moment it was not because of renaissance splendor but because he had noticed a single lighted window on the top floor, and he knew it had to be Sarah's.

Sarah had done her best to keep her thoughts occupied that afternoon but nothing had held her attention. She had flipped through countless television stations, then thumbed through one of Joy's magazines. She had not even attempted a book. Finally she jammed the Discman earphones into her ears and listened to the new Emmylou Harris her grandfather had sent her for Christmas while she practiced knitting, something Joy had insisted she learn and which Sarah found pleasantly soothing. Not long after sunset she felt the baby squirm, felt a tiny foot prodding at her somewhere under her diaphragm. She put down her knitting and jotted down the event in her notebook, then read through all the previous notations she had made over the past month, all the reassuring signs of life. She said a silent prayer of gratitude the way she always did when he moved, and offered up another one for his safe journey into this world.

Finally, she put everything aside and just sat and waited, listening. It was a long drive from the Gare du Nord, well over an hour, easily two if the traffic coming out of the city was heavy, and she knew she shouldn't be expecting them until evening, but she couldn't help herself. Joy had reserved a room for them at the inn in the village, and she thought perhaps they might check in there first, put away their bags, but she hoped not. It was awkward, the two of them arriving together; she had asked Joy to send John up alone, hoping her grandfather would understand.

The time trudged slowly by. Never had she remembered anticipating a moment as fervently as this one. She had tied back her hair loosely with a ribbon and put on small pearl earrings she had bought in Paris. She had agonized over what to wear, arguing the issue quite heatedly with Joy, and in the end she let Joy's judgment prevail because she wasn't sure of herself anymore, wasn't sure of anything at all except how much she needed him and longed for the shelter of his arms.

Then at last she heard the taxi on the drive. With her heart fluttering, she sat there waiting for them to be greeted and guided through to the back of the kitchen and up the staircase to the top floor. The footfalls paused at the top of the stairs and there was a whispered exchange. She could make out his low voice, and Joy's, and then there was only the sound of his steps approaching.

The door opened gently.

He caught sight of her face just as she glanced up at him, and once again, as if seeing her for the first time, he was struck by the depth of her green eyes and her puzzling beauty. She smiled, and he closed the door and then paused to look at her in the soft glow of the fire.

"Sarah," he said quietly.

"Hello, John."

Her eyes followed him as he briefly glanced around, then dropped his coat over a chair and approached the foot of her bed.

"I don't know how much you've been told," he said.

She paused, confused. "About what?"

"About me."

"Nothing."

"Nothing at all?"

"Only that Grandpa was going to see you. That you were in England." She paused again, her eyes softening, yet wary. "And that you were arriving this evening."

His face warmed to a tender smile. "Can I come near you?"

She answered him with an amused smile. "Would I ask you to come all this distance to stay at the foot of the bed?"

"But you didn't ask me."

"Only because I didn't feel I had the right to."

"But you do."

She studied the look in his eyes.

"I'm divorced, Sarah."

Her mouth quivered. "You're divorced?" she repeated.

"Yes."

He pulled the chair over to the side of her bed and sat down. "I wrote you."

"You did?"

He smiled at the incredulity in her voice.

"You thought I wouldn't try to see you again?"

"I didn't know . . . the way it all ended . . ." Her voice trailed off but her eyes locked onto his. They were both thinking of Will, and the flood, and Sarah reached out and took his hand. It was cold, and she closed her hands around his.

"I'll tell you about it another time," he said. He lifted her hands to his lips and kissed the tips of her fingers. "We have a lot to talk about."

She nodded and said, "Yes," but her voice caught in her throat.

"Don't cry," he said, leaning in to kiss her cheek. "I love you, Sarah. Do you believe that?"

"Yes," she whispered faintly, no louder than a breath.

"Joy tells me it's a boy."

"Yes. We had tests done. I wanted to know."

Tenderly, he pulled back the blanket and looked at her, and she guided his hand to her swollen belly.

"I did this to you."

"Indeed you did," she said.

"I shouldn't be feeling like this," he said gruffly, withdrawing his hand.

"Come closer to me."

He leaned over her, his hands braced on either side of her face, and kissed her deeply.

"Get into bed with me," she whispered through the kiss.

He pulled back. "Will I hurt you?"

She gave a soft laugh. "Well, I wasn't proposing anything very energetic."

He removed his shoes and then stood to pull off his sweater. Watching him, she said, "You can take off more than that, you know."

He gave her a quizzical look.

"Go on." She grinned. "And do it slowly."

"Should you get the doctor's permission?"

"What? To see you undress?"

"And after that?"

"Honestly, John," she sighed. "I've been so bored lying here for six weeks."

He laughed at her, and then he unbuttoned his shirt and slipped it off his shoulders. He stood in the firelight, bare-chested, smiling at her.

"Oh my goodness," she breathed. "Just the sight of you."

He glanced down self-consciously at his body. "I'm thinner than I used to be."

"Yes, I can see that," she said soberly. "Have you been ill?"

He walked over to the chair where he had hung his coat and withdrew the letters from an inside pocket.

"Here," he said, advancing toward the bed. "Maybe we can start here."

She took them from him and examined the envelopes. A troubled look passed over her face and she lifted her eyes to his, her brow wrinkled in a deep frown.

"He kept these?" she whispered.

John had stripped off his jeans and was sliding into the bed next to her.

"Come here," he said, reaching an arm around her.

"I can't believe this," she mumbled, laying her head against his shoulder.

"I'm not giving them to you as an indictment of his actions. I'm giving them to you so you'll know where I've been with my life, and how important you are to me."

This stayed her anger, and she looked up at him with softened eyes.

"So you did care?"

"More than you'll ever know."

It was after three in the morning when John returned to the inn, and Jack was still awake watching television from his bed. Jack's eyes followed him as he dug out his pajamas and began to undress.

"How is she?" Jack asked as he flipped off the TV.

"She looks very good." And then, after a moment of deliberation, added, "Looking forward to seeing you."

"Did she say what time tomorrow I could go up there?"

"Whenever you wake up."

Jack glanced at his watch, noted the late hour, commented that Sarah might not want him up there too early after such a late night. There was a recriminating edge to his voice, but John ignored it. Not long after midnight, Sarah had fallen asleep with John's arms around her, and he had stayed and watched over her like he'd promised to do. After adding another log to the fire, he had read a little, but mostly he just sat and watched her sleep. Much later he crept into her studio to take a look at her watercolors, and he felt a flush of pride, as if already he were making her his own, appropriating her as part of himself.

An uneasy silence hung between John and the old man while John brushed his teeth and got into bed and switched off the light. The darkness magnified the tension, and both of them lay stiff and motionless in their beds until Jack's rasping cough broke the silence.

"Hope I don't keep you awake," Jack muttered, and he rolled toward the wall.

"Don't worry about it," John answered.

There was another silence and then John said, "I'm going back to Cambridge tomorrow." He heard Jack twist around in his bed, could feel the old man's eyes on him in the darkness. "I need to make arrangements so I can come back and stay for a while."

There was a drawn-out silence, and then John said, "Sarah and I are going to get married as soon as the baby's born. We were hoping you'd stay around until then."

There was not a sound from Jack's bed. After a long while he turned back to the wall and mumbled, " 'Course I will." John could tell by the tone of his voice that the old man was pleased.

46

Upon returning to Cambridge, John walked straight into a phone store and bought himself a cell phone. Then he walked out and dialed her number. They spoke countless times each day, in the morning and evening, and during the night if she was afraid to sleep. He never minded when she called, even if he was hard at work or in the middle of a discussion with other mathematicians. Only Sarah had his number and the phone was always nearby, so that whenever it rang his hand would shoot out and whatever he had been doing was instantly put on hold.

He assured her he would be back in a week; in the meantime he was trying to ready the house for her and their son. It was comfortable but not at all equipped for a family. He had already found a crib, a car seat, and a stroller, but they were secondhand, and he hoped Sarah wouldn't mind. She teased him sweetly and told him not to worry, said Victoria had promised her some of Justine's things, and they would manage fine. Twice he sent her flowers — red roses and, two days later, an exotic arrangement of sunflowers and wild grasses. Both times she telephoned him straightaway, and he didn't need to see her face, could hear the sheer delight in her voice and imagine it in her eyes.

But despite all their precautions and plans, John did not make it to Sarah's side in time to witness the birth of his son. Sarah went into labor the day before he was to leave Cambridge. She called him before she left for the hospital, saying the ambulance was on its way and Joy and her grandfather would accompany her. He was not to worry, she said, but there was undisguised apprehension in her voice.

John was in the Cock and Bull having dinner with a colleague and his wife when she called. Drained of color, he shot up from the table, grabbed his coat, and flew out the door with the phone to his ear. He took a taxi all the way from Cambridge to London, hoping to catch a flight to Paris, but the driver told him access to Heathrow was choked with traffic because of a petrol lorry accident, and he thought the train would be the surer bet. John caught the last Eurostar out of Waterloo Station. When he finally had his ticket and was waiting to board, he fished the phone out of his pocket and called Sarah.

His hand was shaking and his voice had dried up, and when Joy answered he could hardly speak.

"She's okay," Joy said.

"Is she really? You're not just saying that . . ."

"No, Daddy, she's just fine. They've got her on a monitor, and the baby's heartbeat is strong and steady. Stay cool."

John sank to a chair in the waiting lounge and dropped his head into his hand.

"Thank God," he said with a deep sigh of relief.

"But the labor's going quickly, so if you want to see that little guy of yours make his way into this world you'd better get yourself here as fast as you can."

Just then there was an announcement that his train was ready to board, and John exacted a promise from Joy that she would call him every half hour to let him know their progress.

With his reflection staring back at him from the window, he stood in the train's snack bar and drank several glasses of wine to quiet his nerves, but he was terrified. He wanted to tell someone his son was being born but given the way he looked, wild-eyed with trembling hands, he did not wonder that people averted their eyes or stood at a distance. He checked his watch every few minutes, and when after half an hour the phone had not rung, he dialed Joy, but there was no answer. He hung up and dialed again but still she did not answer. Suddenly light-headed, he made his way back down the aisle to his seat and lowered his head between his knees.

Finally, the call came. It was Sarah's voice, weak but serene. "I'm holding him. I'm holding our child," she whispered. "Oh John," she said, barely strong enough to speak, "he's so beautiful. He's so beautiful."

John had a chance to say only a few words before Joy snatched the phone away, saying she'd call him later, that Sarah was too exhausted to talk more, but they were both well and doing beautifully.

John flung his head back onto the headrest and suddenly warm tears were streaming down his face. He thought he must have fallen asleep then.

The sound of the ringer woke him, and he answered thickly.

"Sarah?"

But it wasn't Sarah. At first it seemed there was no one on the line, but he could hear rustling and what sounded like sniffling, then Jack's voice.

"John?"

"Hey, Jack, you're a great-grandpa now," John said, rubbing his eyes. But there was no laughter on the other end of the line, no cries of jubilation. An alarm rang out in John's brain and his head flooded with heat.

"What's wrong?" he shouted. "What's happening? Damn it, talk to me!"

The anger in John's voice roused Jack to respond.

"She hemorrhaged," he said, "Sarah did. They did their best to stop it. She just . . . she just faded . . ." Then his voice broke.

John felt as if he couldn't breathe. He shot to his feet and bolted down the wagon and out the pneumatic doors to the baggage racks where the air was cooler. He shouted into the phone trying to get somebody to talk to him but all he could hear were voices in the background and somebody crying. Nobody seemed to hear him.

The train stopped just then. A town named Ashford. From there they would enter the long tunnel under the English Channel, and for twenty minutes phone communication would be cut.

He stood in the aisle against the baggage

racks for the rest of the journey. When the train emerged from the tunnel, he tried to call several times but no one answered. There seemed to be nothing anybody had to say anymore.

It was a terrifying loneliness he felt that night crouched in a corner on a suitcase, jostled by the train, watching people pass by with curious stares. He did not know it was possible to feel such emptiness.

When he reached the hospital he wasn't sure where to go. With a steady voice, he gave Sarah's name to the receptionist, but they had a hard time finding it because of the way he pronounced it. There was a moment of confusion, and then the receptionist said, *"BREE-den, ah oui."* He didn't know any French and didn't know how to ask what had happened, so he just took the room number she wrote down for him on a piece of paper and walked in the direction she pointed.

It took him a while to find the elevator, and then he wondered if maybe they'd misunderstood because there were patients on this floor, mothers with babies. As he scanned the room numbers on his way down the hall he began to feel hopeful. He hurried, picking up his stride, his heart surging in his chest, muttering prayers under his breath, and then he was there in her doorway. For a moment he was confused. Her face was colorless against the white sheet and there were tubes in her arms and monitors blinking overhead. But then she turned her head toward him and smiled weakly.

"John," she sighed, and in an instant he was beside her, taking the hand she held out to him.

"Sarah," he whispered. "My precious Sarah."

"Have you seen him?" she mumbled weakly.

"Don't talk, just rest."

"Have you seen him?"

"Not yet. I came straight to you. They told me . . ."

"I know. I'm sorry."

He hushed her, kissed her lips.

"Joy tried to call back . . ."

"It's all right," he whispered. "It's okay now. I'm here."

"I just lost a little too much blood, that's all. But I'll be all right now. Now that you're here." She smiled again and touched his chin with her finger. "He's gorgeous. He looks like you."

He looked into her eyes and saw so much love there he could hardly breathe, didn't know what to do.

"John . . ." she began.

"You just rest now."

"No," she insisted weakly. "I have to tell you this. Before I . . ." She smiled at him. "Before I believe it never happened."

"What?"

She paused, her eyes searching his. "I must have been very close to death."

"I know."

"It wasn't a dream. It really wasn't."

"What?"

"I think I was gone from here for a while."

"But you're back. You're safe now."

"What I'm trying to say is . . ." She faltered. "I was with Will." She smiled then. "He wasn't that terrible little whiny baby he used to be. . . ." She laughed weakly. "He was beautiful, the way you and I had always seen him inside. It was like I was in the presence of this enormous energy. So full of life. I got the feeling he knew about everything, about us, and it was like he was thanking me, thanking us, for having loved him. I don't remember much else, but I know, as surely as you are with me now, he was with me then."

John looked into her eyes and smiled.

"Do you believe me?" she said, curling her fingers around his cheek.

"I believe you, Sarah."

"You do?"

"Of course I do."

They exchanged a look of perfect complicity.

"Now." Sarah beamed. "Go see your son."

He returned her smile, then buried his lips in her neck. "In a minute," he murmured. "First things first."

About the Author

Janice Graham's previous novel, *Firebird,* was an international best-seller and translated into eighteen languages. A native of Kansas, Graham has lived in France, Greece, Israel, and Los Angeles, where she studied film at the University of Southern California. Her screenwriting credits include the feature film *Until September.* She and her daughter, Gabrielle, now divide their time between Paris and Wichita, Kansas.

The Classic
Military Vehicles Story

Chris McNab

The Classic
Military Vehicles Story

The History Press

Published in the United Kingdom in 2011 by
The History Press
The Mill · Brimscombe Port · Stroud · Gloucestershire · GL5 2QG

British Library Cataloguing in Publication Data
A catalogue record for this book is available from the British
Library.

ISBN 978-0-7524-6204-2

Cover images: *Front*: A British Chieftain tank. *Back*: A Willys
'Jeep' armed with three Vickers K machine guns. (both images
courtesy of Cody Images).

Typesetting and origination by The History Press
Printed in China

CONTENTS

ACKNOWLEDGEMENTS

There are several people I would like to thank for their assistance in producing this book. As always, I much appreciate the friendship and support of Jo de Vries at The History Press, and to all the design and editorial team there. Special thanks go to Ted Nevill of Cody Images, who always manages to produce an excellent selection of photographs under short timescales.

The roots of the internal-combustion engine go back deep into history. Elements of what would become the world's principal motive power are detected as far back as the 13th century, at least in concept. Yet in practical terms it was really the second half of the 19th century in which the internal-combustion engine became both an efficient design and a production reality. During the 1860s, engineers such as the Belgian Jean Joseph Etienne Lenoir, Frenchman Alphonse Beau de Rochas and Germans Nikolaus Otto (helped by the future famous names Gottlieb Daimler and Wilhlem Maybach) and Karl Benz, amongst others, made the internal-combustion engine a practical alternative to steam power.

Furthermore, on 29 January 1886, Karl Benz patented the first petrol-powered automobile, propelled by a four-stroke engine. By 1888 the Benz Motorwagen was in production, and a revolution in personal and eventually commercial transport took place.

◀ A de Dion-Bouton motorcycle, here converted rather implausibly into a military vehicle by bolting a Maxim machine gun to the front. The conversion was made in 1899 by the man pictured here, one F.R. Simms. (Cody Images)

Despite the German lead, mass production of automobiles, based on line assembly technologies, was actually an American invention, pioneered by the Oldsmobile Company in 1902. Henry Ford later famously refined the principle, the great Model T vehicle rolling off his assembly lines at a rate of several every hour. Once such volume production was copied abroad, the world was on its way to a transport revolution.

The internal-combustion engine ... is ready to carry whatever one wants, wherever it is needed, at all speeds and distances.
General Charles de Gaulle

Often in the history of engineering, developments in the civilian world inspire the military community, and the advent of the automobile is a case in point. At the end of the 19th century, military technology was also undergoing huge changes. The invention of breech-loading machine guns, rifles and artillery had exponentially transformed the volume of firepower a modern army could generate. Increased firepower meant increased ammunition consumption, which in turn demanded more efficient, scalable logistics. Railways – another transport revolution in that most innovative of centuries – could take ammunition and troops so far, but alternative means were required to shift them from the railhead to the battlefront. Steam-powered tractors and trucks had both entered service by the end of the

1860s, but by the early 1900s petrol- and diesel-powered vehicles were starting to take over and expand possibilities.

Although for many decades to come most soldiers' equipment would still be drawn towards battle by horses, this new breed

of vehicle offered exciting new options for improving the flow of war materiel. To this day, logistics remains the primary function of the bulk of the world's military vehicles.

As we shall see, internal-combustion powered vehicles provided the possibility of a whole new breed of mobile weapons systems. It was a relatively natural step to marry firepower with vehicle, and once embraced by the military, the automobile revolution met a whole world of tactical and utility requirements, in turn producing staff cars, tanks, armoured cars, artillery tractors, transporters, communications vehicles, ambulances, armoured personnel carriers, amphibious assault vehicles, mine-clearers and numerous other types. As such vehicles proliferated, the battlefield was utterly reshaped in terms of speed of manoeuvre and the firepower deployed, and mechanization became central to victory.

This book will describe a journey through the landmarks of military vehicle design since the beginning of the twentieth century to the present day. The technological evolution within that time period is astonishing, stretching from vehicles that offered walking-pace maximum speeds and the firepower of a rifle, up to modern combat vehicles capable of high speeds on both land and water and the capabilities to destroy entire city blocks in a few seconds. In telling this story, however, we will also acknowledge the human truth that no matter how powerful the vehicle, there is always a human being inside whose survival depends upon it.

In 1899, a photograph was taken of a potentially new generation of fighting vehicle. It consisted of a de Dion-Bouton four-wheel motorcycle, looking like a cross between a pram and a car and powered by a diminutive rear-mounted petrol engine, but with a Maxim machine gun bolted to a front bracket by one F.R. Simms (see Introduction – the rider in the photograph on p.7). The machine gun was to be operated by the driver, who in the photograph decorously steers the vehicle one handed while aiming the weapon. A modicum of armoured protection for the rider came from a shield mounted around the gun.

To modern eyes, the de Dion-Bouton fighting vehicle appears almost laughable. Yet it is an important innovation, not least because it represents the concept of combining weapons and vehicles, providing a mobile platform with greater firepower than a horse-mounted cavalryman, and without all the logistical hassles of producing bulky fodder for a hungry animal. Others were more ambitious, however. They saw the potential for creating *armoured* vehicles, machines that not only projected firepower, but at the same time protected the crew inside from return fire.

◄ *This German Ehrhardt BAK 1906 armoured car is little more than a truck covered with armour plate and surmounted with a turret holding a 50mm cannon. Such were typical designs of the early twentieth century. (Cody Images)*

◄ *The French CGV 1906 armoured car had a strikingly boxy design, but could deliver a decent (for the time) road speed of 45km/h (28mph). Significant numbers were exported to Russia. (Cody Images)*

Did you know?
Many early armoured vehicles were armoured in name only – the metal on the 1904 Austro-Daimler armoured car, for example, was a mere 4mm thick, scarcely enough to stop a common rifle bullet.

What we see from the 1890s, therefore, was the emergence of what we today call the armoured car. Military designers took the chassis of civilian or sporting vehicles and built upon them armoured superstructures, complete with weapons

15

The US also produced several varieties of armoured car during the World War I years. Here is an Armoured Car No. 2, dated to around 1916. (Cody Images)

The French Renault FT 17 was a particularly important French light tank/armoured car, as it introduced the fully rotating gun turret, hence providing the vehicle with a 360-degree fire capability. (Cody Images)

(typically machine guns) projecting through ports or mounted in turrets. In 1900, the British John Fowler & Company clad a steam traction engine in armour plate and used it for battlefield logistics during the Boer War in 1901–02. Furthermore, in 1904 the Austrian engineer Paul Daimler took a standard car chassis and surrounded the passenger compartment with thin armour plate, topping off the whole superstructure with a rear-positioned revolving turret fitted with a single Maxim machine gun or two Schwarzlose machine guns. It was manned by a crew of four, and its 30kW (4hp) 4-cylinder engine could power it to a maximum road speed of 45km/h (28mph). Auguring the future of military vehicles, the 'Austro-Daimler' also had four-wheel drive, giving it a decent off-road capability. Two years later

and the French produced a similar vehicle in the form of the Charron, Giradot & Voigt (CGV) 1906. This was constructed along similar lines to the Daimler armoured car, but its turret was armed with a single French 8mm machine gun.

By the time World War I broke out in 1914, armoured cars had become part of the arsenal of most European nations, being produced by the likes of Schneider (France), Vickers (Britain) and Ehrhardt (Germany). The latter, in 1906, manufactured an armoured car that even incorporated an upward-firing 'anti-balloon canon', creating the world's first mobile anti-aircraft vehicle. Many of these armoured cars were intended for light scouting duties in colonial outposts. Typically, they were heavy and slow, and did not cope well with the particularly difficult terrain.

The limitations of early armoured cars were revealed during the global conflict that erupted in 1914. While useful on roads, they were simply unable to cope with the mud and tortured landscape into which many fronts descended. (They still found applications in flat, mud-free environments, such as the Middle East.) The true significance of the conflict for wheeled vehicles was in logistics. Horse-drawn supply columns still dominated, but armies increasingly turned to the power of diesel and petrol to transport ammunition, equipment and supplies to depots near the frontlines. Many of the vehicles used were simply requisitioned civilian types. Germany, for example, appropriated or put into reserve 3,000 tractors, 7,700 heavy trucks and 50,000 cars. At a more ad hoc level, the British also used adapted London buses as crude troop transporters.

A column of British trucks rolls towards the frontline. The truck at the front appears to be the Leyland Three-Tonner, thousands of which were used in the war by the British Army and Royal Flying Corps. (Cody Images)

19

A convoy of Ford Model T pick-up trucks, in British service, moves through African landscape in 1917. Ford vehicles were used in a range of military roles in World War I, from haulage through to field ambulances. (Cody Images)

Did you know?

At the battle of the Marne in September 1914, the French ordered 600 Parisian taxi drivers to deliver 6000 troops to the battlefront.

By far the greatest producer of trucks used for military purposes during the conflict was the United States. The Packard 3-ton Army Truck – originally intended as a gun tractor but repurposed as a troop and supplies carrier – was actually in service before the war began, and it served throughout the conflict. The official wartime government-produced trucks, built according to specifications from the Quartermaster Corps, were known as 'Liberty trucks', and came in 1.5-ton (Class A) or 3–5-ton (Class B) versions, entering service in 1917. Other US manufacturers such as White, GMC and

▶ *Requisitioned civilian types made up a large part of the military vehicles on the Western Front. The London double-decker bus here has been repurposed to deploy carrier pigeons. (Cody Images)*

22

◀ 'Little Willie', the forerunner of the British Mk I tank, was powered by a 78kW (105hp) Daimler engine, and its outer shell was actually boiler plate rather than armour. (Cody Images)

◀◀ During World War I, trucks were soon applied to combat roles as well as logistical tasks. Here what appear to be Thorneycroft trucks are mounted with 13pdr 9cwt anti-aircraft guns. (Cody Images)

Did you know?

Such was the success of the Nash Quad that it led to Nash becoming the world's largest producer of military trucks by the end of the war.

Nash Motors delivered more than 60,000 vehicles for military use, including the Nash Quad, which offered the four-wheel drive capability so useful over the terrain of the Western Front. US trucks were also sold in large numbers to the Allies. Britain, for example, made heavy use of the Ford T cargo truck, adapting it for various utility purposes, including serving as ambulances.

ENTER THE TANK

While trucks and cars became a vital part of behind-the-lines support, on the battlefield itself an armoured vehicle was about to emerge that would change the very nature of land warfare. This vehicle, what we today call the 'tank', would not have been possible without an alternative form of traction to the standard wheel, which delivered a high ground pressure and was therefore unsuitable for use over soft ground. The answer was the 'continuous track', more popularly known as the 'caterpillar track'. Instead of wheels, this system utilized a continuous band of metal links that wrapped around drive wheels. It offered several appreciable advantages, including a low ground pressure, the confidence to negotiate soft terrain and the equal ability to cross trenches. Early experiments with this form of drive dated back to the 1830s, but during the early 1900s the system had been developed to

◀ A boxy American tank/half-track, 'Caterpillar G-9', negotiates a steep slope. The vehicle was made by the Holt Tractor Company, one of the pioneers of the caterpillar track system. (Cody Images)

A British Mk I tank during trials in 1916. Here we can clearly see one of the 6pdr guns mounted in a sponson on the side. The definitive Mk IV version used shorter-barrelled guns. (Cody Images)

a production state by various commercial manufacturers, for applications in industries such as farming and logging. What British military engineers spotted was a way to utilize the continuous track for an entirely different form of armoured vehicle.

In 1915, the Admiralty Landships Committee was formed under the authority of the First Lord of the Admiralty, Winston Churchill, with the purpose of creating a powerfully armed, well-armoured fighting machine to break the deadlock on the Western Front. The first convincing prototype was 'Little Willie', essentially a three-crew armoured box powered by a Daimler 6-cylinder petrol engine to a monotonous top speed of 3.2km/h (2mph). It utilized the continuous-track drive, but was steered mainly by two external wheels connected at the rear. The design was

modified to produce 'Big Willie' in late 1915, which had an improved trench-crossing capability, and it was this model that led to the first production tank in history, the Mk I, of which the British Army ordered 100 in February 1916.

The Mk I was revolutionary. Rhomboidal in shape, with its continuous track running around its outer edges, it had an eight-man crew (four of whom were gunners) and a top speed of 6.4km/h (4mph).

Its outer armour had a maximum depth of 12mm (0.47in.), sufficient to stop most contemporary small-arms fire, although insufficient to withstand a hit from an artillery shell. In its 'Male' version it was armed with two 6pdr cannon mounted in side sponsons and four Hotchkiss machine guns; the 'Female' infantry support version had six machine guns only.

The Mk I tank was infernal to operate, filled with deafening noise and choking gun and exhaust fumes, and it was plagued by mechanical unreliability. Subsequent versions, including the major production model, the Mk IV of 1917, improved the situation progressively, although they remained difficult vehicles to man. But there was no denying their impact on the battlefield, at least in terms of shock value. First used during the battle of the Somme in 1916, and prominently at the battle of Cambrai the following year, the tanks could grind through barbed wire that was impenetrable to infantry, blazing away at close range with cannon and machine gun. The crew remained inside, shielded from the bullets flying around them. Although the early tanks were not battle winning – at least, not yet – they proved that heavily armed, armoured vehicles could have a significant place in fighting wars.

I managed to get astride one of the German trenches... There were some Germans in the dug-outs and I shall never forget the look on their faces.

Captain H.W. Mortimore, who commanded one of the first tanks ever to go into battle, 15 September 1916

◀ The cumbersome French St Charmond tank was an awkward design, the nose of which tended to dig into the ground when the tank was travelling across uneven ground. Here we can see the main armament, a 75mm gun. (Cody Images)

Britain was not the only one to be developing tanks, however. The French were also pushing ahead with their own designs at the same time; in fact, France would produce more tanks (3,870) during the war than Britain (2,693). The first (1917) was the Schneider CA-1, weighing 14.8 tonnes (14.6 long tons), manned by a crew of seven men and armed with a single 75mm gun plus two machine guns. In action, the CA-1 and its improved versions gave a generally poor performance, its fuel tanks being easy to catch fire and struggling manfully when crossing wide trenches or shell-holes. An alternative vehicle that also entered service in 1917 was the St Charmond, unusual for the large portions of hull that overhung the tracks at the front and rear. It again was armed with a single 75mm main gun and multiple (four) machine guns, and just like the Schneider it also waded awkwardly across rough ground.

Yet we must not over-emphasize the failings of these vehicles. These were early days for armoured firepower, and the concept proved itself sufficiently for tanks to enter service with most combatants. The Germans developed the large and unwieldy Sturmpanzerwagen A7V, essentially a chronically unstable iron room armed with a 57mm gun and six machine guns,

Did you know?

The Holt Company also produced a steam-powered tank, which had the unfortunate tendency of turning into a cauldron if a bullet punctured one of the boilers.

◄ *The Schneider Char d'Assaut (CA) tank was another French wartime tank design. It was armed with a 75mm cannon and two Hotchkiss 8mm machine guns, and was manned by a crew of six. (Cody Images)*

► World War I saw motorized logistics used on an extensive scale for the first time. Here we see a group of despatch rides, on Douglas motorbikes, in front of a varied collection of militarized trucks. (Cody Images)

British soldiers have here converted a simple flatbed truck into a mobile weapons platform by adding a Vickers 0.303in. machine gun. Such designs would have been more suited to security duties than trench warfare. (Cody Images)

33

with a road speed of 12.9km/h (8mph) – only about twenty were produced. From America came the Holt Gas-Electric tank, which utilized a Holt petrol engine to power a generator, supplying electricity to drive motors. The types of tank also diversified. French and British designers produced the first light tanks, smaller and lighter armoured vehicles with improved cross-country and on-road performance.

They included the British Medium Tank A 'Whippet' and the French Renault FT-17; the former could do a positively giddy 13.4km/h (8.3mph) on a good surface.

By the end of World War I, therefore, the world's armies had several new war-fighting and utility vehicle types in their arsenal. They included heavy tanks, light tanks, armoured cars, trucks and various logistical vehicles, such as artillery tractors (many of these hefty monsters remained steam-powered). The interwar period would see both vehicles and tactical concepts refined, laying the foundations for the centrality of armour and mechanization in the next world war.

The interwar period reshaped the nature of military vehicles, both tactically and technologically. Britain, France, Germany, the Soviet Union and Italy all began to draw up more ornate doctrines of mechanized and armoured warfare, looking at ways in which new generations of faster, more powerful vehicles could speed up manoeuvre, achieve decisive breakthroughs and support the infantry on the attack.

In the world of tanks, three classes of armoured vehicle emerged: heavy, medium and light. Heavy tanks were designed to smash through enemy defences, and included types such as the French Char 2C and the Soviet T-35 Model 1932. Both of

Near Moscow in 1939, a large body of T-26 tanks conduct manoeuvres. The T-26 was a light infantry support tank, and it was the most numerous vehicle in Soviet armoured service at the time of the German invasion in 1941. (Cody Images)

The M1 Combat Car was a light armoured vehicle used by US cavalry forces from the late 1930s until 1943, by which time it was obsolete. Less than a hundred of all variants were produced. (Cody Images)

these tanks were multi-turret designs; the T-35 Model 32, for example, had one main turret mounting a 76mm howitzer, plus four sub-turrets, each armed with either a cannon or a machine gun. Although the multi-turret approach would persist in some designs into World War II, it was generally dropped across all classes of tank in favour of the single turret, armed with a convincing cannon able to take on both enemy fortifications and opposing tanks.

A step below the heavy tank class was the medium tank. In neat theory, the medium tank was designed to exploit the gaps created by its heavier brethren, using its speed and firepower to push behind the frontlines. Examples of the type include the Vickers Medium Mk II, armed with a quick-firing (QF) 3pdr gun and with a top speed of 21km/h (15mph). Rather more impressive on the speed stakes was the American Christie series of tanks. Despite weighing nearly the same as the Vickers tank, the T3E2 could gallop along off-road at up to 32km/h (20mph), powered by a V12 Curtiss engine. The Soviets went even further, applying the Christie suspension system (which had independent suspension for each wheel) in their BT-2 fast tank – with a maximum speed of 100km/h (62mph), the name was apt.

… the internal combustion engine which, if it is armoured, possesses such a fire power and shock power that the rhythm of battle corresponds to that of its movements.

General Charles de Gaulle

Did you know?
The Soviet T-35 1932 tank was powered by a M-17M 12-cylinder petrol engine that generated 373kW (500hp) and a max speed of 30km/h (18.6mph).

Then came the light tanks category, which sat just above armoured cars. In essence, light tanks served a similar purpose to armoured cars, replacing the traditional mounted cavalry in reconnaissance and fast assault roles. Typically mounted with machine guns or very light cannon, classic examples of the light tank include the Vickers T15 and Matilda, the Italian Fiat 3000 Model 1930 and the Soviet T-26 Model 1933.

The general principle behind the heavy, medium and light classifications was that the heavier vehicles were slower but had more substantial armour and armament, while the lighter vehicles had more insubstantial armour and armament, but the advantages that came with speed. During the 1930s, however, there was a gradual shift in priorities, incomplete by the beginning of World War II in 1939.

Generally speaking, and with much variation between nations, tanks began to acquire greater depth of armour and more powerful guns, essential qualities if they were to survive against both enemy tanks and the new breeds of anti-tank weapons entering service. The German *Wehrmacht*, finally freed from its Versailles Treaty shackles in 1935, embraced this evolution better than most, and entered World War II with one of the most powerful and tactically proficient armoured forces in Europe. The two key German tanks of the 1930s were the PzKpfw II and PzKpfw III. The former emerged in 1934, and was mainly armed with machine guns only (at least during the interwar years), and had an armour depth of 13mm (0.51in.) in

◀ A large group of Soviet BT-7 tanks rolls forward during pre-war manoeuvres. The BT-7 was lightly armed and armoured, but could do a top speed of 86km/h (53mph). (Cody Images)

◄◄◄ Vast formations of PzKpfw Is parade before Nazi dignitaries at Nuremberg in the late 1930s. The display looks impressive, but the Panzer I was virtually outdated by the end of the Poland campaign in September 1939. (Cody Images)

◄ The Spanish Civil War (1936–39) provided the Germans with a testing ground for their concepts of armoured and mechanized warfare. Here we see German motorbike and sidecar combinations leading an SdKfz 265 command tank and a PzKpfw I light tank. (Cody Images)

the Ausf B variant. Between its entering service and the production of the final variant (Ausf F) in 1942, the armour crept up to 80mm (3.1in.) thick. The PzKpfw III medium tank more than doubled its armour depth between 1936, its in-service

date, and 1938, and its firepower went from a 37mm gun to a longer-range 50mm gun by 1939. Just before the outbreak of the war, the PzKpfw IV entered service with a 75mm gun – variants of this vehicle would become the core of the German Panzer force.

The German armoured force set a benchmark against which other armies could be measured. Some emerge from the comparison favourably. The Soviets, for example, upgraded many of their medium tanks from 37mm or 47mm guns up to the 75mm standard during the 1930s, and created one of the greatest tanks of the war in doing so – the T-34 (see next chapter). The French had a robust force of more than 2,600 tanks in 1939, including the Char Léger FCM-36 and the advanced Somua S-35, which had a cast rather than riveted

hull and an armour depth of up to 55mm (2.2in.). Yet only the Char B heavy tank had a 75mm gun, and only 172 of those were produced by 1939. British, Italian, US and Japanese armoured forces were even more heavily dominated by light and medium machine-gun armed types. The scene was set for many unequal struggles.

MULTIPLE TYPES

The interwar period was not only fruitful for developments in tank technology. Indeed, the 1920s and 1930s were also

The tank marks as great a revolution in land warfare as an armoured steamship would have marked had it appeared amongst the toilsome triremes of Actium.

General Sir Ian Hamilton

The Japanese Type 93 Sumida armoured car could be converted from road travel to travel on rails in a matter of about 10 minutes. It was a hefty vehicle used primarily in the Sino-Japanese War (1937–45). (Cody Images)

Did you know?
The PzKpfw IV was the most prolific battle tank in the German armoured inventory – 9,000 were produced between 1939 and 1945.

This diminutive vehicle is a Polish TKS tankette, a two-man armoured car fitted with a single 7.92mm Hotchkiss wz.25 machine gun. These were no match for German armour in 1939. (Cody Images)

notable for increasing the sheer variety of what we classify as military vehicles. For utility vehicles such as trucks and staff cars, the progressive armies abandoned the old policy of using civilian types and oversaw the construction of dedicated military vehicles suited to operating robustly in rough conditions. The Soviets thereby created a range of trucks that would see them through the war and into the Cold War period, vehicles such as the GAZ-AA 4x2 1.5-ton truck, a licence-built copy of the Ford AA Model 1929, and the ZiS-5, which remained in production between 1931 and 1958. The Germans produced a similarly excellent vehicle in the Henschel 33D1, which had a maximum road speed of 60km/h (37mph), and in Britain the likes of Morris-Commercial, Leyland, AEC and Bedford worked up a range of serviceable trucks for needs ranging from light utility to heavy haulage.

Although the Belgian company Fabrique Nationale would later become famous for making small-arms, here we see another of their early products – motorbikes for Belgian Army despatch riders. (Cody Images)

Specialist vehicles also proliferated during the interwar years. As the models and sizes of artillery pieces increased, artillery tractors became more critical to the mechanization of armies. A classic example was the British AEC Matador 0853, a 4x4 wheeled medium artillery tractor powered by a 70.8kW (95hp) AEC 6-cylinder engine;

◄◄ *Fleets of trucks needed drivers to man them. Here a British Army recruit driver is put through his paces over rough terrain at the Royal Army Service Corps in Feltham in 1939. (Cody Images)*

◄ *This French Citroen half-track is being used as a personnel carrier, its capacity expanded by a seated trailer unit. The drum at the front was meant to help when the vehicle was negotiating ditches. (Cody Images)*

it was generally used for drawing the QF 3.75in. AA gun and the 5.5in. Medium Gun. Wheeled propulsion had its limitations over rough ground, though, so tracked and semi-tracked designs were also developed and fielded. Semi-tracked versions included the German Sdkfz 7 and 9 and the French P 107. The Japanese and Russians, by

contrast, preferred fully tracked artillery tractors, often influenced by agricultural designs but with a military twist in fittings and equipment.

It should be noted that the half-track design proved particularly amenable for the development of what are known today as armoured personnel carriers (APCs), vehicles designed to deploy small squads of infantry safely to the combat zone, and deliver additional firepower when they got there. The awkward-looking British Burford-Kegresse half-track had a drive track made of metal-reinforced rubber, but it could carry up to twelve infantrymen plus its two-man crew at a pace of 35km/h

(22mph). It was armed with one or two 0.303in. Vickers machine guns.

The French adopted a more innovative approach to troop carriage in the Lorraine 38L. It consisted of a fully tracked tractor, which could carry six passengers, plus

▼ *Armoured vehicles soon proved that they had many applications other than war-fighting. This Soviet light tank has been converted into a simple bridgelaying vehicle. (Cody Images)*

▶ The French Laffly W15T was an all-terrain vehicle based on the early S15 artillery tractor model. When it wasn't towing a gun, it could be used as a personnel carrier or reconnaissance vehicle. (Cody Images)

▶▶ Experiments in amphibious tanks began prior to World War II. Here is a Soviet T-37 tank, the first fully amphibious tank to enter mass production and military service. (Cody Images)

a towed covered trailer that held an additional six soldiers. The true pioneers of early APCs, however, were the Germans. In 1939, the 1st Panzer Division received the SdKfz 251 half-track, capable of holding up to twelve personnel and transporting them at a speed of 52.5km/h (32.5mph), with support fire from two 7.62mm MG34 machine guns. What would prove to be so impressive about this half-track, and similar versions developed during the war years, was its versatility as a platform. In total, no fewer than twenty-two special-purpose variants were produced during the vehicle's lifetime, these including communications vehicles, ambulances and rocket launchers.

Looking back to the beginning of the interwar period, the 1920s brought the introduction of history's first practical self-propelled gun, the British Birch Gun, in 1925. Mounting artillery upon a vehicle chassis was attractive to tacticians on many levels, not least because it offered the prospect of engaging the enemy but then quickly moving before return fire could be brought to bear. The Birch Gun took the chassis of a Vickers medium tank and mounted it with an 18pdr field gun. The Mk II version followed shortly after, which swapped the 18pdr for a 75mm field gun,

Did you know?

Between 1936 and 1939, the Soviets built 42,000 GAZ-A staff cars, which were essentially licence-built copies of the American 1927 Ford Model A.

the new gun permitting the elevation range necessary for it to engage both ground and aerial targets. Few Birch Guns were built, and there was little interest in integrating them substantially into the British Army, so they were pulled from service in 1931. It would take wartime conditions for the British to revisit the self-propelled gun concept.

The list of specialist vehicles produced between 1918 and 1939 is a substantial one. It includes mobile workshops, ambulance vehicles, tank transporters, communications vehicles and bridging trucks. Yet while the technologies of military vehicles were developing rapidly, many authorities were still uncertain about the applications of armour and mechanization in modern warfare. The Germans, at least in practical implementation, were probably the most advanced in theory and training, and the events of 1939 and 1940 would dispel all illusions about the centrality of vehicle power on the battlefield.

The opening German campaigns of the war, in Poland in 1939 and Western and Northern Europe in 1940, were defined by what mainly post-war historians labelled *Blitzkrieg* ('Lightning War'). At its core, this group of tactical principles is based around focused, fast penetrations by armoured units through weak points in the enemy frontline, the tanks punching deep into the enemy rear areas to encircle army formations, destroy communications and unsettle the tactical response. Following the breakthrough were mechanized and traditional foot-slogging infantry, who would consolidate the gains.

The first two years of the war seem to be the ultimate vindication of *Blitzkrieg*, as previously mighty opponents of Germany fell in a matter of weeks. Panzer forces used specialist command-and-control vehicles such as the Panzerbefehlswagen III Ausf E to coordinate the tanks and other units on the battlefield. (This tank actually had a dummy gun fitted on the turret, to avoid drawing the enemy's attention to the vehicle's command role.) Using superior powers of movement, the German Panzer IIIs and IVs inflicted very heavy losses on Allied light and medium tanks, although at the same time learnt that the light PzKpfw Is and IIs were too insubstantial to take a place in the vanguard. In North Africa in 1940 and 1941, the Germans also took a brutal toll of British/Commonwealth Matilda, Valentine and Stuart tanks, not least because the Panzer forces operated in close cooperation with anti-tank guns.

In June 1941, Hitler widened his imperial ambitions when he invaded the Soviet Union in Operation Barbarossa. Although

◄ Japan's tanks were generally poor-quality types with little in the way of decent armour or armament. The Type 89A Chi-Ro tank seen here had a maximum armour depth of just 17mm (0.66in.). (Cody Images)

▶ A PzKpfw IV tank, here seen painted white for snow camouflage during operations in the Ukraine. The Panzer IV was the workhorse tank of the German Army, and its chassis was used for a variety of other vehicles, including tank-destroyers and the Wirlbewind anti-aircraft vehicle. (Cody Images)

the first months of the German campaign cut swathes of destruction through Soviet forces, and was brought to a stop only before gates of Moscow in December 1941, for the Panzer arm there was also a shock in the form of one of the greatest tanks in history – the T-34.

DEFINING TANKS

The T-34 had entered production in 1940. Riding on the Christie suspension system and particularly wide tracks, it delivered very low ground pressure, ideal for traversing the snows and mud of Russia's seasonal extremes, and at speeds of up to 53km/h (33mph) – faster than both the Panzer III and IV. It had thick armour (up to 80mm/3.1in.), the presented depth of which was increased by the hull and turret having steeply sloped sides to deflect enemy shot. Most importantly, it was armed as standard with a decent 75mm gun.

In short, the T-34 was fast, powerful and well-armoured. Many German tank crews watched in dismay as their shot bounced off the T-34's steel, or they were outmanoeuvred and outgunned in action. Furthermore, in 1943 the Soviets began producing an even more formidable variant, the T-34/85, which had an 85mm gun and thicker armour around the turret and hull. Only the poor state of training among Soviet tank crews prevented the T-34 from

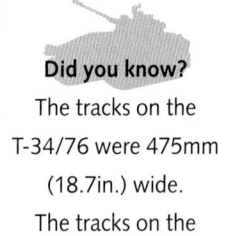

Did you know?
The tracks on the T-34/76 were 475mm (18.7in.) wide. The tracks on the early Panzer IVs, by contrast, were just 360mm (14.2in.) wide.

The British tank here is the Matilda, which served the Allies well in reconnaissance roles during the campaigns in North Africa, and also in some Pacific campaigns. Its principal armament was a 2pdr cannon. (Cody Images)

◄ The US M3 Lee/Grant tank served in both the American and British armies and featured a dual turret design: the hull-mounted side turret held a 75mm gun, while the top turret had a 37mm gun. The high profile unfortunately made the tank easy to target. (Cody Images)

having a crushing effect on German forces. To make matters worse for the Axis, the T-34 was quick to produce, and including post-war manufacture more than 84,000 rolled out of Soviet factories.

Germany's answer to the T-34, and other high-volume Allied tanks such as the US Sherman, came in the form of improved versions of the PzKpfw IV and also some of the most impressive tanks in history – the PzKpfw V Panther and the PzKpfw VI Tiger. Regarding the Panzer IV, this core tank went through numerous upgrades to armour and weaponry, the ultimate incarnation of the latter being the 75mm KwK 40 L/28, which was perfectly capable of disposing of a T-34. The Panther tank was even more formidable. It was designed specifically in response to meeting not only the T-34, but also the Soviet KV-1 heavy

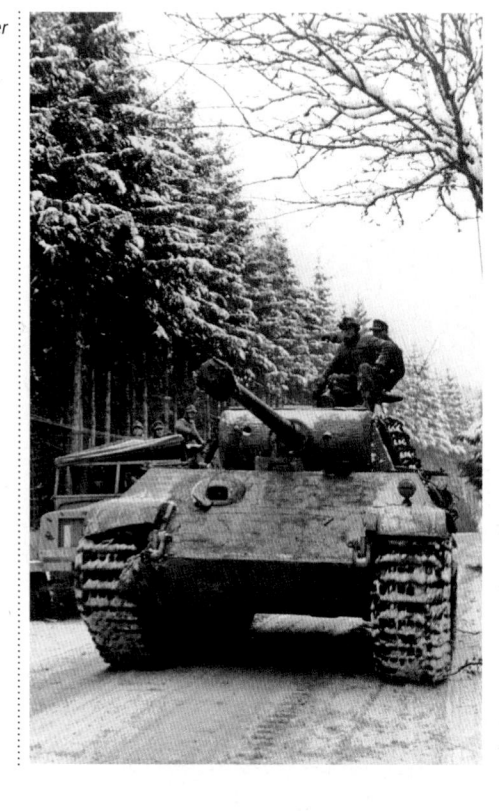

Did you know?

The Panther had a five-man crew, who consisted of driver, radio-operator/hull machine gunner, commander, gunner and loader.

tank, a slow-moving massively armoured monster which later, in the KV-2 variant, even had a 152mm gun and armour up to 110mm (4.33in.) thick. The Panther imitated the sloping armour, low profile and wide tracks of the T-34, and its powerful Maybach engine could push it to 46km/h (29mph). It was also armed with the long-barrelled 75mm gun, with seventy-nine rounds of ammunition carried internally.

The Panther was thrown into action, too early, in 1943 at the battle of Kursk, where mechanical problems plagued its performance. It never entirely freed itself from technical issues, but improved versions of the Panther became some of the feared armoured vehicles on all fronts, accounting for hundreds of Allied tanks.

The Panther's potential claim as the war's greatest tank had a contender in the Tiger.

◀ *The formidable Tiger tank was the last thing many Allied tank crews saw. Its combat strength lay in its 88mm gun, which could penetrate virtually all Allied armour of the time.*
(Cody Images)

Did you know?

The M3 had a length of 4.45m (14ft, 10in.), weighed 14,700kg (32,413lb), had a maximum armour depth of 51mm (2in.) and could travel at a max speed of 58km/h (36mph).

The Tiger's development actually began before the war, but when it emerged on the battlefield in 1942 in North Africa there was nothing to touch it. It was a huge vehicle, weighing 55 tonnes (54 long tons) and with armour equalling the depth of that on the KV-2. Its bulk and weight made it slow, but it was armed with an 88mm gun that delivered exceptional reach and penetration. Like the Panther, it suffered from its fair share of mechanical issues during the early years of operation, but it became one of the Allies' worst nightmares, particularly with the creation of the Tiger II variant, which had thicker armour and a more potent 88mm gun. In one incident, not untypical, in Normandy in 1944 a single Tiger took out twenty-five Allied tanks before it was finally destroyed. Only limited Tiger production numbers and growing Allied air superiority controlled the Tiger's effects.

Apart from the American M26 Pershing tank introduced at the very end of the war, with its 90mm gun, and the Sherman Firefly (see below), the Western Allies made few tanks that directly matched a Panther or Tiger in terms of capabilities. British tanks such as the Covenanter, Crusader, Churchill and Cromwell were nonetheless effective when used intelligently (which they were often not), and huge numbers of American vehicles, also supplied in large numbers to British and Soviet forces through Lend-Lease (the programme under which the US supplied Britain, the Soviets, France and other Allied nations with materiel during 1941–45), helped tip the balance of armoured warfare in the Allies' favour.

◄ The M4 Sherman tank was available in huge numbers to Allied forces, and could hold its own against a Panzer IV. One of its unfortunate design attributes was that it could be hard to escape from if hit and burning. (Cody Images)

Light armour was particularly numerous in Western Allied armies. For example, the M3 Light (Stuart) Tank, served in both American and British forces – in the latter it was nicknamed the 'Honey'. Lightly protected, and armed with a 37mm gun, it was more irritating than dangerous to heavy tanks, the Stuart was soon taken out of frontline combat, but like the legions of other light vehicles and armoured cars used in the war, it proved excellent for reconnaissance and infantry support duties. Some of these vehicles did acquire firepower heavy enough to worry a medium tank – the British AEC Mk III was fitted with the same 75mm gun as mounted on many Cromwell and Churchill tanks. Other examples include the US M8 and T18E2 Boarhound, and (on the opposing side) the German SdKfz 234. Combined with fleets of scout cars with lighter armament, including the M20 Armoured Utility Car and the Daimler Scout Car, infantry were rarely far away from some form of armoured vehicular support.

The greatest of all the Allied armoured vehicles, however, was the M4 Medium (Sherman) tank. A good all-round medium tank, the basic Sherman M4A1 had a 75mm M3 gun, a maximum armour depth of 62mm (2.4in.) and a speed of 34km/h (21mph). Its profile was a bit high, and it had the unfortunate capacity to burn easily when hit by an enemy shell. But with US industrial might behind it, the Sherman was produced in decisive numbers – about 50,000 (all variants). Later versions such as the M4A3 and British Sherman Firefly were even fitted with powerful, long-barrelled 76mm guns capable of taking out a German Tiger or Panther.

▶ The Sherman Firefly was a regular Sherman fitted with a 17pdr (75mm) high-velocity gun, sufficient to destroy even a German Tiger or Panther. They were put to good use during the advance through Normandy in 1945. (Cody Images)

▶▶ A British Churchill tank grinds through the tough bocage terrain in Normandy, 1944. Despite being a large tank, it could move fast – in fact it had to be regulated to 61km/h (38mph) to stop it damaging its tracks and suspension. (Cody Images)

SPECIALIST AND UTILITY VEHICLES

Tanks such as the Sherman, T-34 and Panzer IV provided the chassis for a very large number of specialist vehicles, including assault guns, tank-destroyers, self-propelled guns, rocket launchers, mine-clearing vehicles, armoured flame-throwers and bridge-layers. The Churchill and Sherman tanks in particular were converted into some real oddities, including the Sherman DD (Duplex Drive), a Sherman tank transmuted into an amphibious vehicle via a collapsible fabric screen and two propellers mounted at the rear.

Tanks themselves required whole fleets of support machines to keep them in action, particularly in the form of recovery and engineering vehicles. The hull and chassis of the Sherman tank, for example, were used as the platform for an A-frame crane and winch with a 27,210kg (60,000lb) pull capacity, this American vehicle was known as the M32. German armoured units made a similar conversion of Panther tank to produce the Bergepanther tank recovery vehicle.

Half-tracks also came of age in World War II, and not only in the APC role that they established in the interwar period. The German SdKfz 250 and 251 platforms

Did you know?

The Churchill ARVE (Armoured Vehicle Royal Engineers) could perform a number of pioneer duties depending on the variant, ranging from laying log roads and filling trenches with bundles of brushwood, to destroying enemy bunkers with a 290mm spigot mortar.

◄ An International Harvester TD-18 tractor pulls a US 155mm howitzer through the jungles of the Solomons in 1943. The terrain on most Pacific islands meant that heavy tractors such as these were in high demand. (Cody Images)

The Morris Quad CMP was an Allied artillery tractor, typically used to pull 17pdr or 25pdr field guns. The CMP initials stood for Canadian Military Pattern. (Cody Images)

The German vehicle here is the eight-wheeled SdKfz 232 radio-command vehicle; the wire frame fitted over the top of the car is a long-range radio antenna. The eight-wheel configuration made these vehicles highly mobile. (Cody Images)

were mounted with a broad variety of weapon systems, such as turret-mounted 20mm cannon (SdKfz 250/9) and 75mm Pak 40 anti-tank guns (SdKfz 251/22). For the Allies, the defining half-track was the Carrier, Personnel Half-track M3, produced in quantities approaching 43,000. With a lively cross-country capability and a top speed of 64km/h (40mph), the initial model could carry up to thirteen occupants and could be reconfigured to all sorts of useful utility and combat configurations. For instance, the M4 81mm Motor Mortar Carriage (MMC) did exactly what it stated, the rear cargo bay holding an 81mm that could be fired either mounted or dismounted. The T19 version, meanwhile, had nothing less than a 105mm M2A1 howitzer on the back, making an improvised self-propelled gun. Other versions included field ambulances and engineer vehicles.

World War II spawned a whole new generation of light, multi-purpose utility vehicles. On the Allied side, the most famous of these was undoubtedly the Willys MB Jeep, manufactured by Willys and the Ford Motor Company between 1941 and 1945. These tough, fast, four-wheel drive vehicles, with their iconic shape, were applied across numerous utility roles from serving as staff cars to handling battle casualties, and many versions were mounted with machine guns for light defence. Similar vehicles in wartime service included the Volkswagen Kübelwagen (German), Humber Heavy Utility Car (Britain), and the GAZ-67B (Soviet Union).

Light but fully tracked vehicles were also developed to carry out minor resupply

◀ The Bren Gun Carrier was a useful British/ Commonwealth light utility and reconnaissance vehicle. Here Canadian soldiers have adapted the carrier to take a Vickers machine gun. (Cody Images)

At Salerno in Italy, a German SdKfz 10 ascends some tricky terrain. The SdKfz was a light utility vehicle and troop transporter; here we see it pulling a light anti-tank gun, while the gun crew sit in the back. (Cody Images)

◄ These Special Air Service (SAS) troopers are driving one of the most famous light utility vehicles of the war – the Willys 'Jeep'. Here they have armed the Jeep with three Vickers K machine guns. (Cody Images)

and reconnaissance duties. The British, for example, utilized the Universal Carrier Mk I built by Vickers-Armstrong. This vehicle was powered by a 63.4kW (85hp) 8-cylinder Ford V8 engine and could carry four people (including two crew) inside a light armoured box, with defensive armament provided in the shape of a 0.303in. Bren Gun (hence the vehicle's popular name, the 'Bren Gun Carrier'), and sometimes a 14mm Boys anti-tank rifle. A similar vehicle produced by the Americans was the M28 Weasel, which was appreciated for its ability to lug cargo over almost any terrain, including snow and mud, and for its amphibious abilities – it could achieve a maximum water speed of 6km/h (4mph).

Wartime innovation proved that a core vehicle could be adapted to a multitude of applications, and the world of trucks

was no exception. Improved techniques of industrial mass production ensured that the truck was the primary means of frontline resupply (although horses were still used in huge numbers, particularly on the Eastern Front). The Axis powers were actually the least well served in terms of truck volumes during the war: Germany produced nearly 346,000 trucks between 1939 and 1945, alongside Italy's 83,000 and Japan's 166,000. Looking at the Allies, the British manufactured a respectable 481,000 and the Soviets a weak 197,000, but both these powers were supported by the vast

◄ *The Hotchkiss H35 was a light tank adopted into French service in the mid-1930s. It was a small vehicle just 4.22m (13ft 10in.) long, and despite upgrades in 1939 it performed poorly during the battle of France in 1940. (Cody Images)*

◀◀ *US Lend-Lease provided the Red Army with many of its trucks. Here Soviet infantry in 1945 are riding American GMC 6x6 2½-ton vehicles, powerful heavy lifters. (Cody Images)*

◀ *Dodge trucks fulfilled a huge variety of purposes during World War II. The WC 54 vehicle here is serving as an ambulance during the advance into Germany in 1945. (Cody Images)*

➤ *Conditions on the Eastern Front put the harshest strain on trucks. Soviet trucks, such as the ones seen here, were very basic vehicles, but coped well with sub-zero temperatures. (Cody Images)*

➤➤ *The Soviet T40A was designed as an amphibious tank, but following its poor performance in the Winter War against the Finns it was converted to land operations only. (Cody Images)*

output of the United States – 2,382,000 units, with large numbers exported as part of Lend-Lease.

The US vehicles included some of the great names of automotive history: the Dodge WC series, the GMC 6x6 and the

formidably powerful Mack NO, a 6x6 vehicle stretching 7.5m (24ft 8in.) long and weighing in at 7.5 tonnes (7.4 long tons). The Germans also had some very fine trucks, such as the Büssing-Nag 454 and the Opel Blitz, but they simply weren't available in the massive truck fleets enjoyed by the Allies.

TAKING TO THE WATER

A distinctive innovation of the World War II years was the rise of the amphibious vehicle. The sheer diversity and extent of the war's theatres, which ultimately stretched from Scandinavia down to the South Pacific waters, meant that successfully negotiating water obstacles was essential for both overland advance and for coastal invasions. On the whole, Germany made limited investment in amphibious assault vehicles.

From 1942 it introduced small numbers of the Land-Wasser-Schlepper amphibious tractor onto the Eastern Front and North Africa, which could cross short expanses of water with twenty passengers on board while also towing a floating cargo trailer. A lighter, but more prolific, German amphibious vehicle was the Volkswagen Schwimmwagen (Types 128 and 166). This useful little vehicle was essentially a Kübelwagen fitted with a flotation body and a chain-driven propeller fitted to the rear of the 'hull'. The angle of the front wheels acted as the rudder.

For the Allies looking across oceans and seas to reclaim occupied territories, the need to develop amphibious vehicles was much more imperative. The primary duty of such craft was to transfer troops and materiel from offshore vessels to invasion

Did you know?

The Schwimmwagen had a maximum water speed of 11km/h (7mph), a useful pace for crossing a contested waterway under fire.

◄ *US amphibious power is evident as a large number of LVT 4 amphibious assault vehicles make the run-in to the beach of Iwo Jima in February 1945. The tracks themselves delivered the propulsion through water. (Cody Images)*

Did you know?

The DUKW performed as well on land as on water, with a range of 640km (400 miles) on a single fuel tank and a maximum road speed of 80km/h (50mph).

beaches, as quickly and securely as possible, then fight on land if necessary. In terms of wheeled vehicles, the British developed the 12-tonne (11.8-long ton) Terrapin Mk 1 as an amphibious cargo transporter, and the Americans produced the Ford General Purpose Amphibious (GPA), basically a waterborne version of the Willys Jeep. The most famous of all, however, was another American vehicle, the DUKW 'Duck'. More than 21,000 of these useful 6x6 vehicles were built by GMC from 1942. Looking distinctly more like a boat than a truck, it could carry twelve troops or 2.3 tonnes (2.26 long tons) of equipment across water at a speed of 10km/h (6mph) for a range of 93km (58 miles). The DUKW was used extensively across most Allied theatres, including the D-Day landings in Normandy on 6 June 1944.

The pressures to perfect amphibious warfare were nowhere greater than in the Pacific. US Marine and Army forces were, from 1942, fighting an 'island hopping' campaign across the planet's biggest expanse of water, putting troops and equipment onto tiny scraps of land in the face of blistering resistance and difficult coastal terrain.

The Landing Vehicle, Tracked (LVT) series of amphibious assault vehicles were an ideal solution to conducting these operations successfully. They were fully tracked craft, the tracks providing both a method of propulsion through the water and good traction on soft beaches or muddy coastal regions. The original LVT 1 was capable of carrying eighteen fully equipped soldiers or 2,041kg (4,500lb) of cargo, but its lack of armour was soon revealed as a major

◄ A British despatch rider on a BSA motorcycle stops to talk with the crew of a Humber Light Reconnaissance Car (LRC). As its name suggests, the LRC was used by reconnaissance troops, who relied mainly on its fast 72km/h (45mph) top speed to get it out of trouble. (Cody Images)

issue on the contested Pacific beaches. Therefore subsequent LVTs in the series received increasingly heavy armour and firepower, turning them into true assault vehicles. The LVT(A), for example, was mounted with the turret from an M3 tank, complete with its 37mm gun. (More typical armament was combination of 0.3in. and 0.5in. Browning machine guns fixed into swivelling shield mounts.) Such vehicles were a critical ingredient in the success of American amphibious actions in the Pacific, and they were also used in Italy and Northern Europe in the final months of the war in those theatres.

Amphibious vehicles, as we have seen, were just one example of the impressive innovation shown by military engineers and designers during World War II. In a war defined by manoeuvre and the quest for tactical advantage, military vehicles were now the critical factor in land forces warfare. Not only were they at the vanguard of major advances, but they were also central to logistics, battlefield engineering, command-and-control (in the form of radio cars), medical evacuation, amphibious assault and numerous other duties. The war ended in Europe in May 1945, and in the Pacific the following September. The lessons learnt in World War II were taken forward into the vehicle designs of the Cold War, where they would achieve new levels of sophistication in a computerized age.

In a sense, the basic types of military vehicle changed little in the second half of the 20th century from those established during World War II. The Cold War battlefield was still a place of tanks (of various weights), armoured cars, APCs (in their broadest categories), trucks, light utility vehicles and so on. What changed dramatically was the lethal potential of even the smallest vehicles through the invention of modern anti-tank guided missiles (ATGMs), which also brought the corresponding need for advanced armour and protection systems. In turn, these developments also brought about a new military vehicle type – the infantry fighting vehicle (IFV) – a sort of midway point between the APC and what became known as the main battle tank (MBT). All these changes took place in the context of increasing computerization of war-fighting and logistical technologies, increasing the capabilities of Cold War military vehicles exponentially compared to their World War II predecessors.

Looking first at tanks, which from the 1950s had to operate in the increased threat environment presented by ATGMs, what we see is a progressive development of armour, armament, mobility and fire-control. Armour now had to cope with the shaped-charge warheads of ATGMs, as well as more effective tank shells, such as the high-explosive anti-tank (HEAT) and the later armour-piercing, fin-stabilized, discarding-sabot (APFSDS). For this reason, during the 1960s–80s, armour tended to

The US M60A2 tank had a weapon that could fire both conventional shells and MGM-51 Shillelagh anti-tank guided missiles. The vehicle was not a success, however, and was withdrawn from service in the early 1980s. (Cody Images)

Armor – The Combat Arm of Decision

Motto of the US Army Armor Branch

An Iraqi T-55 tank lies destroyed north of Kuwait City in 1991. Soviet-era Iraqi armour was completely outclassed by coalition tanks, and also fell easy prey to coalition strike aircraft. (Cody Images)

Did you know?

In the 1970s, the British introduced their Chobham multi-layered, composite armour, designed to defeat shaped-charge warheads. First fitted to the Chieftain tank, its exact composition is still a secret.

become both heavier (i.e. thicker) and more multi-layered in design to cope with more sophisticated warheads. In the 1980s explosive reactive armour (ERA) made its appearance. ERA consisted of explosive panels on the outside of the tank

that detonated when struck by a shell; the outward force of the ERA blast was intended to counter the inward impact of the enemy shell or missile. The threat of nuclear, biological and chemical (NBC) warfare also meant that many tanks had to be fitted with the required survival systems for operating in radioactive or poisonous environments.

As armour became harder to puncture, so tank guns increased in their power, range and lethality (aided by the ammunition types described above). A good example of this shift can be seen in the British Centurion tank of the 1950s. Between 1945 and 1959 its main armament was progressively upgraded from 76mm to 83.8mm to 105mm. Centurions were eventually replaced in the 1970s by the Chieftain tank, which had a 120mm gun

and was wrapped in the new Chobham armour. Soviet forces also upgraded their firepower. The great series of Soviet postwar MBTs – vehicles such as the T-54, T-55, T-62 and T-72 – took on heavier armament, working up from the 100mm guns of the T-54 and T-55 to the 125mm guns of the T-64, T-72 and T-80.

▲ The AMX-30 is a French MBT, but here it is seen in Saudi Arabian service. It is armed with a 105mm gun, plus a coaxial 20mm cannon, and it is protected by a full NBC suite. (Cody Images)

➤ *The M60A1 Armoured Vehicle-Launched Bridge (AVLB) is fitted with a scissors-type bridge that can be emplaced across an 18m (60ft) gap in just two minutes. Retrieval takes 10 minutes. (Cody Images)*

Did you know?
Gyroscopic gun stabilization was introduced into Cold War tank gun systems. It meant that a tank gun could maintain its aim point even when the tank was moving over rough ground.

The United States moved with the trend also. In the early post-war years, and apart from small numbers of heavy tanks such as the M103 with its 120mm gun, the US Army fielded three principal medium tanks – the M46, M47 and M48 – which

were armed with 90mm guns. Yet with the introduction of the M60 in 1956, the Army switched to the 105mm gun, and versions of the M48 were also upgraded to this calibre.

As MBTs were up-gunned, they were also beneficiaries of profound changes in fire-control systems. Optical range-finders were introduced on tanks such as the M47 and German Leopard 1, then in the 1960s

◄ The M1 Abrams virtually represents perfection in tank design. Its only drawback is the voracious fuel consumption from its gas turbine engine, although this same engine can push the vehicle to speeds of more than 70km/h (43.5mph). (Cody Images)

laser range-finders began to appear. A decade later, and sophisticated fire-control computers started to transform armoured warfare gunnery, automatically adjusting the aim point to compensate for factors such as wind speed, air temperature, ammunition type and even barrel condition, dramatically increasing the first-round hit probability.

Many Cold War MBTs fall into the category of 'classic' – the Soviet T-72; the British Chieftain and later Challenger; the Israeli Merkava; the French AMX-30. To illustrate how far MBT technology has come since 1945, however, the US M1 Abrams is a perfect example. Entering service in 1983, the M1 was a big vehicle of more than 57 tonnes (56 long tons), but driven by a 1,119kW (1,500hp) Lycoming gas-turbine engine it could develop a maximum speed of 67km/h (42mph). Its sophisticated

The British Chieftain was one of the great tanks of the Cold War era, with an excellent long-range gun. Here we are looking down the business end of the 120mm L11 series rifled gun. (Cody Images)

Many of our tanks were hit. We had never come up against anything like it before.

Israeli tank crewman, having encountered anti-tank missiles in the Yom Kippur War, 1973

Chobham-type armour was resistant to all but the heaviest anti-tank weapons. The initial main gun was a 105mm rifled type, but with the 1990 M1A1 variant this was upgraded to a 120mm smoothbore gun that, allied to its impressive computerized fire-control suite, could engage targets with first-round kills out to 3,000m (3,280yds). Standard equipment included a commander's independent thermal viewer, position and navigation control, internal diagnostic systems, integration into networked command-and-control and full NBC protection. Such vehicles are a long

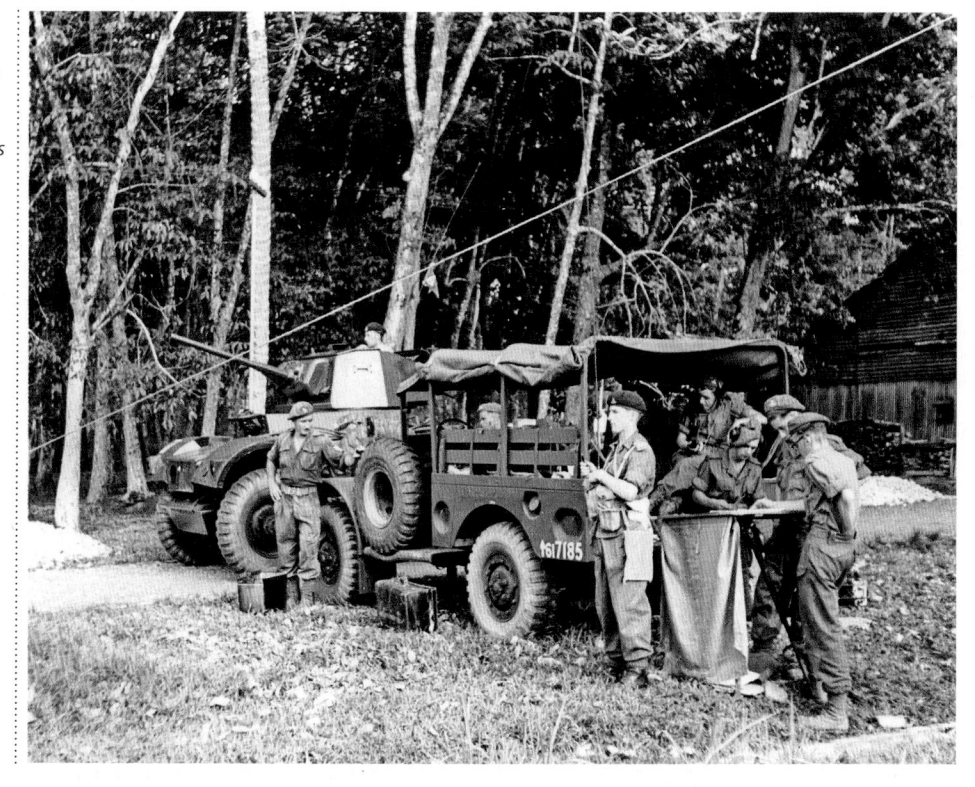

▶ *During counter-insurgency operations in Malaya in 1952, a British Daimler armoured car parks alongside a Dodge truck that is being used as a mobile command post. (Cody Images)*

way from the welded or riveted steel machines of the World War II era.

APCS AND IFVS

The end of World War II put the final nail in the coffin of horse-drawn military logistics, and while footslogging would remain a part of infantry life to this day, the requirements of manoeuvre warfare meant that larger numbers of soldiers would be deployed to the frontlines in APCs. Crudely categorized, modern APCs fell into two types – wheeled and tracked. Tracked APCs offered superior off-road capability but lower speeds on-road, whereas the reverse was true of wheeled variants. The Cold War armies, therefore, tended have a mix of both types.

The greatest of the Cold War APCs, at least in terms of distribution and influence, has to be the US M113. Designed to be airportable, the M113 was essentially a powered metal box, the outer walls made of aluminium armour. It could carry eleven troops plus its two-man crew, was armed with a single pintle-mounted 0.5in. machine gun, and had a maximum road speed of 68km/h (42mph), and was also amphibious.

Although basic, the M113 demonstrated an incredible ability to be adapted and modified to multiple and various purposes. Just a few of its variants included mortar carriers, smoke generators, anti-aircraft vehicles (equipped with both multi-barrel cannon and surface-to-air missiles), cargo transporters, engineer and recovery vehicles and command posts. It demonstrated what would be a distinctive trend of post-war APCs – the ability to transform

Did you know?
The M113s were amongst the most mass-produced military vehicles in history. More than 80,000 of the type have gone into service to date.

US infantry pour from the back of an M41 APC in Korea. APCs are designed to give infantry a fast, protected journey to wherever they are needed, and provide fire support as appropriate. (Cody Images)

their combat capability by adding the latest combat systems. All of a sudden, light armoured vehicles became a genuine threat to MBTs and supersonic jets, even as they performed traditional logistical and infantry-deployment roles. What this led to was the creation of dedicated IFVs, vehicles designed to serve like an APC but offer greater firepower in attack and support roles.

Soviet-era vehicles formed the armoured contingent of many Cold War armies, particularly those in the Middle East. Here is a BMP-1 formerly in the service of the Iraqi Army. (Cody Images)

The Soviets led the way with vehicles such as the BMP-1 in the late 1960s. It was a tracked, fully amphibious vehicle capable of carrying three crew and eight additional troops, but what separated it from any of the Western vehicles around at the time was its extensive turret-mounted armament – one 73mm cannon, an externally mounted Sagger ATGW, and a 7.62mm coaxial machine gun. Here was

Did you know?

The AT-4 Sagger wire-guided anti-tank missile was used heavily by the Egyptians during the 1973 Yom Kippur War against Israel. Some sources say that 800 Israeli tanks were lost to the missile.

a light armoured vehicle that delivered as much combat force as utility.

The appearance of the BMP-1, and other similar types, prompted Western forces to develop their own ranges of IFVs, the turreted configuration offering a diverse spectrum of weapon mounts. During the 1970s, European IFVs included the German Marder and the French AMX-10P, while the United States produced the Armored

Infantry Fighting Vehicle (AIFV), which was essentially an M113 with improved armour, fully amphibious capability and a turreted 25mm Oerlikon cannon. Like many IFVs, the AIFV also had firing ports in the hull so all the soldiers carried inside could shoot outwards. The greatest of the American IFVs, however, has been the Bradley M2/M3 of the 1980s, with its advanced armour system plus one 25mm Bushmaster Chain Gun, one 7.62mm coaxial machine gun and two TOW anti-tank missile launchers. The British equivalent would be the Warrior Mechanised Combat Vehicle (MCV), produced from the mid-1980s and armed with a 30mm Rarden cannon. IFVs also come in wheeled varieties, such as the

Did you know?

The Warrior MCV has a crew of three, plus it can carry seven fully equipped soldiers. Its armour type is classified but it has full NBC protection and night-vision equipment for each of its crew members.

The Alvis Striker was a tracked anti-tank missile launcher, and part of the Scorpion family of vehicles. It was armed with ten Swingfire anti-tank guided weapons (ATGWs), fired from a five-missile launcher unit.

US Marine Corps' eight-wheeled LAV-25, which has seen service in mortar, anti-tank, air defence, recovery, command-and-control, logistics, fire-support and electronic warfare variants. As experience in war zones such as Iraq and Afghanistan has proven, IFVs can provide a dramatic firepower advantage and increase the survivability of the troops they carry inside.

It should be noted that there are several more categories of modern armoured combat vehicles other than those described above, but space does not allow for more than a brief summary. IFVs, to some extent, stole the thunder of traditional armoured cars, hence the newer Cold War generations carved their niche by offering greater levels of fire support, similar to those of medium tanks. The French Panhard ERC 90 F4 Sagaie, for example, is a six-wheeled vehicle armed with a 90mm gun with full computerized fire-control. Vehicles offering similar firepower include the Canadian Cougar Wheeled Fire Support Vehicle and the American Dragon Armored Fighting Vehicle.

Artillery was also increasingly mechanized, with numerous types of self-propelled guns on both tracked and wheeled mounts (good examples are the French GCT 155mm and the South African G6 Rhino), and also tactical missile launchers such as the formidable Vought M270 Multiple Launch Rocket System (MLRS). The latter was capable of destroying a football pitch-sized area of ground in seconds with a twelve missile barrage of submunition-loaded rockets firing to ranges of 300km (186 miles). Against aircraft threats, light armoured vehicles and also trucks were mounted with SAM systems and multi-barrel/multiple radar-controlled

A British FV107 Scimitar armoured vehicle conducts a patrol in Bosnia in the 1990s. The Scimitar bears a resemblance to the FV101 Scorpion Light Tank, but it is armed with a 30mm Rarden cannon instead of a 76mm gun. (Cody Images)

Did you know?

During the 1991 Gulf War, Iraqi forces struck by the MLRS found the experience of airburst shrapnel warheads so traumatic that those who survived called the system 'Black Rain'.

➤ The SA-6 Gainful consists of three SA-6 surface–to-air missiles mounted on the modified chassis of a ZSU-23-4 air defence vehicle. The missiles can reach out to a range of 22km (13.7 miles). (Cody Images)

air-defence cannon. Battle-tested in conflicts including several Arab-Israeli wars and major Indo-Pakistan tank battles in the 1970s; all such armoured systems conspired to make the modern battlefield more lethal than ever.

LIGHT AND HEAVY LOGISTICS

Changes in the world of military utility vehicles since the end of World War II have been less visibly dramatic than those that have occurred in armoured fighting vehicles. Yet the Cold War era did introduce important transformations in capability, and also some new formats. There have also

◄ 'Jeep'-type vehicles extended their service well into the Cold War. Three US soldiers here stare from their Jeep across the Berlin Wall during the 1960s; an M60 machine gun is mounted on the back. (Cody Images)

The legendary 'Humvee' is an extremely versatile infantry platform, capable of taking various different weapons configurations. The vehicle here has a .50-cal Browning M2HB in a dedicated weapons system on the roof. (US Army)

been some post-war vehicles justifiably described as classics. Probably the two most recognisable are the British Land Rover and American High-Mobility, Multi-Purpose Wheeled Vehicle (HMMWV), the latter commonly known as the 'Humvee'.

The Land Rover Half-Ton was, from the 1960s to the 1980s, the standard British Army light utility vehicle, derived from Land Rover's commercial Series IIA. Its four-wheel-drive configuration, and its resilience in the face of all manner of

punishment, made it a popular addition to the British armed forces. The Humvee, by contrast, emerged after the military Land Rover had been in service for twenty decades. It replaced a range of existing small utility vehicles, and also became a major combat vehicle for both the US Army and the Marine Corps, with weapons mounted including Mk 19 grenade launchers, M2, M249 and M240G/B machine guns, and even TOW missile systems.

Regarding logistics, military trucks began a steady shift from simple workhorses to advanced vehicular platforms. During the 1950s, many military trucks, particularly in the Soviet Union, were war surplus stocks, but during the 1960s and '70s new designs were introduced such as the KrAZ-255B, Ural 375D (both Soviet), M813 (United States) and Land Rover One-Tonne (UK).

What was distinctive about these vehicles was that they variously incorporated design features that would later become standard fit, as armies moved away from militarized civilian trucks to purpose-built military vehicles. These features included driver-operated tyre-pressure adjustment, fully enclosed cab with NBC protection, multi-type brake systems and even amphibious capabilities (such as the American M520 Goer and the British Stalwart).

Trucks also became platforms for roles other than logistics. The redoubtable US M35 series of trucks, over its impressive

Good logistics is combat power.
Lieutenant-General William G. Pagonis

The M35 series of trucks has given its logistical capabilities to the US Army from the 1950s to the present day. This specific cargo variant is the M44A2. (Cody Images)

The huge weight of modern MBTs requires equally impressive tank transporters. The vehicle here is a Unipower 8x8 transporter, capable of pulling an entire Abrams tank on its trailer. (Cody Images)

60-year plus lifespan, variously transmuted into fuel transporters, engineering vans, wrecker and construction vehicles and even heavily armed gun trucks, acting as escorts to US convoys travelling through the Vietnamese hinterland during the Vietnam War (1963–75). In time, the militarization of trucks would lead to their being used in a broader range of combat roles, particularly as mounts for rocket-launchers, cruise missiles, SAM and tactical nuclear missile systems. Because of their increasingly combat-oriented profile, many trucks began to receive armoured cabs – the Soviet Ural 4320B cab could shrug off fire even from mighty 12.7mm (0.5in.) machine guns. Modern trucks, therefore, contribute more to the operational life of armed services than just shifting supplies from A to B.

While the largest of trucks could transport entire tanks, at the small end of the scale the post-war period also saw investment in

So-called 'KP cars' were manufactured by both Volvo and Scania, and featured an unusual tower design for the machine gunner. They were used by Swedish UN personnel in the Congo in the 1960s. (Cody Images)

Logistics ... as vital to military success as daily food is to daily work.
Captain A.T. Mahan

numerous light utility transports designed to improve small-unit logistical capabilities. Some types bordered on the ingenious. One such example was the M561 Gama-Goat (again American), a six-wheel vehicle split into a front powered section and a coupled rear section. The flexible coupling between the two halves meant the Gama-Goat could haul itself across the most convoluted terrain, it was also amphibious. These light utility vehicles lifted the load from the soldier's backs and the flow of supplies to the frontline was much improved.

SECURITY

The Cold War was a time in which many armies, particularly those with membership of NATO, were heavily involved in peacekeeping operations, facing situations somewhere between humanitarian aid

Did you know?

Introduced in 1956, the US M274 Mechanical Mule was essentially nothing more than a chassis, an engine, and a seat and controls for one driver, yet it could usefully haul a 450kg (1000lb) load on its flatbed.

and outright combat. For this reason, the post-war period to the present day has seen the increasing use of security vehicles – essentially unarmed or lightly armed utility vehicles with armour protection from insurgent attack or riot. In the UK's long-standing deployment in Northern Ireland, the affectionately titled Humber 'Pig' was a regular feature, taking up

to eight occupants and with duties that included riot control (in which it was fitted with window grilles, additional armour and anti-barricade equipment) and casualty evacuation. Another, heavier, option was the Alvis Saracen six-wheel APC, which for peacekeeping duties often had its machine-gun armament removed. Other popular security vehicles of note are the German Sonderwagen SWI, the British Sandringham 6 (essentially a six-wheel armour-clad Land Rover) and the American Commando Ranger. Security vehicles are still very much a part of armed forces, their relevance undiminished by the end of the Cold War in 1989.

◀ *White-painted vehicles of United Nations Interim Force in Lebanon (UNIFIL) go on patrol. The vehicle at the rear is the 6x6 Sisu XA-180, an APC with capacity for two crew and 10 passengers. (Cody Images)*

In 1991, a US-led military coalition launched Operation Desert Storm, the campaign to eject the Iraqi forces of Saddam Hussein from occupied Kuwait.

The land campaign saw modern American and British armour utterly dominate the older Soviet-era armoured vehicles, although as much through superior training

This Saudi multiple-launch rocket system (MLRS), like others of its type, has devastating area-fire potential. Each missile from its launcher can dispense submunitions (cluster bombs) over dozens of square metres of land. (Cody Images)

US soldiers wait to collect fuel containers air-dropped in Afghanistan. Their collection vehicles are the 6x4 M-Gator Military Utility Vehicle. (Cody Images)

In Operation Desert Storm, such was the US and British superiority in tank gunnery that the first, and last, thing many Iraqi tank crews saw of the enemy was a muzzle flash on the horizon, seconds before the shell hit.

as advanced technology. The role of the tank seemed confirmed, and several new/upgraded MBTs entered the field around this time, including the M1A2 Abrams, the Challenger 2, the Chinese Type 90, the Russian T-90 and the French LeClerc, with third-generation gunnery, NBC, armour and navigation systems.

Since then, however, MBTs have acquired a significant question mark over their future, seen by some as out-of-date monsters rendered obsolete by the firepower of IFVs and issues of cost and long-haul transportation. At the time of writing, therefore, few countries in the world are investing in designing brand new tanks, although more are working on upgrading existing tanks to modern requirements.

The weight of emphasis has now shifted very much to the IFVs and other lighter, easily deployable armoured vehicles, such as the Bradley, LAV-25 and Warrior introduced in the previous chapter. Such vehicles have been improved with all manner of hi-tech equipment. Blue Force Tracking systems mounted on the dashboards, for example, show the occupants the positions of all friendly and enemy forces in the area in real time, the information beamed down from satellites and aircraft.

As we can see, military vehicles have now achieved ultimate sophistication and firepower. Yet heated and politically sensitive debates have been stirred by the experience of fighting in Iraq and Afghanistan since 2001. Light vehicles such as Humvees and 'Snatch' Land Rovers – a standard Land Rover Defender 110 fitted with an additional armour kit – have proved especially vulnerable to improvised

◀ A US Army Bradley sits under shelter and camouflage in desert conditions. The Bradley is a state-of-the-art infantry fighting vehicle (IFV) armed with a 25mm chain gun and TOW anti-tank missiles. (Cody Images)

Did you know?

In US forces, the Boomerang Mobile Shooter Detection System – which can be mounted on the corner of a Humvee or Bradley – can compute the exact position from which an enemy gunman fired a shot.

explosive devices (IEDs), which typically tear such soft-skinned vehicles apart. In response, more armies are now designing Mine Resistant Ambush Protected (MRAP) vehicles, which act in traditional APC/IFV roles but have far greater resistance to destruction from IEDs. These vehicles have resilient armour set at angles that deflect explosive force away from the vehicle, whether the explosion comes from directly underneath or from an IED set high on a telegraph pole. Anti-shred tyres also

Did you know?

Modern self-propelled guns such as the German Panzerhaubitzer 2000 can deliver Multiple Rounds Simultaneous Impact (MRSI) volleys, firing multiple shells at different trajectories within a few seconds, all the shells arriving on target at the same precise moment.

Sgt Chris Freeman ... squeezed the trigger and the SABOT round sliced into the second T-72. It exploded in a flash of fire and smoke...

Captain Jason Conroy, an Abrams tank commander in Iraq, 2003

prevent the vehicle grinding to a halt if the tyres are hit. MRAP vehicles include the BAe Caiman, the Force Protection Cougar H and HE, and the Force Protection Buffalo. It is likely that MRAP principles will filter into all manner of vehicles, from armoured cars to trucks.

Controversy over the right type of military vehicle for the battlefield has also dogged

A US Stryker armoured fighting vehicle provides a powerful support vehicle for American infantry teams. The metal cage around this vehicle is designed to pre-detonate incoming shaped-charge warheads. (Cody Images)

some of the most promising types of recent times. Regarding amphibious vehicles, the US Marine Corps' Expeditionary Fighting Vehicle (EFV), previously known as the Advanced Amphibious Assault Vehicle (AAAV), represents astonishing abilities on both land and water. It is self-deploying and seagoing, and can travel across water carrying seventeen Marines at a speed of 47km/h (45mph), then drive straight onto land to deploy both the soldiers and its turret-mounted 30mm II Bushmaster cannon. It has composite armour, plus protection systems from mines and NBC conditions. Despite its qualities, however, at the time of writing its future is in question, as the US armed forces seek to rationalize its inventory based on predictions of future combat conditions.

It is difficult to say which of the very latest vehicles will become 'classics', not least because the era of the 'unmanned ground vehicle' (UGV) is very much on the horizon. These are tactical and logistical vehicles that, depending on the type, can either be driven by a remote operator or can autonomously drive themselves to a given destination, using GPS guidance, advanced sensors and massive computer power to negotiate obstacles. The US Army's Multifunction Utility/Logistics and

◄ A USMC Amphibious Assault Vehicle (AAV) takes the plunge during amphibious operations. The fully tracked vehicle can transport up to twenty-five soldiers in its hold. (Cody Images)

You can have all the armour in the world on a tank, and a tank can be blown up. And you can have an up-armoured Humvee, and it can be blown up.

Secretary of Defense Donald Rumsfeld

Equipment Vehicle (MULE), for example, is an autonomous system that uses a 3D laser-radar ground mapping system to negotiate everything from trees to trenches, and even distinguishes between living and inanimate things according to their heat signatures. Powered by a hybrid electric/ diesel powerplant, with each wheel driven by separate electric hub motors, the vehicle has astonishing manoeuvrability, and can take supplies into the most dangerous areas without risking crews.

The MULE, and similar vehicles in production, are just the tip of the iceberg. It may well be that in 50 years time the great age of human-driven military vehicles will be largely behind us, at least in modern armies. Such is the irresistible nature of technological progress. The lineage of such vehicles will nonetheless stretch back to when inventors first strapped machine guns to cars, or when lozenge-shaped tanks lumbered over the battlefields of France.

◄ A vision of the future? The US Army 'The Multifunction Utility/Logistics and Equipment' (MULE) vehicle is fully robotic, and can drive itself to a given destination while autonomously negotiating obstacles. (US Army)

BIBLIOGRAPHY

Church, John, *Military Vehicles of World War 2* (Poole, New Orchard Editions, 1982)

Foss, Christopher F., *Tanks and Combat Vehicles Recognition Guide* (London, HarperCollins, 2000)

Gudmundsson, Bruce I., *On Armor* (Westport, CT, Praeger, 2004)

Jackson, Robert, *Tanks and Armored Fighting Vehicles – Visual Encyclopedia* (London, Amber Books, 2009)

McNab, Chris, *Military Vehicles* (Miami, Lewis International, 2003)

McNab, Chris, *Tools of Violence – Guns, Tanks and Dirty Bombs* (Oxford, Osprey, 2008)

Van Creveld, Martin, *Technology and War* (New York, Macmillan, 1991)

Wright, Patrick, *Tank* (London, Faber & Faber, 2000)

Decorative finishes

Most paints and staining mediums can be used to decorate plaster. Acrylic paints are ideal. They are quick drying and can be used in many ways: direct from the container; diluted with water to form washes; and mixed with specially manufactured mediums and with materials such as sand to create textures.

Brushes can be used in ways other than simply coating the surface evenly with paint. The dry brush technique allows you to apply highlights. First load your brush with paint and then brush off the excess on a cloth or piece of paper; next draw the brush over the surface and only the high points will pick up the paint. Stippling is another technique. Hold your brush vertically and dab downwards.

However, paintbrushes are not the only implements you can use to apply paint. You can spatter your cast by loading a toothbrush with watery paint, drawing back the bristles and releasing them.

Sponges can be used in two ways which will recreate the pattern of their surface texture on the cast: either dab a color on top of another or dab a dry sponge on top of wet paint to remove some of the color. Cloths can be used to wipe paint over the surface highlights of a cast.

Working area

Cover your working area with newspaper – it is the easiest way to clear away spilled plaster and is essential for decorative techniques such as spattering. Always have cleaning materials on hand; use mineral spirits to clean oil-based products and soap and water for water-based ones.

Acrylics and spray paints are ideal for plaster. Use toothbrushes, sponges and cloths as well as paintbrushes to apply paint.

Metallic paints come in many different forms and produce beautiful finishes.

Latex is a flexible mold-making material which picks up fine surface detail.

Powder paint is used to make colored plaster.

Scrim adds strength to large casts.

10

MIXING PLASTER

A good mix of plaster is essential for any plaster project. A bad mix results in a weak plaster — that is, if it sets at all! To produce a good mix, the correct amount of plaster needs to be added to the water. Weighing and measuring play no part as the process itself indicates when to stop adding plaster. This method is foolproof, easy to learn and always produces a good mix.

Feel the heat

When plaster and water are mixed together, an exothermic reaction takes place, i.e. heat is given off. You can feel this after the plaster sets: place your hand on it and feel its warmth. At this stage, the plaster is vulnerable and should not be disturbed. It will start to cool after a few minutes and although it will still be wet the plaster can be handled again. The time it takes to dry out completely depends on the size of the cast and the surrounding temperature.

Knock – don't wash

Working with plaster is a messy activity. Always make sure that both you and your work area are adequately protected before you start. Always clean your mixing bowl and tools after the plaster has set. Simply press the sides of the mixing bowl inwards and the set plaster will crack and fall away from the side of the bowl. Similarly, wait until the plaster has set on your tools and then scrape it off.

Disposal

You should never pour wet plaster down the sink or drain or wash wet plaster off under a running faucet. When the plaster has gone down the drain, it will almost certainly set, resulting in blocked pipes. If you wish to wash off wet plaster, always have a bucket of water on hand to do this. At the end of the work session, allow the solid stuff to settle to the bottom, pour the water down a land drain and dispose of the solid waste in the household garbage can.

1 Gently sprinkle the plaster as close to the surface of the water as possible. Disperse it slowly and evenly over the surface.

2 The plaster sinks to the bottom, but as you add more, it will gradually start to rise above the surface of the water to form peaks. This is the characteristic to look for.

3 When peaks start to form, allow them to settle for a few seconds to see if they sink back into the water. If the peaks remain, mix the plaster into the water, getting rid of any lumps.

5 A good example of a bad mix: not enough plaster has been added to the water. The plaster is transparent and immediately runs off the spoon.

1 Sprinkle some powder paint onto the surface of the water and mix well. Add enough color to obtain the desired tone.

4 Your mix should be smooth and creamy. To test for a good mix, withdraw a spoon slowly. The plaster should not run off the spoon and it should be opaque.

Coloring plaster
When making a colored mix of plaster, the color should be mixed with the water before adding the plaster. Any water soluble paint can be used, but it is easiest to use powder paint, as in this example. When you add the color, you should keep in mind that once the plaster is mixed, the color will be lighter than the powder.

2 Add plaster as instructed before and mix well to make sure the color is evenly dispersed.

12

CASTING

A plaster cast is made using a mold. This is a negative impression of an original (the positive). There are many different types of mold, but the casting technique is the same for all. Wet plaster is poured into the mold and is left to set; the cast (set plaster) is then removed. Some molds can be used over and over again, but in this section we look at taking casts from molds which are discarded after use.

Ready-made molds
A wide variety of ready-made molds come to us in the form of packaging – for example, yogurt cups and the clear hard plastic shapes used to hold items in place on display cards. Look out for these – you will be amazed by the plethora of interesting shapes you can cast from them. They are useful for experimenting with different decorative finishes – or you may even cast an interesting object in its own right!

1 To determine how much plaster to mix, fill the mold with water and then pour the water into the mixing bowl. Make up your mix of plaster as described on page 10.

2 Pour in the plaster slowly and evenly until the mold is half full. Let the plaster settle and then gently shake the mold from side to side to ensure that you get an even distribution.

3 Fill the mold with plaster. If you pour in too much plaster, use a spatula to level off the top. Hold the mold firmly and gently agitate to expel any air bubbles.

4 When dry, carefully remove the cast from the mold. If necessary, cut the flange with scissors and peel the plastic from the cast.

5 Use sandpaper to smooth away rough edges.

Tip You may need to support the mold to keep it level if it is an awkward shape. Use lumps of Plasticine or pieces of wood where necessary. Always replace the mold onto its support carefully after agitating the mix to expel air bubbles.

Press molds

You can push all sorts of objects into a thick bed of clay or Plasticine and pour plaster into the negative spaces.

1 Knead the Plasticine to soften it. Roll out a thick slab.

2 Coat your object with dishwashing liquid to prevent it sticking. Push it into the Plasticine.

13

3 Build a wall around the impression with strips of Plasticine. Use a modeling tool to blend where the wall joins the base to ensure an effective seal, both inside and out.

4 Take a cast. Release it by peeling away the Plasticine.

14

LATEX MOLDS

Latex is a flexible mold-making material which picks up fine surface detail from a positive. Here we demonstrate how to make a one-piece mold which will peel off easily. Once it has been made – and it is straightforward to do – multiple casts can be taken which opens up the possibilities for making and decorating.

Laying on the coats

A latex mold is made by painting on latex. The first coats are very liquid so fine detail can be sought. The following coats have thickener added so both strength and thickness can be built up. However, if too much thickener is added, the mold will not be as flexible. Use an old brush because if the latex sets on the bristles, it will be ruined. Between applying coats, keep your brush in the pot of latex to stop it drying out, and be quick to wash brushes in hot soapy water when you have finished. Keep the lid firmly on the latex pot to avoid a skin forming.

Undercuts

Undercuts (gaps between the object and the baseboard on which it rests) allow latex to flow underneath and thus prevent the easy removal of a mold. Latex is a very flexible material and is able to stretch over minor undercuts, but it is important to reduce them to a minimum. Before starting to make a mold, fill any undercuts with Plasticine.

The support jacket

Latex is a flexible material and therefore needs support. When a cast is taken, the mold is held firm by a specially made plaster support jacket. It prevents distortion when the plaster is poured in and ensures the plaster surface sets level.

Building a wall

Roll out a thick slab of Plasticine or modeling clay and cut it into strips: the width should be the depth of the positive (the object you have made a mold from) at its highest point plus 1in (2.5cm). Position these to make a wall approximately 1in (2.5cm) from the positive and smooth the clay into the baseboard to make a tight seal.

A latex fish mold

This example uses the fish relief (see page 82). Any undercuts should be filled with Plasticine.

1 Paint the first coat of latex onto the fish and onto the baseboard to make a flange all the way around. Leave it to dry. Paint on another five coats of latex, allowing each to dry before applying the next.

2 Make up a mix of latex and latex thickener and paint on three coats, again allowing each to dry in between.

3 Build a wall of Plasticine around the fish at the outer edge of the latex flange.

4 Pour the plaster in slowly and evenly; rushing may result in a collapsed wall. Tap the baseboard to expel any air bubbles.

5 When the plaster has set, remove the Plasticine wall and gently slide the whole unit off the baseboard. Turn it over.

6 Hold the latex flange and gently pull the fish out of its plaster case. The latex is very strong and flexible, so it can be pulled and stretched.

7 Peel off the latex mold and wash it in soapy water. Replace the mold in the plaster case.

Tip Integrate hanging hooks as part of the casting process to ensure a strong fixing. Bend a piece of wire and hang it in the plaster from a length of doweling which rests on either edge of the support jacket.

16 CARE AND REPAIR

No matter how careful you are, accidents will happen and plaster objects are especially vulnerable to breakage. However, if a plaster cast does break or get damaged, do not despair – everything is repairable. Two techniques are shown here which can be used to repair any plaster object. If the broken fragment is available, it is straightforward; otherwise, plaster is modeled to the required shape.

Superglue

The simplest method of repairing cracks and broken fragments is to use superglue.

1 Wet the crack by pushing in a wet brush. Hold the tube above the crack and gently squeeze so the glue falls into the crack.

2 Push the head onto the neck and hold it in place and at the same time wipe off any excess glue with a damp cloth.

3 Wet the exposed areas of plaster on both the object and the fragment which has broken off.

4 Squeeze some superglue onto the fragment and push it into place. Hold firmly in position for a few seconds until the glue has set.

Health and safety

- Always wear barrier cream and rubber gloves when working with plaster and latex as they can be skin irritants; use soapy water to wash any areas of the body which come into contact with them.

- A dust mask may be worn if the air becomes filled with plaster dust.

- Work in well-ventilated areas to avoid fumes from latex and spray paints.

- Take great care when using scalpels and metal cutters, cutting away from the body; never cut towards yourself.

Applying new plaster

Broken fragments can easily be lost or they may be shattered into tiny pieces. In this case, you must repair your object by applying layers of new plaster. The exposed plaster on the ornament needs to be thoroughly soaked with water before applying new plaster. Otherwise, the plaster on the ornament will draw out the water from the newly applied plaster and it will not set properly. Use a softer type of plaster for repair work as it is easier to form it into the required shape once it has set.

2 Make a mix of plaster and leave it to thicken. Use a brush to lay it on around the wire. Keep building up the thickness of plaster in this way.

4 Sand the repair to the necessary shape, blending it in with the overall shape. This can now be painted to finish the repair.

1 This ornament has a wire support embedded in the plaster and new plaster is built up around this. Wet the exposed areas of plaster.

3 When you have built up the shape, use a wet brush to level the repair with the surrounding surface. Leave it to dry.

ANIMAL KINGDOM

The use of a paper template is an easy way to model clay or Plasticine shapes in relief. This technique is used to model the Chameleon Clock and the Farm Animals. Once you have mastered this technique, you can carry on to make all kinds of animals, or indeed any relief shape. The Teddy Bear is cast from a bought mold and is painted with great precision to show its finely modeled forms and surface to its best effect. The Vatican Lions are plaster blanks and their surfaces are treated to give the impression of prolonged exposure to the elements.

Miniature versions of the lions to be seen outside the Vatican in Rome can be finished to resemble the weathered color of the originals. The sandstone and lichen surface is replicated by applying acrylic paint with different techniques and building up the color in stages. Placed either side of a doorway, they will exude a magnificence despite their smaller scale.

VATICAN LIONS

2 Dip a paintbrush into some white paint and then brush it out on some paper, leaving the brush relatively dry. Drag it across the surface so paint is picked up on the high points.

MATERIALS

Plaster lions
Acrylic paint:
yellow ochre,
white, raw sienna
and emerald green
Copper paint
Green patina paint

EQUIPMENT

Small palette
Paintbrushes
Toothbrush
Wide mesh
cloth/natural
sponge

1 Apply yellow ochre paint to the whole lion, creating an opaque Leave it to dry.

3 Using raw sienna paint, repeat the technique to obtain a dry brush. Hold the brush vertically and dab it to achieve a stippled effect. An uneven application will look more natural.

4 Apply more white paint unevenly, using an open weave cloth. Gradually build the paint up over the whole surface.

There are many metallic paints available which produce extremely realistic results. This lion has been painted copper using a paint that contains ground metal. If you wish to achieve a weathered look, apply a coat of green patina paint while the second coat of copper is still sticky.

5 Mix some watery green paint and use a toothbrush to spatter it over the whole surface. Repeat the effect with watery yellow ochre paint.

This free standing pig is made starting with a simple drawing of a pig – children's illustrated books are a good source of inspiration. The pig is formed in modeling clay, from which a latex mold is made. The plaster cast is painted in bright colors in keeping with its highly stylized form. It can be a lone pig or it could be the first of a farmyard set.

FARM ANIMALS

MATERIALS

Modeling clay
Copper wire
Copper sheet
Plaster
Latex
Acrylic paint: red, yellow, green, blue, white and black
Gold powder
Spar varnish
Doweling wood

EQUIPMENT

Rolling pin
Baseboard
Modeling tools
Marker pen
Small pointed pliers
Mixing bowl
Sandpaper
Paintbrushes
Small mixing dish

1 Roll out a ¾in (19mm) thick slab of clay.

2 Lay a copy of the template provided on top of the clay. Using a modeling tool, cut through the clay, carefully following the outline of the template.

3 Keep the template on top of the clay and use a modeling tool to trace the drawn lines to produce indentations on the clay's surface.

4 Wet the clay and use a wide-ended modeling tool to press the clay down at an angle to follow the form of the body as it rises up and away from the leg.

5 Use a combination of modeling tools and your fingers on the wet clay to develop the pig's form, using the indentations on the clay's surface as guidelines.

7 Use pliers to form a spiral of copper wire for the tail. Bend the wire at right angles to this and bend again as shown.

9 Smooth the edges of the cast with sandpaper. You are now ready to paint your pig.

6 When the modeling is complete, you are ready to make a latex mold (see page 14).

8 When you cast the pig, incorporate the tail by suspending it from a skewer resting on either side of the mold.

Photocopy this template or draw your own design.

24

10 Mix red and white paint to produce pink and cover the whole surface of the pig.

11 Paint white onto the legs, nose and ears.

12 While the paint is wet, brush some red paint into the crevices where the body meets the legs and blend in. Blend red paint over the whole surface to achieve a variety of pink tones.

13 Mix black and white paint together and apply gray patches over the pig's body. When dry, paint with spar varnish.

14 To make a coxcomb, cut out a triangle from a sheet of copper. Make a series of parallel cuts along one edge to produce a comb-like effect.

Make a cow from a thick layer of clay and sandpaper the bottom of the legs so that it is freestanding. By adding a stick to the cockerel, it can be used to adorn plant pots.

26   This teddy bear was cast into plaster from a purchased rubber mold. It was meticulously modeled and the cast is decorated with equal precision. Because more than one teddy bear can be cast, you can make several, each unique with different color combinations. This project is a good exercise in painting fine detailed surfaces, for which you need a very steady hand.

TEDDY BEAR

Use a cardboard box with a hole cut in the lid to suspend the mold.

2 Paint a very watery mix of burnt sienna over the base coat so the color sinks into the crevices. Avoid making drip marks.

MATERIALS

Rubber mold
Plaster
Acrylic paint:
Naples yellow,
burnt sienna,
yellow, green,
white, black, red
and blue

EQUIPMENT

Small mixing dish
Paintbrush
Mixing bowl

1 Paint a thin base coat of Naples yellow over the bear's body and allow it to dry.

3 Paint the vest yellow. Dip your brush into the yellow paint, dry most of it off with a rag and then brush across the body so the high points of the surface pick up the paint.

5 Paint the eyes with burnt sienna; paint the star on the ball with Naples yellow and the circles red. Finally, carefully paint a blue stripe around the ball.

4 Add white to yellow to make a light tone and paint the nose, paws, eyes and the inside of the ears. Carefully paint vertical stripes on the vest.

This teddy bear has black fur and a bright red vest. The striking colors produce a very different effect from that of the brown bear.

28 Change is the theme of this clock – the time is constantly changing and the chameleon changes the color of its skin. The clock face is sculpted in modeling clay with the aid of templates and cast into plaster using a latex mold. The battery-powered clock mechanism, which has an integral hanging hook, is easily obtained and attaches to the back of the clock face.

2 Draw your design of the clock face on paper using the chameleon template provided.

CHAMELEON CLOCK

MATERIALS

Paper
Modeling clay
Plaster
Latex
Acrylic paint: green, yellow and blue
Gold powder
Spar varnish
Clock mechanism

EQUIPMENT

Rolling pin
Modeling tools
Marker pen
Mixing bowl
Sandpaper
Palette
Baseboard

1 Roll out some modeling clay on the baseboard to a thickness of ¾in (19mm).

3 Lay the clock face template on top of the clay and cut around it with a modeling tool. Cut out an extra chameleon using the template provided.

4 Keep the templates on top of the clay and use a modeling tool to trace the drawn lines to produce indentations on the clay's surface. Mark the center point of the clock face.

6 Place a modeling tool vertically on the center mark and rotate it to enlarge the hole.

8 Use the sharp end of a modeling tool to add contrasting textures to the body. Only slight pressure is needed to produce such marks.

5 Place the cut out chameleon on top of one of the chameleons on the clock face. Use a modeling tool to blend the clay along the cut edges of these two sections. This end will be the top of the clock.

7 Wet the surface of the clay and, using the indentations as guidelines, start to model the chameleon form. A wet finger run over the surface helps to consolidate the shape.

9 Select a wide-ended modeling tool and run it around the inside rim of the clock face to produce a bevel, smoothing it out with wet fingers. Shape the other chameleon as before.

30

10 When the modeling is complete, make a latex mold (see page 14) and take a plaster cast. Smooth the edges with sandpaper.

12 Paint yellow in the gaps between the turquoise. A touch of orange paint blended into the top of each yellow stripe gives an illusion of form. Paint the other chameleon in the same way.

14 Paint the circumference of the clock mauve and fill in the areas not already painted blue. When the paint has dried, turn the clock over and paint the back blue.

11 Paint dark turquoise stripes on the chameleon. Note how they do not follow the direction of the indented marks. When dry, paint parts of these stripes with a lighter color turquoise.

13 Paint the clock face blue, using as many coats as necessary to obtain a thick even color. Allow the paint to dry between coats.

15 Working in a well-ventilated area, paint the whole of the clock, back and front, with a coat of spar varnish.

16 Mix some gold powder and varnish to a creamy consistency and paint a decorative border around the clock.

17 To install the clock mechanism, push the central spindle through the hole in the center and screw down the hands.

MARK LA TROBE
Egyptian cats
The marbled effect was achieved by adding a water-based dye to the plaster. The dye was not mixed fully into the plaster but folded in loosely.

MARK LA TROBE • Three shelves
Staining with diluted furniture wax produces the effect of old plaster, from a dark oak color to the off-white of clear wax.

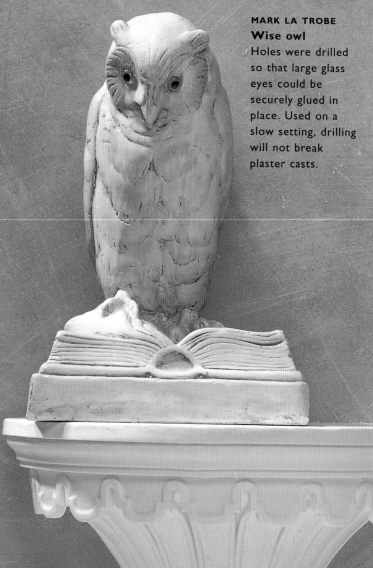

MARK LA TROBE
Wise owl
Holes were drilled so that large glass eyes could be securely glued in place. Used on a slow setting, drilling will not break plaster casts.

GALLERY

Animals have inspired artists throughout the ages. Here we see cats rendered in plaster in the Egyptian tradition. Animals have also been used to adorn buildings and fountains, as exemplified by the griffin and lion heads. Whether purely ornamental, like the majestic lounging lion, the wise owl and the cockerel wall plaques, or cast as utilitarian bookends, animals make a dramatic decorative statement.

MARK LA TROBE
Dog bookends
Meticulously modeled and stained with diluted furniture wax, these dogs are difficult for the beginner to sculpt, but a simpler version is within everybody's capabilities.

PAMELA STEWART-PEARSON

Two cockerels

A wood carving was the original for these reliefs. They were painted with acrylic paint with gilded wax applied on top.

MIKE WELLS

Lounging lion

Over a sprayed base coat of brown paint, gold wax was applied with a cloth and buffed when dry.

◀▼ BERNARD CLAYDON
Griffin and lion's head
The original figures were modeled in clay, from which silicone rubber molds were made. The turquoise and verdigris colorings were achieved by using an airbrush.

MARK LA TROBE
Lion's head
This cast is based on a fountain head design, and is an example of the many pieces of classical sculpture which are now available as plaster casts.

Painting the plaster cast as naturalistically as possible is the primary aim in this chapter. The press mold technique is used to make an attractive Mini-veg Panel. A latex mold is made of one side of a fossil, a plaster cast taken and this is then colored to replicate the surface of the original. Platicine is modeled freehand to make the Sunflower Candleholder and Plant Pot Stick; the plaster casts are painted with bright colors to reflect the ambience of their inspiration. Bought rubber molds are used to cast different fruits which are painted in a way

ORGANIC ORIGINS

that will convince the eye but unfortunately not your teeth! Blending paint together is further explored when decorating the blank plaster swag. This is also shown with a metallic finish to demonstrate the various effects you can achieve.

A latex mold was made from a found object – a fossil – and then cast into plaster. As it is a one-piece mold, you must choose the best side of the fossil to work from. In this project, we replicate the surface coloring of the original fossil as closely as possible. The finished fossil makes an attractive ornament or a useful paperweight.

FOSSIL

Granite spray paints are widely available. This fossil was sprayed blue granite and the crevices emphasized with black paint.

2 You are now ready to make a latex mold (see page 14) and take a cast.

MATERIALS

Fossil
Plasticine
Plaster
Latex
Acrylic paint: black, white and yellow
Whitewash powder
Blue granite spray paint

EQUIPMENT

Mixing bowl
Paintbrush
Toothbrush
Sponge
Small mixing dish
Baseboard

1 Fill in the undercuts of the fossil with Plasticine and build halfway up the fossil.

3 Mix white and black acrylic paint to produce a mid-tone gray and cover the surface of the plaster cast. Leave it to dry.

4 Dab black acrylic paint onto the surface with a sponge. Use a ragged rather than a straight edge of the sponge.

6 Brush on a coat of watery yellow paint and while wet use a sponge to dab whitewash powder on top. Leave it to dry.

7 Remove the excess whitewash with a damp sponge.

5 Make a watery mix of light gray. Use a toothbrush to spatter the paint onto the surface. Leave it to dry.

40 A plaster blank of ribbons, fruit and flowers – known as a swag – is painted to produce a brightly colored decorative element. It looks good on its own or several can be joined to make a chain of swags to sweep across a wall. The naturalistic sunflower head could be incorporated with other elements to make an alternative type of swag.

FLOWER SWAGS

MATERIALS

Plaster swag
Plaster sunflower
Acrylic paint:
green, crimson,
yellow, blue, brown
and white
Bronze paint
Ruby red metallic
paint

EQUIPMENT

Palette
Paintbrush

1 Use bright colors to paint the individual elements of the swag. Dark orange was painted over a lighter orange and then blended in.

2 Paint the individual elements systematically, using the same color for each type.

3 As more and more elements of the swag are painted, the colors intensify as they contrast with or complement each other.

4 Bright red bows at either end of the swag provide a strong compositional device for this multicolored decoration.

6 Add white to the tip of each petal and blend in to produce a gradation of tone running from top to bottom. Paint the center brown. Pick out the high points with white and blend in.

Over a bronze base coat, apply metallic ruby red paint using a dry brush so that only the high points pick up the paint.

5 Mix green and white and paint the leaves. Paint a darker green in the crevices and a touch of white on the tip of each leaf. Paint the petals yellow.

42 Fruit has remained a popular subject for artists for centuries. In this project, plaster casts of a pear, orange and apple are made from bought molds and then painted using acrylic paints. To obtain a naturalistic look, a variety of shades of color should be applied to each fruit and blended in. It is a good opportunity to practice color mixing. While painting, it is helpful to have a selection of fruits to refer to.

FRUIT

MATERIALS

Rubber molds
Plaster
Acrylic paint:
green, yellow, blue,
red and white
Spar varnish

EQUIPMENT

Mixing bowl
Small mixing dish
Paintbrush

1 Mix a base coat for the pear from green and yellow paint. Leave it to dry.

2 Paint on different shades of green: add blue to darken the green or yellow to lighten it.

3 Cover the surface with patches of various shades to recreate the surface of a pear.

4 Paint the surface of the pear with spar varnish. Use even strokes and avoid drip marks.

5 Paint the other fruits in a similar way: the base color for the orange is a mixture of red and yellow; red for the apple. Blend white highlights into the fruit and darker lowlights. Paint both with spar varnish.

Instead of using spar varnish, apply an oil-based varnish such as Japan gold size and then a coat of gum arabic. This will produce a crackle glaze.

44

A sunflower is modeled from Plasticine using a variety of modeling tools. A latex mold is then made from which multiple casts can be taken – each can be decorated in different ways. The candleholder makes a good table decoration and the plant pot stick is an unusual feature for a flower pot – it adds dazzle when a plant is not flowering.

SUNFLOWERS

MATERIALS

Plasticine
Latex
Plaster
Acrylic paint:
Turner's yellow,
cadmium yellow,
cadmium red, blue,
green and white
Doweling wood

EQUIPMENT

Baseboard
Modeling tool
Rolling pin
Mixing bowl
Paintbrush
Small mixing dish
Film cannister

2 Shape a piece of Plasticine into a basic leaf shape and curl one end under. Use a modeling tool to draw the veins. Attach this to the central element securely.

1 Knead the Plasticine and make a semi-spherical shape. Push a plastic film cannister into the center to make a socket for the candle. Any object with the correct diameter can be used.

3 Roll a ball of Plasticine, pinch one of the edges and tease it out to make a petal. Arrange petals all around the central element, attaching them securely.

4 Blend the Plasticine seams. With a pointed modeling tool, make holes in the central area.

6 Take plaster casts from your molds. Mix Turner's yellow and cadmium yellow with a touch of red and paint the petals of both of the sunflowers.

7 Apply green paint to the leaf and the doweling. Mix brown by adding blue and red to the yellow and paint the flower centers. Paint white on the high points and darker yellow on the low points of the petals, and a lighter green on the leaf.

5 Model a smaller sunflower using simpler shapes but no large leaf. Use doweling to create a cavity for a stick to be attached when it has been cast into plaster. Now make a latex mold of each flower (see page 14).

46

This attractive wall panel is made by casting small varieties of vegetables into plaster using the press mold technique. Plasticine is wrapped around each vegetable to make a negative of its form and pick up surface detail. If the Plasticine molds are handled carefully, they can be reused many times.

MINI-VEG PANEL

MATERIALS

Plasticine
Plaster
Scrim
Galvanized wire
Mini vegetables
Vegetable oil
Acrylic paint
Gloss and matt
varnish

EQUIPMENT

Kitchen knife
Scissors
Baseboard
Strips of timber
2in (5cm) oval nails
Rolling pin
Paintbrush
Mixing bowl
Palette

1 Roll out a slab of Plasticine about ½in (13mm) thick, and push the corn into its surface. Fold the Plasticine around its form, pressing well.

2 Trim the Plasticine level where it meets. Carefully open the Plasticine just enough to remove the corn. Return the Plasticine to its original form.

3 Brush a coat of vegetable oil inside the mold and fill with plaster. When it has set, gently peel back the Plasticine to remove the cast. Repeat this process for the other vegetables.

4 Make a frame to fit around the baseboard. Tack the frame together with nails – the frame needs to be easily dismantled. Seal the gaps between baseboard and frame with Plasticine.

6 Pour plaster into the frame. While the plaster is still wet, lay the scrim on top. Gently push it slightly below the surface.

8 Remove the plaster panel by dismantling the frame. Arrange the vegetable casts on the panel in a pleasing composition and then draw around each.

5 Cut some scrim slightly smaller than the area inside the frame. Coat the baseboard and the inside surfaces of the frame with vegetable oil.

7 Bend two pieces of wire to make hanging hooks. Place them in the wet plaster, carefully lifting up the scrim to slip the two curled sections underneath. Rest the circular parts on the frame.

9 Use a kitchen knife to score the underside of each vegetable cast and its corresponding position on the panel. This will ensure a good fixing.

48

10 Mix a small quantity of plaster and when it has thickened to a cream cheese consistency, apply it to a scored area on the panel. Press the cast on top of it. Repeat to adhere all the casts.

12 Brush wet plaster along the plaster join between the casts and the panel. Leave it to dry thoroughly.

14 Paint carrots orange. Paint red and white rings across them to give the impression of indentations and highlights.

11 Use a modeling tool to trim off the excess plaster which squeezed out between the casts and the panel.

13 Paint the background to resemble wood grain. Apply a variety of browns in long continuous strokes across the board. Add a couple of circular wood knots.

15 Paint tomatoes and chillies a deep red. Paint corn yellow; when dry, lightly brush white paint onto the high points.

16 Paint the stalks of chillies green and the leaves of cauliflowers in two shades of green, keeping the stalky parts of the leaf a lighter green than the rest.

17 Paint okra the same shades of green but blend the colors well and paint the high points with a dark green. Use vertical brushstrokes in varying shades of brown and red for onions.

18 Apply matt varnish to the board and vegetables such as okra and gloss varnish to vegetables such as tomatoes.

THE WORKS • Rock mirror
The original form for this mirror was made using real pebbles, and the plaster cast replicates their texture.

SARAH WILLIAMS • Spiral wall plaque
The rich colors used in medieval manuscripts and images from folk art inspired the design of this relief. It was painted with acrylic paint and gold leaf.

GALLERY

The organic world provides a wealth of inspiration. The rock mirror is an excellent example of using actual organic objects as the starting point for a plasterwork. It is interesting to see how the two leaf mirrors each display a different facet of the leaf shape. The brightly colored plaque uses a spiral as its central motif, an abstract representation of the cycles of nature. Fruit and flowers are used imaginatively and to great effect in the other plasterworks.

MARK LA TROBE • Swag, fruitbowl and wreath
These wall plaques were modeled in clay from which silicone rubber molds were made. The subsequent plaster casts have light colored wax applied to them; when dry the wax was buffed to produce a surface shine.

THE WORKS
Leaf mirror
The mirror surround was painted with cobalt blue and then coats of gilt cream were brushed on daily. It was then varnished.

INTERIOR DESIGNS

There is an abundance of blank plaster casts available for decoration. A lot if not most of these are based on traditional classical designs, such as the Column. The Column has been chosen to demonstrate the most complex decorative technique in this book: marbling. The Uplighter, although of a classical design, allows you to attach an electric light fixture to it; this is given an antiqued finish. The traditional Fleur-de-Lys is here modeled in Plasticine and a variety of colored casts are taken from the latex mold. The picture frame and bows are decorated with bright flat colors in a variety of striking designs. The Rosettes are stained with powder paint and coated with a textured gel which belies the smooth surface of the plaster cast.

Show off your favorite photograph or picture in this highly decorative picture frame. Acrylic paint is used and sealed with spar varnish. All the colors can be found using only the primary colors – red, blue and yellow – together with white. The painted surface is then highlighted with gold.

GOTHIC FRAME

2 When you paint the very deep red, you will need to have a steady hand to avoid brushing paint onto areas that have already been painted.

MATERIALS

Plaster picture frame
Acrylic paints: yellow, red, blue and white
Gold powder
Spar varnish

EQUIPMENT

Small paintbrush
Palette
Small mixing dish

1 Follow the color scheme shown, starting with yellow paint. Then paint the turquoise and mauve areas. It does not matter if you go over the edges at this point.

3 Paint the remaining areas of the frame with a dark blue, including the back. Paint evenly and avoid leaving brush marks. If the coat is too streaked, repaint when dry.

4 In a small mixing bowl, mix some varnish and gold powder to a creamy consistency. Use a paintbrush to highlight details.

6 Leave it to dry completely. In a well-ventilated area, seal the entire frame with a coat of clear spar varnish.

5 Brush off the excess paint on a sheet of paper until the brush is relatively dry. Drag it lightly across the surface of the frame to leave a light deposit.

Use superglue to stick the glass and hanging hook onto the back. Place the picture face down on the glass with a piece of card on top and secure them in position with tape.

58 There are many plaster casts of architectural features available ready to be decorated and used for interior decoration. The finish on the uplighter gives the impression that it is an old architectural feature. Rosettes look effective on cornicing around the top of a wall or the architrave around a door. The textured finish shown here belies the smooth surface of plaster.

UPLIGHTER AND ROSETTES

2 Rub off excess wax with a cloth. Leave the wax to dry.

MATERIALS

Plaster uplighter
Plaster rosettes
Antique wax
furniture polish
Mineral spirits
Textured acrylic gel
Acrylic paint:
bronze yellow,
Naples yellow,
burnt umber,
black and white
Blue and red
powder paint

EQUIPMENT

Small jar
Paintbrushes
Soft cloth
Small mixing dish

1 Dilute antique wax with mineral spirits to make it liquid enough to apply with a paintbrush. Brush it onto the plaster, taking care to avoid drip marks.

3 Use a soft cloth to buff the whole of the uplighter to produce an aged-looking surface.

4 Apply textured acrylic gel evenly over the surface of a rosette. Mix bronze yellow with Naples yellow and apply a base coat. Paint on a wash of darker tone.

5 Stipple on burnt umber, reaching into the crevices. Before the paint dries, soften the edges with a dry brush. Repeat this technique using gray paint. Apply creamy yellow paint to the high points using a dry brush.

Dampen the rosette and sprinkle it with colored powder paint. Brush off the excess powder after ten minutes. The dampened plaster will absorb some of the color.

60

The traditional image of the fleur-de-lys was originally found in architecture, but has been adopted by Western culture – for instance, it is used on flags, coats of arms, fabric designs, etc. Its relief format makes it an ideal shape for casting from a latex mold. Colored plaster is used for the cast and then a metallic finish is applied.

FLEUR-DE-LYS

MATERIALS

Plasticine
Latex
Plaster
Red, green and blue
powder paint
Silver and gold
acrylic paint or wax
Mineral spirits

EQUIPMENT

Pencil
Modeling tools
Paintbrush
Mixing bowl
Baseboard
Small mixing dish

1 Make a copy of the template provided. Place it on the board and draw around it.

2 Build up the forms inside the drawn lines with Plasticine. Use a modeling tool to keep the Plasticine hard against the lines.

3 Continue to model the form, applying the Plasticine with your fingers and defining the shape with a modeling tool.

4 With the basic form of the fleur-de-lys filled in, use the blade of a wide-ended modeling tool to slice the excess Plasticine off the main form to create a smooth angular surface. Use a smaller tool to define the more detailed areas of the form.

6 Finish the blue plaster cast by painting the side elements with silver paint. Finish the red fleur-de-lys by painting the central element with gold paint. Apply gold paint to one of the beveled sides of each element of the green cast.

5 Dip a finger in mineral spirits and run it over the surface of the form to produce a smooth surface. You are now ready to make a latex mold (see page 14). Cast the fleur-de-lys using blue, green and red colored plaster (see page 11).

Ribbons and bows are available in many different styles and can be used as individual decorative elements or to frame other plasterworks such as a swag. Here, they are shown with a bold scarlet finish, in softer blue and yellow colors, and in a striking tartan.

RIBBONS AND BOWS

2 This tartan has thick ultramarine stripes with thin pairs of black stripes in between.

MATERIALS

Plaster bows
Acrylic paint: blue, purple, crimson, ultramarine, black, yellow and hooker's green

EQUIPMENT

Paintbrush
Small mixing dish

1 Apply a base coat of hooker's green. Work out your tartan design. The important thing is to paint the stripes in regular, repeating patterns.

3 The final touch is made by mixing a small amount of green with yellow and painting a pattern of light stripes on the bow.

4 Paint this ribbon yellow on top and blue on the underside. Follow the flow of the bow as you apply the yellow. Paint the crevices on the knot with brown.

6 Paint crimson over the whole surface and allow it to dry. Brush purple into the crevices and the high points of the knot.

5 Paint the underside of the ribbon light blue.

Time and patience is required to achieve this marble effect. Before you start, familiarize yourself with the various colorings and patterns of different types of marble – look at marble floors and walls of buildings and sculpture and plinths in museums. Note pattern details which interest you and make a drawing of your proposed decoration.

MARBLED COLUMN

MATERIALS

Plaster column
White eggshell paint
Fine wet and dry sandpaper
Scumble glaze
Oil paint: burnt sienna, raw sienna, chrome yellow, Indian red, white and ultramarine
Mineral spirits
Satin varnish
Beeswax

EQUIPMENT

Paintbrushes
Hog bristle brush
Badgerhair brush
Sable brush (No. 1)
Dust brush
Feather
Rag
Newspaper
Soft cloth

2 Use a cloth to apply scumble glaze over the entire surface of the column: when paint is applied, it will stay wet longer, allowing it to be manipulated to achieve the desired effect.

1 Seal the column by painting on two coats of eggshell paint, allowing the first coat to dry before applying the second. When dry, smooth the surface with wet and dry sandpaper. Clean with a dusting brush.

3 Dilute burnt sienna oil paint with mineral spirits to produce a very thin wash and brush on quickly. Follow this with a thin wash of raw sienna.

4 While the paint is still wet, stipple with a hog bristle brush to soften the surface. With a badgerhair brush, lightly stroke the paint surface in all directions to remove the brush marks.

5 Soak some twisted newspaper in mineral spirits and dab it on: this will break up the paint surface. Use the badgerhair brush to soften this.

6 Mix burnt sienna with chrome yellow paint and make a thin wash. Stipple it onto the base of the column, then blend in with a hog bristle brush by stippling in all directions. This dark tone will give the base of the column some visual weight.

Before you begin marbling, make a drawing of the column and its proposed decoration to refer to.

7 Mix Indian red, burnt sienna and a touch of ultramarine with mineral spirits and a dab of scumble glaze. Use a sable brush to add veins between the light and dark areas.

8 Stipple the veins with the hog bristle brush and then soften them with the badgerhair brush, following the direction of the veins. Add more veins.

9 For variety, charge your brush with ultramarine on one side and a mixture of raw and burnt sienna on the other. Dilute the colors more to obtain a lighter tone for these secondary veins.

10 Following the course of the large veins, paint fine veins in a predominantly blue tone mixed from burnt sienna and ultramarine. Stipple and soften with the hog bristle and badgerhair brushes.

11 Dampen a rag with mineral spirits and wipe off areas of the base color – large and small – around the veins to reveal the white plaster.

12 Dip a feather in a thin wash of white oil paint and drag it across the surface using a jittery motion. This produces a very subtle effect.

13 Paint the whole of the column with a wash of raw sienna. Stipple and soften with a hog bristle and badgerhair brush as before and allow it to dry. Coat with satin varnish.

14 A final polish with beeswax enhances all the colors and hides any remaining brushstrokes.

GALLERY

MARK LA TROBE • Bows
A coating of wax produces
one of the most effective
but simple-to-do antique
finishes.

◄ FUNKY ECLECTICA
Pewter mirror
Art Nouveau designs were
the inspiration for this
mirror. The original was
made in wood and gesso,
from which a silicone
mold was made. Silver
and bronze powders were
used for the finish.

Plaster has long been used as a building material, and the different periods in history provide a wide range of architectural designs for us to draw upon. The capital, rosette and shelf are directly derived from classical originals; the bows are traditional decorations but have a more modern feel to them; Art Nouveau inspired one of the mirrors while old church carvings inspired the other; Gothic and Baroque traditions inspired the box and small plaques.

▲► CLIFTON LITTLE VENICE
Soane rosette and
ionic capital
Cast in lightly colored
and plain white plaster,
these classic architectural
features can transform
a room.

▶ **MIRABILIS DESIGN • Church mirror**
With reference to 10th-century church carvings
this mirrored candleholder was modeled
in clay, from which a latex mold was
made. It was then given a subtle finish
using acrylic paint.

▲ **OFER ACOO**
Gothic
wall plaques
An interest in
Gothic architecture inspired these
reliefs. They were painted with acrylic
colors and gold highlights added.

FUNKY ECLECTICA • Blue baroque box
The artist modeled this relief in clay and cast
it into plaster using a one-off mold. Its rich
decorative finish was produced using tinted
shellac and bronze powders.

OCEAN WORLD

The paint effects used in this chapter seek to emulate the glistening and shimmering effect of water and its associated sea objects. The Starfish and Scallop come as plaster blanks and are decorated with pearlized paint. The paint effects used on the Shell Tiles also invoke that sense of the sea, even though one of the tiles is decorated using a teabag! The Sculpted Shell and the Tropical Fish are modeled with different surface textures which show how effectively a latex mold picks up detail. The Jumping Fish is cast from a bought mold and decorated with layers of washes which emulate the fish's scales.

The starfish and scallop shell shown here are decorated in complementary colors enriched with pearlized paint and glitter. Both shapes have a flat back: a hanging hook can be glued to the back to hang them on a wall or they can simply be left as they are and placed on a shelf. Alternatively, you can decorate a few of each shape and arrange them as a frieze.

STARFISH AND SCALLOP

2 Fill the indentations on the high points with pearl white paint.

MATERIALS

Plaster starfish
Plaster scallop
Acrylic paint: blue,
yellow, red and
white
Pearl white paint
Blue glitter gel
Gold wax

EQUIPMENT

Paintbrush
Small mixing dish
Cloth

1 Mix a deep orange and paint a generous coat onto the whole surface of the starfish.

On a surface painted with pink pearlized paint, wipe gold wax lightly. Buff with a soft cloth when dry.

3 Paint the scallop shell blue and allow it to dry. Rub a darker blue into this base coat.

4 Rub some blue glitter gel onto the surface and allow it to dry.

5 Rub some gold wax onto the surface so that it reaches both the high points and the crevices.

Alternatively, apply turquoise pearlized paint and gold wax to pick out the ridges of the shell.

76 This fish relief was cast from a purchased rigid plastic mold and therefore did not need support while the plaster set. It is decorated using acrylic paint. The color on the main body is built up using washes (watery mixes of paint) and is effective in emulating fish scales.

JUMPING FISH

2 Mix an orange wash and paint the fins, gills and lips. Take care not to go over the edges onto the main body of the fish.

MATERIALS

Plastic mold
Plaster
Acrylic paint: blue, yellow, lime green and red
Spar varnish

EQUIPMENT

Mixing bowl
Small mixing dish
Paintbrush

1 Mix a green wash and paint the scales of the fish.

3 Paint dark red to pick out the detail on the fins.

4 Paint a wash of lime green over the scales to add highlights.

5 Apply a wash of blue at random over the scales to break up the color and add lowlights.

Finish the piece with a coat of varnish to protect the surface and reproduce the effect of shimmering scales.

A stylized shell is decorated to reflect glistening shells on a beach. First the shell is modeled in Plasticine as a relief, i.e. the underside is flat, making it suitable for a one-piece latex mold. Each plaster cast can be decorated using the same technique, changing the base color for variety. When hanging in a cluster on a bathroom wall, they exude a beach flavor.

SCULPTED SHELL

MATERIALS

Plasticine
Latex
Plaster
Paperclip
Blue pearlized paint
Blue acrylic paint
Gold wax
Gold glitter

EQUIPMENT

Modeling tool
Paintbrushes
Cloth
Mixing bowl
Palette

1 Knead the Plasticine to make it pliable and model an elongated shell shape. Create an opening at one end with your fingers.

2 Place the shape on your work surface and, applying light pressure, twist the form back and forth to create a flat back. Press the Plasticine with your fingers to create indentations to run around the shell from the opening to its tip.

3 Roll out some very thin worms of Plasticine and place them on the ridges. Use a modeling tool to make a pattern of indentations on the surface.

5 Paint an even coat of pearlized blue paint all over the shell, taking care to avoid drip marks. Leave it to dry.

6 Dip a cloth in gold wax and rub it lightly across the surface so that the color is picked up by the high points of the shell.

4 You are now ready to make the latex mold (see page 14). When casting into plaster, incorporate a hanging hook (see page 15).

When dry, buff the shell with a soft cloth. The pearl in the paint and the gold will be enhanced when light falls on the shell.

Alternatively, paint the shell blue and sprinkle with gold glitter while still wet. Shake off the excess when dry.

80

These shell tiles can be interspersed with plain tiles on the walls of a bathroom. Pearlized paints produce a shimmering radiance; crackle glazing gives the impression of old paintings and hand-made crafts; staining with tea, plain or fruit flavored, gives a more subtle and unusual effect. Tiles can be bought or made using the same method as for the mini-veg panel (see page 46).

SHELL TILES

2 While the paint is still wet, use a brush loaded with white pearl paint to produce swirls of color.

MATERIALS

Plaster tiles
Tea bag
Antique wax
furniture polish
Mineral spirits
Oil-based varnish
(Japan gold size)
Gum arabic
Acrylic paint: blue,
pink and white
White pearl paint

EQUIPMENT

Small mixing dish
Paintbrushes
Small jar
Soft cloth

1 Brush a generous coat of light blue paint onto the background area of the tile.

3 Mix pink with pearl white, dilute to make a wash and apply to three of the shells. Mix blue with pearl white and apply to the remaining shells. Use water to blend in the background area.

4 Finish the shell in the same way as the uplighter (see page 58). Apply a coat of Japan gold size to the tile and allow it to dry. Brush on a coat of gum arabic.

6 Pour hot water over a tea bag and dab it on the surface. Keep dipping the bag into the tea water to keep it moist and to freshen the tea color.

5 Apply blue paint on top: the paint will immediately crack and produce a rough, hand-painted effect. For a smoother look, apply the coat of paint first.

82 Two methods of producing a relief are shown here. The fish relief is modeled direct in clay and provides the opportunity to experiment with modeling tools to create different surface textures. The fish tank is made by cutting out simple profiles from slabs of Plasticine and positioning them in a wooden frame. You must remember to work in reverse: what is on the righthand side when making will be on the left of the cast.

TROPICAL FISH

MATERIALS

Plasticine
Modeling clay
Latex
Plaster
Galvanized wire
Vegetable oil
Acrylic paint: red, turquoise, blue and white
Gold powder
Spar varnish

EQUIPMENT

Rolling pin
Baseboard
Modeling tools
Mixing bowl
Paintbrush
Old marker pen
Strips of timber
2in (5cm) oval nails
Small mixing dish

1 Roll out some modeling clay, making it thicker in the middle than at the edge. Lay a copy of the template provided on the clay and cut round it with a modeling tool.

2 Bevel the edge and smooth it with a wet finger. Use a wide-ended tool to slice off the top of each fin to lie lower than the main body.

3 Flatten the area between the ridge marks drawn on the surface. Smooth these areas out with a wet finger so that these three ridges stand out.

5 Shape the eye and create eyelash marks. Cut out a wedge for the mouth and bevel it. Make the teeth: notice how their shape has been determined by the shape of the modeling tool.

6 Using a serrated-edged modeling tool, hold it at an angle on each of the raised ridges and press lightly. With the sharp edge of a modeling tool, make a series of crosshatched lines on the fins and the tail.

4 Roll a small ball of clay and stick it in position for the eye, wetting the surface of the fish first. Blend the edges with a modeling tool to fix the join and smooth over with a wet finger.

7 Press an old marker pen into the surface of the clay in between the ridges on the fish. You are now ready to make a latex mold (see page 14). Cast the fish relief into plaster. You are now ready to decorate the fish.

9 Model a wavy shape of Plasticine 1in (2.5cm) thick and position it at the top of the frame. Cut out two ¹/₂in (13mm) thick fish shapes and place these in the frame. Cut out thin wave shapes and place these around the fish.

11 Smooth the edges with sandpaper and then paint the whole tank blue. Paint darker blue into the recessed areas.

8 To make a fish tank, make a wooden frame around the baseboard and seal the gaps between the frame and the board with Plasticine in the same way as for the mini-veg panel (see page 46).

10 Coat everything with vegetable oil to prevent sticking and pour in the plaster slowly and evenly, incorporating hanging hooks.

12 Paint the whole fish with scarlet red and allow it to dry.

13 Brush deep violet red into all the crevices of the fish.

14 Mix some gold powder and spar varnish and paint the lips, teeth and eyelids. Paint patterns on the body in contrast with the indentation marks.

15 Add white to turquoise and paint the whole fish. Use turquoise straight from the tube to brush into the crevices. Apply gold powder and varnish as before but in different patterns.

SHOELESS JOE • Shell box and starfish box
Plaster casts were taken from an original shell and starfish and glued onto wooden boxes. The painted surface of the boxes was broken up by sanding to produce a weather-beaten look.

BERNARD CLAYDON
Seahorses, heraldic dolphin and pisces plaque
The original reliefs were modeled in clay, from which silicone rubber molds were made. The smooth and even finish on the seahorses was achieved by using an airbrush. The others were handpainted.

► THE WORKS • Shell clock

Shells were bonded to a dome-shaped base to make
the original. The verdigris finish was achieved by
painting the cast dark red/brown and then
sponging on turquoise randomly. Finally, it
was brushed with gilt cream diluted with
turpentine.

The variety of forms that exist
below the sea are brought to life
in this section. The wooden boxes

GALLERY

and mirror have a driftwood quality, a fitting match for their shell
and starfish attachments. Sea creatures are very easy to model
and cast, either as individual elements or as wall plaques, and
together with shells make attractive border decorations. The
anchor is a splendidly rendered traditional seafaring symbol.

SHOELESS JOE
Starfish mirror
The rough-hewn timber frame was white-washed to reflect sun bleached beaches. Plaster casts were made from real starfishes and bonded to the frame. The natural sisal hanging rope further develops the seashore theme.

BERNARD CLAYDON
Humpback whale
The original whale was modeled in clay, from which a silicone rubber mold was made. The smooth and even finish was achieved by applying the color with an airbrush.

THE WORKS
Shell mirrors
Shells were bonded to papier mâché frames, the smaller frame having a rope surround attached. The plaster casts were painted with burgundy colored paint with gilt cream brushed on top.

JOHN DE VEUVE • Anchor
Modeled in clay, a rubber silicone mold was then taken. The mottled paint effect was achieved by applying the paint with an airbrush.

HEAVENLY BODIES

Stars, moons and suns are ideal shapes to make and cast, and can be used in a variety
of ways. The Star Brooches are extremely easy to make and are cast directly from
pastry cutters. The Eclectic Mirror is made by applying the plaster freehand with a
variety of objects then embedded in it. The Twilight Box is made in a similar way, but
instead of plaster, spackle is used into which a star and moon shape are embedded
before the spackle sets. Sun, moon, star and cloud shapes are perfect subject matter
for a mobile. Each is painted with a hazy coloring to give them a far away look.
The Sun Wall Plaque is decorated in five different ways, clearly demonstrating the
wide variety of effects which can be achieved.

These brooches will add an extra sparkle to everyday dress. Molds for the shapes are formed using baking cutters and Plasticine to contain the plaster when it is poured. The casts need to be removed with great care to avoid breaking them. Superglue is used to attach the brooch fasteners to the back of the casts.

STAR BROOCHES

2 Carefully peel away the Plasticine, keeping the cutters in position. Hold the cutters and gently push the plaster cast and the small cutter through the large one.

MATERIALS

Plaster
Plasticine
Vegetable oil
Superglue
Brooch fasteners
Acrylic paint: gold, blue and silver
Bronze spray paint
Gold wax

EQUIPMENT

Pastry cutters, large and small
Rolling pin
Mixing bowl
Sandpaper
Small mixing dish
Paintbrush
Cloth

1 Coat the inside of each cutter with vegetable oil. On a bed of Plasticine place a small cutter inside a larger one. Pour plaster into this mold and gently agitate to expel any air bubbles.

3 Hold the plaster cast and gently push the small cutter up through the cast. Use sandpaper to smooth the edges and glue a brooch fastener to the back.

4 Cast two solid shapes from the larger pastry cutter using the same technique. Smooth the edges with sandpaper.

5 Apply superglue to one of the stars and place the other on top, lining up the points of the top star between the points of the lower star.

7 Make a solid cast of the small pastry cutter. Smooth the edges and then glue a brooch fastener to the back.

9 Alternatively, use bronze spray paint to decorate the double star. Make sure that the spray reaches into the crevices between the two stars, but also avoid making drip marks.

6 Hold the two stars firmly together until the glue has set and then glue a brooch fastener to the back.

8 Paint the first star cast gold and the smallest star silver. Paint the double star blue and allow it to dry. Use a cloth to rub gold wax onto the surface.

All the mobile elements were cast from purchased rigid molds. Hanging hooks were embedded as part of the casting process. They are decorated using a sponge to produce a hazy effect – this gives the impression they are out of focus and a long way away. All the colors have been mixed with white to make pastel shades.

SKY MOBILE

2 Paint the cloud with a mixture of yellow and white paint. Allow all the elements to dry.

MATERIALS

Plastic molds
Plaster
Acrylic paint:
white, blue, red, yellow and gold
Doweling wood
Chain or ribbon
Paperclips

EQUIPMENT

Small mixing dish
Paintbrush
Sponge
Toothbrush
Mixing bowl

1 Apply base coats to both sides of all the elements. Mix pink from red and white for the star; mix mauve from red, blue and white for the sun; and pastel blue from blue and white for the moon.

3 With a sponge dab white paint onto the surface, including the back. Allow it to dry.

4 Dab pastel yellow paint onto both sides of each element. Allow it to dry.

5 Load a toothbrush with gold paint and spatter the surface of each element.

6 Join two pieces of wood to form a cross. Attach each element to the cross with a length of chain or ribbon. Hang the whole mobile from the ceiling.

96 A nighttime theme of moon and stars was chosen for this project. However, you could use other plaster casts – ready-made ones or those cast from molds you have made or bought. Choose casts that will complement each other and produce a pleasing design. Do not select big and cumbersome casts as they will make the box difficult to handle.

2 Mix some spackle to the consistency of cream cheese and spread it over the lid.

TWILIGHT BOX

MATERIALS

Box with lid
Plaster casts of
moon and 2 stars
Spackle
Spray paint: black,
silver and red
Gold wax

EQUIPMENT

Spackle knife
Mixing bowl
Cloth

1 Arrange the plaster casts on the lid of the box until you get a pleasing composition.

3 Apply spackle to the back of the moon and two stars, position them on the lid and push down to obtain a good fixing.

4 Use a wet spackle knife to smooth the spackle around the edges of the casts, closing up any gaps.

6 Spray silver paint horizontally so the spray is not aimed at the surface but falls on top of it with the high points becoming coated with silver.

7 Alternatively, spray a red base coat and with a cloth dipped in gold wax wipe over the high areas of the lid.

5 When the spackle has completely dried, spray the lid, sides and bottom of the box with black paint. Allow it to dry.

This mirror surround is made by applying plaster freehand. The plaster mix is left to thicken to the consistency of cream cheese before laying it. Plaster blanks and glass beads embedded in the plaster make a highly decorative and original mirror surround. It gives you the opportunity to creatively use some of those interesting objects you have collected over the years!

ECLECTIC MIRROR

MATERIALS

Plaster
Corrugated cardboard
Newspaper
Mirror
Plaster casts: sun, moon and 3 stars
Glass beads
Black acrylic paint
Gold and silver powder
Spar varnish
Paperclip

EQUIPMENT

Mixing bowl
Palette
Paintbrush
Cloth

1 Cut corrugated cardboard to the same size as the mirror and lay it on top of the newspaper. Mix some plaster. Hold the cardboard in position and apply the plaster around, and just covering, the edge of the cardboard to create a border 2in (5cm) wide.

2 While the plaster is still wet, carefully lay the mirror on top, applying light pressure to embed the mirror in the plaster. Allow the plaster to set.

3 Mix up a small amount of plaster and apply it along the top of the mirror. Lay a selection of your plaster casts and beads in the wet plaster and apply light pressure to ensure a good fixing. Run your finger along the inside edge of the plaster to make it even all around the mirror.

4 Continue creating the border around the mirror. Mix only a small amount of plaster at a time; otherwise it will be wasted.

6 Paint the whole surface, back and front, with black paint. Mix silver powder with spar varnish and apply over the whole frame with a dry brush.

7 Mix together gold powder and spar varnish and paint onto parts of the beads and embedded objects in a variety of patterns.

5 Wipe away the excess plaster and leave it to set. When dry, turn the mirror over and peel off the newspaper and cardboard. Place a bent paperclip in a small amount of plaster at the top end to form a hanging hook.

This project encompasses Plasticine modeling, mold making, taking a cast and decorating. The cast can be decorated in a variety of ways: a bright yellow stippled finish emulates the shimmering sun in a blue sky and a solid bright yellow finish makes an even bolder statement; the cheerful ambience of the plaque is enhanced using silver or gold; and a sparkling sandstone finish gives a more natural effect.

SUN WALL PLAQUE

2 Roll two worm shapes for the eyebrows, two balls for the cheeks and a smaller ball for the nose. Push them into the surface to form a face, blending them in with your fingers.

MATERIALS

Plasticine
Plaster
Latex
Acrylic paint:
yellow, cadmium
blue, Prussian blue,
white and silver
Textured acrylic
glitter gel
Red oxide paint
Gold wax

EQUIPMENT

Mixing bowl
Saucer
Modeling tool
Paintbrush
Small mixing dish
Sponge
Cloth

1 Knead the Plasticine and pat it out into a ½in (13mm) thick circle. Lay it on top of a saucer and add the rays of the sun, pushing them well into the rim.

3 Use a modeling tool to shape the facial details. You are now ready to make a latex mold (see page 14). Take a cast.

4 Paint the background areas between the sun's rays and the rim of the plaque a bright blue.

6 Paint the face yellow, reaching into all the crevices. Take care not to go over the edges onto the blue background.

7 Use a dry brush to emphasize the high points on the surface of the face with white paint.

5 Use a sponge to dab white paint on top of the blue.

8 Alternatively, mix a light blue from white and blue paint and with a sponge dab it onto the surface. Make sure that the paint reaches into all the crevices.

10 Mix white and yellow paint to make a lighter shade. With a sponge, dab it lightly onto the surface of the face.

11 Finally, stipple bright yellow paint over the entire surface.

9 Enhance the high points of the face with darker blue paint by dragging a relatively dry brush across the surface.

Gold wax rubbed over red oxide paint creates a cheerful ambience.

12 Another alternative is to paint the background with deep Prussian blue.

13 Paint the face with silver. Apply another coat of silver when dry to strengthen the effect.

14 To produce a sparkling sandstone effect, brush textured acrylic glitter gel over the whole surface of the plaque.

◄ **BERNARD CLAYDON**
Ivory moon and gold star
The original moon and star were modeled in clay and silicone rubber molds made. The smooth and even colors were achieved by applying the finish with an airbrush.

▼ **SARAH WILLIAMS**
Heart wall relief
Brightly colored folk art inspired the design of this relief. It was handpainted with acrylic paints.

▲▶ BERNARD CLAYDON
Verdigris stars
The original stars were
modeled in clay. A
combination of applying
paint with an airbrush and
handpainting was used to
create a verdigris effect.

▲ THE WORKS • Sun clock
The precise and
symmetrical design on this
clock was painted on top
of a white base coat using
cobalt blue paint and gilt.

GALLERY

There is a limited selection of shapes
available to us up in the sky, but the vast
variety of plaster objects that exist which
use these forms is truly amazing. The sun and moon were the inspiration for a variety of wall
plaques, mirrors and clocks. Stars have been blended with sun rays in other wall plaques and can be
combined most effectively with hearts to form a border design for a mirror.

▲ THE WORKS
Squirls mirror
The original for this mirror surround was a wood frame with star plaster blanks, string spirals and hearts made from Plasticine bonded to the surface. A verdigris finish was applied.

◄ ALAN WALLIS DESIGN
Sun mirror
The plaster cast was painted light green over which gold paint was applied. This was then rubbed back to reveal the paint underneath it in a patinated effect.

▶ **THE WORKS · Squirl heart**
The finish for this heart is verdigris: dark red/brown paint was brushed on and turquoise sponged randomly on top. A coat of diluted gilt cream was then applied.

▲▶ **BERNARD CLAYDON**
Yellow sun and gold sun
The originals for both of these suns were modeled in clay. The smooth and even finishes were achieved by applying the color with an airbrush. They were then varnished.

In this chapter, you learn the important technique of taking a one-piece (two-dimensional) mold from a three-dimensional object, in this case a Classical Statue. The intricately modeled Buddha Panel is cast from a ready-made mold. Two techniques are used to color it, both of which produce an aged quality. The Cherubs are decorated in both metallic and bright, natural colors. A blank

FACES AND FIGURES

plaster cast of a Greek Bust is given a simplified marble finish, as well as the almost surreal porphyry which clearly demonstrates the impact you can achieve from different decorative techniques. The Cherub Mirror is made using spackle into which plaster casts of cherubs are embedded. The black and gold finish produces an antiqued gold mirror surround.

110

A plaster cast of a Greek or Roman sculpture adds classical elegance to any room. Although usually decorated to complement their classical elegance, here it takes on a somewhat surreal air. The cast is first coated with matt spray sealer to prevent the paint from being absorbed by the plaster and then paint is spattered on. It is important to apply each color evenly to the surface.

GREEK BUST

2 Use a toothbrush to spatter the cast with watery black paint and then again with white paint.

MATERIALS

Plaster bust
Acrylic paint:
purple, black, red,
white and gold
White spray paint
Silver marble spray
paint
Matt spray sealer

EQUIPMENT

Paintbrush
Sponge
Toothbrush

1 Cover the head thoroughly with matt spray sealer. Brush on purple acrylic paint using loose cross-hatched strokes. While the paint is still wet, dab the paint surface with a sponge.

3 Mix white and red to produce a deep pink color and spatter onto the surface as before. Repeat the technique using gold paint. Leave it to dry.

4 Apply matt spray sealer to seal the surface.

There are many different colored marble sprays: white, black and maroon base coats with silver and gold marble veins. Experiment with different combinations and qualities of veins on a remnant of plaster before tackling the bust.

5 Special marble sprays are now available. Spray a white basecoat evenly over the whole bust. Use silver marble spray to add veins and blend these in more realistically by spraying a small amount of white on top.

112

Cherubs are widely available as casts and molds. The winged cherub was sprayed black and gold enamel paint applied to the highlights with a cloth. Spray paint allows an even base coat to be achieved. The base color of the other cherubs is a watery mix of acrylic paint, with highlights of gold and bright colors.

CHERUBS

2 Dip a cloth in gold enamel paint and run it over the surface of the cherub so that the high points are coated with gold.

MATERIALS

Plastic molds
Plaster cherub
Plaster
Black spray paint
Gold enamel paint
Acrylic paint: red,
white, yellow, blue,
green and black
Gold powder
Spar varnish

EQUIPMENT

Cloth
Paintbrush
Small mixing dish
Mixing bowl

1 In a well-ventilated area, spray the cherub black. Spray evenly backwards and forwards to avoid creating runs and drip marks.

3 Mix white and red to make a flesh color. Mix a darker tone and paint the crevices. Paint the wings turquoise, the hair yellow and the trumpet black.

You can have a lot of fun painting cherubs in a less traditional manner!

4 Mix gold powder with spar varnish and paint the trumpet. Brush gold lightly over the hair, wings and high points of the body with a dry brush.

114

This intricately modeled Buddha panel is the very essence of Indian art. It is an object for contemplation, not only of the subject matter but also the detailed modeling in each of the panels – each tells a story. A plaster cast is taken from a purchased plastic mold and then decorated. The antiqued metal finish enhances the relief forms and also gives the panel a museum-like quality.

BUDDHA PANEL

2 Mix burnt umber and Payne's gray paint and cover the whole of the panel. Leave it to dry.

MATERIALS

Plastic mold
Plaster
Acrylic paint: burnt umber and Payne's gray
Bronze yellow paint
Iridescent bronze paint
Gold paint
Antique silver powder
Spar varnish

EQUIPMENT

Mixing bowl
Paintbrush
Sponge
Small mixing dish

1 Pour the plaster into the mold slowly and evenly. When it has set, turn the mold and cast over and gently lift the mold off the plaster cast.

3 Mix bronze yellow and irridescent bronze paint. Dip a sponge in the paint and wipe it across the relief so that it picks out the high points.

4 Dip a sponge into gold paint and rub this over the central panel, with the high points again picking up the paint.

5 For an alternative finish, paint a mixture of antique silver powder and spar varnish onto the outer edge panels.

116

A three-dimensional ornament is transformed into an attractive wall plaque using a one-piece mold. A ledge of Plasticine is built around the object and undercuts are filled in to enable easy removal. The finish is verdigris, a term used to describe the surface of copper, bronze or brass objects which have been exposed to the elements. This coloring was chosen to complement the classical form.

CLASSICAL STATUE

MATERIALS

Statuette
Plasticine
Corrugated cardboard
Latex
Plaster
Bronze enamel paint
Acrylic paint: blue, green and yellow
Water-based white paint
Whitewash powder
Rubbing alcohol

EQUIPMENT

Mixing bowl
Paintbrush
Toothbrush
Cloth

1 Knead the Plasticine to make it more pliable. Cut a piece of corrugated cardboard to the height and width of the statuette and place it underneath.

2 Fill the space between the cardboard and the underside of the statue with Plasticine and build halfway up the statue. You are now ready to make the latex mold (see page 14).

3 Take a cast and brush on a coat of bronze enamel paint. When it is dry, apply a watery mix of blue and green acrylic paint over the whole surface.

4 Mix white paint, light blue and bright green acrylic, whitewash powder and rubbing alcohol to form a paste. Brush all over the surface and leave it to dry.

6 Lightly brush the surface with water and sprinkle whitewash over. Wipe off the excess.

5 Use a cloth to dab on some light blue acrylic paint and leave it to dry. Make a watery mix of lime green acrylic and spatter it over the surface with a toothbrush.

118

The diamond hanging format of this classical style mirror adds a sense of drama and the gold finish makes it look antique. The frame and base are foamboard, available from art material suppliers, but if you wish to use a mirror larger than 15in (38cm), use a wood frame. The cherubs are bonded to the frame using spackle, which takes longer to set and sets harder than plaster.

CHERUB MIRROR

MATERIALS

Plaster cherubs
Foamboard
Mirror
Galvanized wire
Double-sided
adhesive tape
Spackle
Black spray paint
Gold enamel paint
Decorative paper
Brown package tape
Aerosol spray glue

EQUIPMENT

Cutting mat
Scalpel
Fine marker pen
Straight edge/ruler
Pliers
Mixing bowl
Spackle knife
Cloth

2 Place this frame on top of the other piece of foamboard and line up the edges. Holding a pen at an angle, trace the inside square and then cut it out.

1 Cut two pieces of foamboard 2in (5cm) larger than the mirror. Place the mirror centrally on top of one piece and cut the board around the mirror.

3 On the larger frame make two slits 4in (10cm) from the same corner. Cut two lengths of wire and bend double. Push each loop through a slit so it projects 1in (2.5cm) on the other side. Bend the ends to lie flat.

4 Place double-sided tape along the edges of the smaller frame. Position the larger frame on top with the edges lined up and press to ensure the tape sticks.

6 Turn the frame over with the hanging hooks behind at the top. Arrange the cherubs on the frame in a pleasing design. Remove the casts, keeping them in the same composition.

8 Apply some spackle to the underside of a cherub, position it on the frame and push to obtain a good fixing.

5 Rest the mirror on the flange you have created to make sure it fits. Trim the foamboard if necessary.

7 Support the frame above the work surface. Mix some spackle to the consistency of cream cheese and spread a layer over the frame.

9 Add more spackle if necessary under the wings and wherever else the cherub does not come into contact with the spackle.

10 Where a cherub hangs over the edge of the frame, apply spackle underneath and level off to the frame edge to strengthen.

11 Turn the frame over and secure the two hanging hooks with some spackle. Use a knife to trim off excess spackle along the flange of the frame. Leave it to dry thoroughly.

12 In a well-ventilated area, spray the back and front of the frame with black spray paint. Make sure one side is dry before turning the frame over.

13 Insert the mirror and secure in place with brown package tape.

14 Spray the back of the mirror with adhesive and smooth decorative paper over. Cut to the right size.

15 Dip a cloth in gold paint and gently wipe across the surface of the cherubs so that the paint is picked up by the high points and the crevices remain black.

CLIFTON LITTLE VENICE
Greek head
A coating of black paint
was rubbed off before it
had completely dried;
notice how the paint has
been trapped in the
crevices to produce the
stone effect.

▲ DOPPELGANGER • **Piggy**
back climbing figure
This piece was inspired by
an actor seen rescuing a
person in a movie. The
plaster cast was lightly
stained and varnished.

► **MATTHEW LEE • Roccoco wall clock**
This clock was inspired by Spanish and Italian church interiors. The original surround was modeled in clay, from which a mold was made. The plaster cast was painted black and then applied with gold.

Classical sculpture from around the globe provides perhaps the greatest inspiration of all. The human form has been rendered throughout history by artists: the calm figure of Buddha; the beauty of Greek and Renaissance sculpture; the dramatic masks of Roman theater; the perenniel figure of the cherub; and the experimental figurative sculpture of the 20th century.

▲ **MARK LA TROBE • Cherubs**
Gold ink was painted over these cherubs. Before drying, it was rubbed off the body, leaving a residue in the crevices.

MIKE WELLS
Cherub mirror
A base color was sprayed on and gold wax was applied to achieve an antiqued effect.

MIKE WELLS • Eye
Gold wax rubbed over a base coat of black paint produces an alternative effect to that of classical sculpture.

▼ MARK LA TROBE • Buddha
Car paint spray was used to create this extremely authentic metallic finish.

MARK LA TROBE • Nose and mouth
These plaster casts, taken from classical sculpture, were coated with clear wax and then buffed to produce a creamy surface shine.

MARK LA TROBE
Roman masks
Taken from Roman
originals, these have a very
convincing verdigris finish.
They were painted copper
and then powder color
applied to produce the
matt finish.

INDEX

CREDITS

Quarto would like to thank the following individuals who took part in the step-by-step demonstrations:

Ofer Acoo, Errol Allen, Clare Baggaley, Mary Fellows, Sandra Hurst Chico, Dhyan Jennings, Mark La Trobe, Karen Nettlefield, John Plowman, Mike Wells, Debbie Worth

Quarto would also like to thank all those who kindly submitted items for the gallery, including: Ofer Acoo, Clapton, London; Alan Wallis Design, courtesy of Ruth Gill Interiors, Crouch End, London; Kristina Bieganski at Funky Eclectica, Shepherd's Bush, London; Bernard Claydon, Brighton, Sussex; Clifton Little Venice, Maida Vale, London; John De Veuve at Rough Arts, Westcliffe-on-Sea, Essex; Rae and Lee Fether at The Works, Kentish Town, London; Mark La Trobe at Plasterworks, Islington, London; Matthew Lee at Larnaca Works, Grange Wale, London; Simon Sprecher at Doppelganger and Shaun and Nicole Keir-Tomalin at Shoeless Joe, both courtesy of Crocodile Antiques, Muswell Hill, London; Pamela Stewart-Pearson, Esher, Surrey; Julie Taylor and Maddy Petit at Mirabilis Design, Clapham, London; Mike Wells at Divine Decadence, Putney, London; Sarah Williams, Blackheath, London.

Finally, Quarto would like to thank the following suppliers who contributed materials for use in the demonstrations:

Alec Tiranti Limited
27 Warren Street,
London W1P 5DG, UK
Tel & Fax: 0171 636 8565

DecoArt
PO Box 386, Stanford KY 40484, USA
Tel: 606 365 3193
Fax: 606 365 9739

Formby's
825 Crossover Lane,
Memphis TN 38117, USA
Consumer help line: 1-800-F-O-R-M-B-Y-S

Fred Aldous Ltd
PO Box 135, 37 Lever Street,
Manchester M60 1UX, UK
Tel: 0161 236 2477
Fax: 0161 236 6075

Hobby Ceramicraft
Rotherwick, Basingstoke, Hampshire, UK
Tel & Fax: 01256 762461

Modern Options Inc
2325 Third Street,
San Francisco CA 94107, USA
Tel: 415 252 5580
Fax: 415 252 5599

Supercast Ltd
Hawthorn Avenue, Hull HU3 5JZ, UK
Tel: 01482 223398
Fax: 01482 228445

Swanson
1200 Park Avenue,
Murfreesboro TN 37129, USA
Tel: 615 896 4114
Fax: 615 898 1313
Orders: 1 800 251 1402